MARY DOWNING HAHN

Took

a ghost story
graphic novel

Adapted by
Scott Peterson,
Jen Vaughn,
and Hank Jones

Etch
Clarion Books
Imprints of HarperCollins*Publishers*
Boston New York

For Pete, Joan, and Devin for giving me the chance to work on such a cool project.
And for Jen for doing such a great job on the art.
And, as always, here's to Story.
—Scott Peterson

To Kyla Gay for the love, Pete Friedrich for the guidance,
my coworking buds for the support, and all the shadows for the company
—Jen Vaughn

Etch and Clarion Books are imprints of HarperCollins Publishers.

Took
Copyright © 2022 by HarperCollins Publishers LLC
Adapted from *Took* by Mary Downing Hahn
Copyright © 2015 by Mary Downing Hahn
clarionbooks.com

Library of Congress Cataloging-in-Publication Data has been applied for.
ISBN: 978-0-358-53688-8 hardcover
ISBN: 978-0-358-53687-1 paperback

Colorist: Hank Jones
Lettering by Morgan Martinez
Flatters: Frank Reynoso, Laura Martin, and Christiana Tushaj
The illustrations in this book were done in Clip Studio Paint on an iPad.
The text was set in Ashcan, Nightwatcher, and Evil Doings.
Cover design by Catherine San Juan and Pete Friedrich
Interior design by Pete Friedrich

Manufactured in Canada
Friesens 10 9 8 7 6 5 4 3 2 1
45XXXXXXXX

First Edition

took

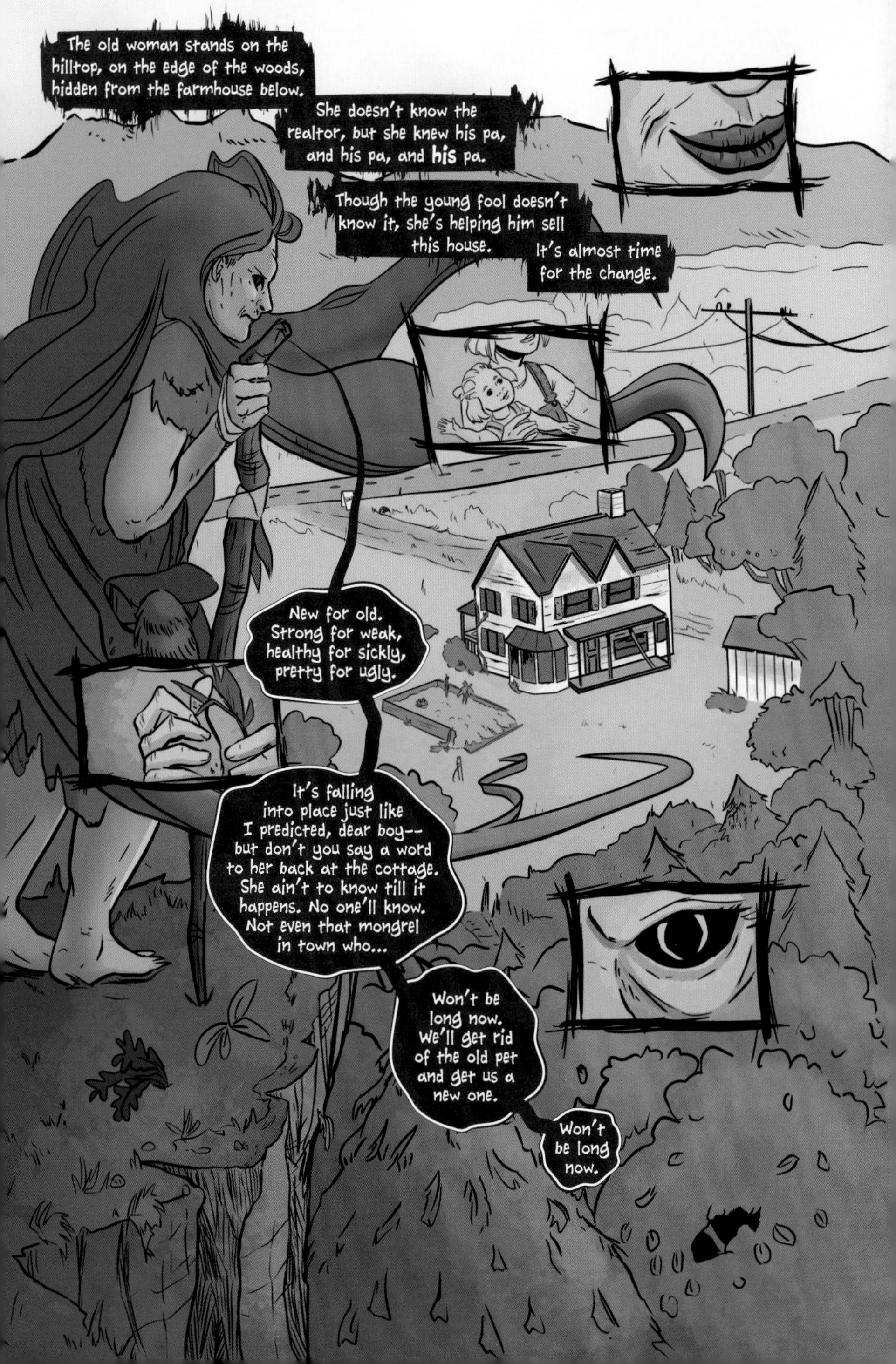
The old woman stands on the hilltop, on the edge of the woods, hidden from the farmhouse below.
She doesn't know the realtor, but she knew his pa, and his pa, and **his** pa.
Though the young fool doesn't know it, she's helping him sell this house.
It's almost time for the change.
New for old. Strong for weak, healthy for sickly, pretty for ugly.
It's falling into place just like I predicted, dear boy-- but don't you say a word to her back at the cottage. She ain't to know till it happens. No one'll know. Not even that mongrel in town who...
Won't be long now. We'll get rid of the old pet and get us a new one.
Won't be long now.

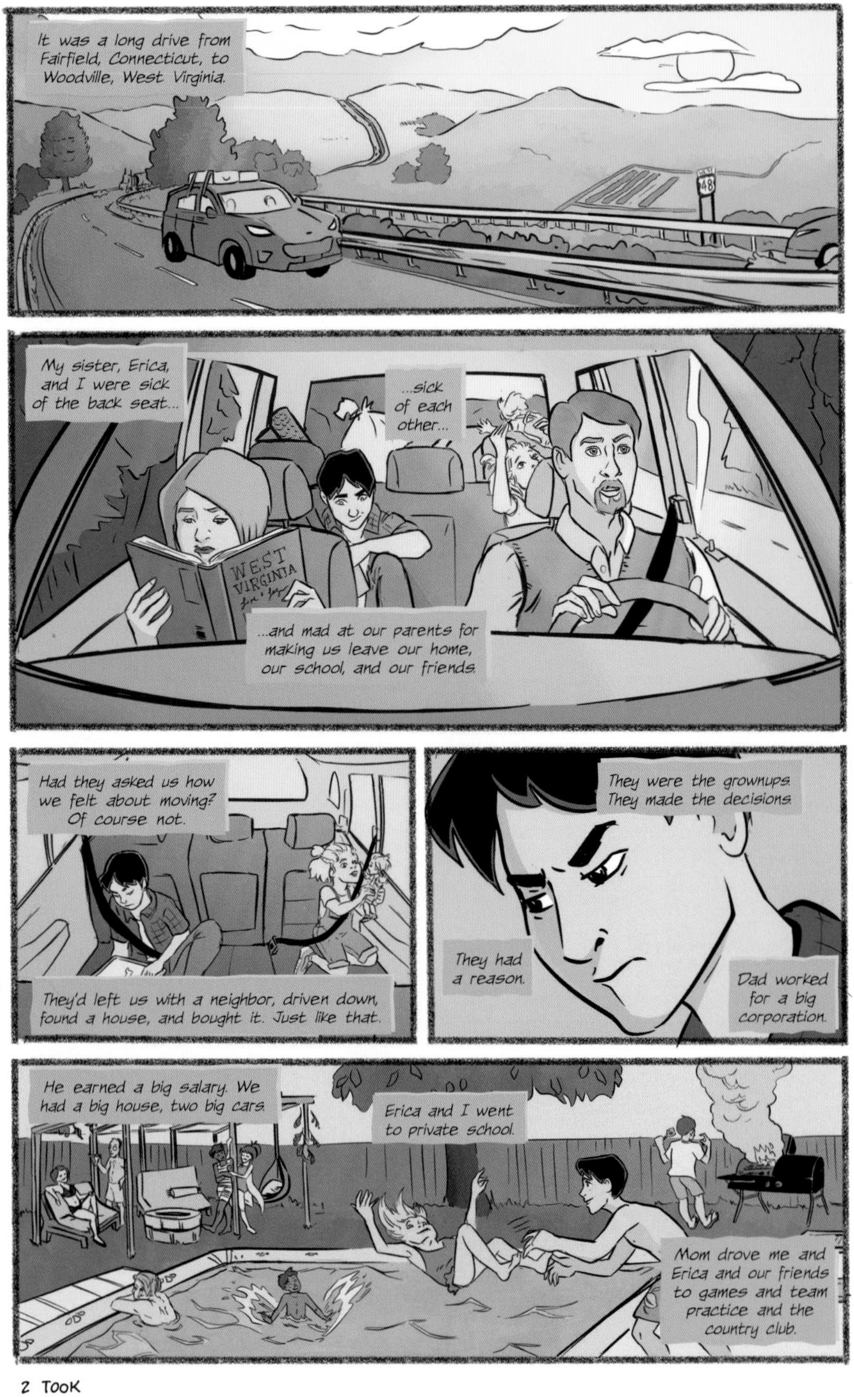
It was a long drive from Fairfield, Connecticut, to Woodville, West Virginia.
My sister, Erica, and I were sick of the back seat...
...sick of each other...
WEST VIRGINIA
...and mad at our parents for making us leave our home, our school, and our friends.
Had they asked us how we felt about moving? Of course not.
They'd left us with a neighbor, driven down, found a house, and bought it. Just like that.
They were the grownups. They made the decisions.
They had a reason.
Dad worked for a big corporation.
He earned a big salary. We had a big house, two big cars.
Erica and I went to private school.
Mom drove me and Erica and our friends to games and team practice and the country club.

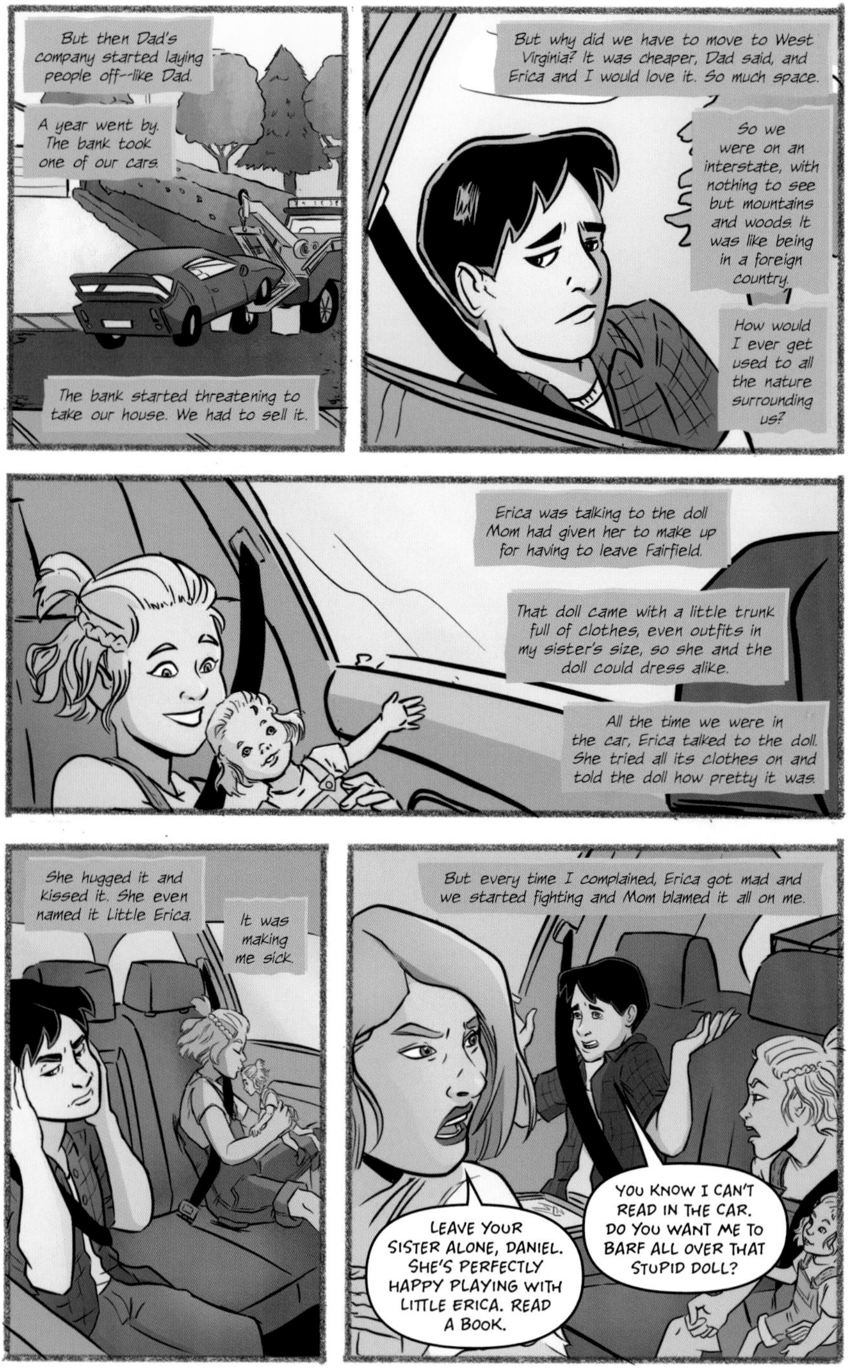
But then Dad's company started laying people off--like Dad.
A year went by. The bank took one of our cars.
The bank started threatening to take our house. We had to sell it.
But why did we have to move to West Virginia? It was cheaper, Dad said, and Erica and I would love it. So much space.
So we were on an interstate, with nothing to see but mountains and woods. It was like being in a foreign country.
How would I ever get used to all the nature surrounding us?
Erica was talking to the doll Mom had given her to make up for having to leave Fairfield.
That doll came with a little trunk full of clothes, even outfits in my sister's size, so she and the doll could dress alike.
All the time we were in the car, Erica talked to the doll. She tried all its clothes on and told the doll how pretty it was.
She hugged it and kissed it. She even named it Little Erica.
It was making me sick.
But every time I complained, Erica got mad and we started fighting and Mom blamed it all on me.
YOU KNOW I CAN'T READ IN THE CAR. DO YOU WANT ME TO BARF ALL OVER THAT STUPID DOLL?
LEAVE YOUR SISTER ALONE, DANIEL. SHE'S PERFECTLY HAPPY PLAYING WITH LITTLE ERICA. READ A BOOK.

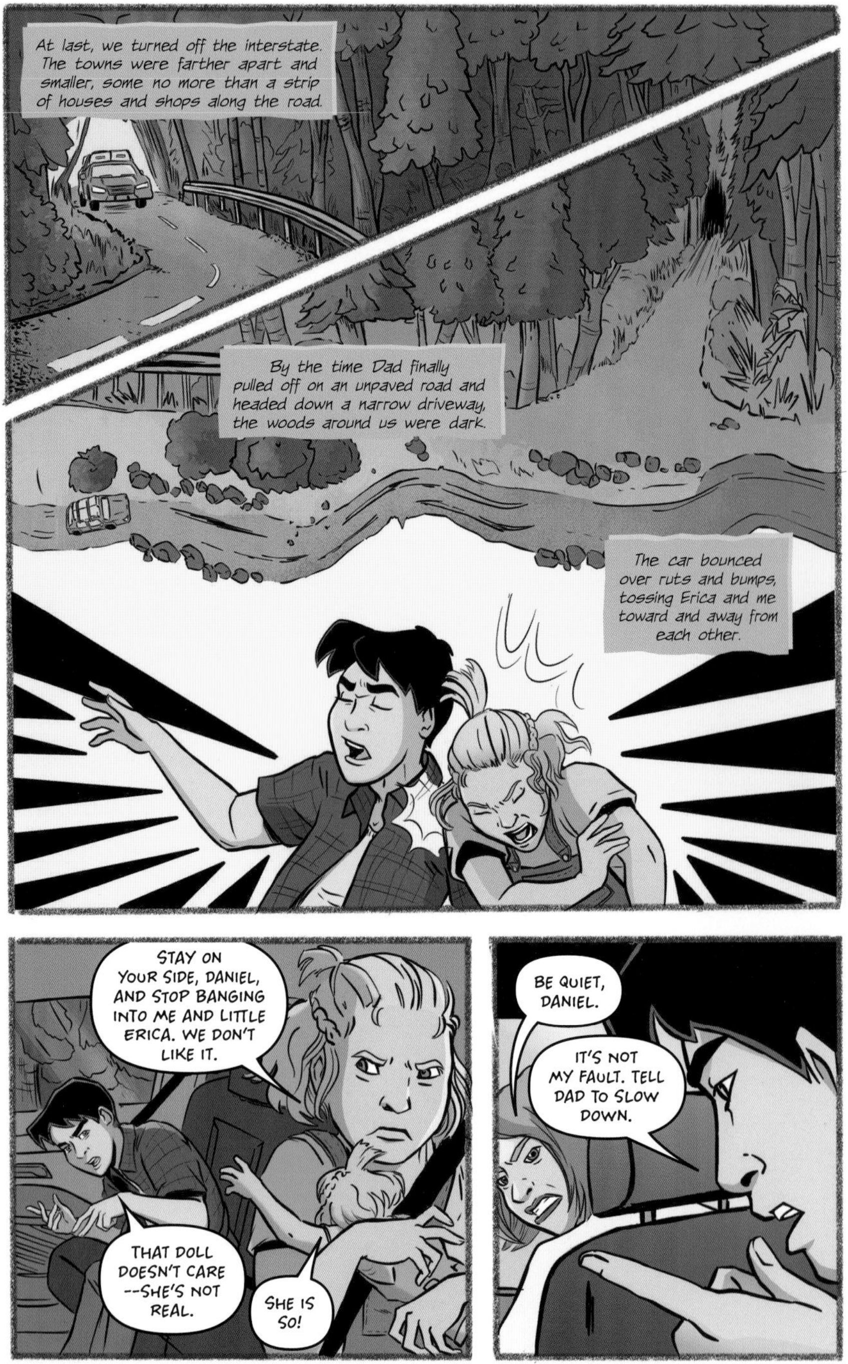
At last, we turned off the interstate. The towns were farther apart and smaller, some no more than a strip of houses and shops along the road.
By the time Dad finally pulled off on an unpaved road and headed down a narrow driveway, the woods around us were dark.
The car bounced over ruts and bumps, tossing Erica and me toward and away from each other.
STAY ON YOUR SIDE, DANIEL, AND STOP BANGING INTO ME AND LITTLE ERICA. WE DON'T LIKE IT.
THAT DOLL DOESN'T CARE --SHE'S NOT REAL.
SHE IS SO!
BE QUIET, DANIEL.
IT'S NOT MY FAULT. TELL DAD TO SLOW DOWN.

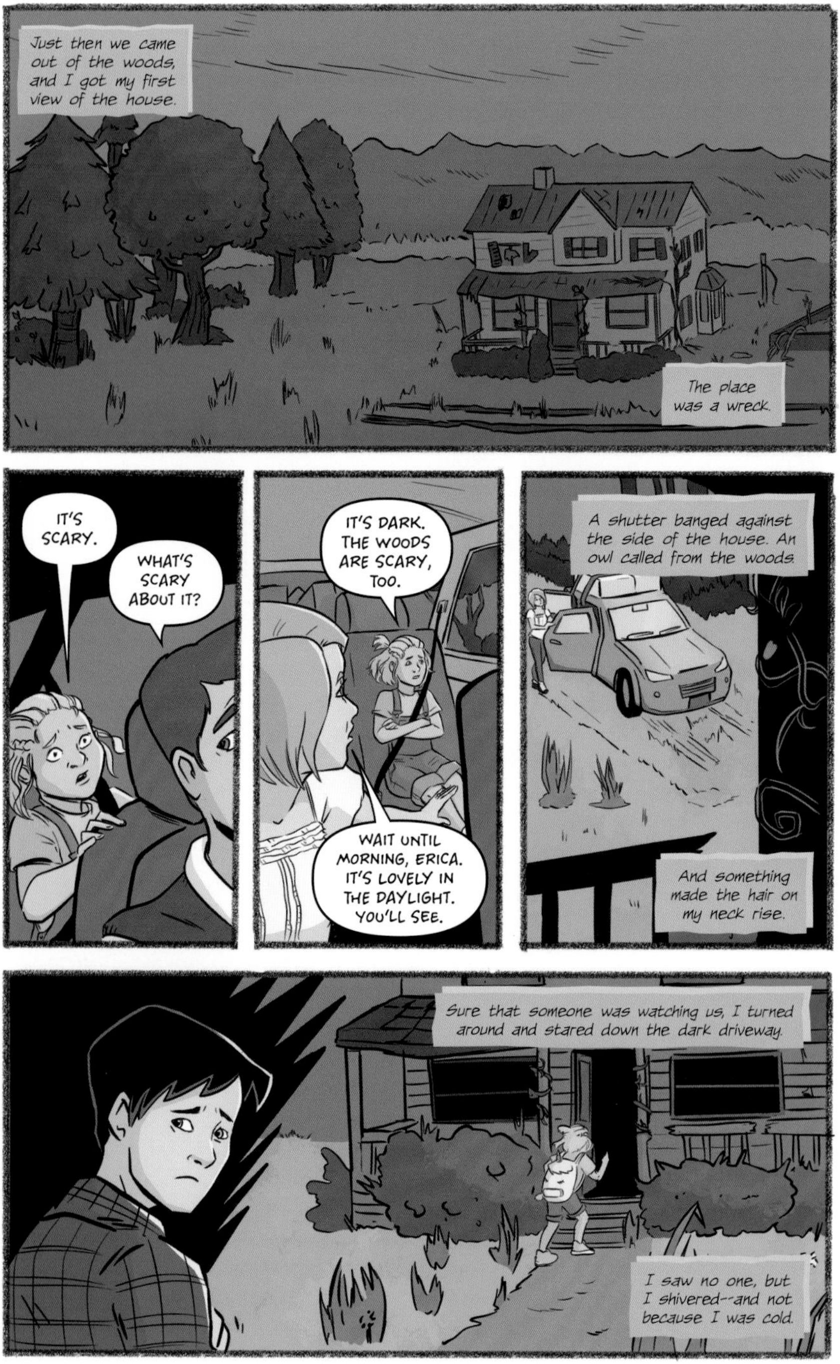
Just then we came out of the woods, and I got my first view of the house.
The place was a wreck.
IT'S SCARY.
WHAT'S SCARY ABOUT IT?
IT'S DARK. THE WOODS ARE SCARY, TOO.
WAIT UNTIL MORNING, ERICA. IT'S LOVELY IN THE DAYLIGHT. YOU'LL SEE.
A shutter banged against the side of the house. An owl called from the woods.
And something made the hair on my neck rise.
Sure that someone was watching us, I turned around and stared down the dark driveway.
I saw no one, but I shivered--and not because I was cold.

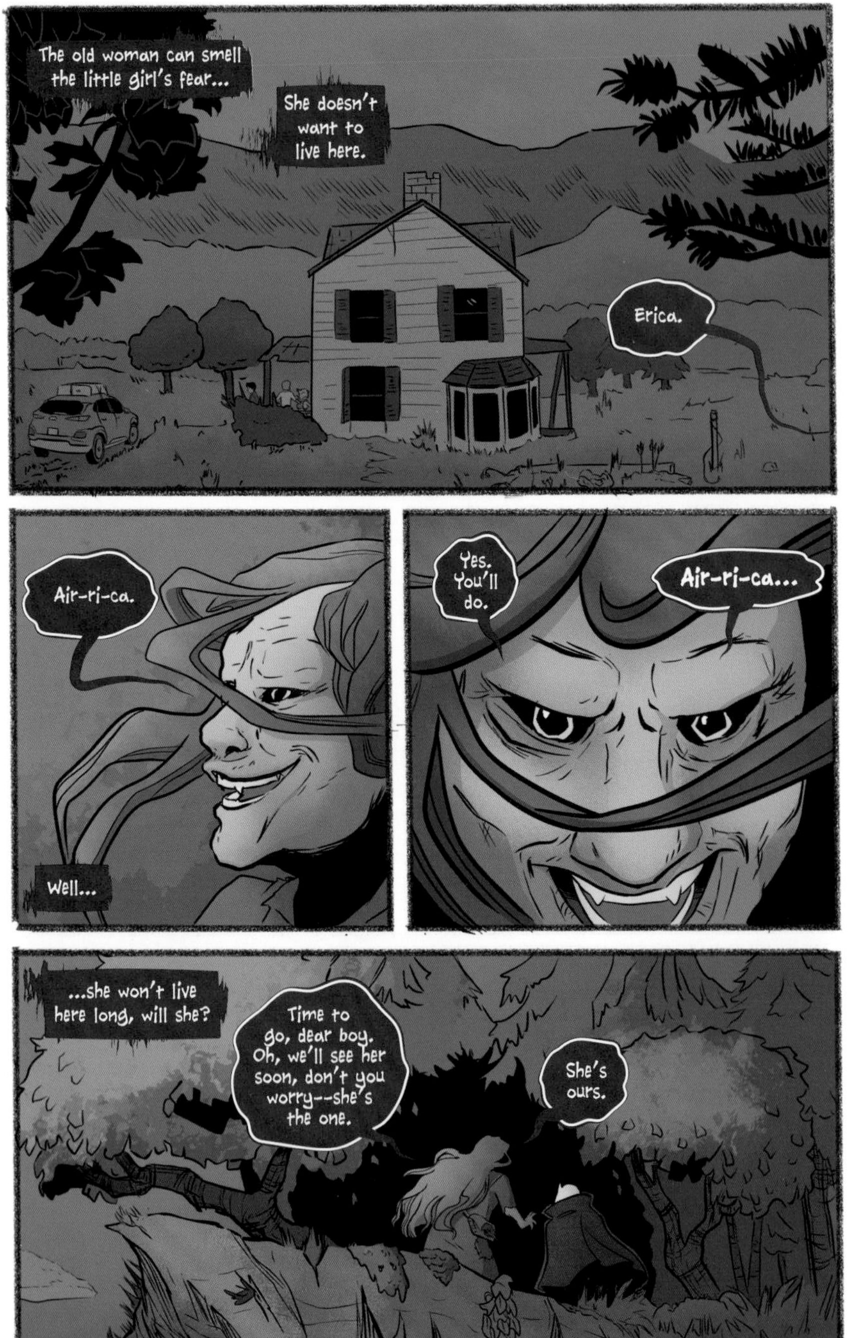
The old woman can smell the little girl's fear...
She doesn't want to live here.
Erica.
Air-ri-ca.
Well...
Yes. You'll do.
Air-ri-ca...
...she won't live here long, will she?
Time to go, dear boy. Oh, we'll see her soon, don't you worry--she's the one.
She's ours.

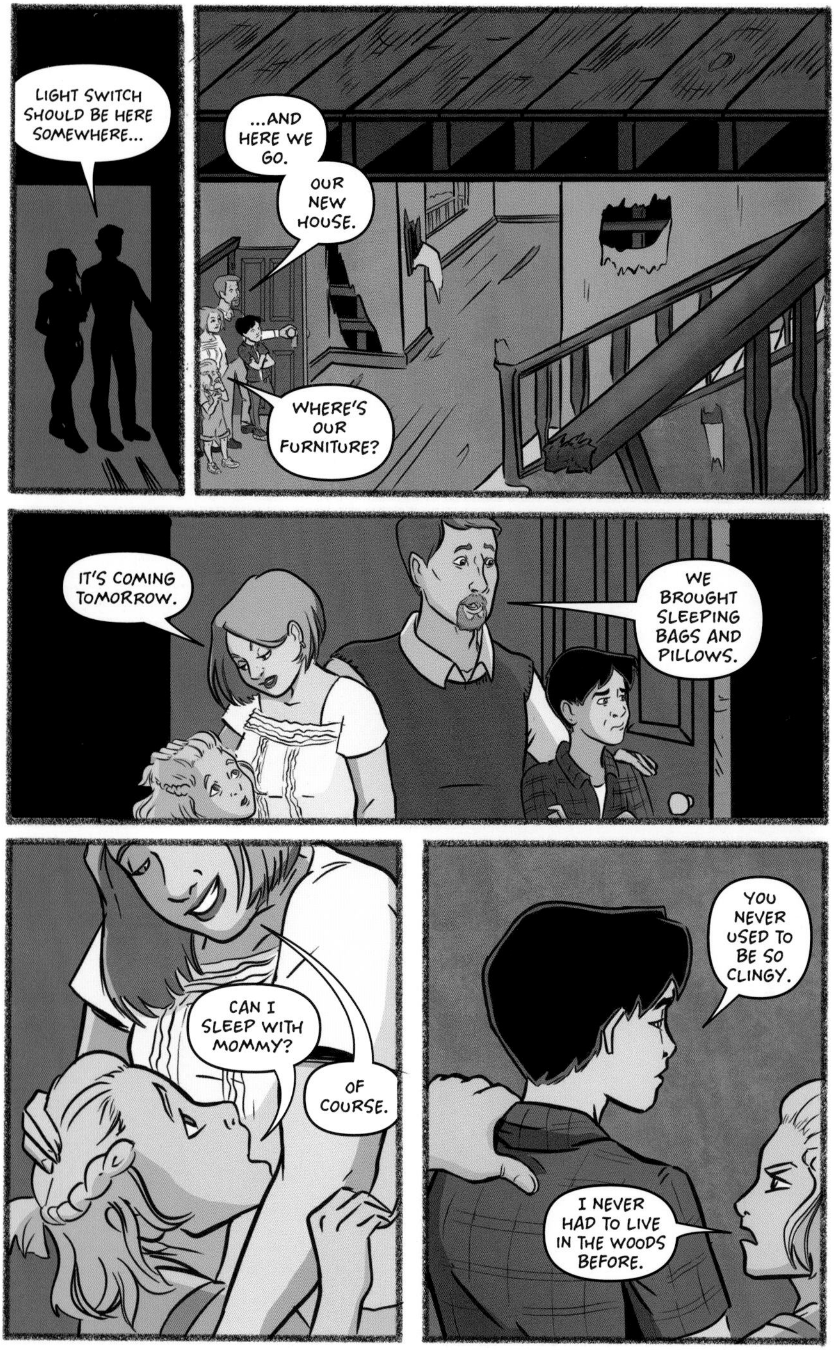
LIGHT SWITCH SHOULD BE HERE SOMEWHERE...
...AND HERE WE GO.
OUR NEW HOUSE.
WHERE'S OUR FURNITURE?
IT'S COMING TOMORROW.
WE BROUGHT SLEEPING BAGS AND PILLOWS.
CAN I SLEEP WITH MOMMY?
OF COURSE.
YOU NEVER USED TO BE SO CLINGY.
I NEVER HAD TO LIVE IN THE WOODS BEFORE.

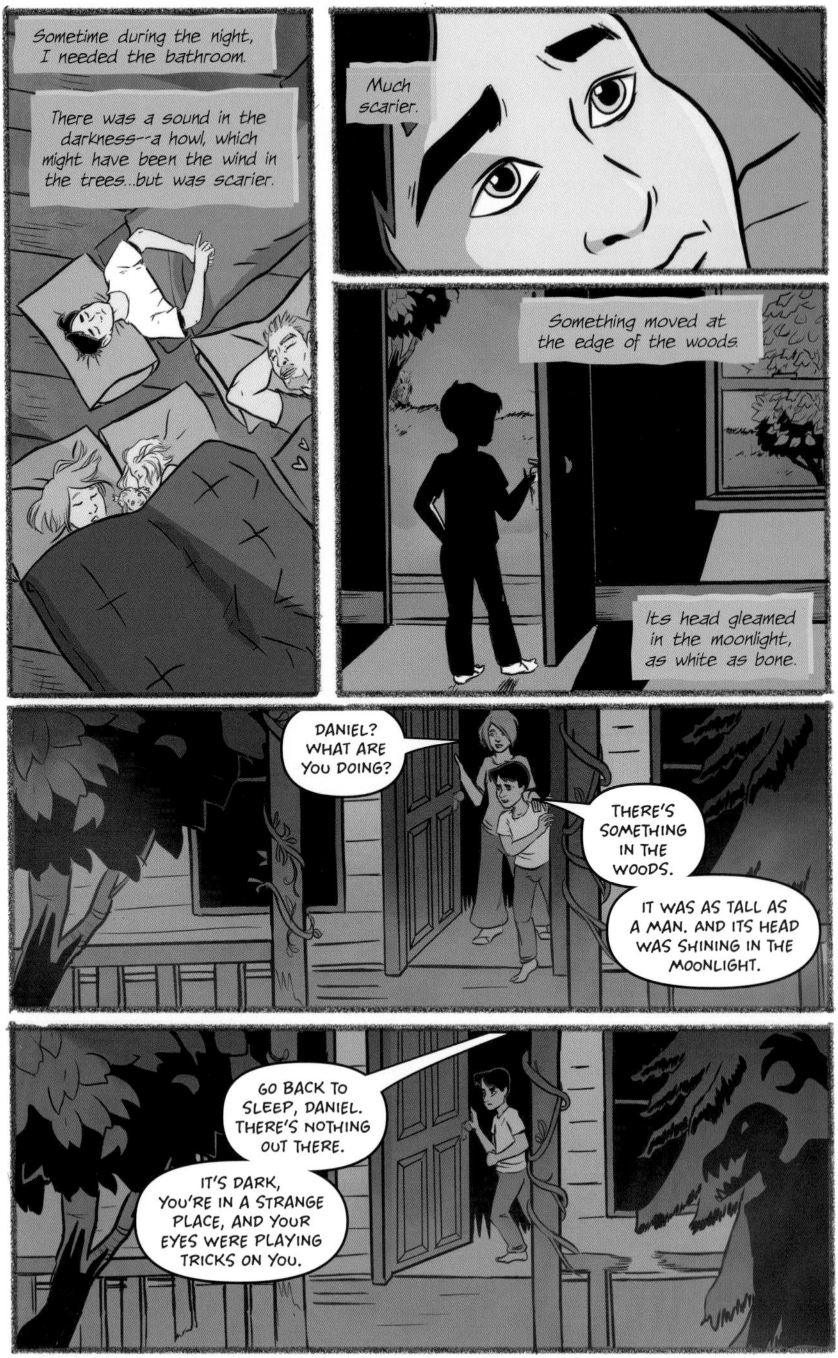
Sometime during the night, I needed the bathroom.
There was a sound in the darkness--a howl, which might have been the wind in the trees...but was scarier.
Much scarier.
Something moved at the edge of the woods.
Its head gleamed in the moonlight, as white as bone.
DANIEL? WHAT ARE YOU DOING?
THERE'S SOMETHING IN THE WOODS.
IT WAS AS TALL AS A MAN. AND ITS HEAD WAS SHINING IN THE MOONLIGHT.
GO BACK TO SLEEP, DANIEL. THERE'S NOTHING OUT THERE.
IT'S DARK, YOU'RE IN A STRANGE PLACE, AND YOUR EYES WERE PLAYING TRICKS ON YOU.

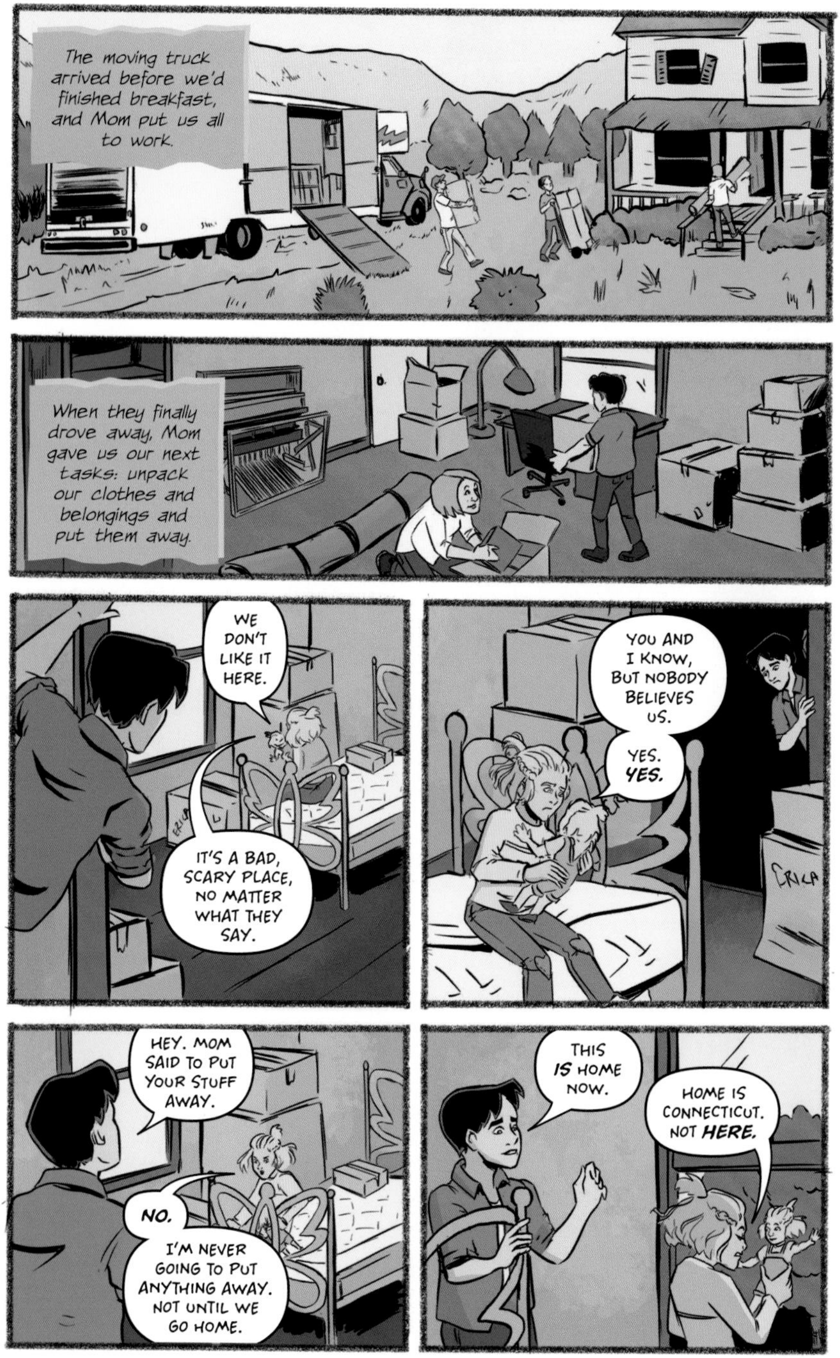
The moving truck arrived before we'd finished breakfast, and Mom put us all to work.
When they finally drove away, Mom gave us our next tasks: unpack our clothes and belongings and put them away.
WE DON'T LIKE IT HERE.
IT'S A BAD, SCARY PLACE, NO MATTER WHAT THEY SAY.
YOU AND I KNOW, BUT NOBODY BELIEVES US.
YES. *YES.*
HEY. MOM SAID TO PUT YOUR STUFF AWAY.
NO.
I'M NEVER GOING TO PUT ANYTHING AWAY. NOT UNTIL WE GO HOME.
THIS *IS* HOME NOW.
HOME IS CONNECTICUT. NOT *HERE.*

LET'S SEE.

IT'S ONLY SEPTEMBER, SO HOPEFULLY I'LL HAVE TIME TO FIGURE OUT HOW THIS MONSTER WORKS BEFORE WE ACTUALLY NEED IT.

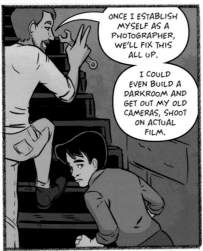

ONCE I ESTABLISH MYSELF AS A PHOTOGRAPHER, WE'LL FIX THIS ALL UP.

I COULD EVEN BUILD A DARKROOM AND GET OUT MY OLD CAMERAS, SHOOT ON ACTUAL FILM.

Nobody noticed as I slipped out the back door.

The house looked even worse in daylight.

What were Dad and Mom thinking? Had they lost their minds? We'd never get the place fixed up.

I felt like siding with Erica.

Maybe between the two of us we could persuade Mom and Dad to go back to Connecticut.

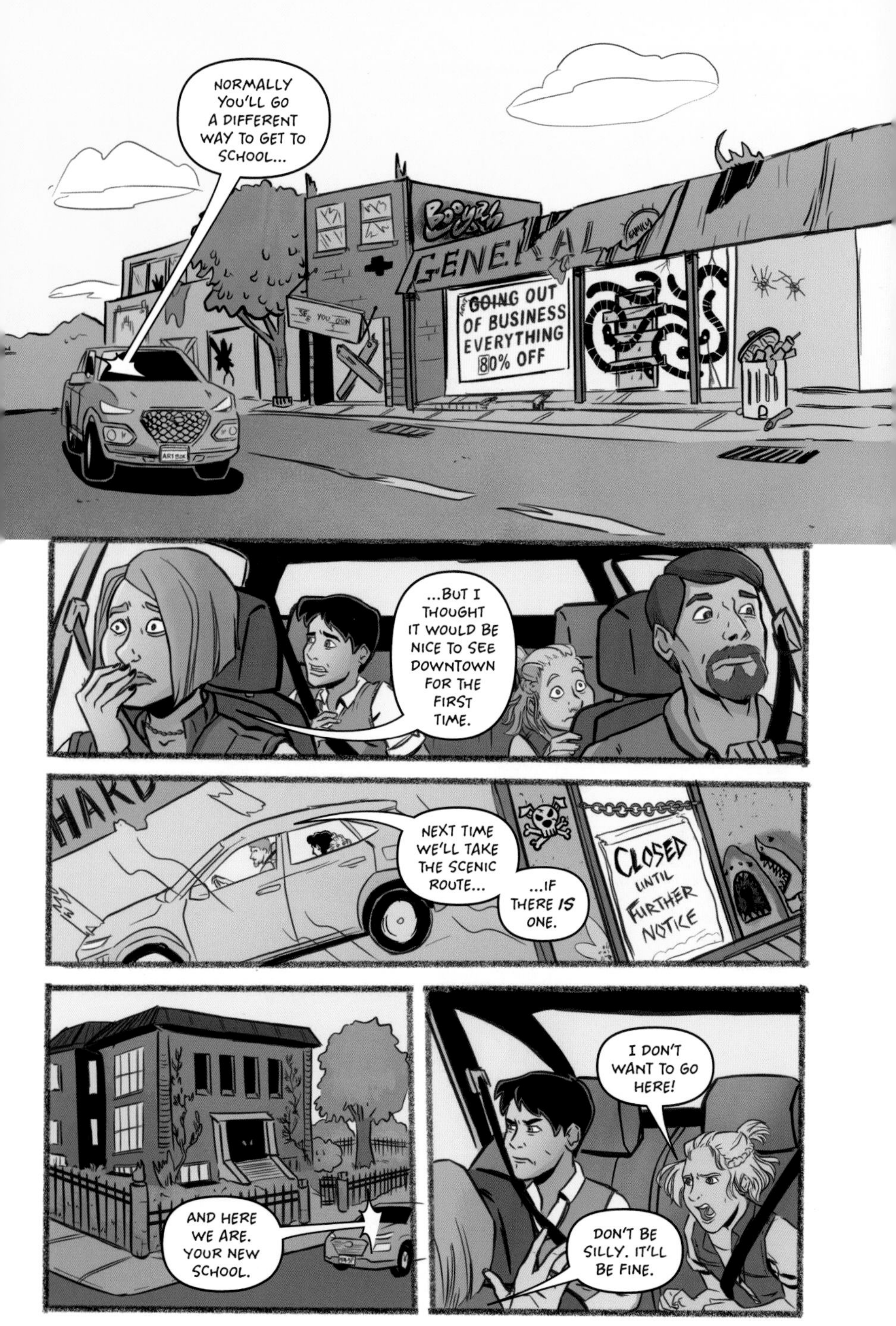
NORMALLY YOU'LL GO A DIFFERENT WAY TO GET TO SCHOOL...
GOING OUT OF BUSINESS EVERYTHING 80% OFF
...BUT I THOUGHT IT WOULD BE NICE TO SEE DOWNTOWN FOR THE FIRST TIME.
NEXT TIME WE'LL TAKE THE SCENIC ROUTE...
...IF THERE *IS* ONE.
CLOSED UNTIL FURTHER NOTICE
AND HERE WE ARE. YOUR NEW SCHOOL.
I DON'T WANT TO GO HERE!
DON'T BE SILLY. IT'LL BE FINE.

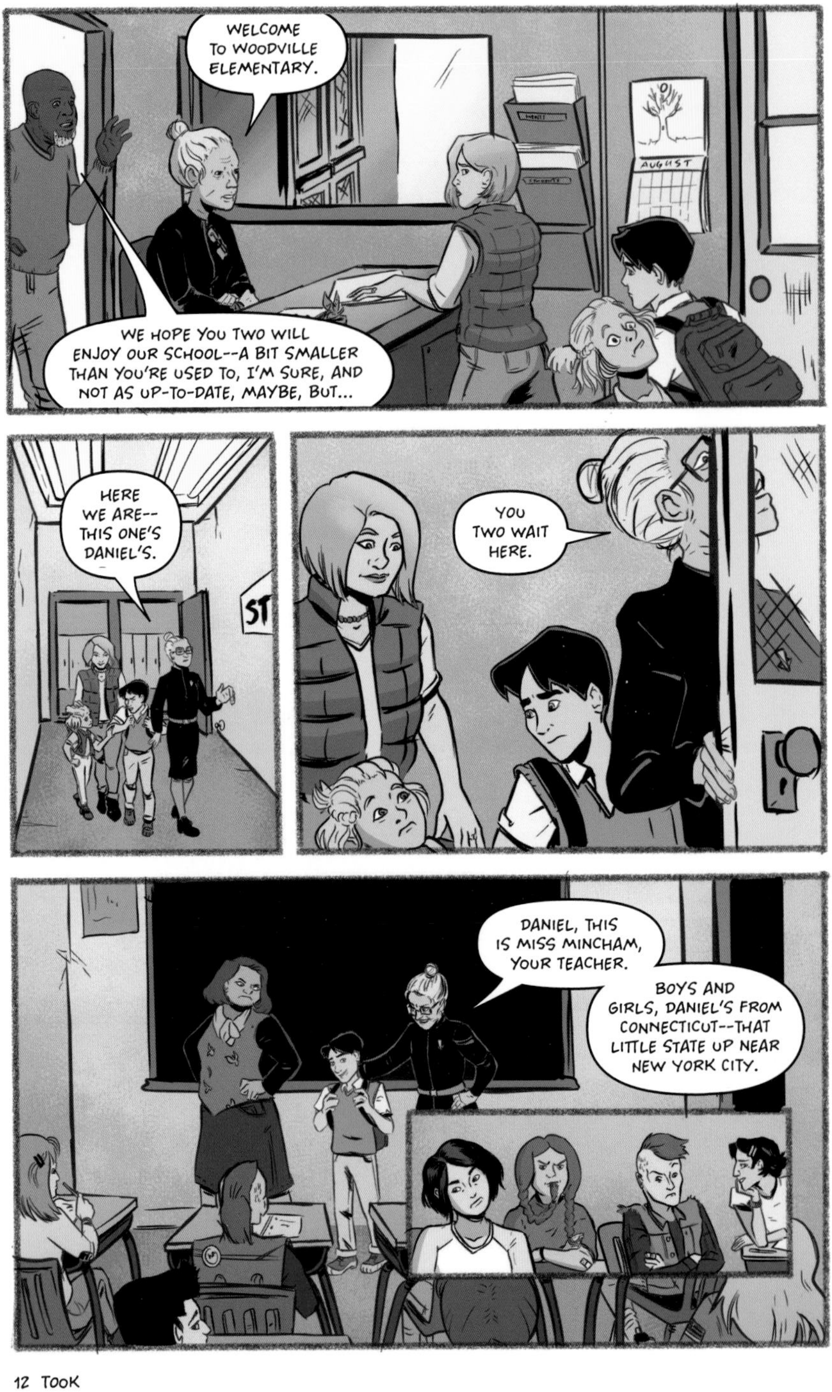
WELCOME TO WOODVILLE ELEMENTARY.
WE HOPE YOU TWO WILL ENJOY OUR SCHOOL--A BIT SMALLER THAN YOU'RE USED TO, I'M SURE, AND NOT AS UP-TO-DATE, MAYBE, BUT...
AUGUST
HERE WE ARE--THIS ONE'S DANIEL'S.
ST
YOU TWO WAIT HERE.
DANIEL, THIS IS MISS MINCHAM, YOUR TEACHER.
BOYS AND GIRLS, DANIEL'S FROM CONNECTICUT--THAT LITTLE STATE UP NEAR NEW YORK CITY.

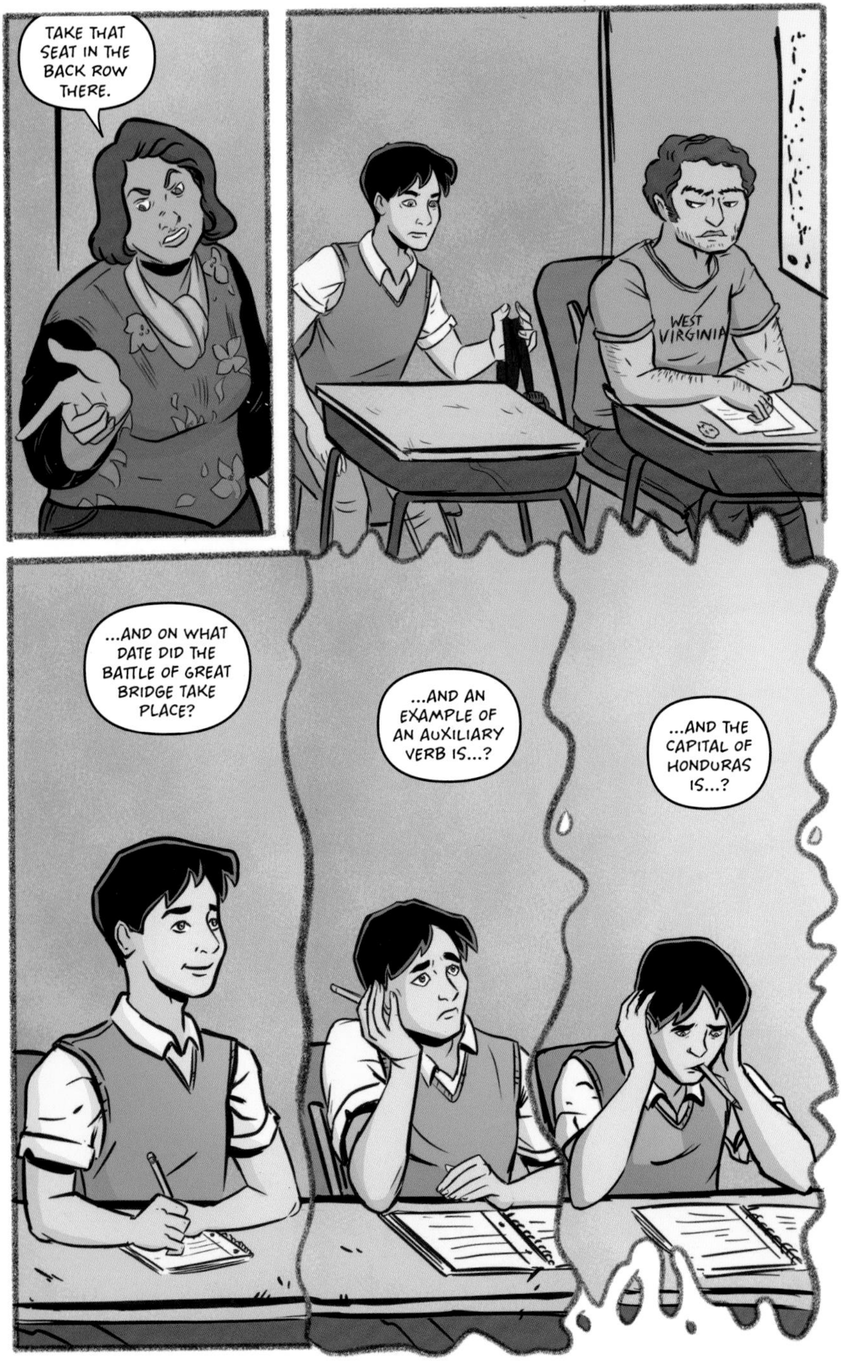
TAKE THAT SEAT IN THE BACK ROW THERE.
WEST VIRGINIA
...AND ON WHAT DATE DID THE BATTLE OF GREAT BRIDGE TAKE PLACE?
...AND AN EXAMPLE OF AN AUXILIARY VERB IS...?
...AND THE CAPITAL OF HONDURAS IS...?

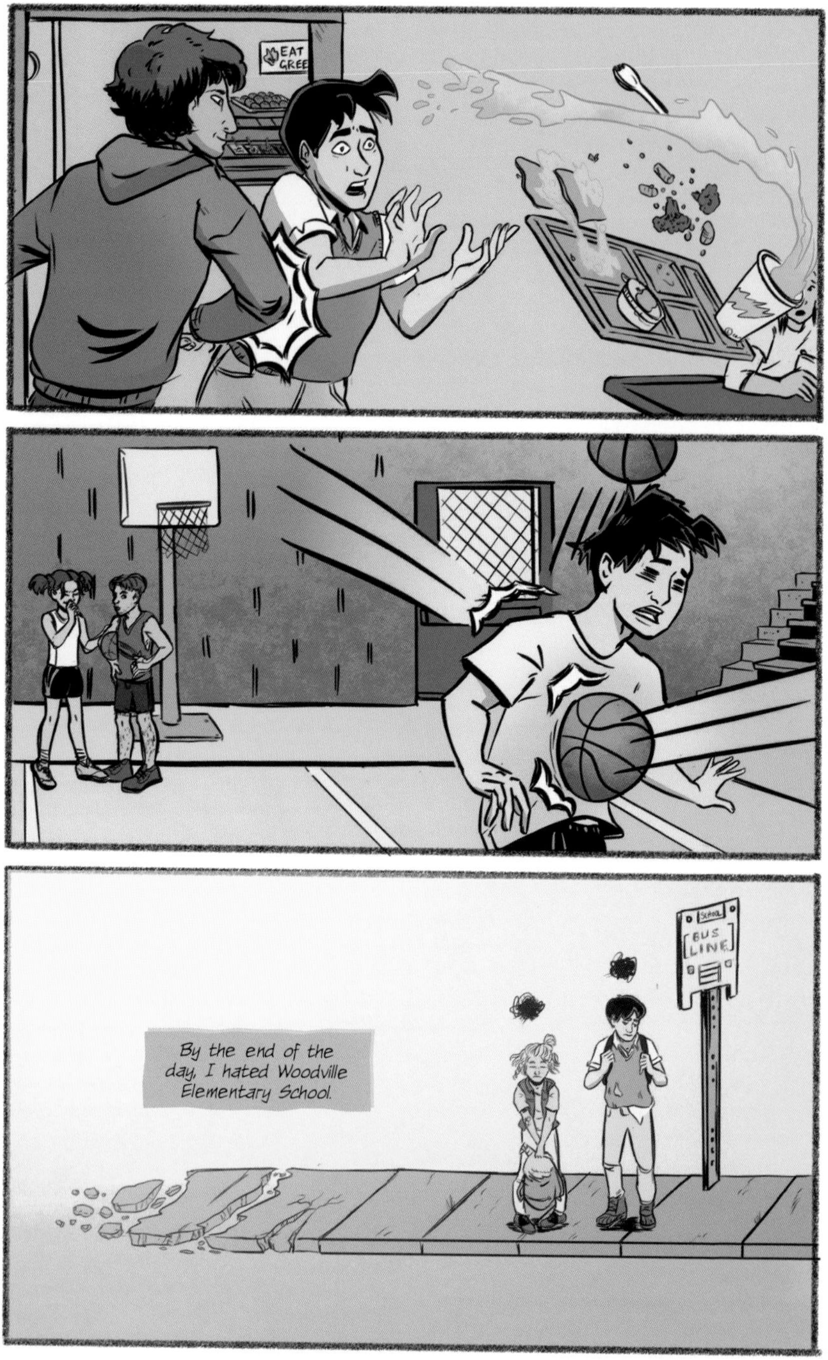
EAT GREE
By the end of the day, I hated Woodville Elementary School.
School
BUS LINE

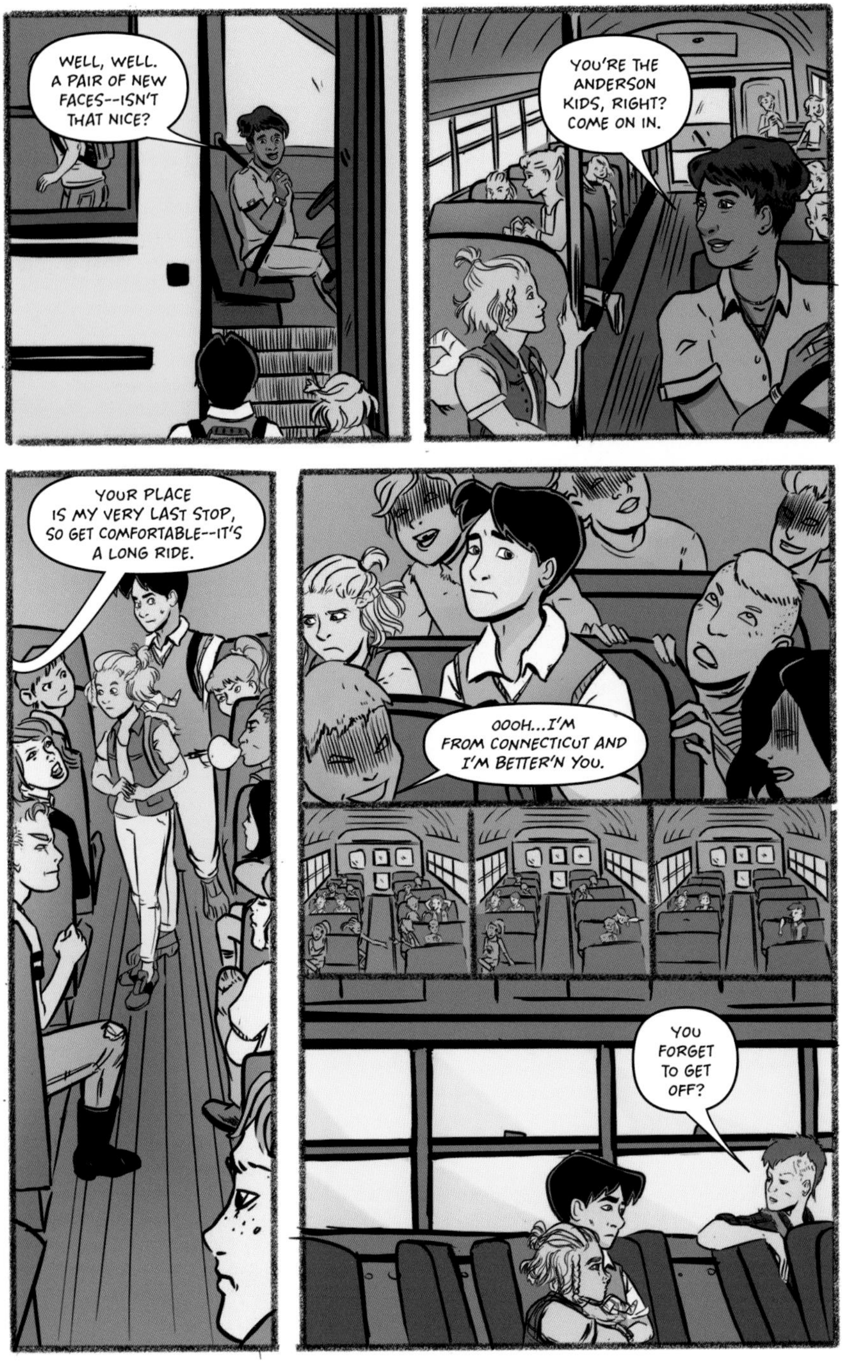
WELL, WELL. A PAIR OF NEW FACES--ISN'T THAT NICE?
YOU'RE THE ANDERSON KIDS, RIGHT? COME ON IN.
YOUR PLACE IS MY VERY LAST STOP, SO GET COMFORTABLE--IT'S A LONG RIDE.
OOOH...I'M FROM CONNECTICUT AND I'M BETTER'N YOU.
YOU FORGET TO GET OFF?

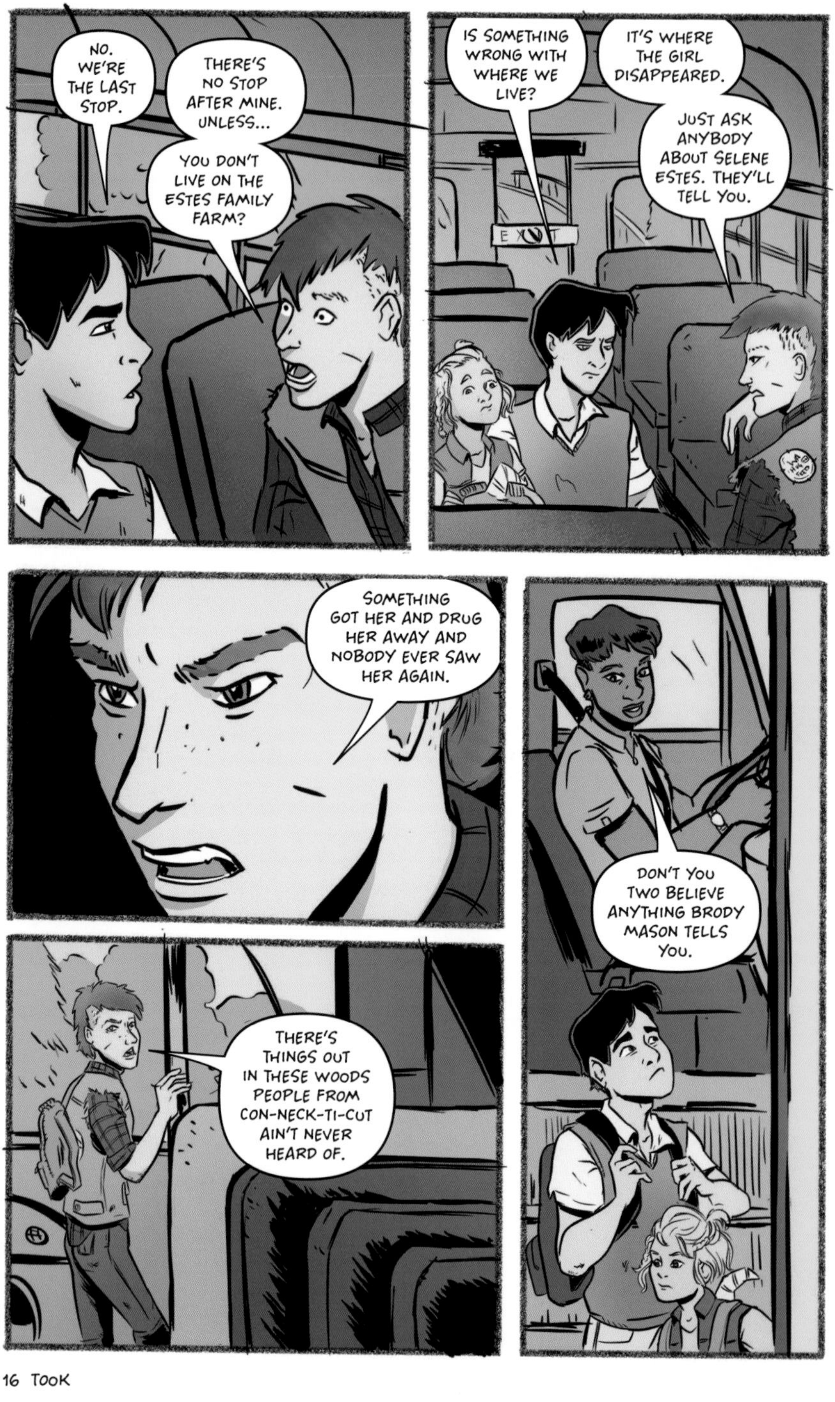
NO. WE'RE THE LAST STOP.
THERE'S NO STOP AFTER MINE. UNLESS...
YOU DON'T LIVE ON THE ESTES FAMILY FARM?
IS SOMETHING WRONG WITH WHERE WE LIVE?
IT'S WHERE THE GIRL DISAPPEARED.
JUST ASK ANYBODY ABOUT SELENE ESTES. THEY'LL TELL YOU.
SOMETHING GOT HER AND DRUG HER AWAY AND NOBODY EVER SAW HER AGAIN.
DON'T YOU TWO BELIEVE ANYTHING BRODY MASON TELLS YOU.
THERE'S THINGS OUT IN THESE WOODS PEOPLE FROM CON-NECK-TI-CUT AIN'T NEVER HEARD OF.

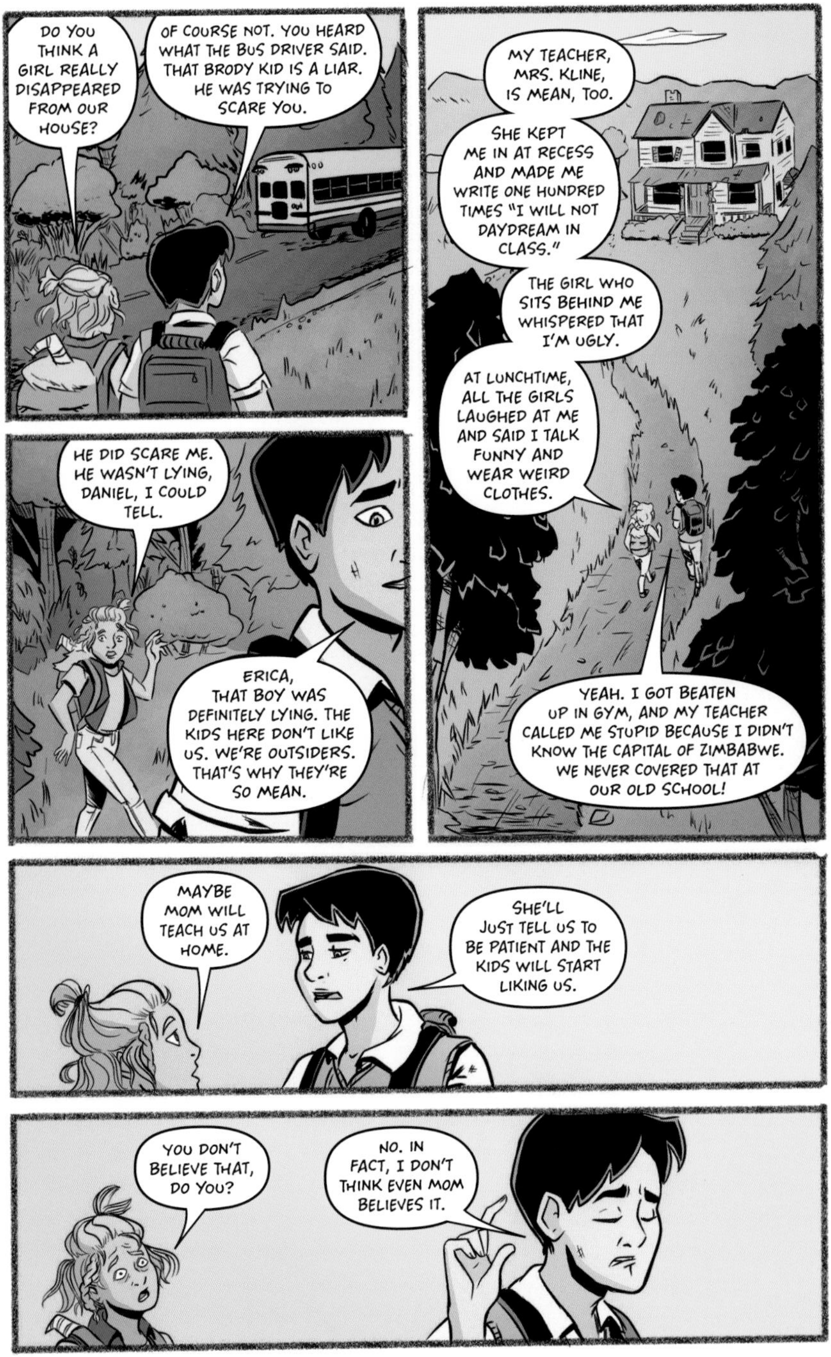
DO YOU THINK A GIRL REALLY DISAPPEARED FROM OUR HOUSE?
OF COURSE NOT. YOU HEARD WHAT THE BUS DRIVER SAID. THAT BRODY KID IS A LIAR. HE WAS TRYING TO SCARE YOU.
HE DID SCARE ME. HE WASN'T LYING, DANIEL, I COULD TELL.
ERICA, THAT BOY WAS DEFINITELY LYING. THE KIDS HERE DON'T LIKE US. WE'RE OUTSIDERS. THAT'S WHY THEY'RE SO MEAN.
MY TEACHER, MRS. KLINE, IS MEAN, TOO.
SHE KEPT ME IN AT RECESS AND MADE ME WRITE ONE HUNDRED TIMES "I WILL NOT DAYDREAM IN CLASS."
THE GIRL WHO SITS BEHIND ME WHISPERED THAT I'M UGLY.
AT LUNCHTIME, ALL THE GIRLS LAUGHED AT ME AND SAID I TALK FUNNY AND WEAR WEIRD CLOTHES.
YEAH. I GOT BEATEN UP IN GYM, AND MY TEACHER CALLED ME STUPID BECAUSE I DIDN'T KNOW THE CAPITAL OF ZIMBABWE. WE NEVER COVERED THAT AT OUR OLD SCHOOL!
MAYBE MOM WILL TEACH US AT HOME.
SHE'LL JUST TELL US TO BE PATIENT AND THE KIDS WILL START LIKING US.
YOU DON'T BELIEVE THAT, DO YOU?
NO. IN FACT, I DON'T THINK EVEN MOM BELIEVES IT.

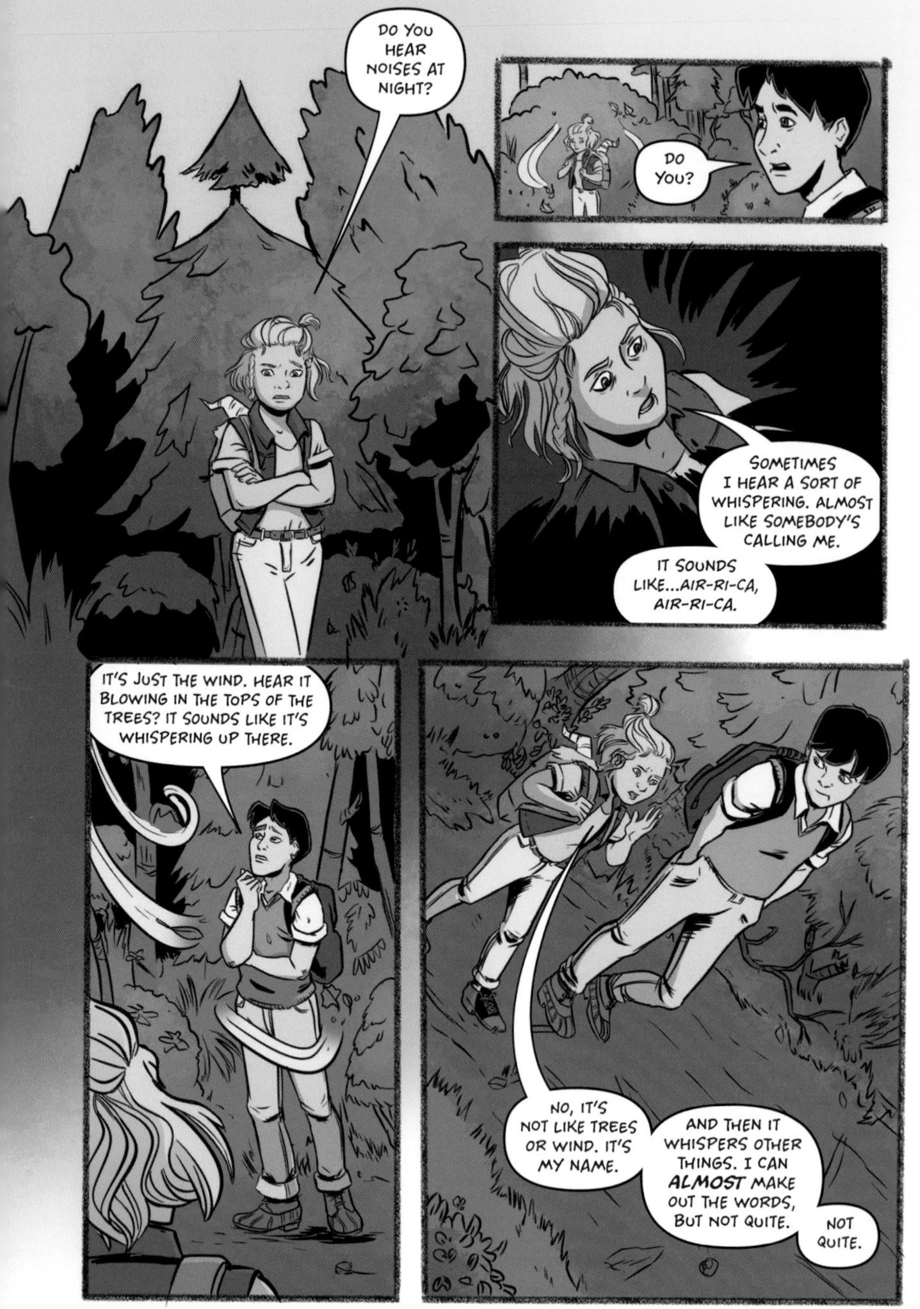
DO YOU HEAR NOISES AT NIGHT?
DO YOU?
SOMETIMES I HEAR A SORT OF WHISPERING. ALMOST LIKE SOMEBODY'S CALLING ME.
IT SOUNDS LIKE...AIR-RI-CA, AIR-RI-CA.
IT'S JUST THE WIND. HEAR IT BLOWING IN THE TOPS OF THE TREES? IT SOUNDS LIKE IT'S WHISPERING UP THERE.
NO, IT'S NOT LIKE TREES OR WIND. IT'S MY NAME.
AND THEN IT WHISPERS OTHER THINGS. I CAN **ALMOST** MAKE OUT THE WORDS, BUT NOT QUITE.
NOT QUITE.

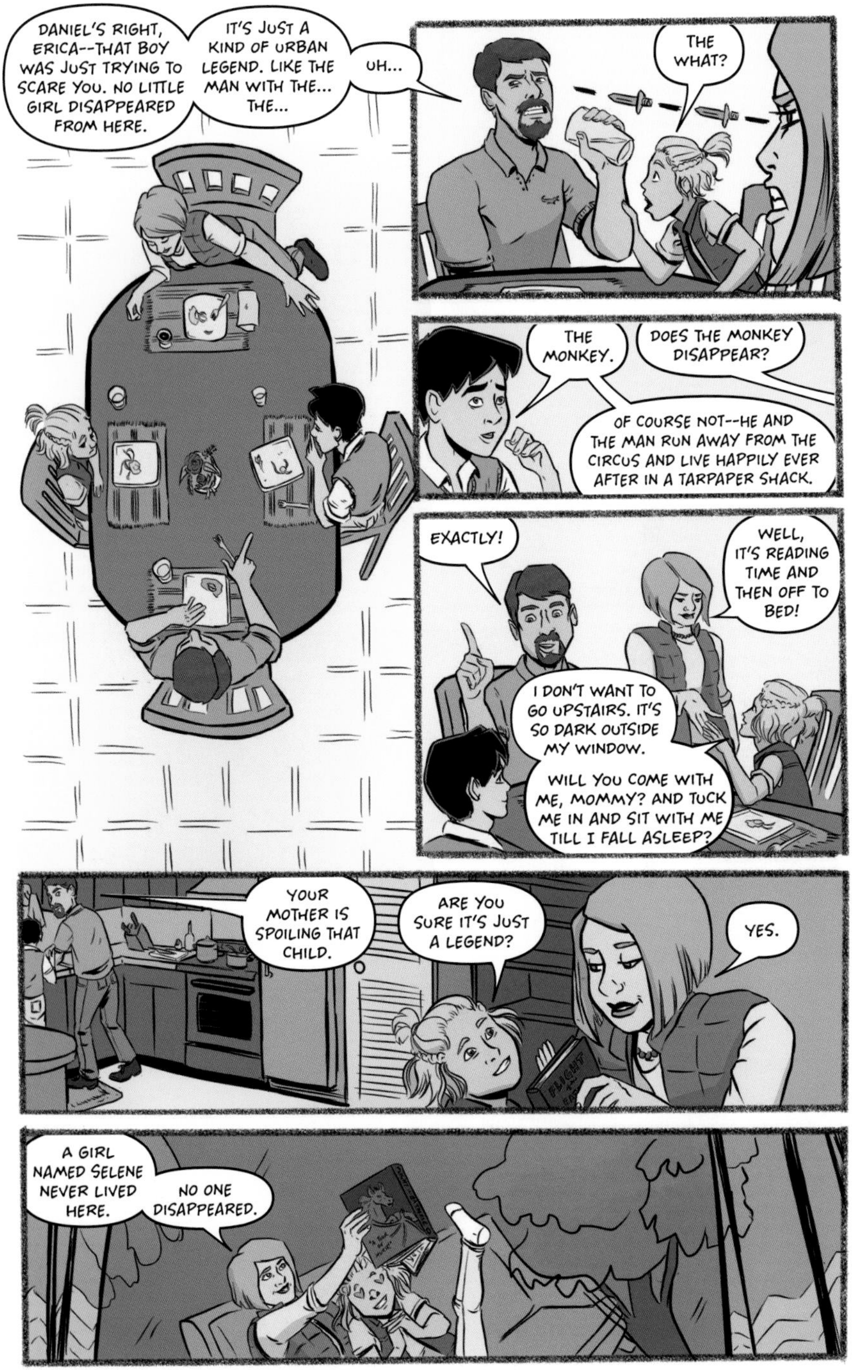
DANIEL'S RIGHT, ERICA--THAT BOY WAS JUST TRYING TO SCARE YOU. NO LITTLE GIRL DISAPPEARED FROM HERE.
IT'S JUST A KIND OF URBAN LEGEND. LIKE THE MAN WITH THE... THE...
UH...
THE WHAT?
THE MONKEY.
DOES THE MONKEY DISAPPEAR?
OF COURSE NOT--HE AND THE MAN RUN AWAY FROM THE CIRCUS AND LIVE HAPPILY EVER AFTER IN A TARPAPER SHACK.
EXACTLY!
WELL, IT'S READING TIME AND THEN OFF TO BED!
I DON'T WANT TO GO UPSTAIRS. IT'S SO DARK OUTSIDE MY WINDOW.
WILL YOU COME WITH ME, MOMMY? AND TUCK ME IN AND SIT WITH ME TILL I FALL ASLEEP?
YOUR MOTHER IS SPOILING THAT CHILD.
ARE YOU SURE IT'S JUST A LEGEND?
YES.
A GIRL NAMED SELENE NEVER LIVED HERE.
NO ONE DISAPPEARED.

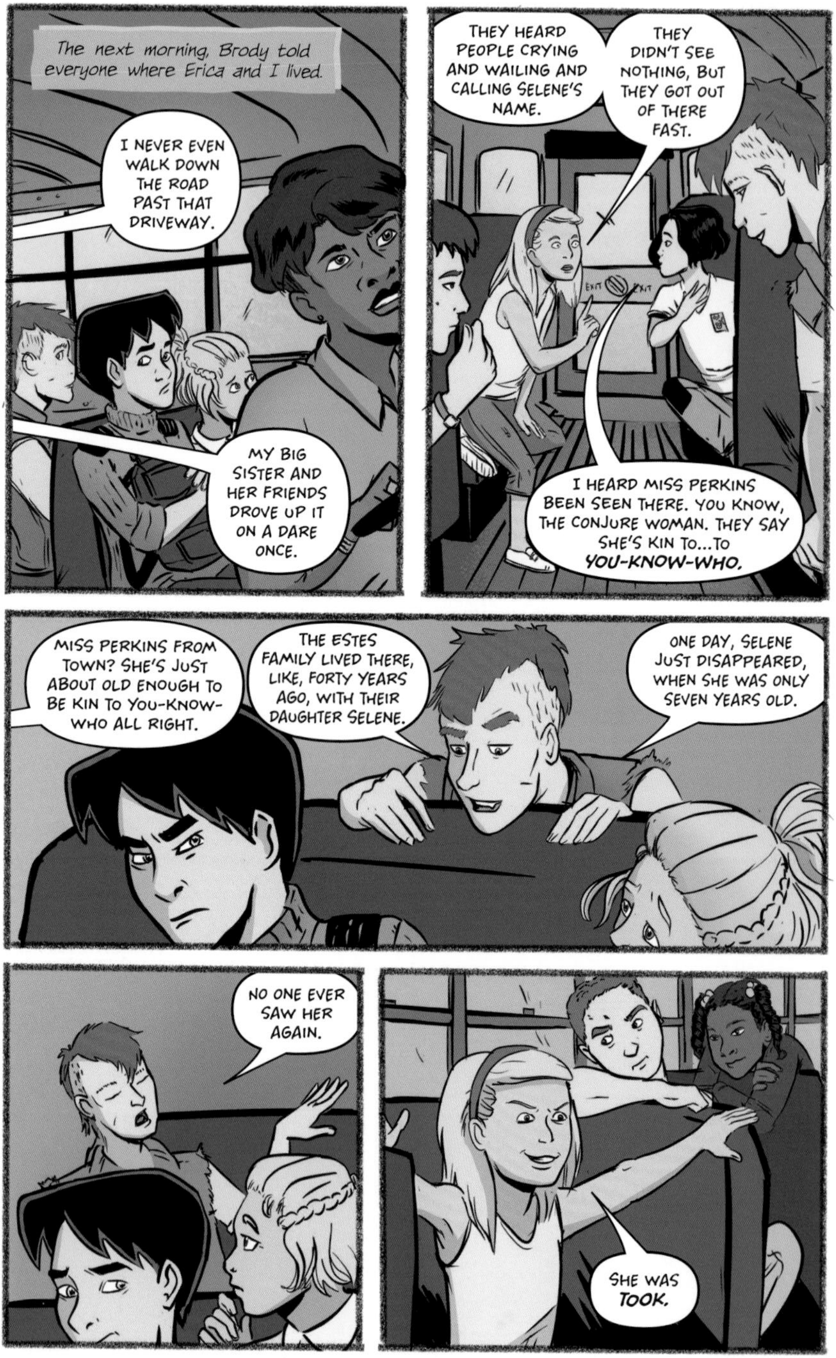
The next morning, Brody told everyone where Erica and I lived.
I NEVER EVEN WALK DOWN THE ROAD PAST THAT DRIVEWAY.
MY BIG SISTER AND HER FRIENDS DROVE UP IT ON A DARE ONCE.
THEY HEARD PEOPLE CRYING AND WAILING AND CALLING SELENE'S NAME.
THEY DIDN'T SEE NOTHING, BUT THEY GOT OUT OF THERE FAST.
I HEARD MISS PERKINS BEEN SEEN THERE. YOU KNOW, THE CONJURE WOMAN. THEY SAY SHE'S KIN TO...TO ***YOU-KNOW-WHO.***
MISS PERKINS FROM TOWN? SHE'S JUST ABOUT OLD ENOUGH TO BE KIN TO YOU-KNOW-WHO ALL RIGHT.
THE ESTES FAMILY LIVED THERE, LIKE, FORTY YEARS AGO, WITH THEIR DAUGHTER SELENE.
ONE DAY, SELENE JUST DISAPPEARED, WHEN SHE WAS ONLY SEVEN YEARS OLD.
NO ONE EVER SAW HER AGAIN.
SHE WAS ***TOOK.***

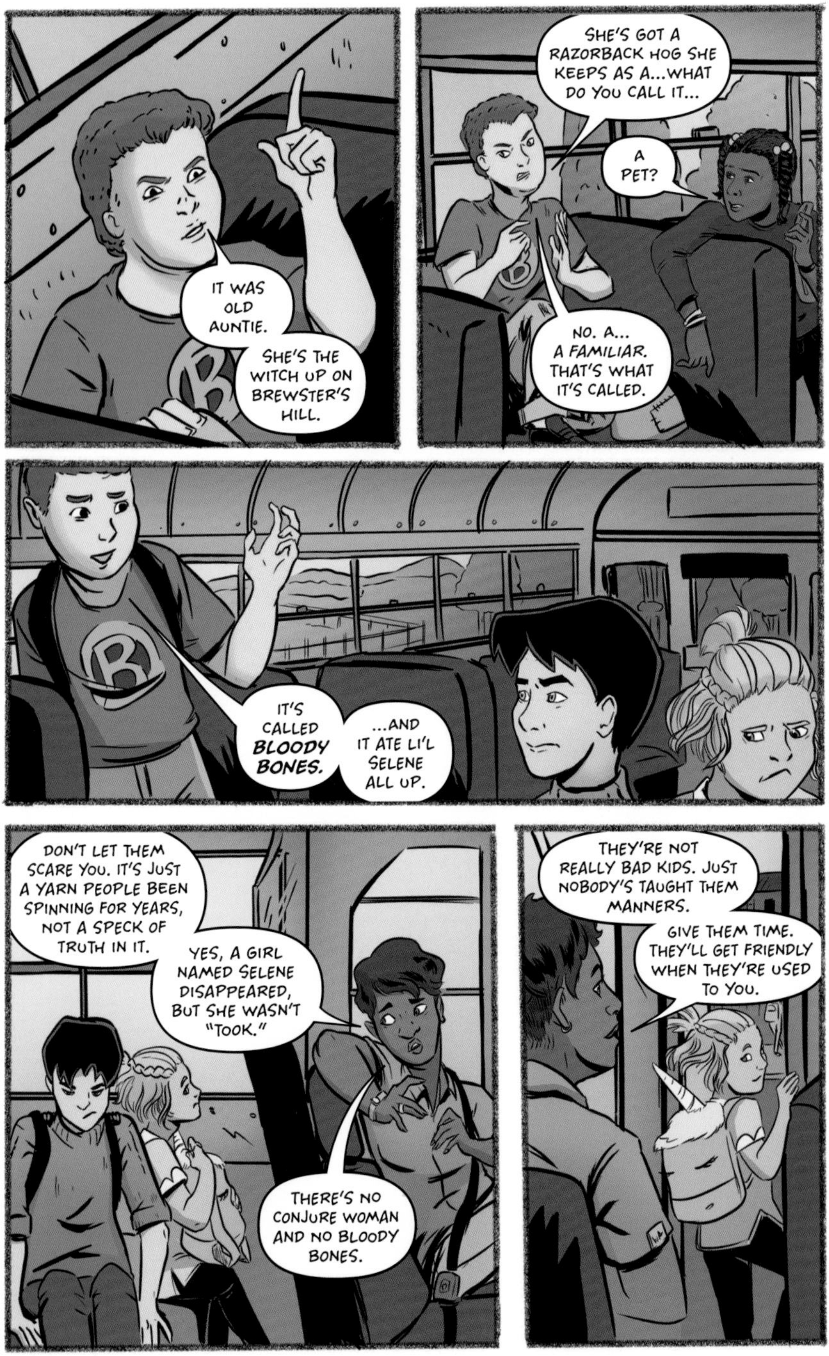
IT WAS OLD AUNTIE.
SHE'S THE WITCH UP ON BREWSTER'S HILL.
SHE'S GOT A RAZORBACK HOG SHE KEEPS AS A...WHAT DO YOU CALL IT...
A PET?
NO. A... A *FAMILIAR*. THAT'S WHAT IT'S CALLED.
IT'S CALLED ***BLOODY BONES.***
...AND IT ATE LI'L SELENE ALL UP.
DON'T LET THEM SCARE YOU. IT'S JUST A YARN PEOPLE BEEN SPINNING FOR YEARS, NOT A SPECK OF TRUTH IN IT.
YES, A GIRL NAMED SELENE DISAPPEARED, BUT SHE WASN'T "TOOK."
THERE'S NO CONJURE WOMAN AND NO BLOODY BONES.
THEY'RE NOT REALLY BAD KIDS. JUST NOBODY'S TAUGHT THEM MANNERS.
GIVE THEM TIME. THEY'LL GET FRIENDLY WHEN THEY'RE USED TO YOU.

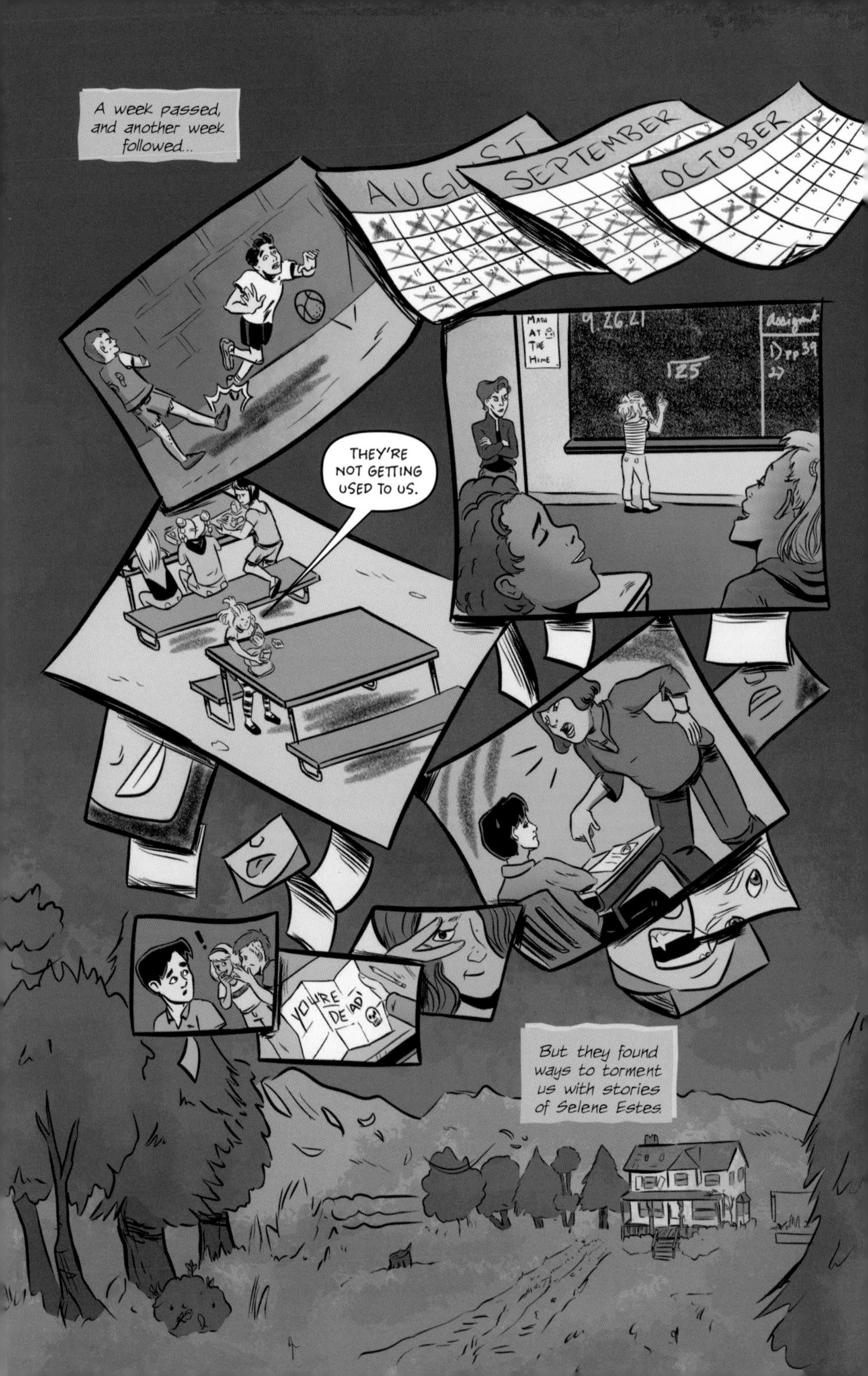
A week passed, and another week followed...
AUGUST
SEPTEMBER
OCTOBER
MATH AT THE HOME
9.26.21
THEY'RE NOT GETTING USED TO US.
YOU'RE DEAD
But they found ways to torment us with stories of Selene Estes.

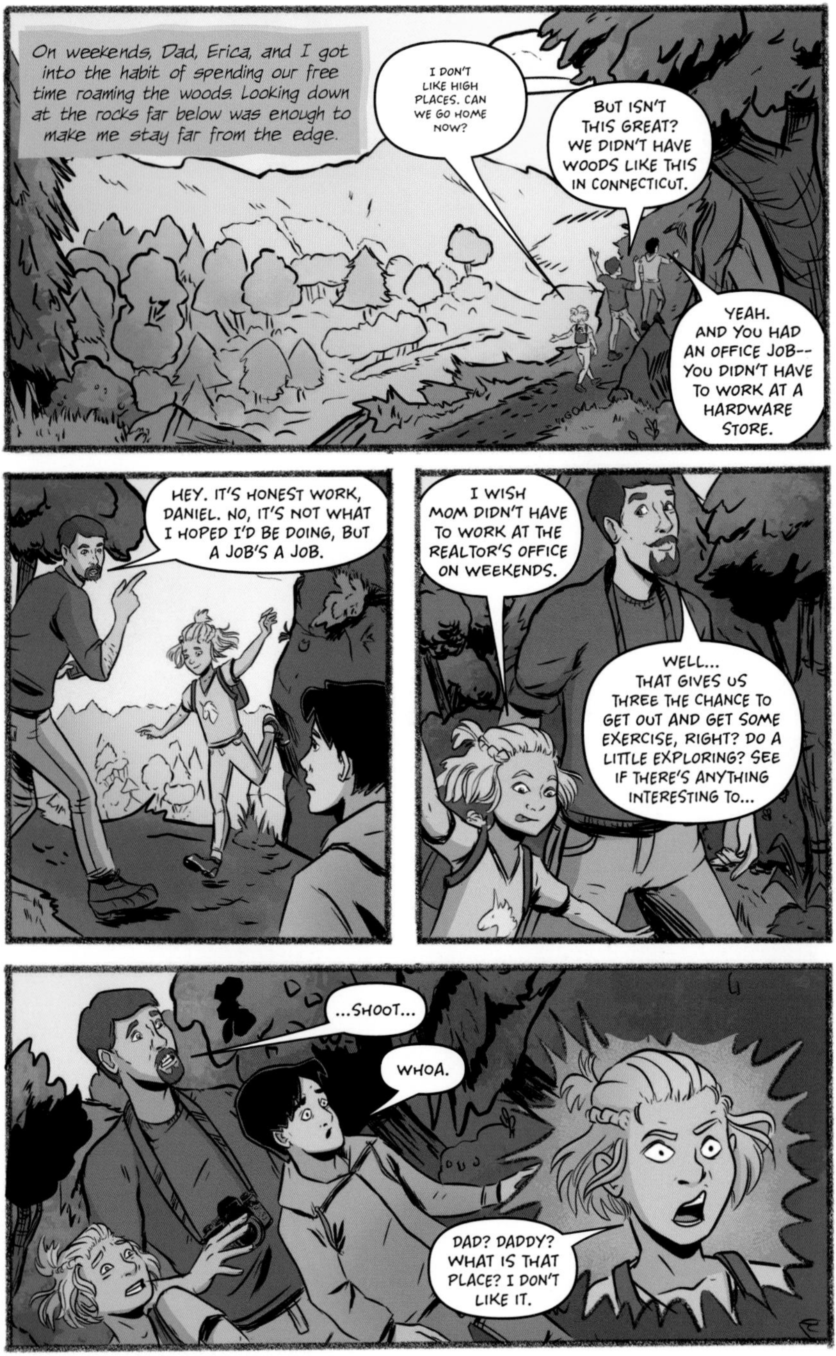
On weekends, Dad, Erica, and I got into the habit of spending our free time roaming the woods. Looking down at the rocks far below was enough to make me stay far from the edge.
I DON'T LIKE HIGH PLACES. CAN WE GO HOME NOW?
BUT ISN'T THIS GREAT? WE DIDN'T HAVE WOODS LIKE THIS IN CONNECTICUT.
YEAH. AND YOU HAD AN OFFICE JOB-- YOU DIDN'T HAVE TO WORK AT A HARDWARE STORE.
HEY. IT'S HONEST WORK, DANIEL. NO, IT'S NOT WHAT I HOPED I'D BE DOING, BUT A JOB'S A JOB.
I WISH MOM DIDN'T HAVE TO WORK AT THE REALTOR'S OFFICE ON WEEKENDS.
WELL... THAT GIVES US THREE THE CHANCE TO GET OUT AND GET SOME EXERCISE, RIGHT? DO A LITTLE EXPLORING? SEE IF THERE'S ANYTHING INTERESTING TO...
...SHOOT...
WHOA.
DAD? DADDY? WHAT IS THAT PLACE? I DON'T LIKE IT.

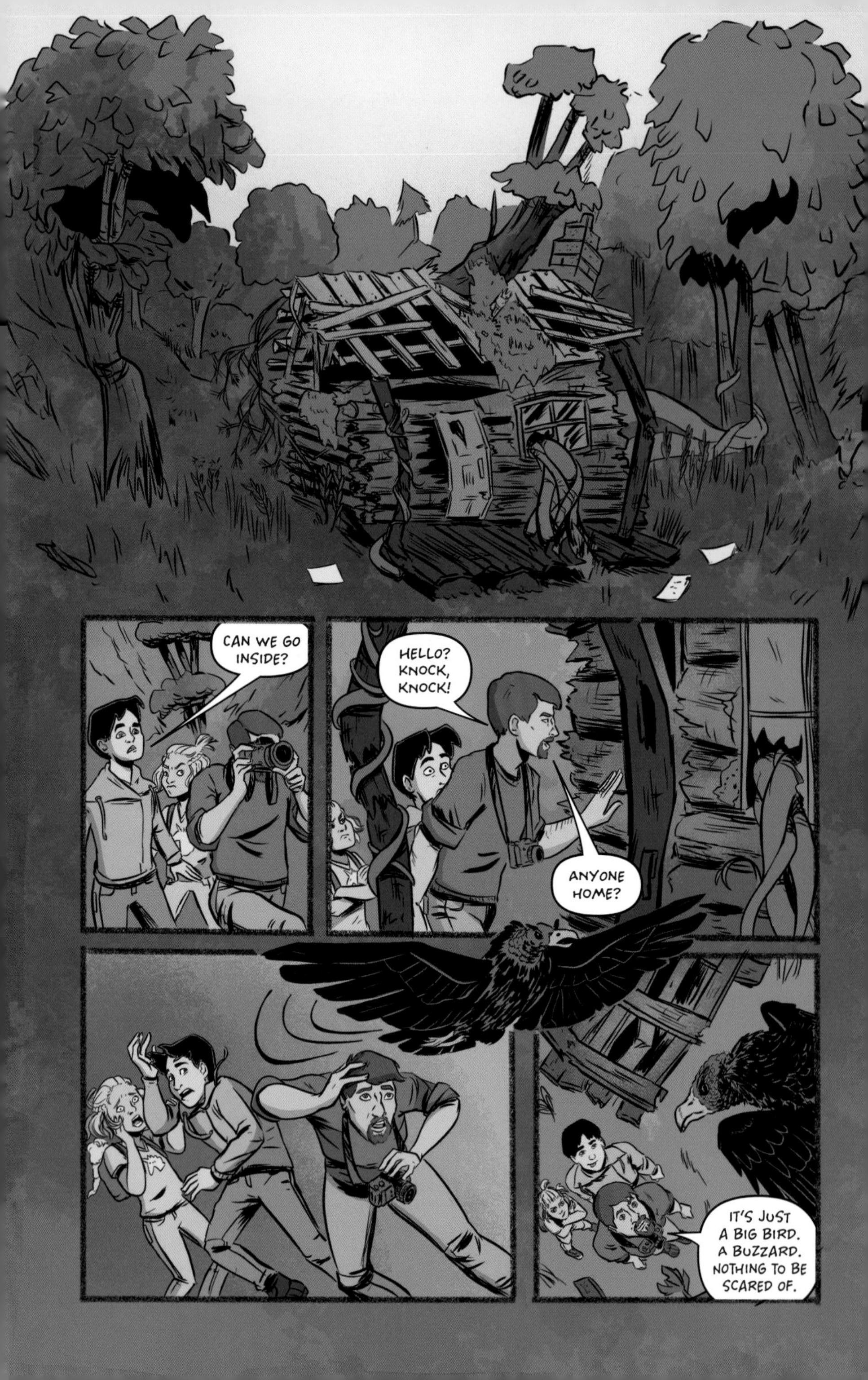
CAN WE GO INSIDE?
HELLO? KNOCK, KNOCK!
ANYONE HOME?
IT'S JUST A BIG BIRD. A BUZZARD. NOTHING TO BE SCARED OF.

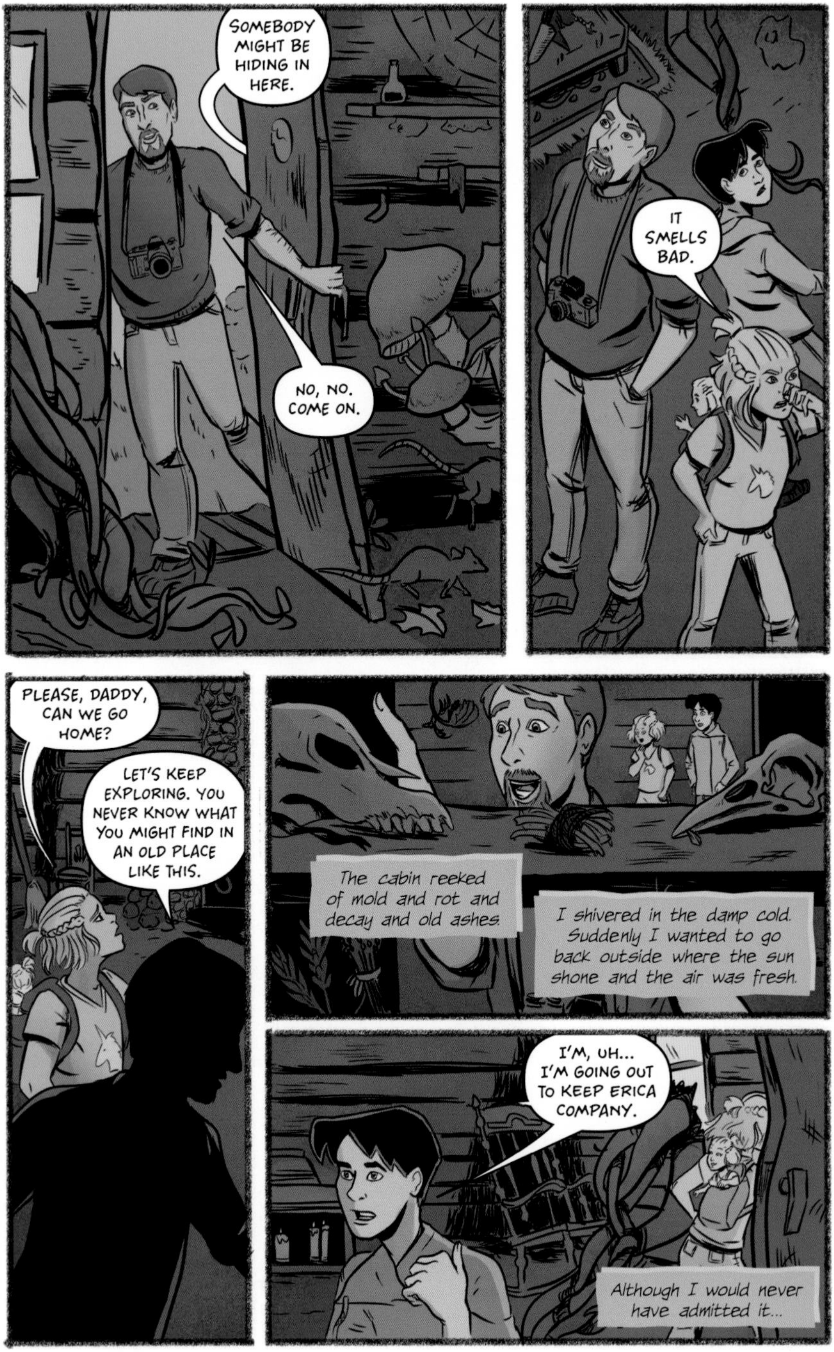
SOMEBODY MIGHT BE HIDING IN HERE.
NO, NO. COME ON.
IT SMELLS BAD.
PLEASE, DADDY, CAN WE GO HOME?
LET'S KEEP EXPLORING. YOU NEVER KNOW WHAT YOU MIGHT FIND IN AN OLD PLACE LIKE THIS.
The cabin reeked of mold and rot and decay and old ashes.
I shivered in the damp cold. Suddenly I wanted to go back outside where the sun shone and the air was fresh.
I'M, UH... I'M GOING OUT TO KEEP ERICA COMPANY.
Although I would never have admitted it...

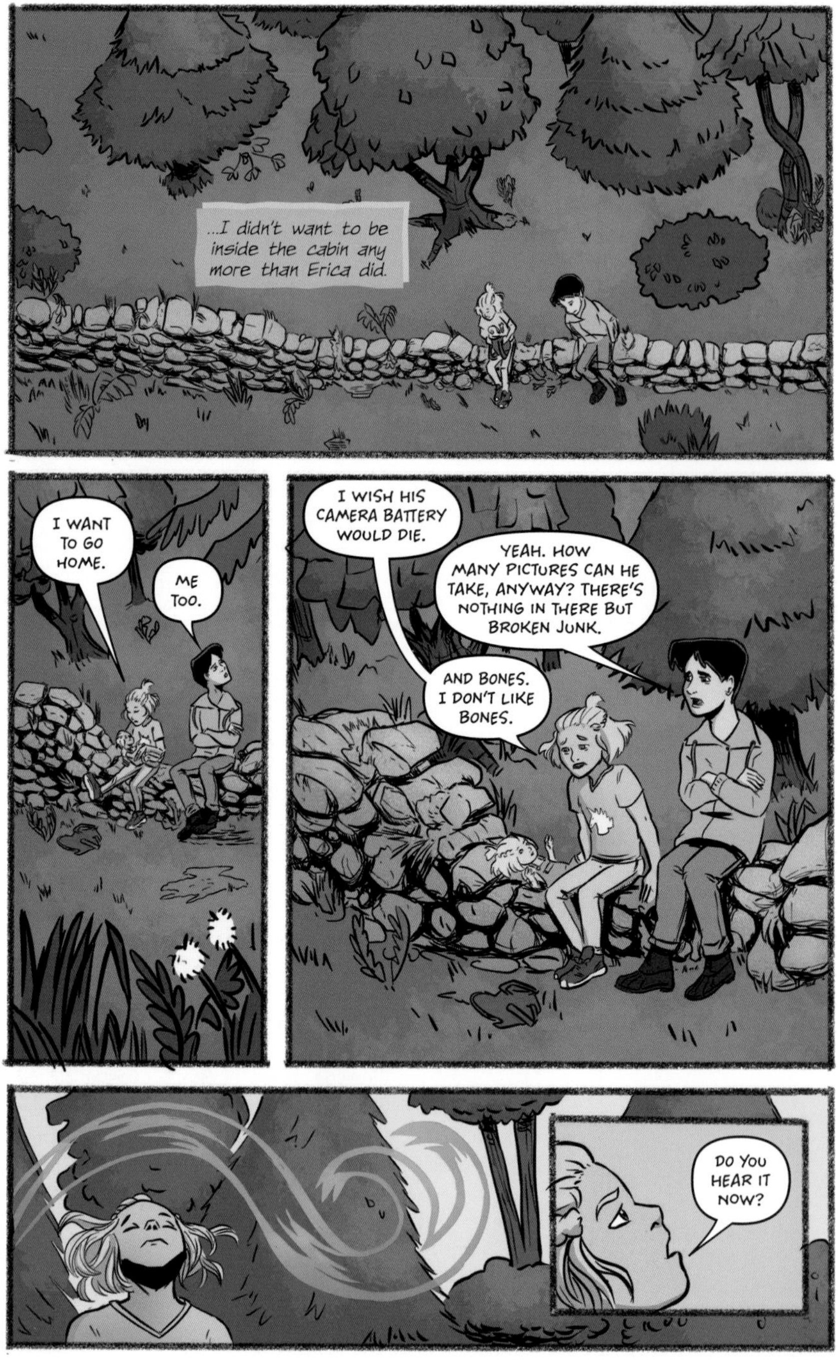
...I didn't want to be inside the cabin any more than Erica did.
I WANT TO GO HOME.
ME TOO.
I WISH HIS CAMERA BATTERY WOULD DIE.
YEAH. HOW MANY PICTURES CAN HE TAKE, ANYWAY? THERE'S NOTHING IN THERE BUT BROKEN JUNK.
AND BONES. I DON'T LIKE BONES.
DO YOU HEAR IT NOW?

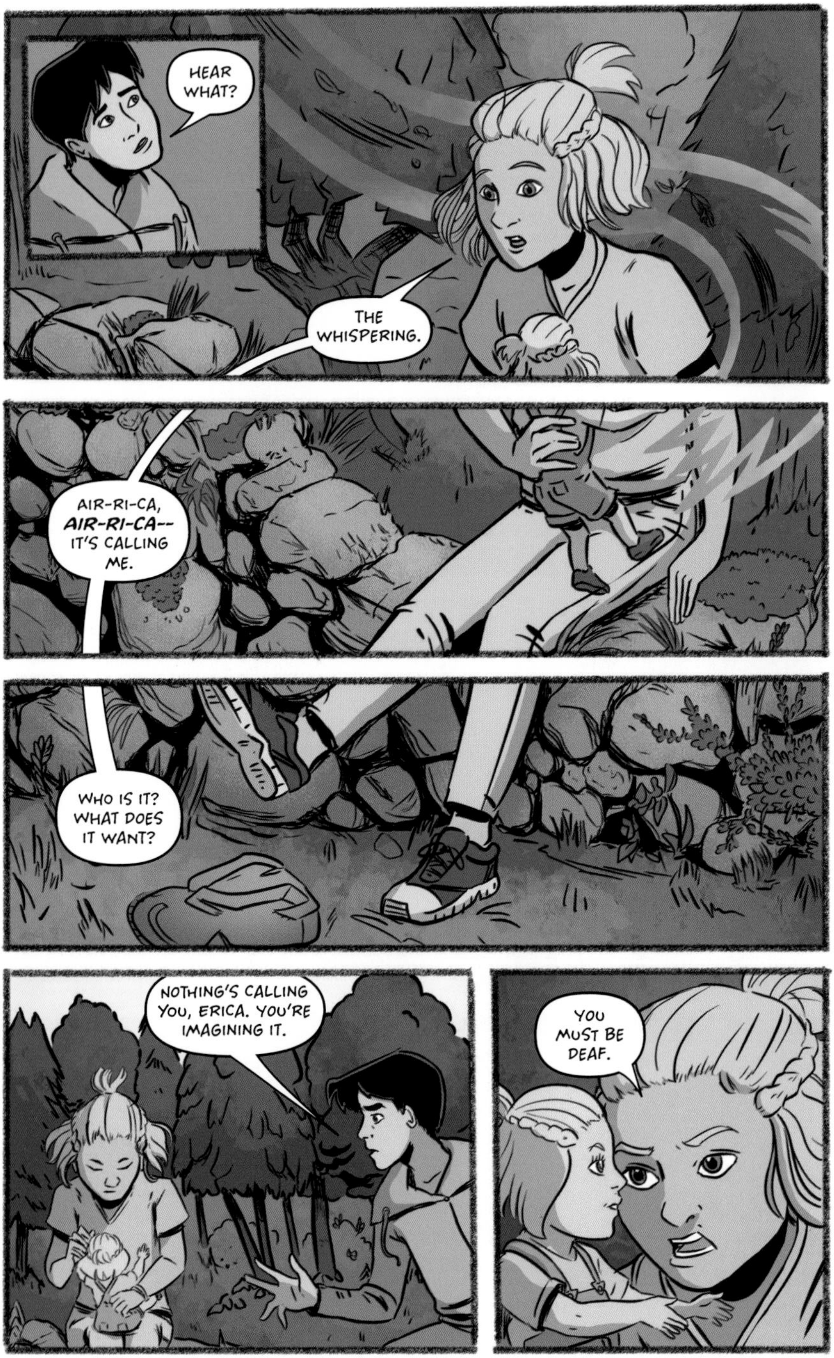
HEAR WHAT?
THE WHISPERING.
AIR-RI-CA, **AIR-RI-CA--** IT'S CALLING ME.
WHO IS IT? WHAT DOES IT WANT?
NOTHING'S CALLING YOU, ERICA. YOU'RE IMAGINING IT.
YOU MUST BE DEAF.

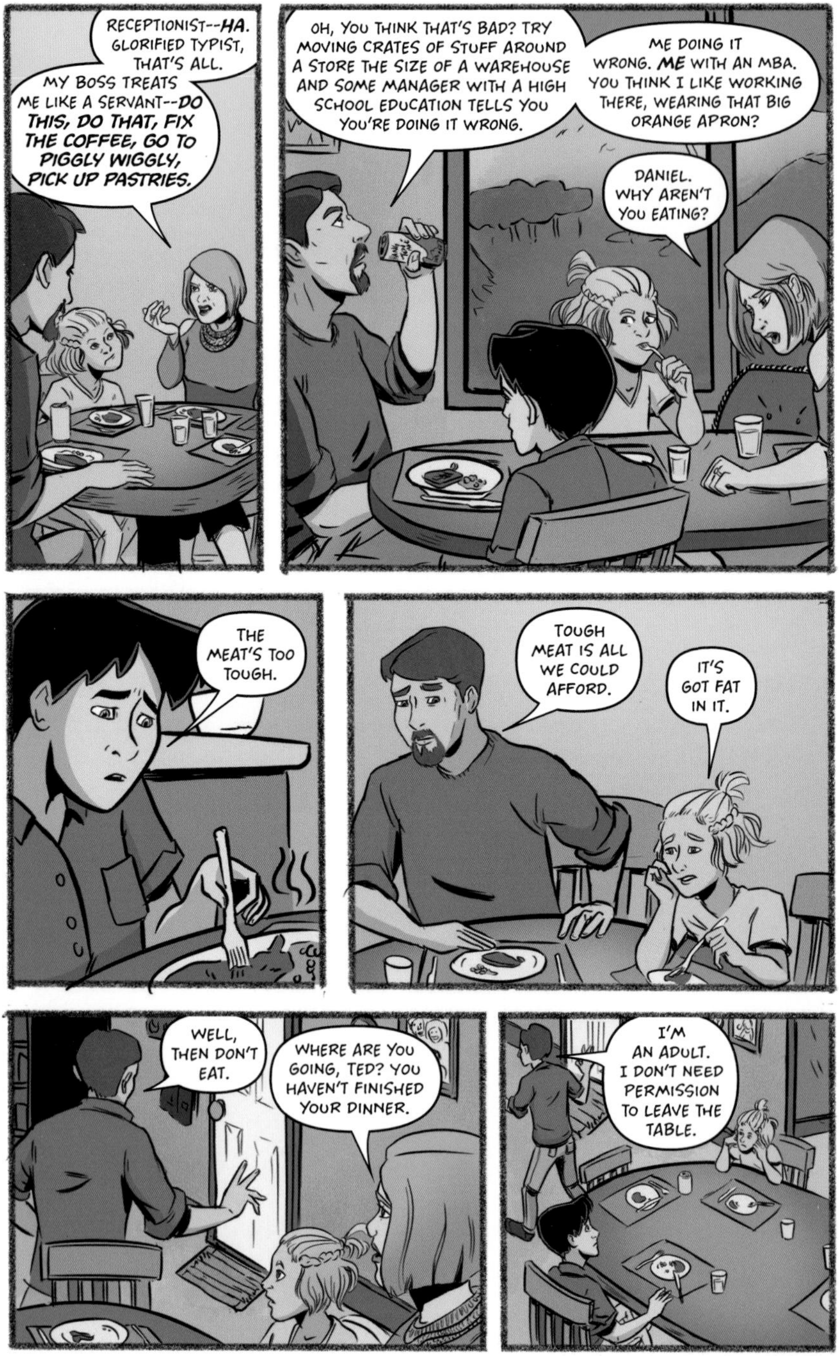
RECEPTIONIST--HA. GLORIFIED TYPIST, THAT'S ALL.
MY BOSS TREATS ME LIKE A SERVANT--DO THIS, DO THAT, FIX THE COFFEE, GO TO PIGGLY WIGGLY, PICK UP PASTRIES.
OH, YOU THINK THAT'S BAD? TRY MOVING CRATES OF STUFF AROUND A STORE THE SIZE OF A WAREHOUSE AND SOME MANAGER WITH A HIGH SCHOOL EDUCATION TELLS YOU YOU'RE DOING IT WRONG.
ME DOING IT WRONG. ME WITH AN MBA. YOU THINK I LIKE WORKING THERE, WEARING THAT BIG ORANGE APRON?
DANIEL. WHY AREN'T YOU EATING?
THE MEAT'S TOO TOUGH.
TOUGH MEAT IS ALL WE COULD AFFORD.
IT'S GOT FAT IN IT.
WELL, THEN DON'T EAT.
WHERE ARE YOU GOING, TED? YOU HAVEN'T FINISHED YOUR DINNER.
I'M AN ADULT. I DON'T NEED PERMISSION TO LEAVE THE TABLE.

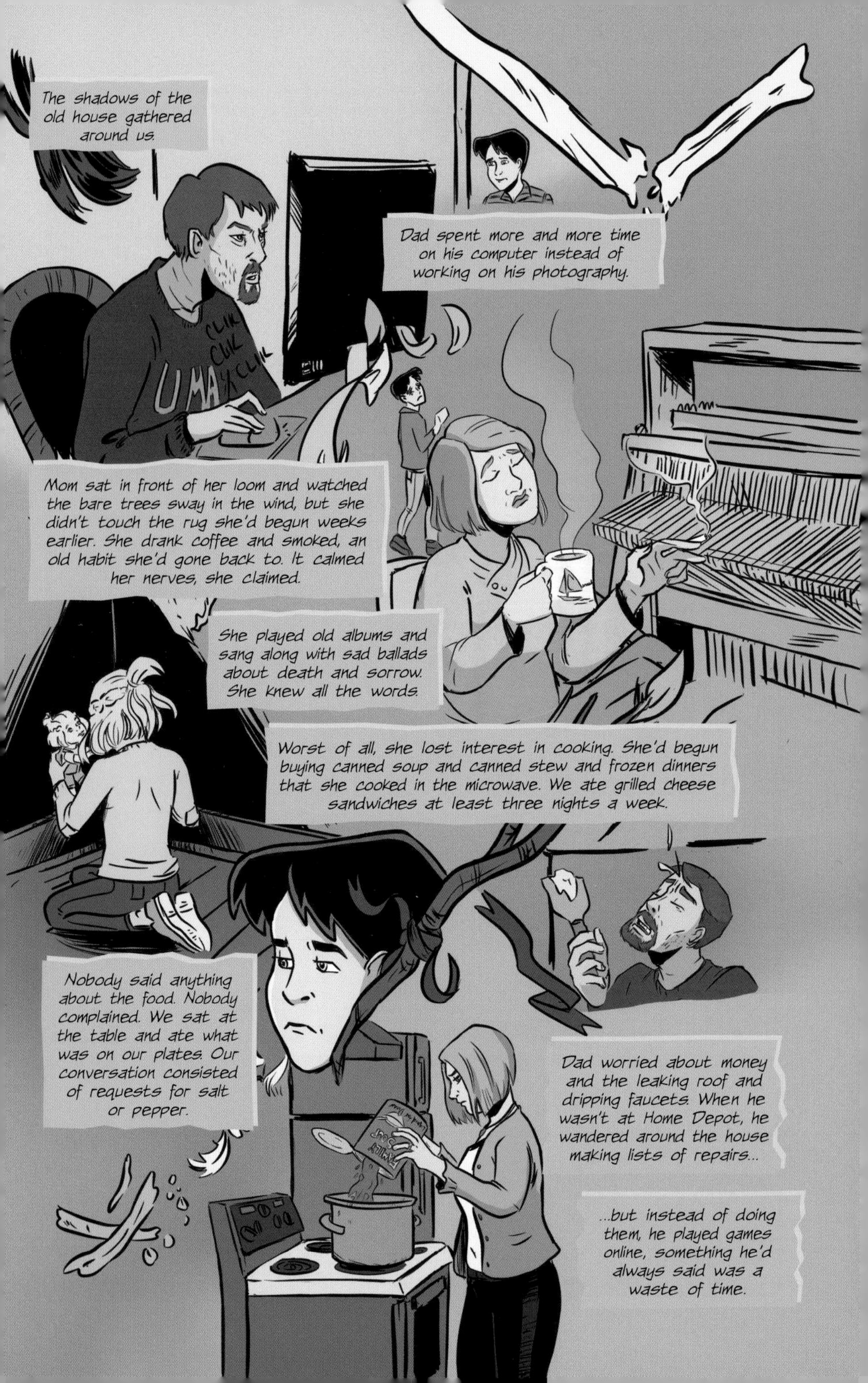
The shadows of the old house gathered around us.
Dad spent more and more time on his computer instead of working on his photography.
CLIK CLIK CLIK
Mom sat in front of her loom and watched the bare trees sway in the wind, but she didn't touch the rug she'd begun weeks earlier. She drank coffee and smoked, an old habit she'd gone back to. It calmed her nerves, she claimed.
She played old albums and sang along with sad ballads about death and sorrow. She knew all the words.
Worst of all, she lost interest in cooking. She'd begun buying canned soup and canned stew and frozen dinners that she cooked in the microwave. We ate grilled cheese sandwiches at least three nights a week.
Nobody said anything about the food. Nobody complained. We sat at the table and ate what was on our plates. Our conversation consisted of requests for salt or pepper.
Dad worried about money and the leaking roof and dripping faucets. When he wasn't at Home Depot, he wandered around the house making lists of repairs...
...but instead of doing them, he played games online, something he'd always said was a waste of time.

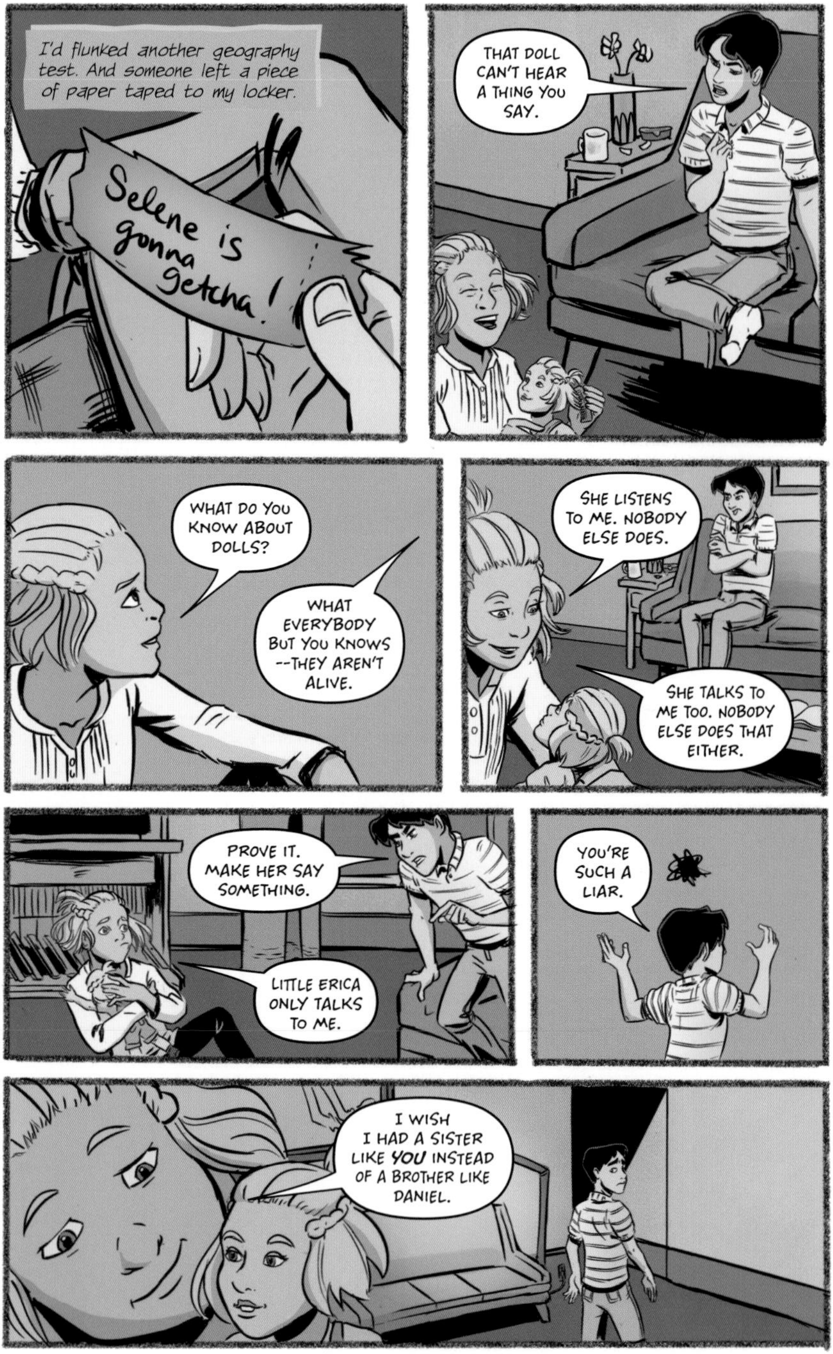

I'd flunked another geography test. And someone left a piece of paper taped to my locker.
Selene is gonna getcha!
THAT DOLL CAN'T HEAR A THING YOU SAY.
WHAT DO YOU KNOW ABOUT DOLLS?
WHAT EVERYBODY BUT YOU KNOWS --THEY AREN'T ALIVE.
SHE LISTENS TO ME. NOBODY ELSE DOES.
SHE TALKS TO ME TOO. NOBODY ELSE DOES THAT EITHER.
PROVE IT. MAKE HER SAY SOMETHING.
LITTLE ERICA ONLY TALKS TO ME.
YOU'RE SUCH A LIAR.
I WISH I HAD A SISTER LIKE *YOU* INSTEAD OF A BROTHER LIKE DANIEL.

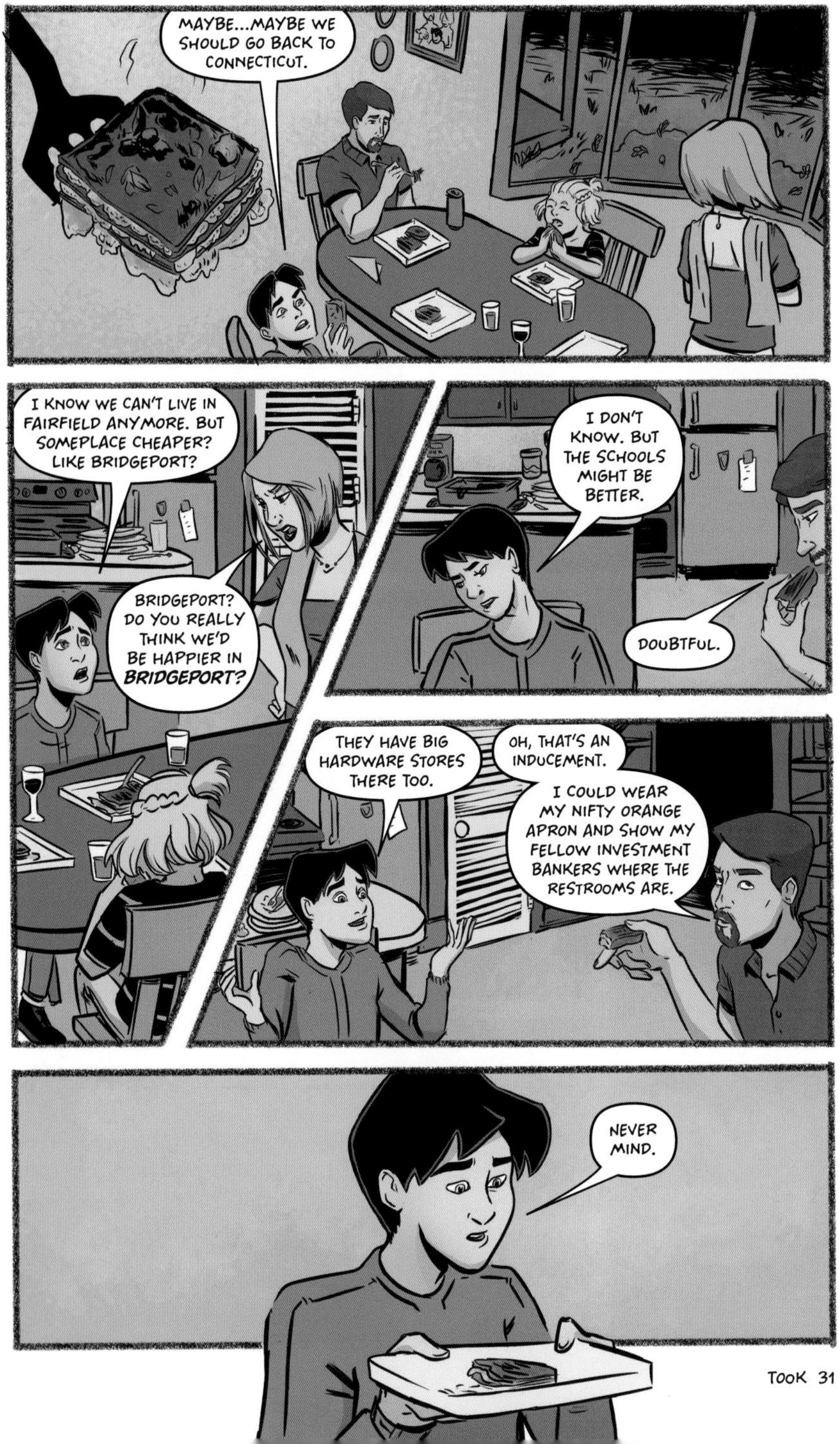

MAYBE...MAYBE WE SHOULD GO BACK TO CONNECTICUT.
I KNOW WE CAN'T LIVE IN FAIRFIELD ANYMORE. BUT SOMEPLACE CHEAPER? LIKE BRIDGEPORT?
BRIDGEPORT? DO YOU REALLY THINK WE'D BE HAPPIER IN BRIDGEPORT?
I DON'T KNOW. BUT THE SCHOOLS MIGHT BE BETTER.
DOUBTFUL.
THEY HAVE BIG HARDWARE STORES THERE TOO.
OH, THAT'S AN INDUCEMENT.
I COULD WEAR MY NIFTY ORANGE APRON AND SHOW MY FELLOW INVESTMENT BANKERS WHERE THE RESTROOMS ARE.
NEVER MIND.

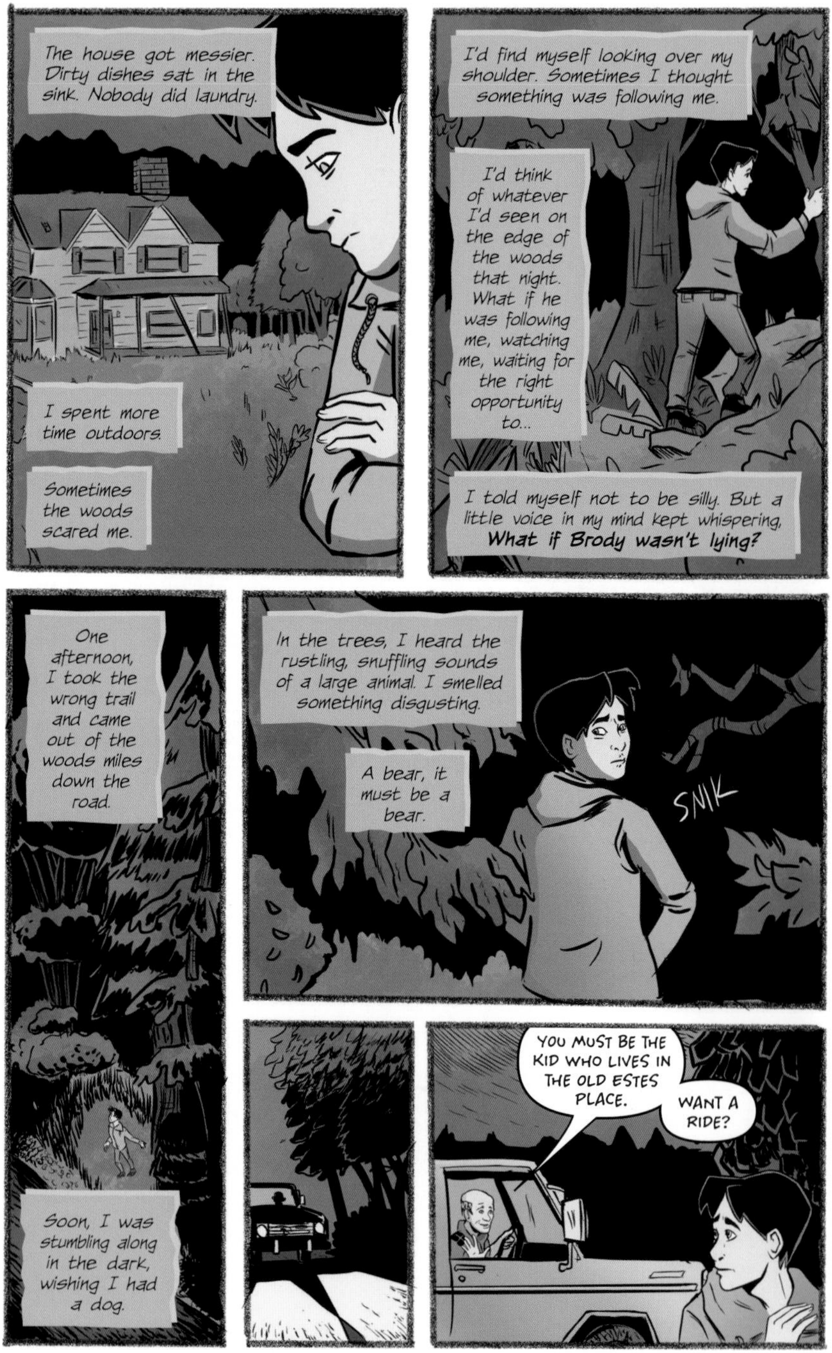

The house got messier. Dirty dishes sat in the sink. Nobody did laundry.
I spent more time outdoors.
Sometimes the woods scared me.
I'd find myself looking over my shoulder. Sometimes I thought something was following me.
I'd think of whatever I'd seen on the edge of the woods that night. What if he was following me, watching me, waiting for the right opportunity to...
I told myself not to be silly. But a little voice in my mind kept whispering, **What if Brody wasn't lying?**
One afternoon, I took the wrong trail and came out of the woods miles down the road.
In the trees, I heard the rustling, snuffling sounds of a large animal. I smelled something disgusting.
A bear, it must be a bear.
SNIK
Soon, I was stumbling along in the dark, wishing I had a dog.
YOU MUST BE THE KID WHO LIVES IN THE OLD ESTES PLACE.
WANT A RIDE?

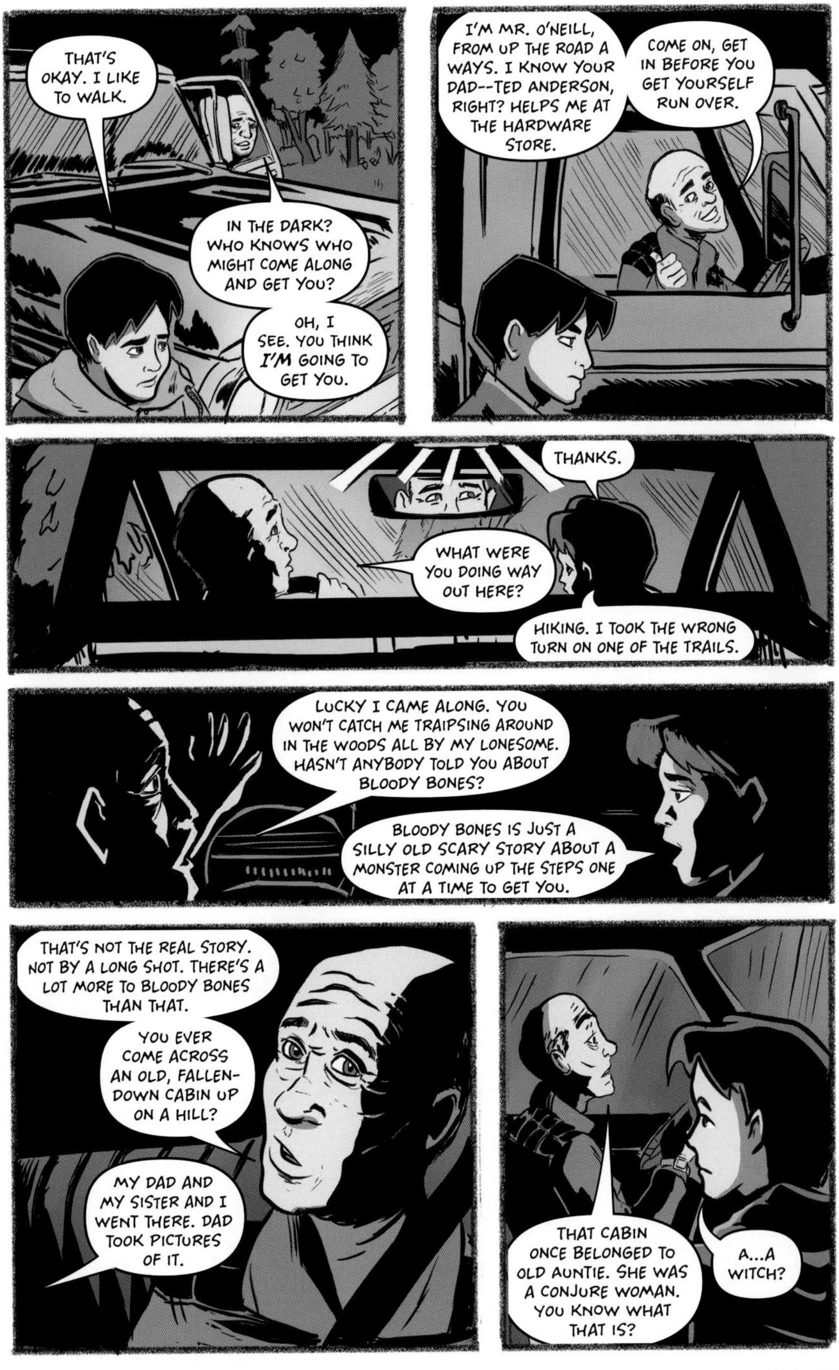
THAT'S OKAY. I LIKE TO WALK.
IN THE DARK? WHO KNOWS WHO MIGHT COME ALONG AND GET YOU?
OH, I SEE. YOU THINK I'M GOING TO GET YOU.
I'M MR. O'NEILL, FROM UP THE ROAD A WAYS. I KNOW YOUR DAD--TED ANDERSON, RIGHT? HELPS ME AT THE HARDWARE STORE.
COME ON, GET IN BEFORE YOU GET YOURSELF RUN OVER.
THANKS.
WHAT WERE YOU DOING WAY OUT HERE?
HIKING. I TOOK THE WRONG TURN ON ONE OF THE TRAILS.
LUCKY I CAME ALONG. YOU WON'T CATCH ME TRAIPSING AROUND IN THE WOODS ALL BY MY LONESOME. HASN'T ANYBODY TOLD YOU ABOUT BLOODY BONES?
BLOODY BONES IS JUST A SILLY OLD SCARY STORY ABOUT A MONSTER COMING UP THE STEPS ONE AT A TIME TO GET YOU.
THAT'S NOT THE REAL STORY. NOT BY A LONG SHOT. THERE'S A LOT MORE TO BLOODY BONES THAN THAT.
YOU EVER COME ACROSS AN OLD, FALLEN-DOWN CABIN UP ON A HILL?
MY DAD AND MY SISTER AND I WENT THERE. DAD TOOK PICTURES OF IT.
THAT CABIN ONCE BELONGED TO OLD AUNTIE. SHE WAS A CONJURE WOMAN. YOU KNOW WHAT THAT IS?
A...A WITCH?

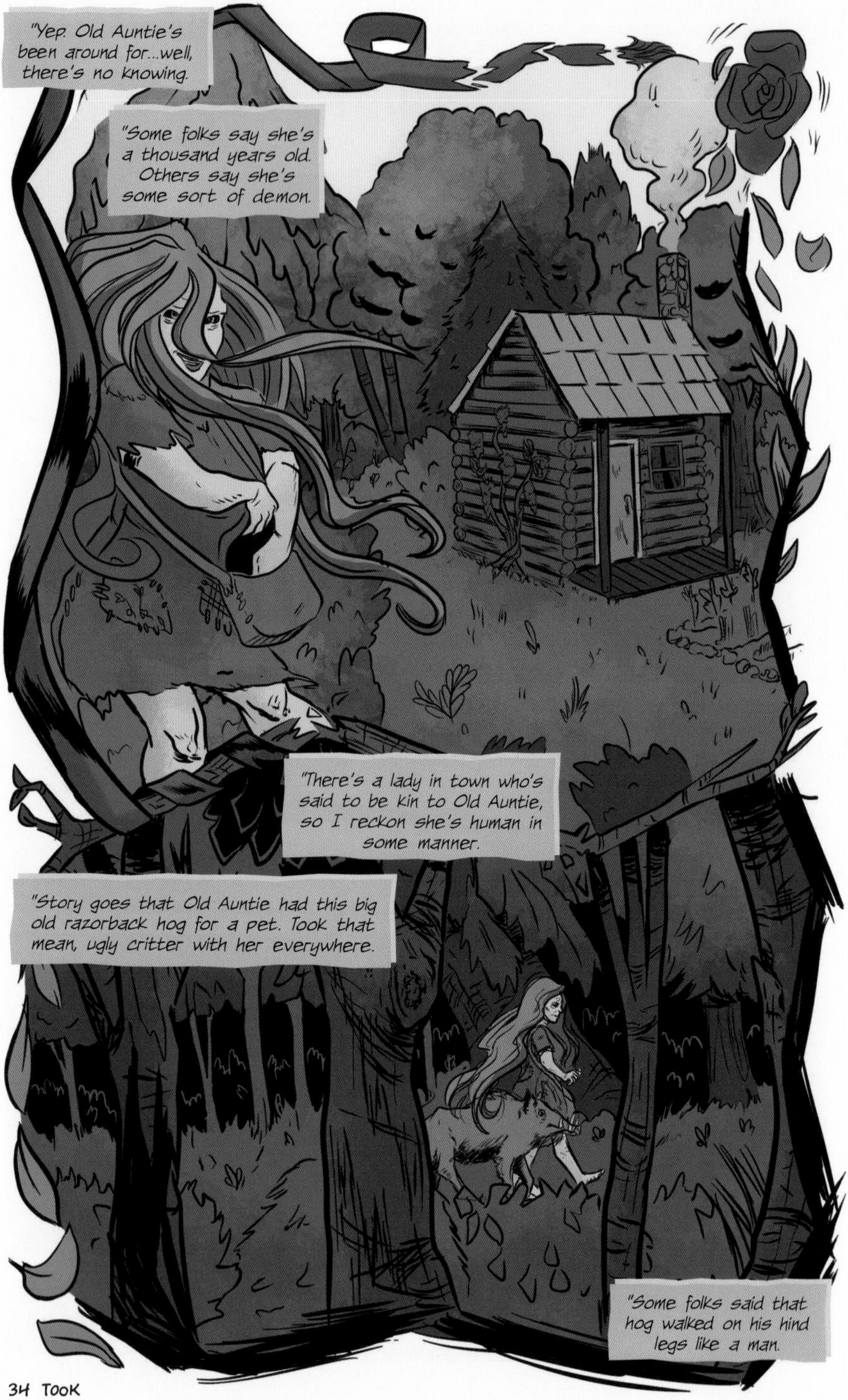
"Yep. Old Auntie's been around for...well, there's no knowing.
"Some folks say she's a thousand years old. Others say she's some sort of demon.
"There's a lady in town who's said to be kin to Old Auntie, so I reckon she's human in some manner.
"Story goes that Old Auntie had this big old razorback hog for a pet. Took that mean, ugly critter with her everywhere.
"Some folks said that hog walked on his hind legs like a man.

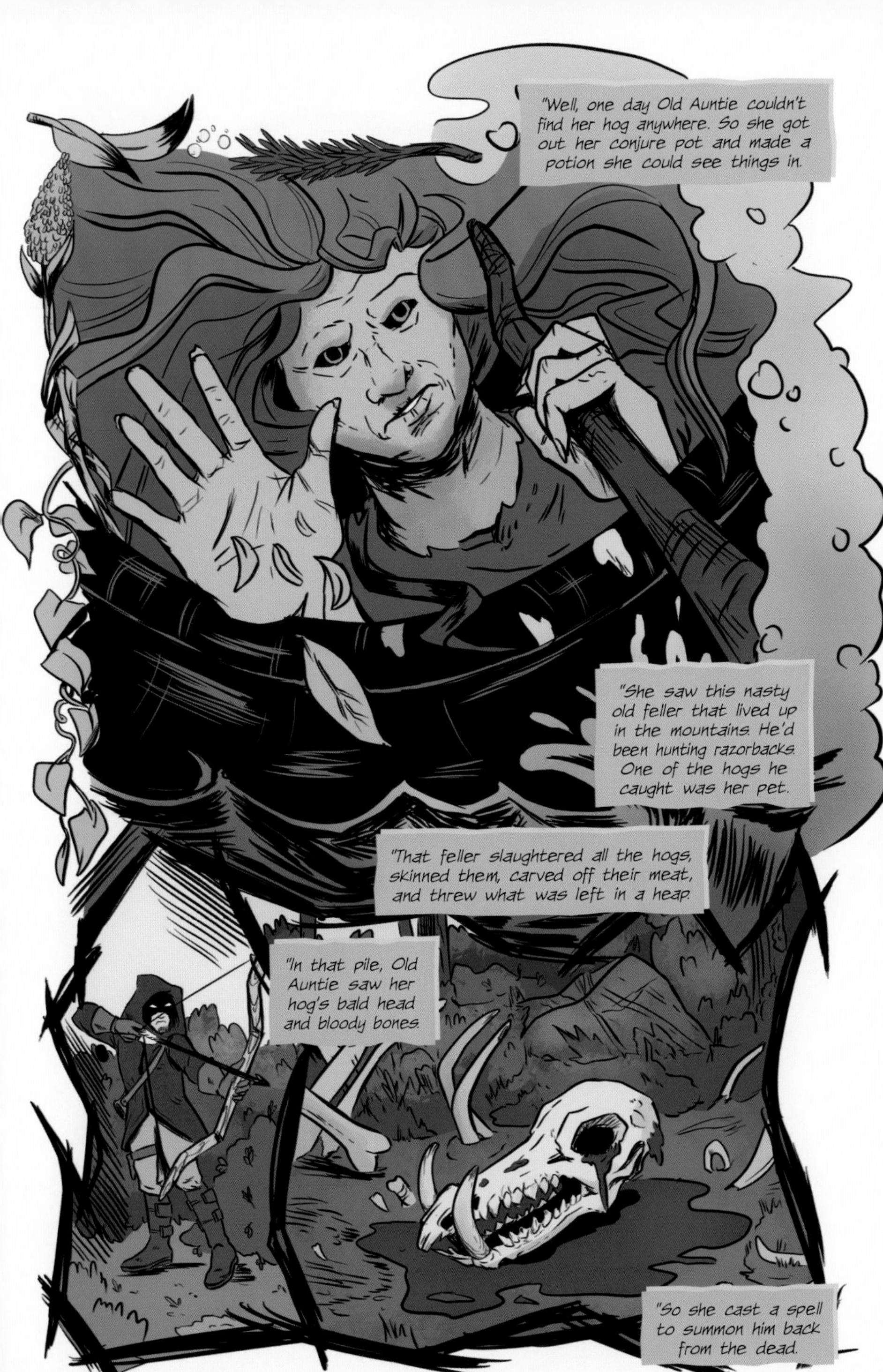
"Well, one day Old Auntie couldn't find her hog anywhere. So she got out her conjure pot and made a potion she could see things in.
"She saw this nasty old feller that lived up in the mountains. He'd been hunting razorbacks. One of the hogs he caught was her pet.
"That feller slaughtered all the hogs, skinned them, carved off their meat, and threw what was left in a heap.
"In that pile, Old Auntie saw her hog's bald head and bloody bones.
"So she cast a spell to summon him back from the dead.

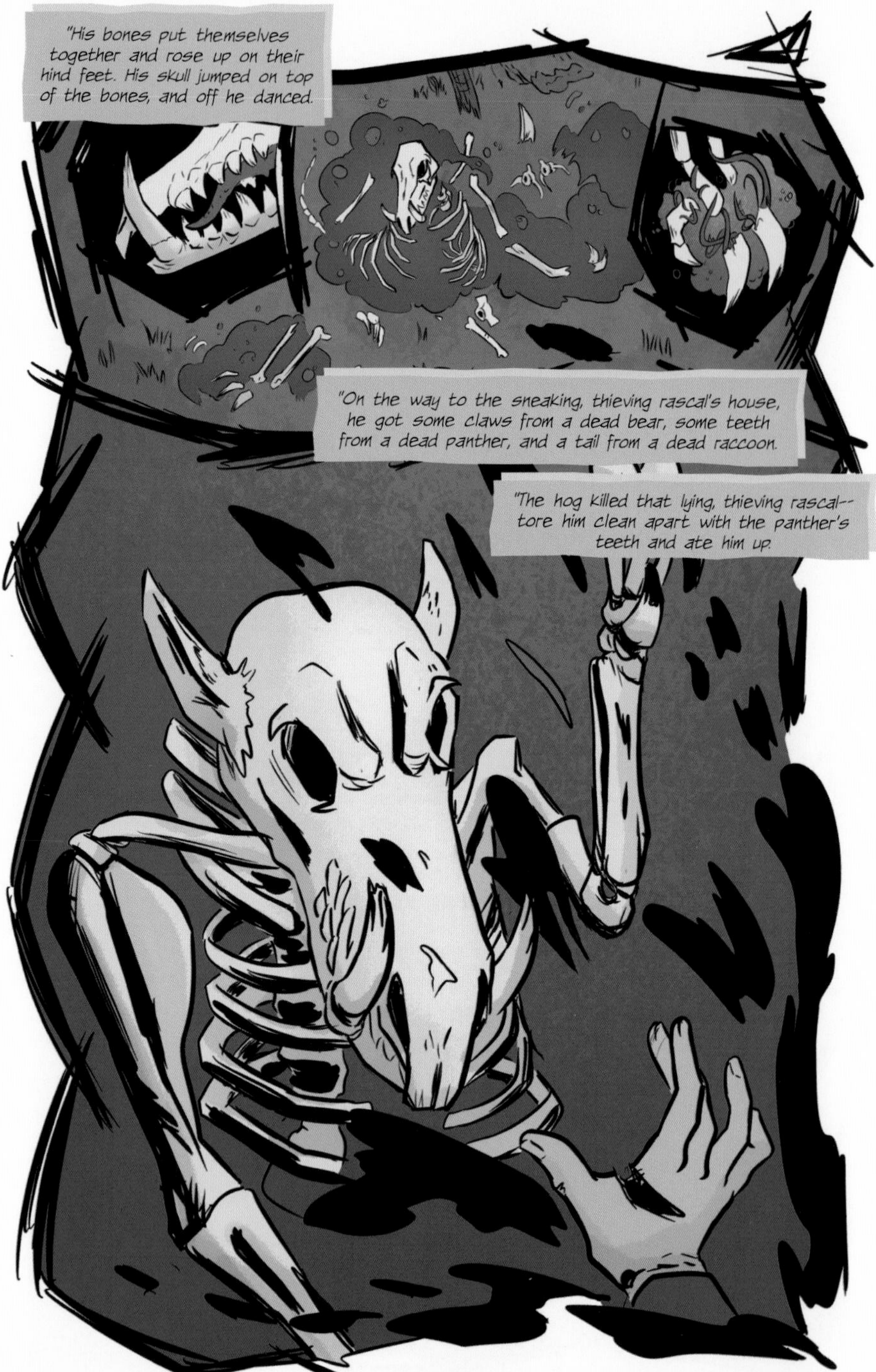
"His bones put themselves together and rose up on their hind feet. His skull jumped on top of the bones, and off he danced.
"On the way to the sneaking, thieving rascal's house, he got some claws from a dead bear, some teeth from a dead panther, and a tail from a dead raccoon.
"The hog killed that lying, thieving rascal--tore him clean apart with the panther's teeth and ate him up.

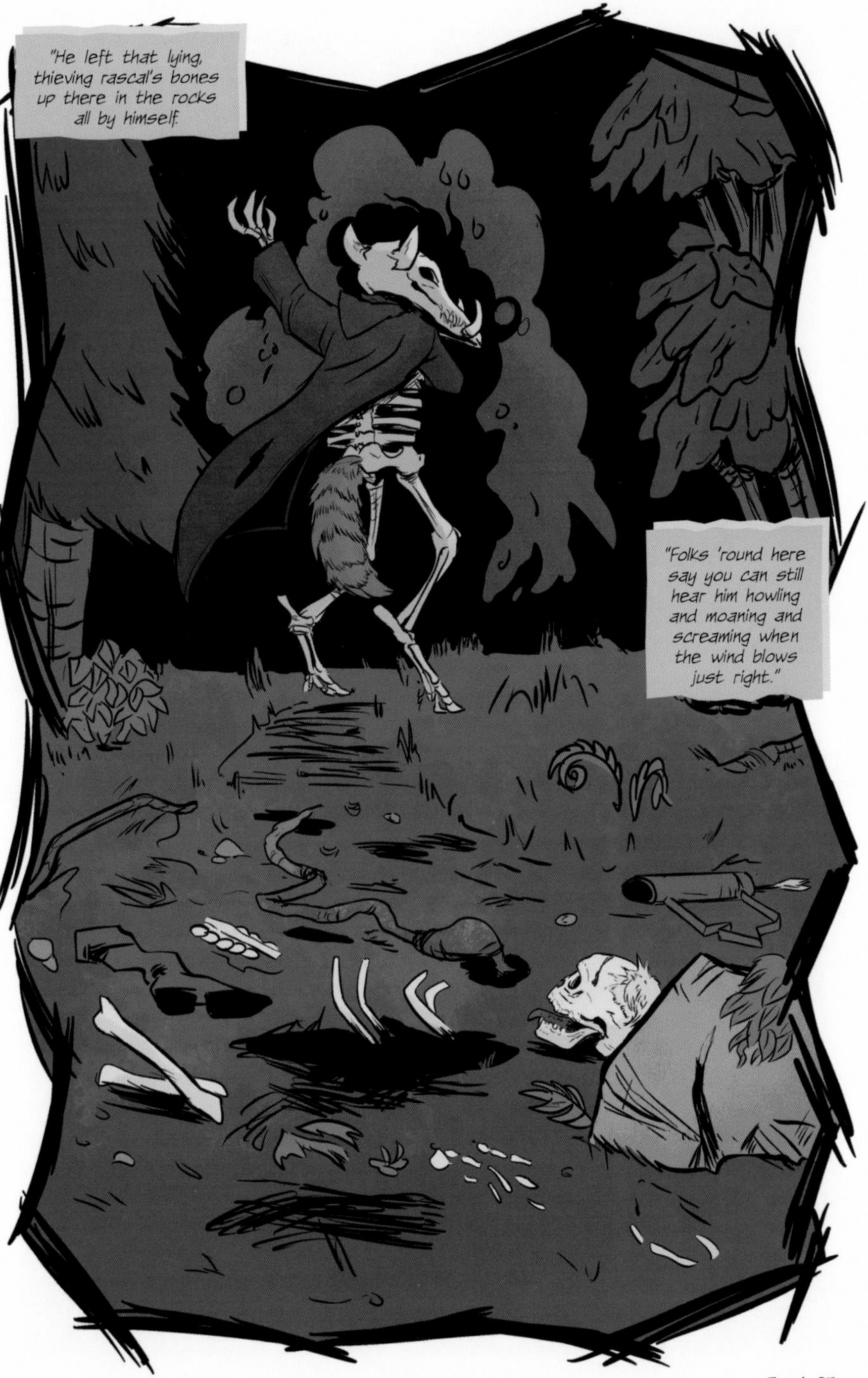
"He left that lying, thieving rascal's bones up there in the rocks all by himself.
"Folks 'round here say you can still hear him howling and moaning and screaming when the wind blows just right."

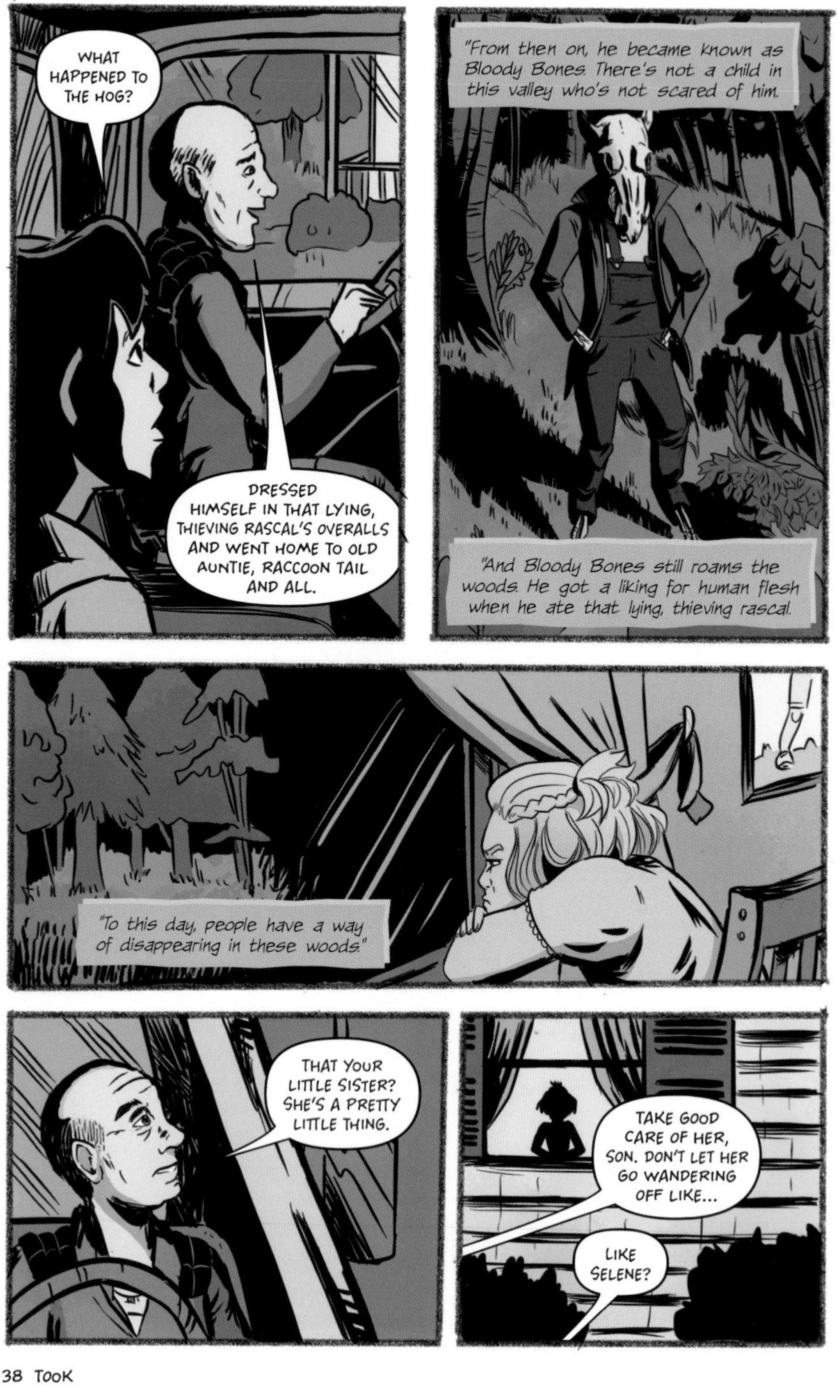
WHAT HAPPENED TO THE HOG?
DRESSED HIMSELF IN THAT LYING, THIEVING RASCAL'S OVERALLS AND WENT HOME TO OLD AUNTIE, RACCOON TAIL AND ALL.
"From then on, he became known as Bloody Bones. There's not a child in this valley who's not scared of him.
"And Bloody Bones still roams the woods. He got a liking for human flesh when he ate that lying, thieving rascal.
"To this day, people have a way of disappearing in these woods."
THAT YOUR LITTLE SISTER? SHE'S A PRETTY LITTLE THING.
TAKE GOOD CARE OF HER, SON. DON'T LET HER GO WANDERING OFF LIKE...
LIKE SELENE?

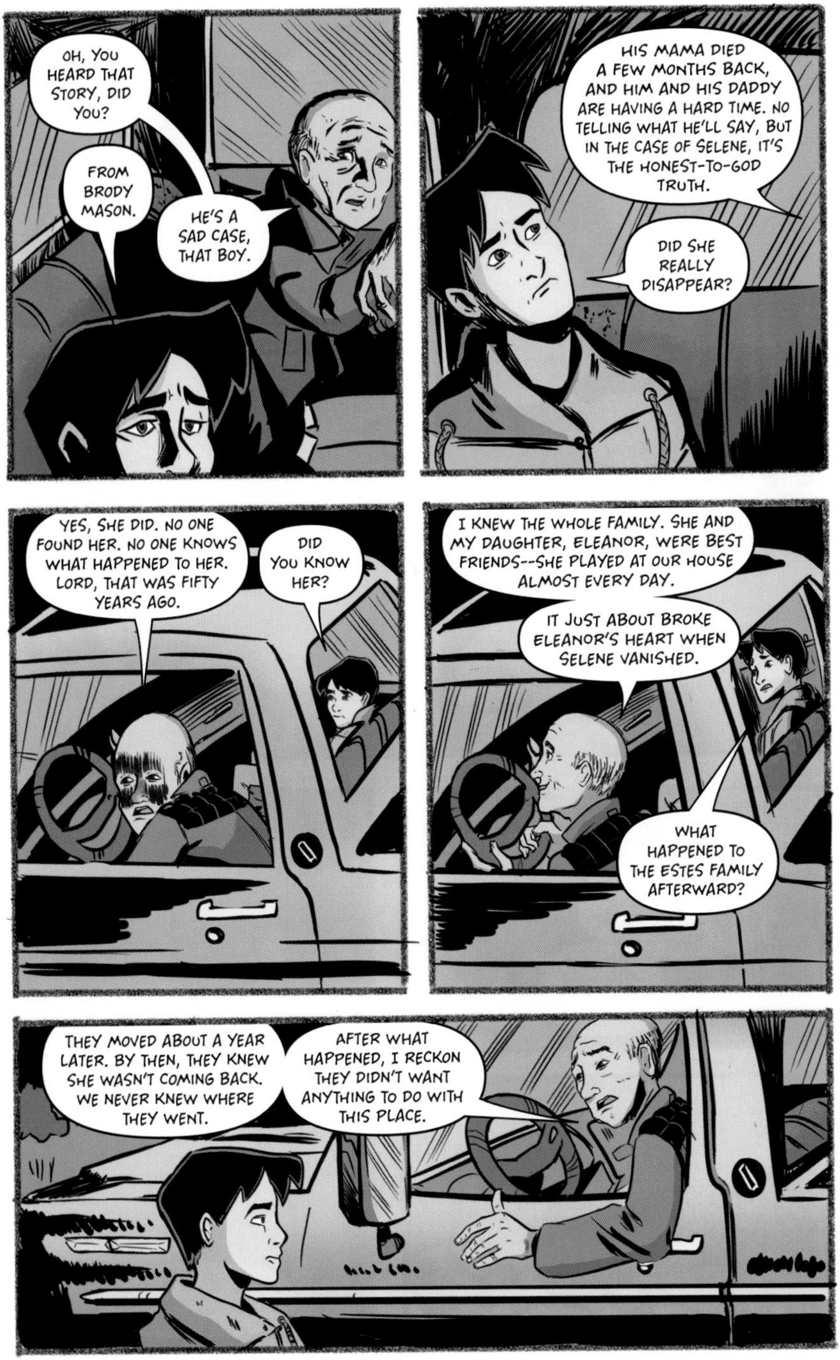
OH, YOU HEARD THAT STORY, DID YOU?
FROM BRODY MASON.
HE'S A SAD CASE, THAT BOY.
HIS MAMA DIED A FEW MONTHS BACK, AND HIM AND HIS DADDY ARE HAVING A HARD TIME. NO TELLING WHAT HE'LL SAY, BUT IN THE CASE OF SELENE, IT'S THE HONEST-TO-GOD TRUTH.
DID SHE REALLY DISAPPEAR?
YES, SHE DID. NO ONE FOUND HER. NO ONE KNOWS WHAT HAPPENED TO HER. LORD, THAT WAS FIFTY YEARS AGO.
DID YOU KNOW HER?
I KNEW THE WHOLE FAMILY. SHE AND MY DAUGHTER, ELEANOR, WERE BEST FRIENDS--SHE PLAYED AT OUR HOUSE ALMOST EVERY DAY.
IT JUST ABOUT BROKE ELEANOR'S HEART WHEN SELENE VANISHED.
WHAT HAPPENED TO THE ESTES FAMILY AFTERWARD?
THEY MOVED ABOUT A YEAR LATER. BY THEN, THEY KNEW SHE WASN'T COMING BACK. WE NEVER KNEW WHERE THEY WENT.
AFTER WHAT HAPPENED, I RECKON THEY DIDN'T WANT ANYTHING TO DO WITH THIS PLACE.

"Say hi to your dad for me."

WHAT HAVE I TOLD YOU ABOUT TAKING RIDES WITH STRANGERS?

HE WASN'T A STRANGER, MOM. DAD KNOWS HIM.

BUT *YOU* DIDN'T KNOW HIM. HE COULD HAVE BEEN LYING. HE COULD HAVE KIDNAPPED YOU.

NEVER DO THAT AGAIN!

SHE'S CRYING.

NOBODY'S HAPPY ANYMORE.

IT'S THIS HOUSE. WE NEVER SHOULD HAVE COME HERE.

DO YOU EVER FEEL LIKE SOMETHING BAD WILL HAPPEN?

LIKE WHAT?

I DON'T KNOW, JUST SOMETHING.

THOSE WHISPERS, THEY'RE GETTING LOUDER. THEY KEEP ME AWAKE AT NIGHT.

ARE YOU SURE YOU NEVER HEAR THEM?

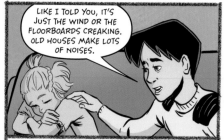

LIKE I TOLD YOU, IT'S JUST THE WIND OR THE FLOORBOARDS CREAKING. OLD HOUSES MAKE LOTS OF NOISES.

THE WIND DOESN'T SAY PEOPLE'S NAMES.

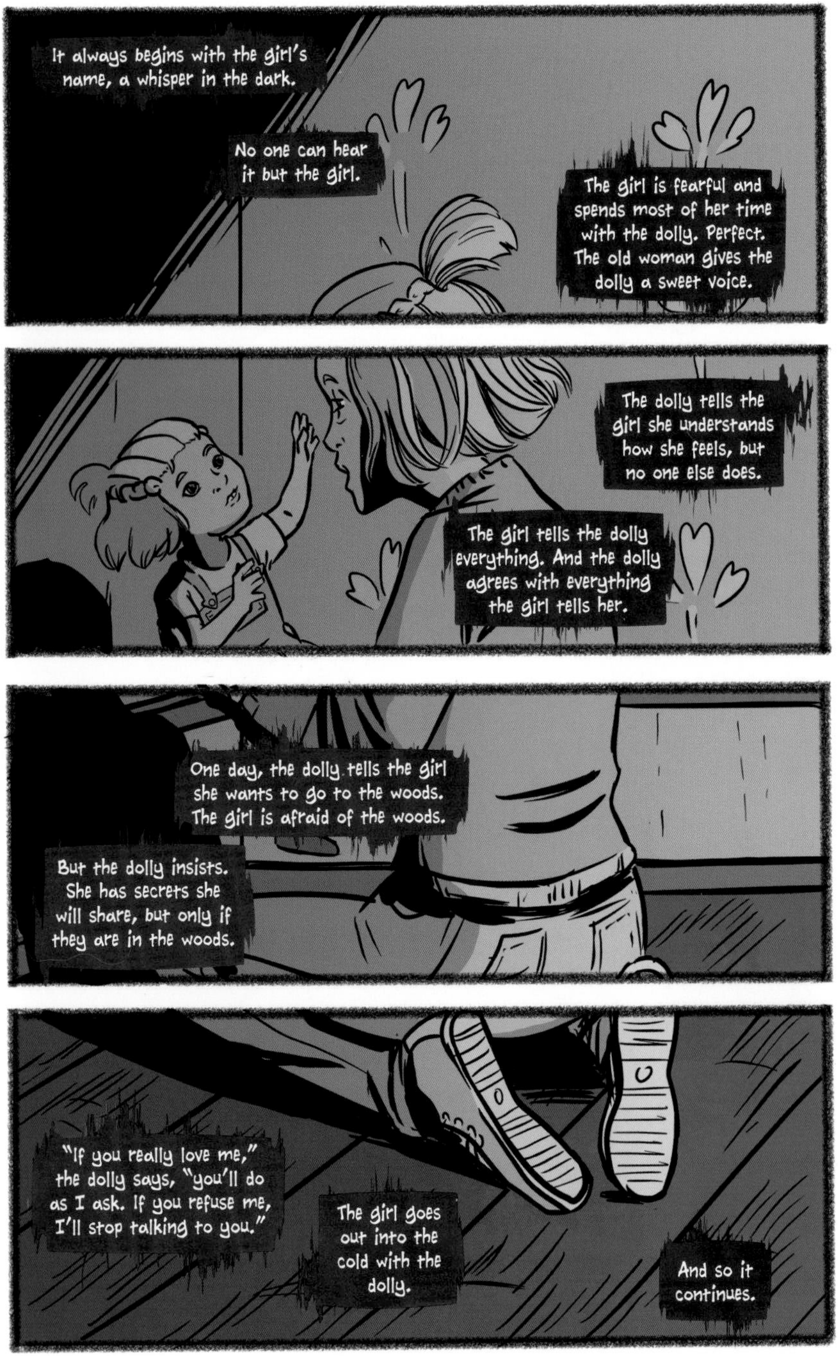
It always begins with the girl's name, a whisper in the dark.
No one can hear it but the girl.
The girl is fearful and spends most of her time with the dolly. Perfect. The old woman gives the dolly a sweet voice.
The dolly tells the girl she understands how she feels, but no one else does.
The girl tells the dolly everything. And the dolly agrees with everything the girl tells her.
One day, the dolly tells the girl she wants to go to the woods. The girl is afraid of the woods.
But the dolly insists. She has secrets she will share, but only if they are in the woods.
"If you really love me," the dolly says, "you'll do as I ask. If you refuse me, I'll stop talking to you."
The girl goes out into the cold with the dolly.
And so it continues.

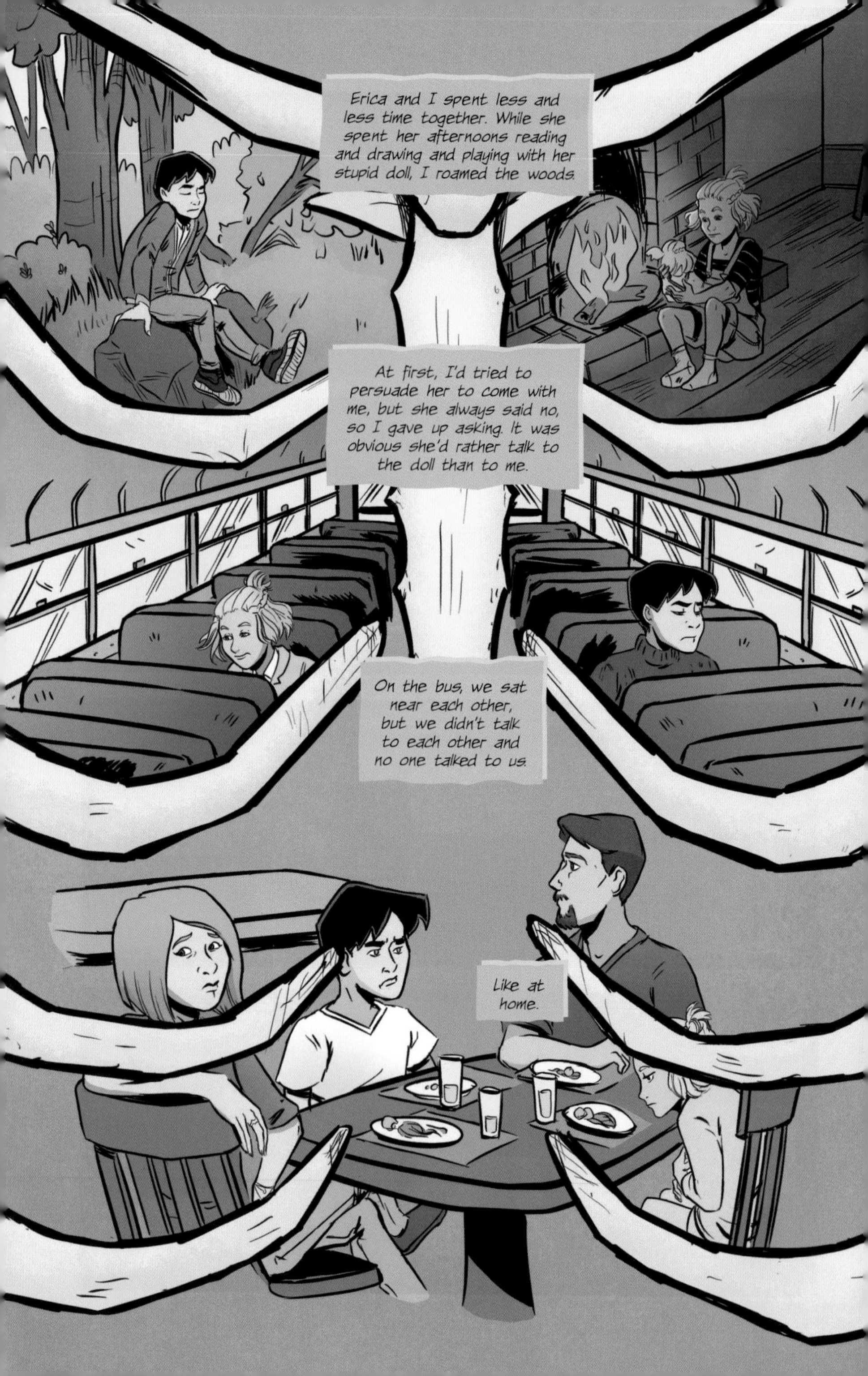
Erica and I spent less and less time together. While she spent her afternoons reading and drawing and playing with her stupid doll, I roamed the woods.
At first, I'd tried to persuade her to come with me, but she always said no, so I gave up asking. It was obvious she'd rather talk to the doll than to me.
On the bus, we sat near each other, but we didn't talk to each other and no one talked to us.
Like at home.

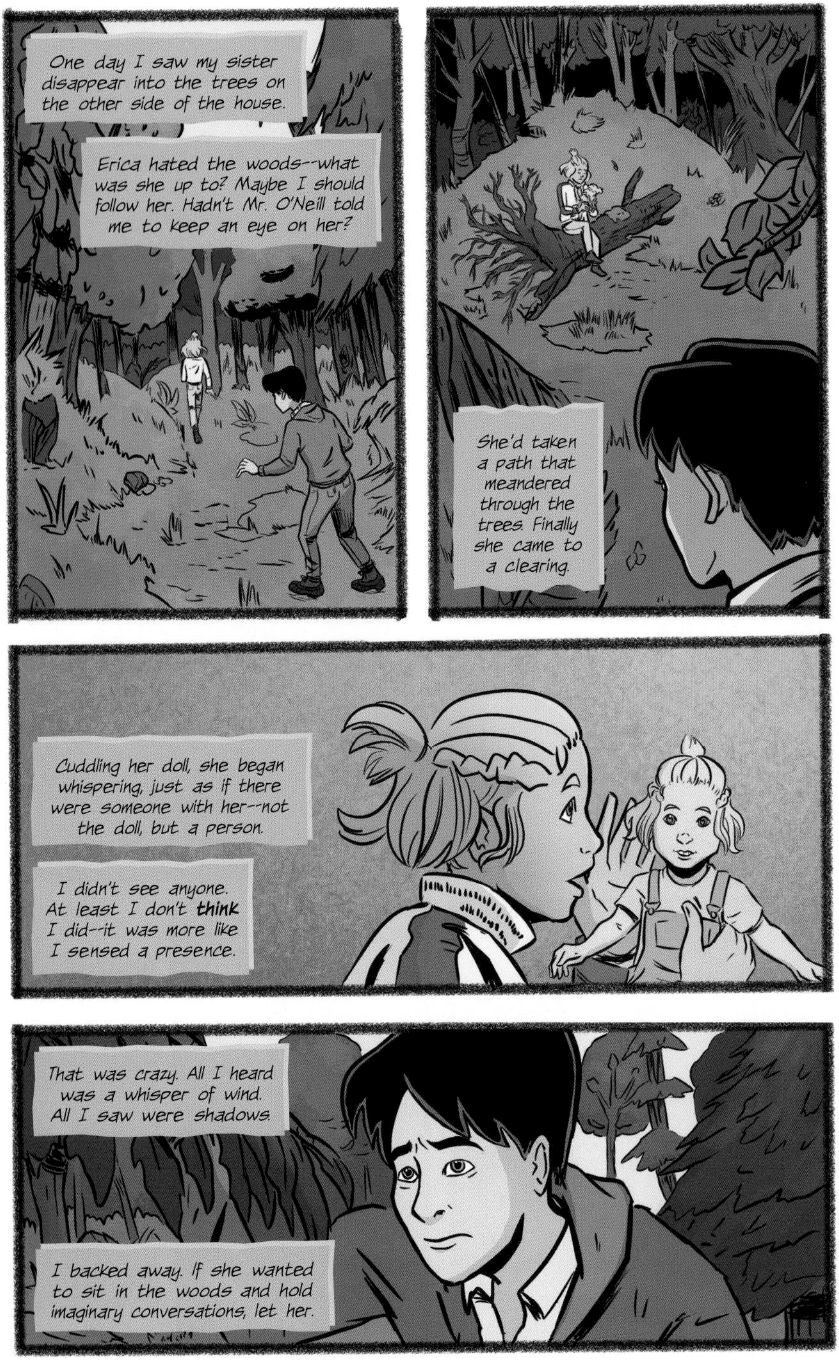
One day I saw my sister disappear into the trees on the other side of the house.
Erica hated the woods--what was she up to? Maybe I should follow her. Hadn't Mr. O'Neill told me to keep an eye on her?
She'd taken a path that meandered through the trees. Finally she came to a clearing.
Cuddling her doll, she began whispering, just as if there were someone with her--not the doll, but a person.
I didn't see anyone. At least I don't **think** I did--it was more like I sensed a presence.
That was crazy. All I heard was a whisper of wind. All I saw were shadows.
I backed away. If she wanted to sit in the woods and hold imaginary conversations, let her.

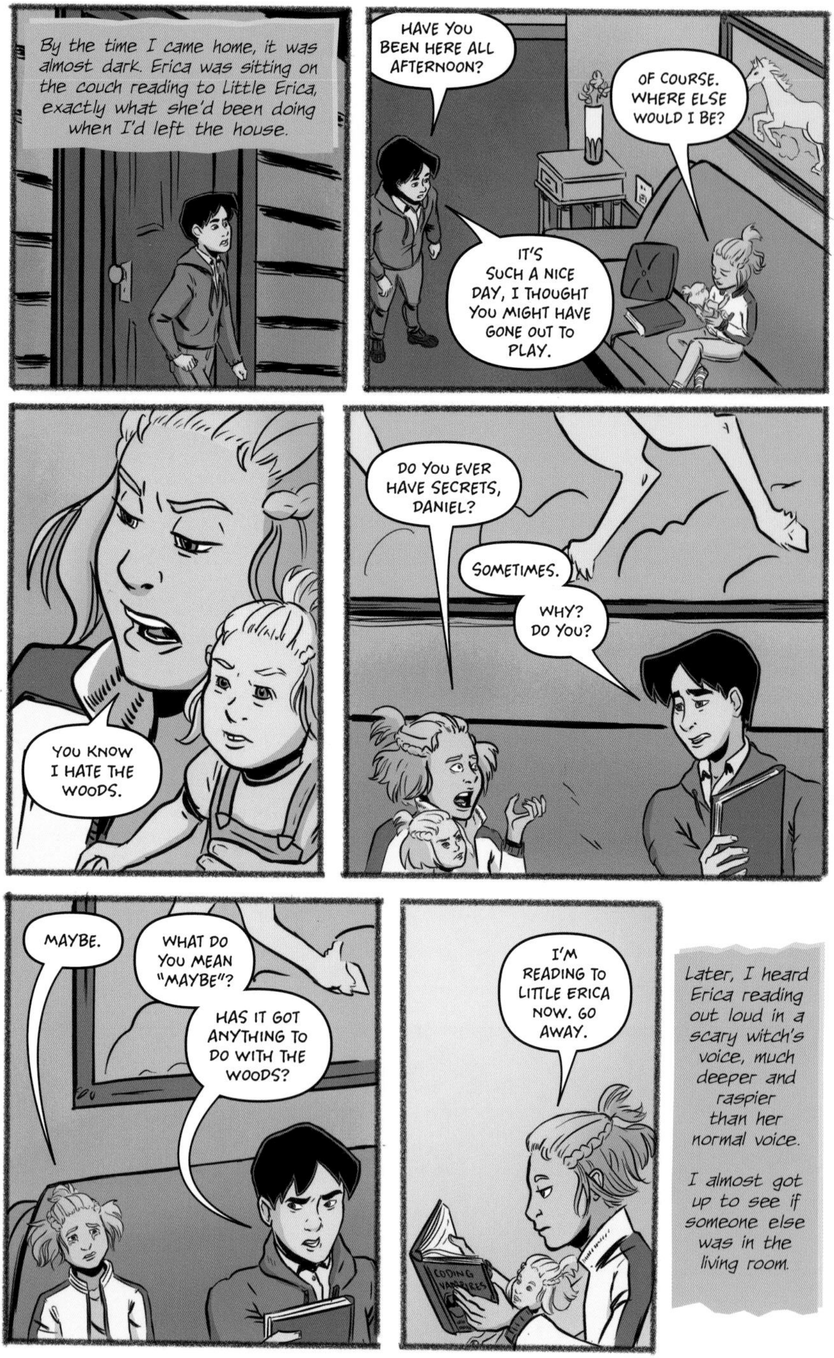
By the time I came home, it was almost dark. Erica was sitting on the couch reading to Little Erica, exactly what she'd been doing when I'd left the house.
HAVE YOU BEEN HERE ALL AFTERNOON?
OF COURSE. WHERE ELSE WOULD I BE?
IT'S SUCH A NICE DAY, I THOUGHT YOU MIGHT HAVE GONE OUT TO PLAY.
YOU KNOW I HATE THE WOODS.
DO YOU EVER HAVE SECRETS, DANIEL?
SOMETIMES.
WHY? DO YOU?
MAYBE.
WHAT DO YOU MEAN "MAYBE"?
HAS IT GOT ANYTHING TO DO WITH THE WOODS?
I'M READING TO LITTLE ERICA NOW. GO AWAY.
Later, I heard Erica reading out loud in a scary witch's voice, much deeper and raspier than her normal voice.
I almost got up to see if someone else was in the living room.

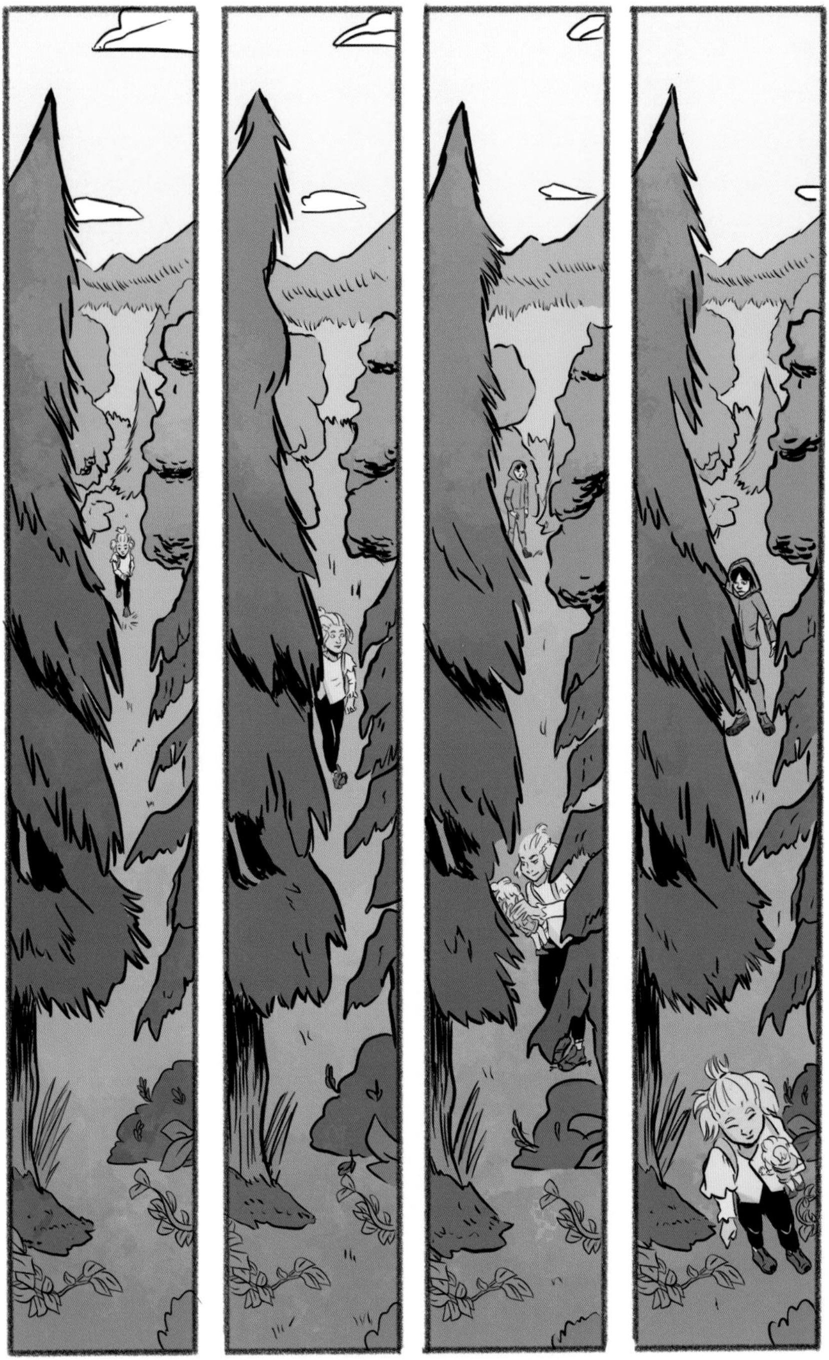

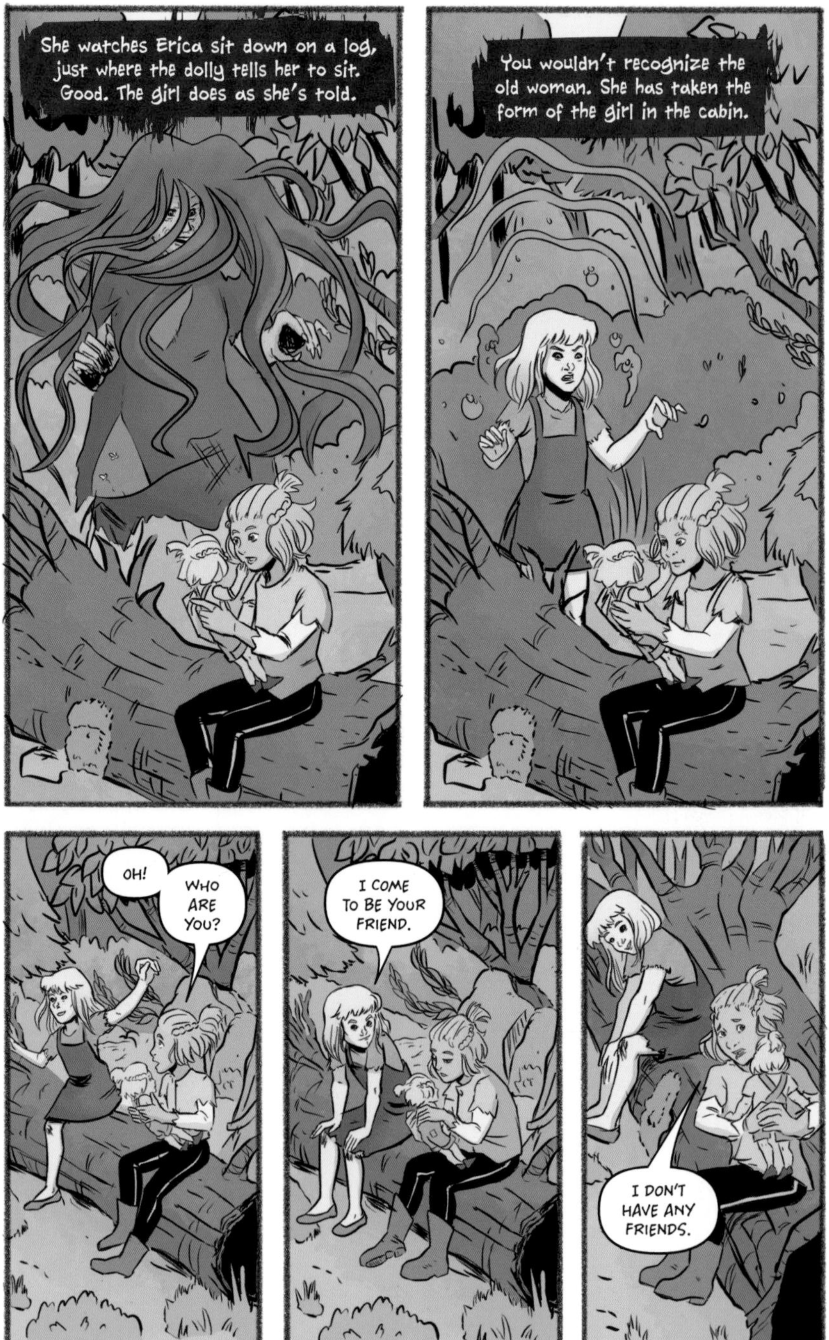

She watches Erica sit down on a log, just where the dolly tells her to sit. Good. The girl does as she's told.
You wouldn't recognize the old woman. She has taken the form of the girl in the cabin.
OH!
WHO ARE YOU?
I COME TO BE YOUR FRIEND.
I DON'T HAVE ANY FRIENDS.

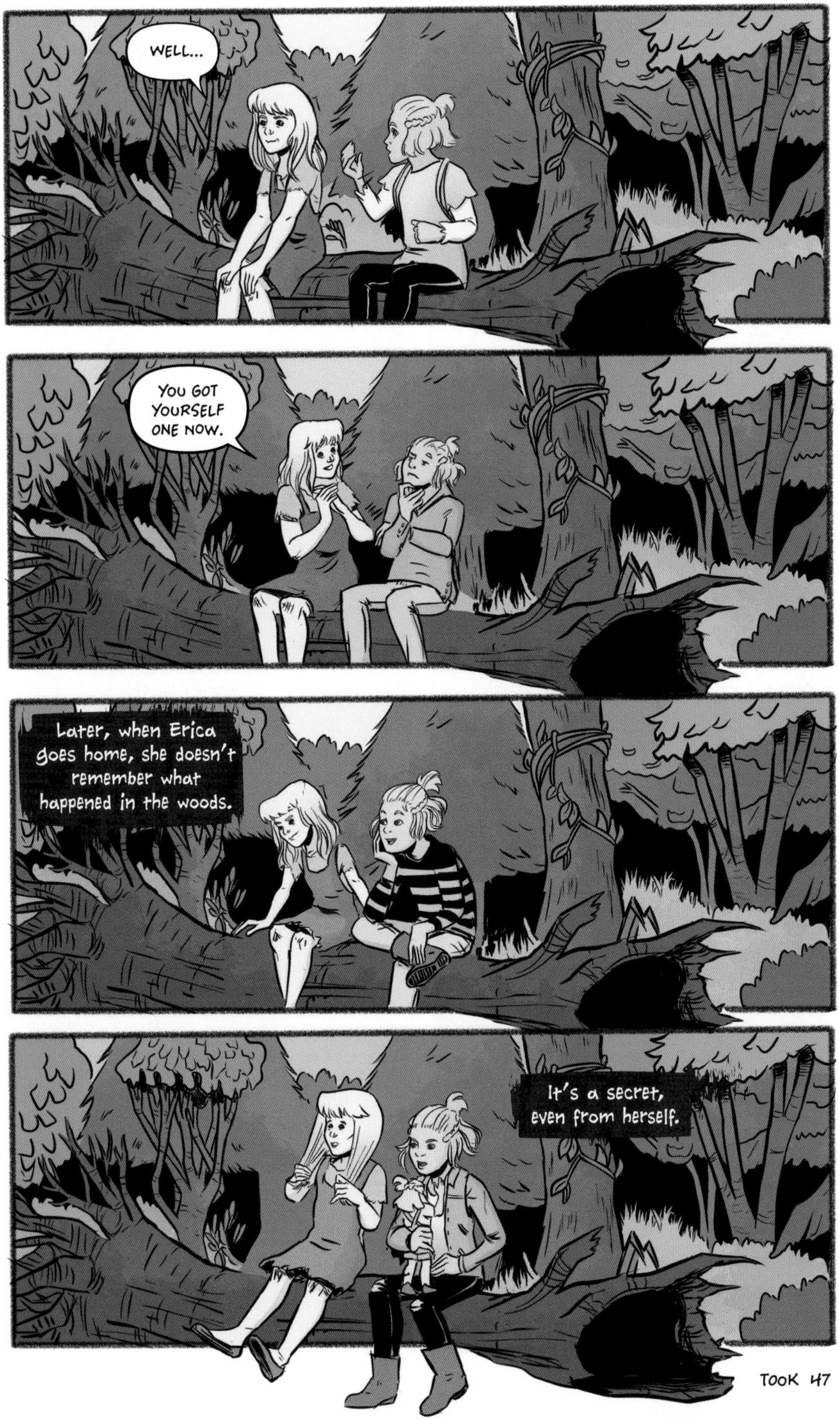
WELL...
YOU GOT YOURSELF ONE NOW.
Later, when Erica goes home, she doesn't remember what happened in the woods.
It's a secret, even from herself.

I LIVE WITH MY AUNTIE IN A PRETTY LITTLE CABIN ON THE TIPPITY TOP OF A HILL. SHE LOVES ME MORE'N ANYBODY EVER DID.

MORE THAN YOUR MOMMY AND DADDY?

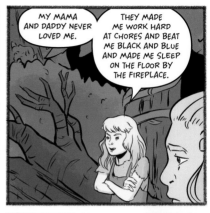

MY MAMA AND DADDY NEVER LOVED ME.

THEY MADE ME WORK HARD AT CHORES AND BEAT ME BLACK AND BLUE AND MADE ME SLEEP ON THE FLOOR BY THE FIREPLACE.

MY PARENTS WOULD NEVER DO THAT.

OH YES, THEY WOULD. YOU'LL SEE.

THEY ALREADY LOVE YOUR BROTHER MORE THAN YOU.

IT'S TRUE. THEY'VE ALWAYS LOVED DANIEL BEST.

MY AUNTIE'S KEEPING AN EYE ON YOU.

SHE LOVES YOU EVEN THOUGH YOU DON'T KNOW IT YET, AND AIMS TO RESCUE YOU AND BRING YOU TO HER CABIN, WHERE ME AND YOU WILL LIVE LIKE SISTERS.

WILL I HAVE TO GO TO SCHOOL?

SCHOOL? NO, INDEED. OLD AUNTIE GOT NO USE FOR SCHOOL. SHE'LL TEACH YOU ALL YOU NEED TO KNOW.

I MUST GO.

The old woman sees the brother watching from the woods. He can't see her, but he knows someone is there.

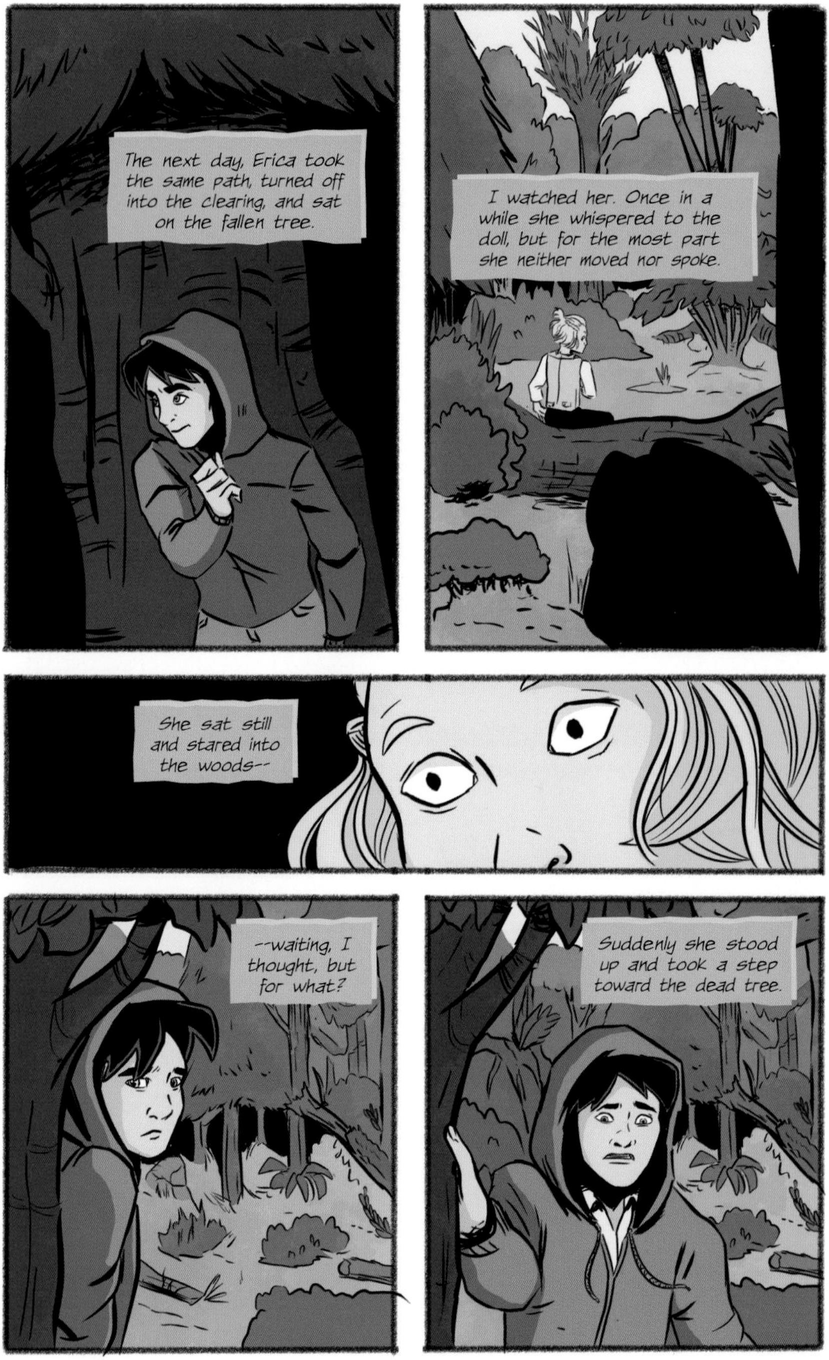
The next day, Erica took the same path, turned off into the clearing, and sat on the fallen tree.
I watched her. Once in a while she whispered to the doll, but for the most part she neither moved nor spoke.
She sat still and stared into the woods--
--waiting, I thought, but for what?
Suddenly she stood up and took a step toward the dead tree.

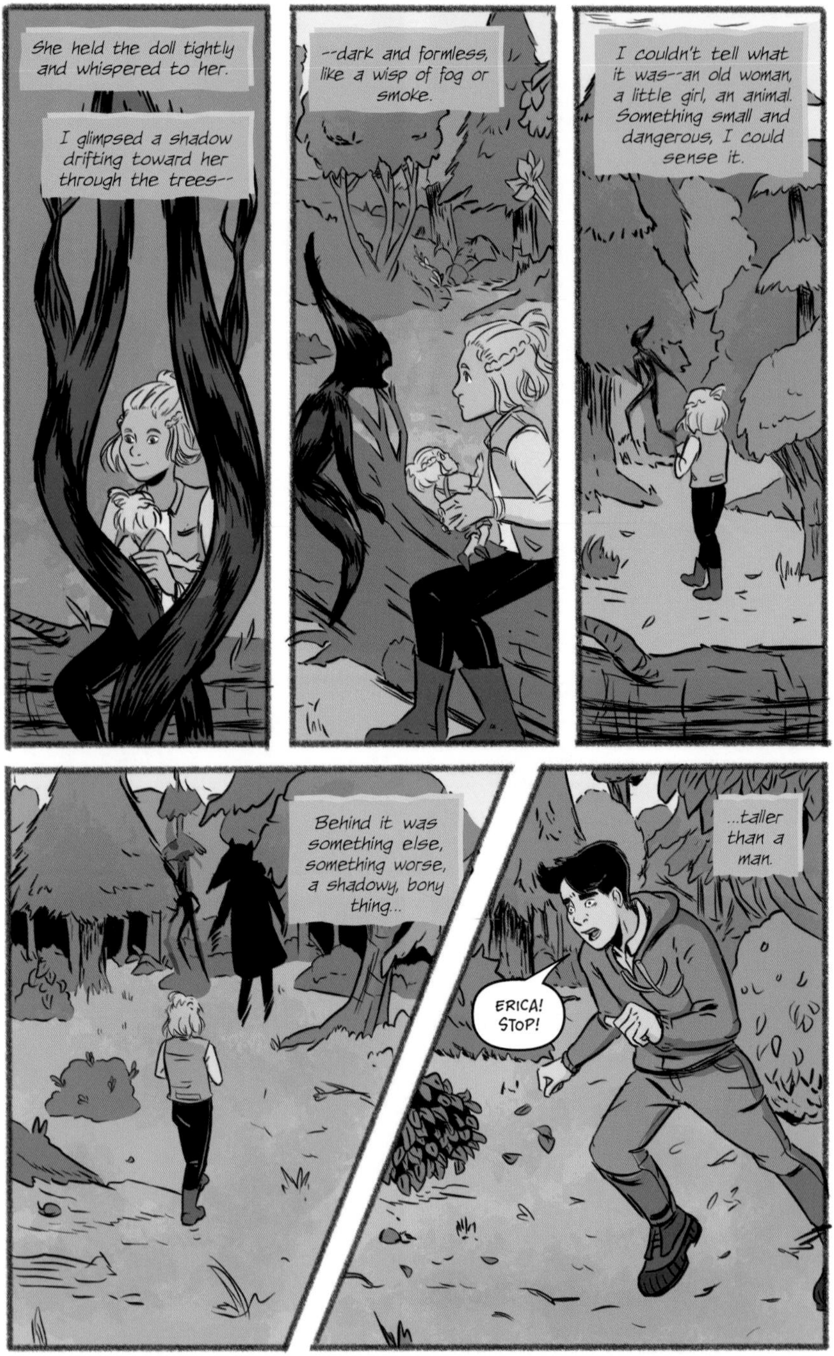
She held the doll tightly and whispered to her.
I glimpsed a shadow drifting toward her through the trees--
--dark and formless, like a wisp of fog or smoke.
I couldn't tell what it was--an old woman, a little girl, an animal. Something small and dangerous, I could sense it.
Behind it was something else, something worse, a shadowy, bony thing...
...taller than a man.
ERICA! STOP!

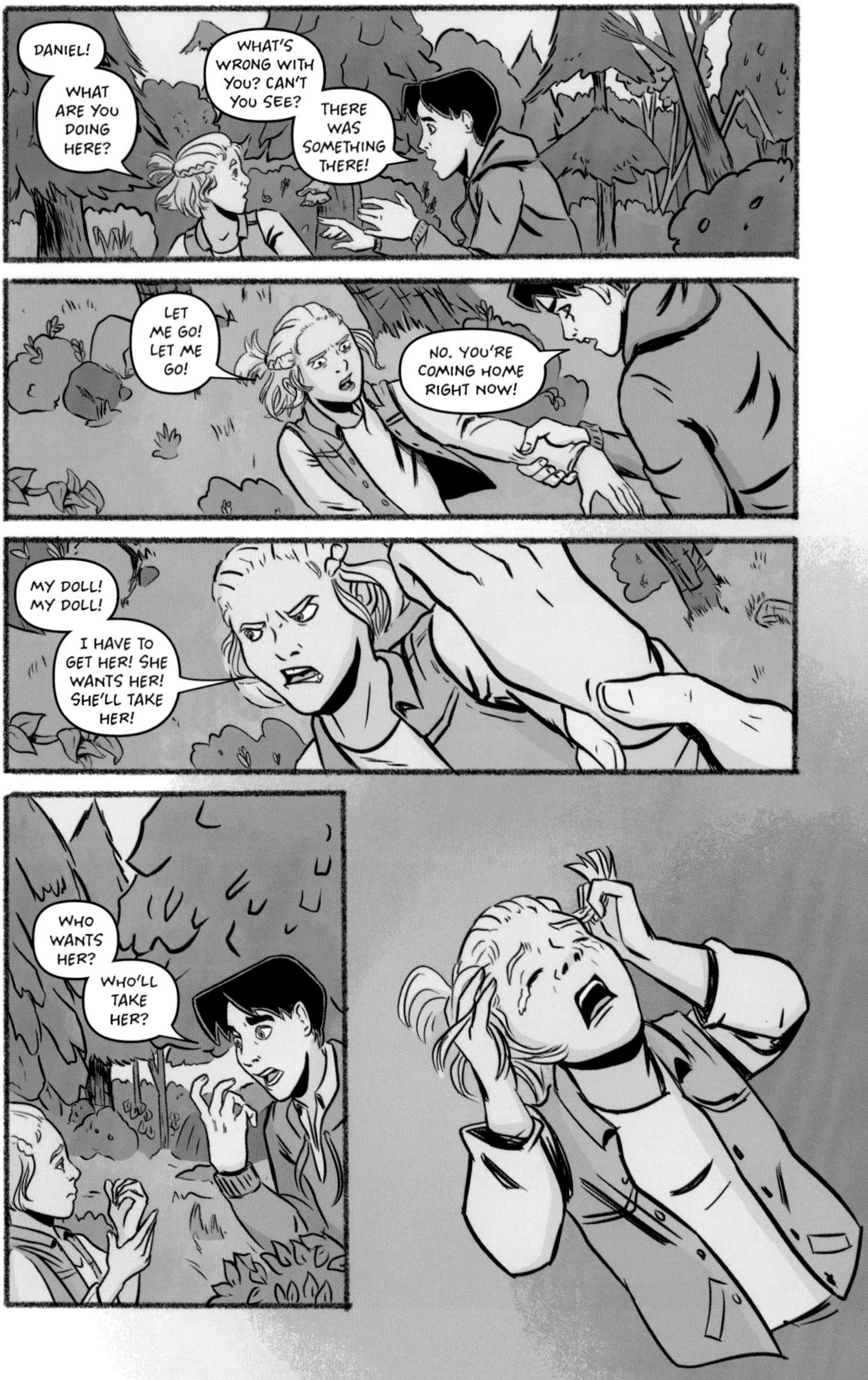
DANIEL!
WHAT ARE YOU DOING HERE?
WHAT'S WRONG WITH YOU? CAN'T YOU SEE?
THERE WAS SOMETHING THERE!
LET ME GO! LET ME GO!
NO. YOU'RE COMING HOME RIGHT NOW!
MY DOLL! MY DOLL!
I HAVE TO GET HER! SHE WANTS HER! SHE'LL TAKE HER!
WHO WANTS HER?
WHO'LL TAKE HER?

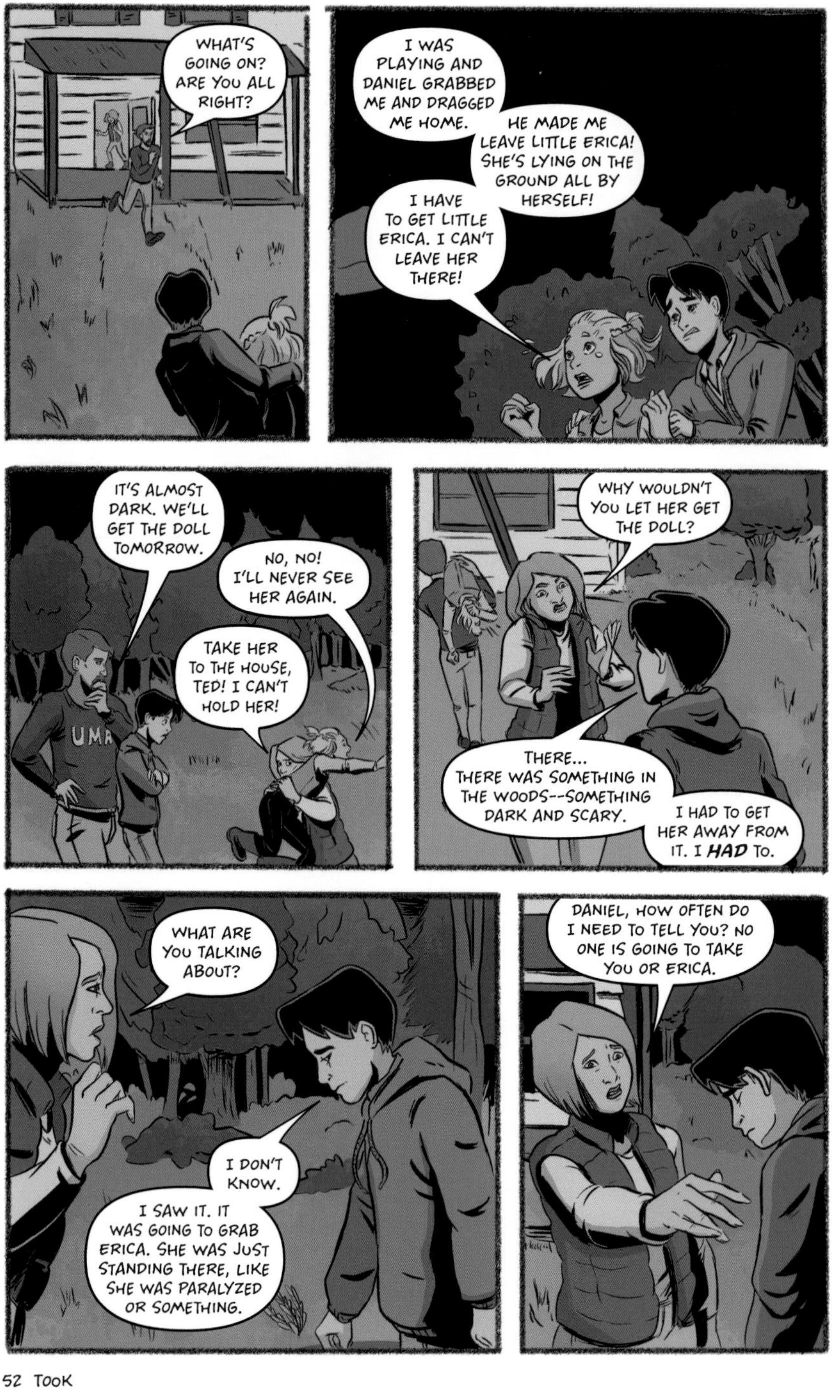
WHAT'S GOING ON? ARE YOU ALL RIGHT?
I WAS PLAYING AND DANIEL GRABBED ME AND DRAGGED ME HOME.
HE MADE ME LEAVE LITTLE ERICA! SHE'S LYING ON THE GROUND ALL BY HERSELF!
I HAVE TO GET LITTLE ERICA. I CAN'T LEAVE HER THERE!
IT'S ALMOST DARK. WE'LL GET THE DOLL TOMORROW.
NO, NO! I'LL NEVER SEE HER AGAIN.
TAKE HER TO THE HOUSE, TED! I CAN'T HOLD HER!
UMA
WHY WOULDN'T YOU LET HER GET THE DOLL?
THERE... THERE WAS SOMETHING IN THE WOODS--SOMETHING DARK AND SCARY.
I HAD TO GET HER AWAY FROM IT. I ***HAD*** TO.
WHAT ARE YOU TALKING ABOUT?
I DON'T KNOW.
I SAW IT. IT WAS GOING TO GRAB ERICA. SHE WAS JUST STANDING THERE, LIKE SHE WAS PARALYZED OR SOMETHING.
DANIEL, HOW OFTEN DO I NEED TO TELL YOU? NO ONE IS GOING TO TAKE YOU OR ERICA.

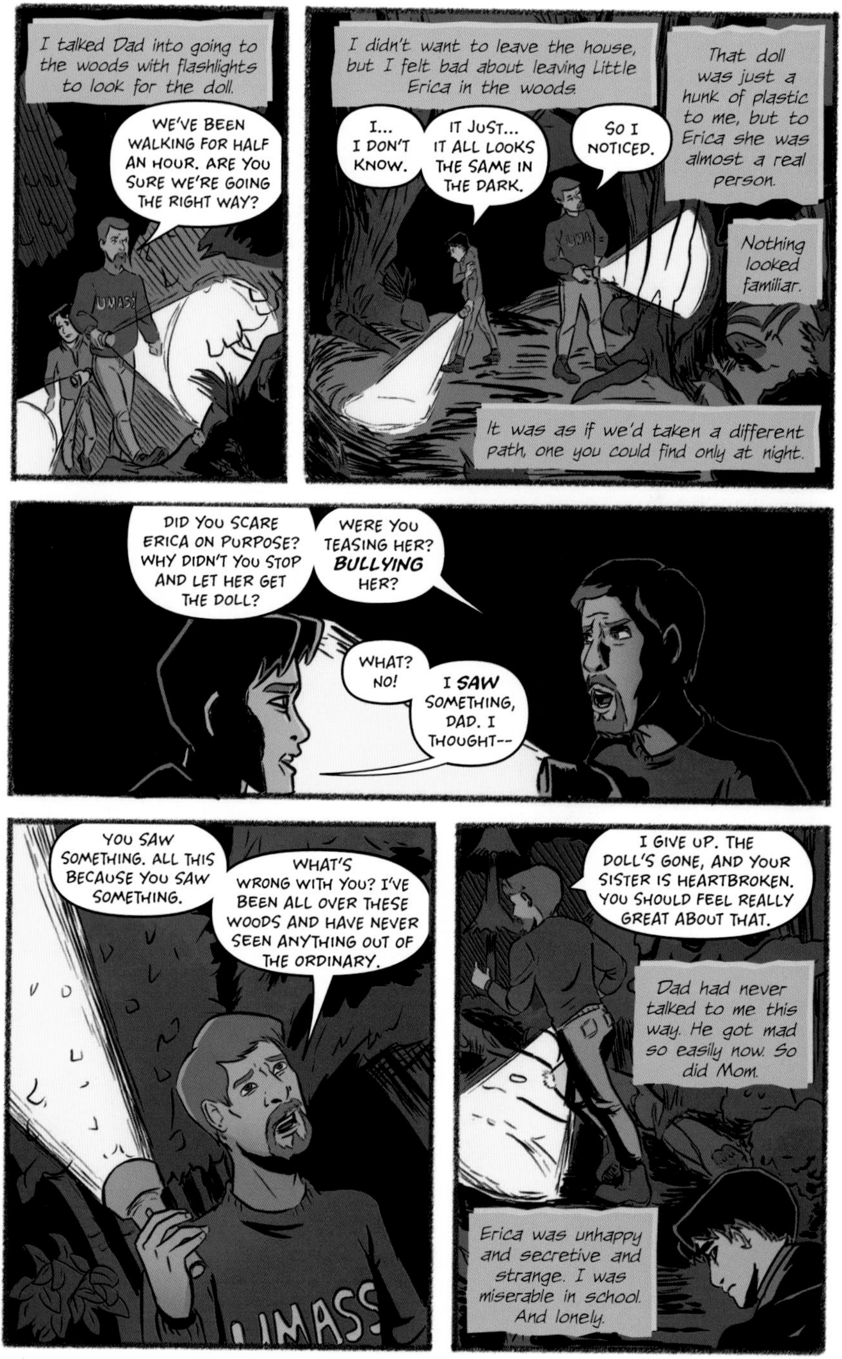

I talked Dad into going to the woods with flashlights to look for the doll.
WE'VE BEEN WALKING FOR HALF AN HOUR. ARE YOU SURE WE'RE GOING THE RIGHT WAY?
UMASS
I didn't want to leave the house, but I felt bad about leaving Little Erica in the woods.
I... I DON'T KNOW.
IT JUST... IT ALL LOOKS THE SAME IN THE DARK.
SO I NOTICED.
That doll was just a hunk of plastic to me, but to Erica she was almost a real person.
Nothing looked familiar.
It was as if we'd taken a different path, one you could find only at night.
DID YOU SCARE ERICA ON PURPOSE? WHY DIDN'T YOU STOP AND LET HER GET THE DOLL?
WERE YOU TEASING HER? BULLYING HER?
WHAT? NO!
I SAW SOMETHING, DAD. I THOUGHT--
YOU SAW SOMETHING. ALL THIS BECAUSE YOU SAW SOMETHING.
WHAT'S WRONG WITH YOU? I'VE BEEN ALL OVER THESE WOODS AND HAVE NEVER SEEN ANYTHING OUT OF THE ORDINARY.
UMASS
I GIVE UP. THE DOLL'S GONE, AND YOUR SISTER IS HEARTBROKEN. YOU SHOULD FEEL REALLY GREAT ABOUT THAT.
Dad had never talked to me this way. He got mad so easily now. So did Mom.
Erica was unhappy and secretive and strange. I was miserable in school. And lonely.

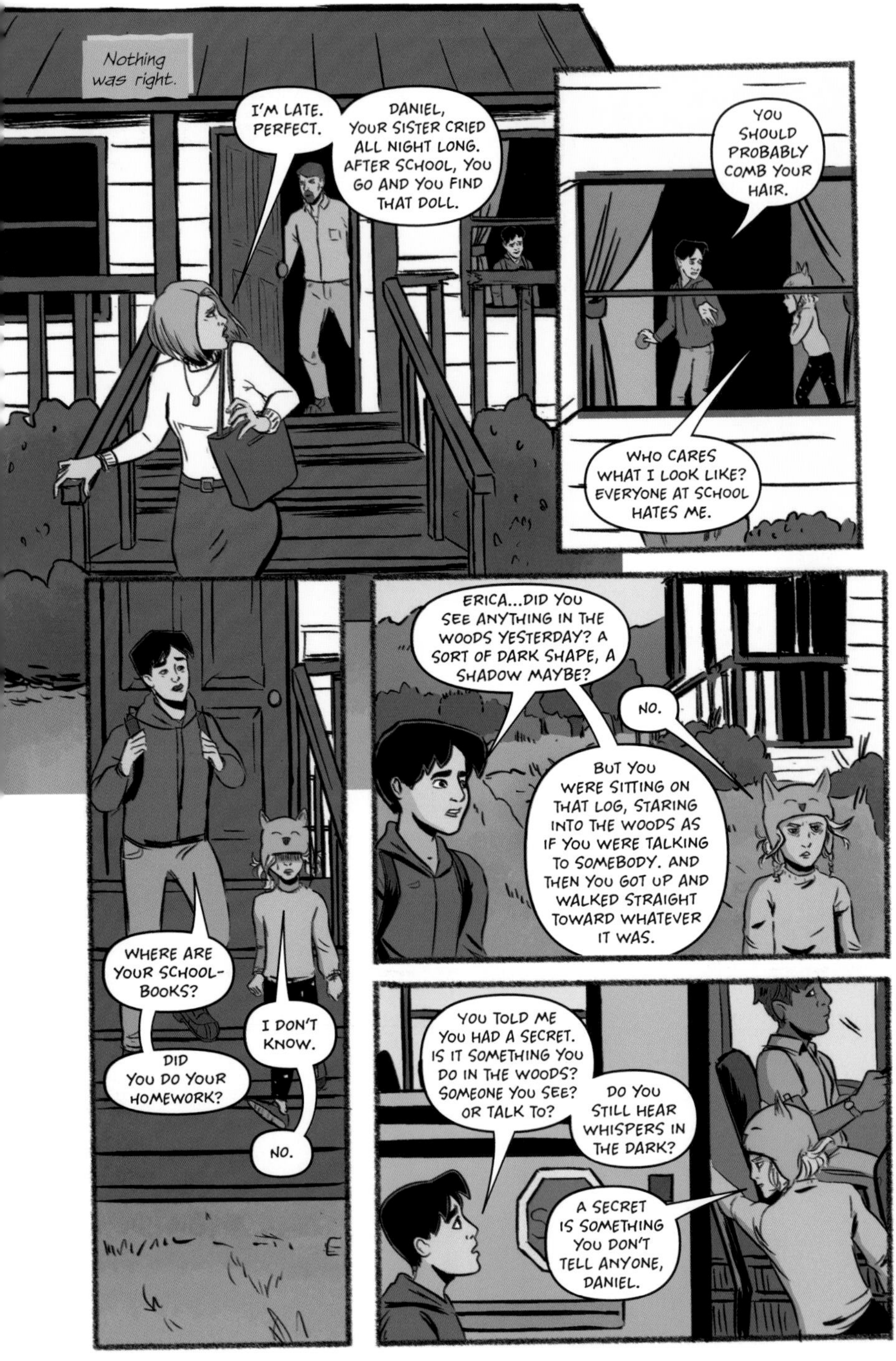
Nothing was right.
I'M LATE. PERFECT.
DANIEL, YOUR SISTER CRIED ALL NIGHT LONG. AFTER SCHOOL, YOU GO AND YOU FIND THAT DOLL.
YOU SHOULD PROBABLY COMB YOUR HAIR.
WHO CARES WHAT I LOOK LIKE? EVERYONE AT SCHOOL HATES ME.
WHERE ARE YOUR SCHOOL-BOOKS?
I DON'T KNOW.
DID YOU DO YOUR HOMEWORK?
NO.
ERICA...DID YOU SEE ANYTHING IN THE WOODS YESTERDAY? A SORT OF DARK SHAPE, A SHADOW MAYBE?
NO.
BUT YOU WERE SITTING ON THAT LOG, STARING INTO THE WOODS AS IF YOU WERE TALKING TO SOMEBODY. AND THEN YOU GOT UP AND WALKED STRAIGHT TOWARD WHATEVER IT WAS.
YOU TOLD ME YOU HAD A SECRET. IS IT SOMETHING YOU DO IN THE WOODS? SOMEONE YOU SEE? OR TALK TO?
DO YOU STILL HEAR WHISPERS IN THE DARK?
A SECRET IS SOMETHING YOU DON'T TELL ANYONE, DANIEL.

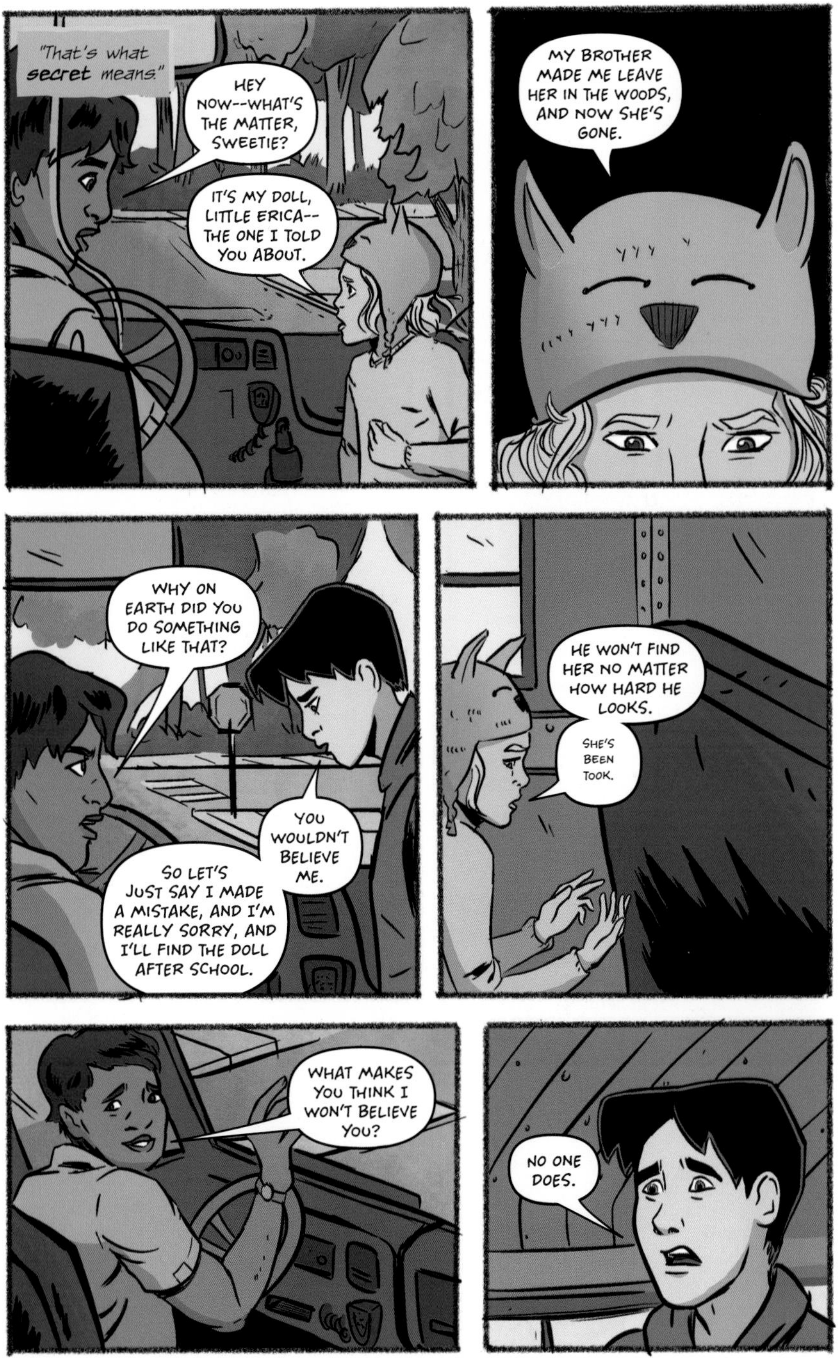
"That's what **secret** means."
HEY NOW--WHAT'S THE MATTER, SWEETIE?
IT'S MY DOLL, LITTLE ERICA-- THE ONE I TOLD YOU ABOUT.
MY BROTHER MADE ME LEAVE HER IN THE WOODS, AND NOW SHE'S GONE.
WHY ON EARTH DID YOU DO SOMETHING LIKE THAT?
YOU WOULDN'T BELIEVE ME.
SO LET'S JUST SAY I MADE A MISTAKE, AND I'M REALLY SORRY, AND I'LL FIND THE DOLL AFTER SCHOOL.
HE WON'T FIND HER NO MATTER HOW HARD HE LOOKS.
SHE'S BEEN TOOK.
WHAT MAKES YOU THINK I WON'T BELIEVE YOU?
NO ONE DOES.

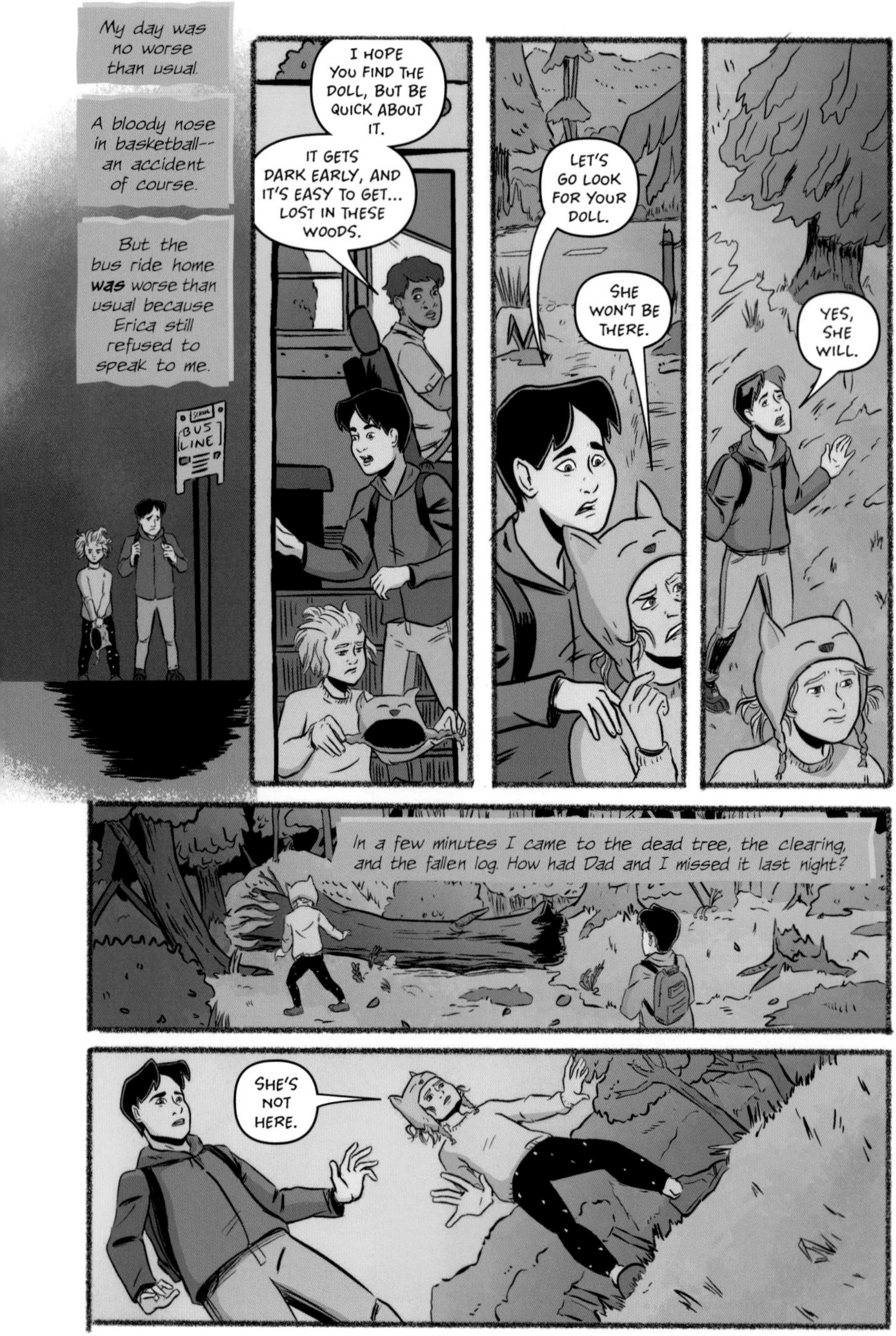
My day was no worse than usual.
A bloody nose in basketball--an accident of course.
But the bus ride home **was** worse than usual because Erica still refused to speak to me.
SCHOOL BUS LINE
I HOPE YOU FIND THE DOLL, BUT BE QUICK ABOUT IT.
IT GETS DARK EARLY, AND IT'S EASY TO GET... LOST IN THESE WOODS.
LET'S GO LOOK FOR YOUR DOLL.
SHE WON'T BE THERE.
YES, SHE WILL.
In a few minutes I came to the dead tree, the clearing, and the fallen log. How had Dad and I missed it last night?
SHE'S NOT HERE.

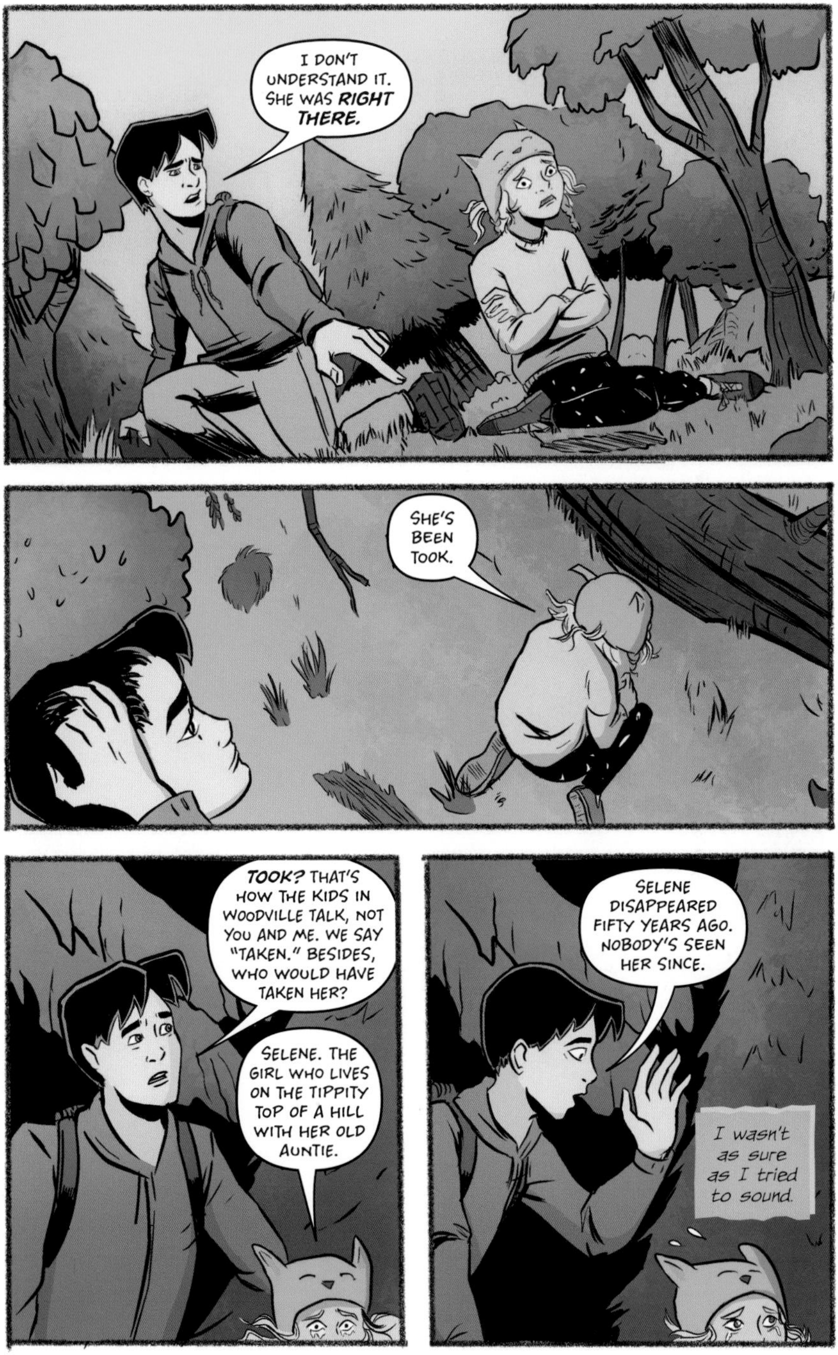
I DON'T UNDERSTAND IT. SHE WAS RIGHT THERE.
SHE'S BEEN TOOK.
TOOK? THAT'S HOW THE KIDS IN WOODVILLE TALK, NOT YOU AND ME. WE SAY "TAKEN." BESIDES, WHO WOULD HAVE TAKEN HER?
SELENE. THE GIRL WHO LIVES ON THE TIPPITY TOP OF A HILL WITH HER OLD AUNTIE.
SELENE DISAPPEARED FIFTY YEARS AGO. NOBODY'S SEEN HER SINCE.
I wasn't as sure as I tried to sound.

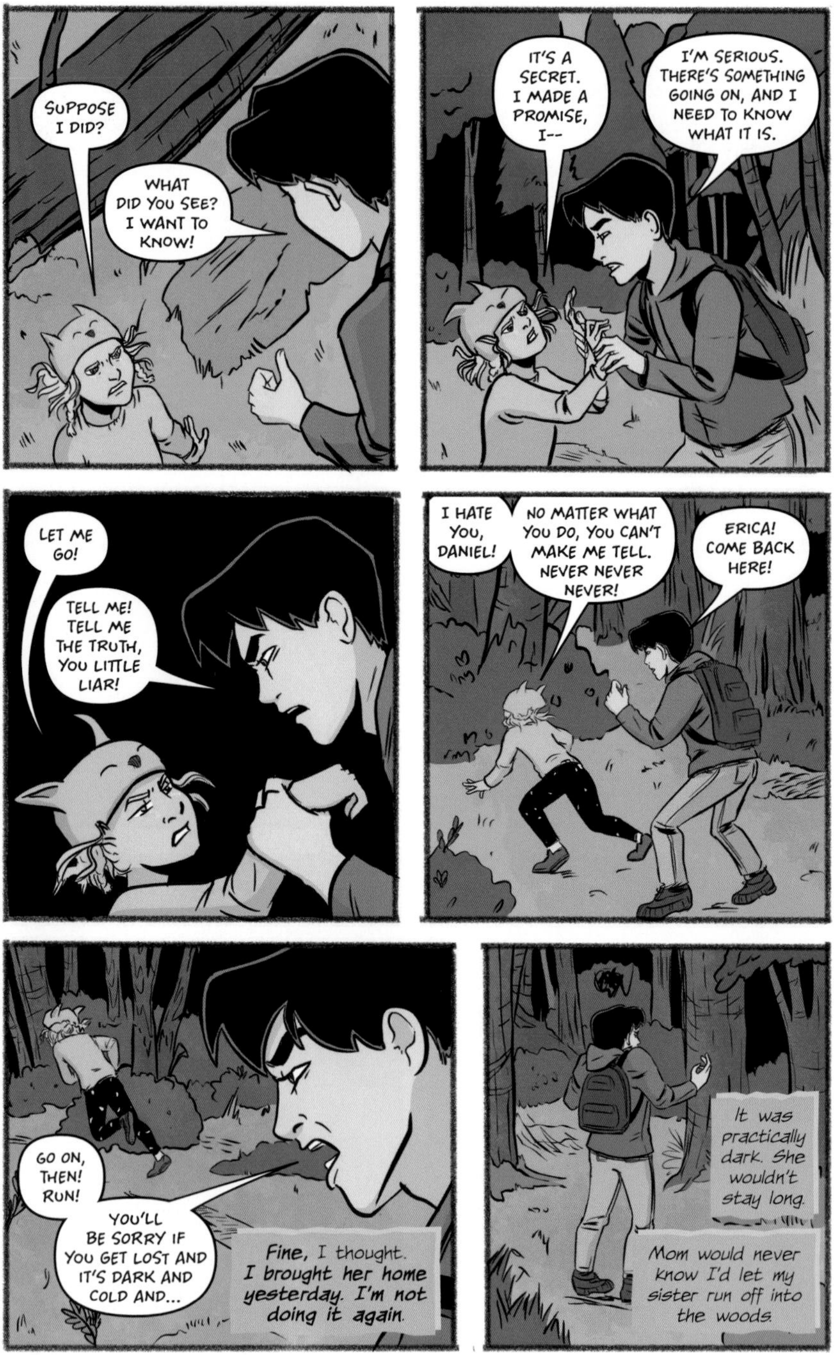
SUPPOSE I DID?
WHAT DID YOU SEE? I WANT TO KNOW!
IT'S A SECRET. I MADE A PROMISE, I--
I'M SERIOUS. THERE'S SOMETHING GOING ON, AND I NEED TO KNOW WHAT IT IS.
LET ME GO!
TELL ME! TELL ME THE TRUTH, YOU LITTLE LIAR!
I HATE YOU, DANIEL!
NO MATTER WHAT YOU DO, YOU CAN'T MAKE ME TELL. NEVER NEVER NEVER!
ERICA! COME BACK HERE!
GO ON, THEN! RUN!
YOU'LL BE SORRY IF YOU GET LOST AND IT'S DARK AND COLD AND...
Fine, I thought. I brought her home yesterday. I'm not doing it again.
It was practically dark. She wouldn't stay long.
Mom would never know I'd let my sister run off into the woods.

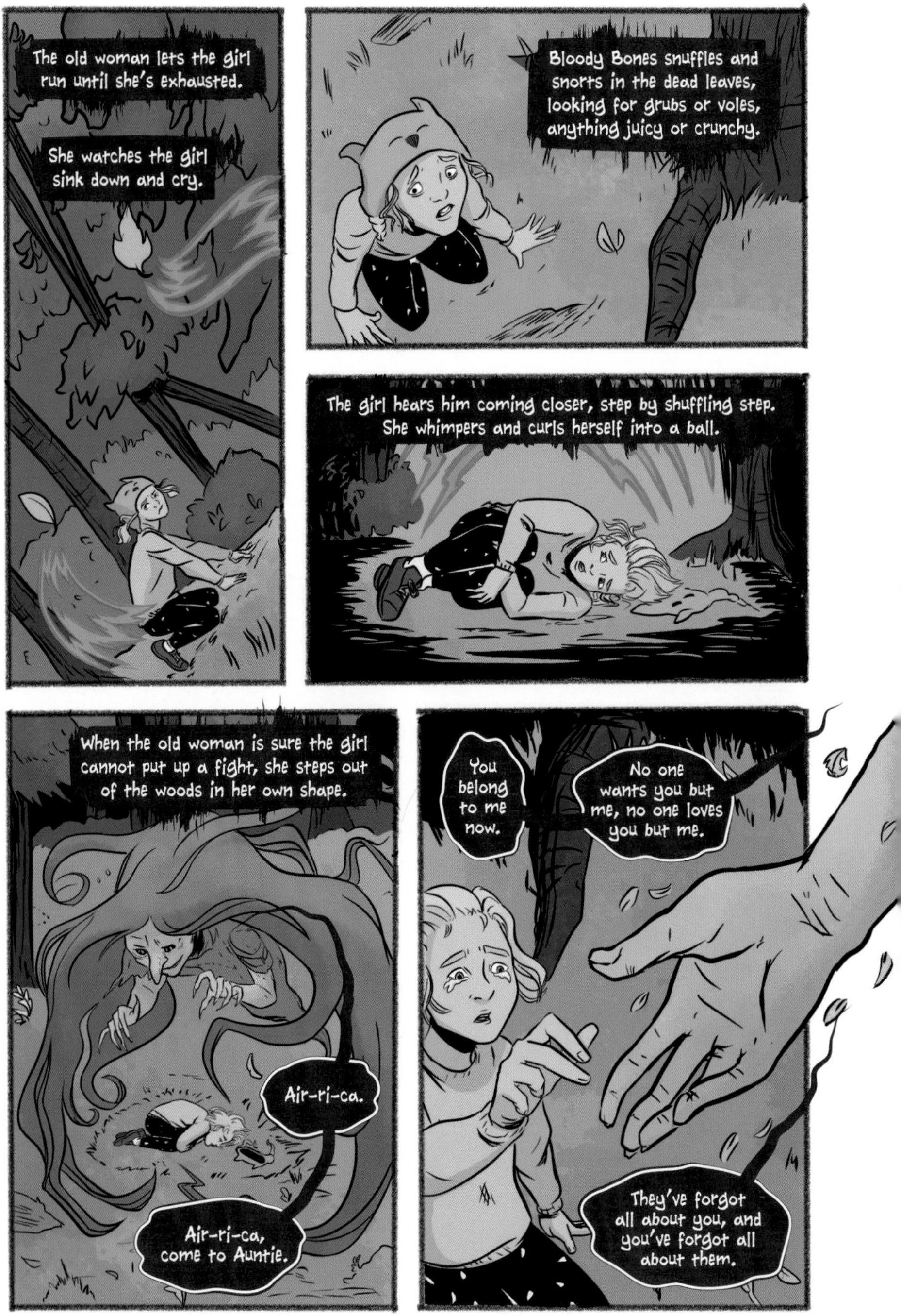
The old woman lets the girl run until she's exhausted.
She watches the girl sink down and cry.
Bloody Bones snuffles and snorts in the dead leaves, looking for grubs or voles, anything juicy or crunchy.
The girl hears him coming closer, step by shuffling step. She whimpers and curls herself into a ball.
When the old woman is sure the girl cannot put up a fight, she steps out of the woods in her own shape.
Air-ri-ca.
Air-ri-ca, come to Auntie.
You belong to me now.
No one wants you but me, no one loves you but me.
They've forgot all about you, and you've forgot all about them.

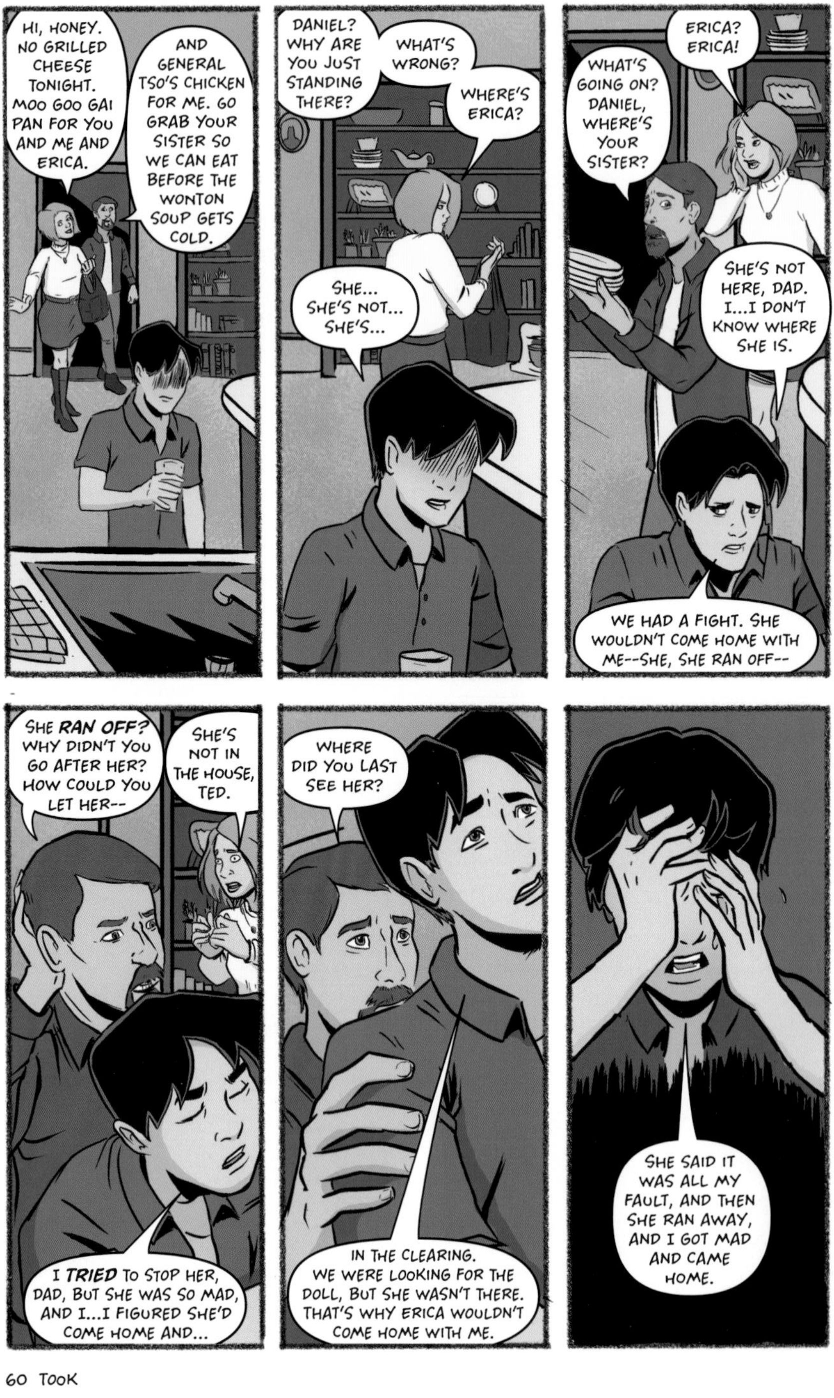
HI, HONEY. NO GRILLED CHEESE TONIGHT. MOO GOO GAI PAN FOR YOU AND ME AND ERICA.
AND GENERAL TSO'S CHICKEN FOR ME. GO GRAB YOUR SISTER SO WE CAN EAT BEFORE THE WONTON SOUP GETS COLD.
DANIEL? WHY ARE YOU JUST STANDING THERE?
WHAT'S WRONG?
WHERE'S ERICA?
SHE... SHE'S NOT... SHE'S...
ERICA? ERICA!
WHAT'S GOING ON? DANIEL, WHERE'S YOUR SISTER?
SHE'S NOT HERE, DAD. I...I DON'T KNOW WHERE SHE IS.
WE HAD A FIGHT. SHE WOULDN'T COME HOME WITH ME--SHE, SHE RAN OFF--
SHE *RAN OFF?* WHY DIDN'T YOU GO AFTER HER? HOW COULD YOU LET HER--
SHE'S NOT IN THE HOUSE, TED.
I *TRIED* TO STOP HER, DAD, BUT SHE WAS SO MAD, AND I...I FIGURED SHE'D COME HOME AND...
WHERE DID YOU LAST SEE HER?
IN THE CLEARING. WE WERE LOOKING FOR THE DOLL, BUT SHE WASN'T THERE. THAT'S WHY ERICA WOULDN'T COME HOME WITH ME.
SHE SAID IT WAS ALL MY FAULT, AND THEN SHE RAN AWAY, AND I GOT MAD AND CAME HOME.

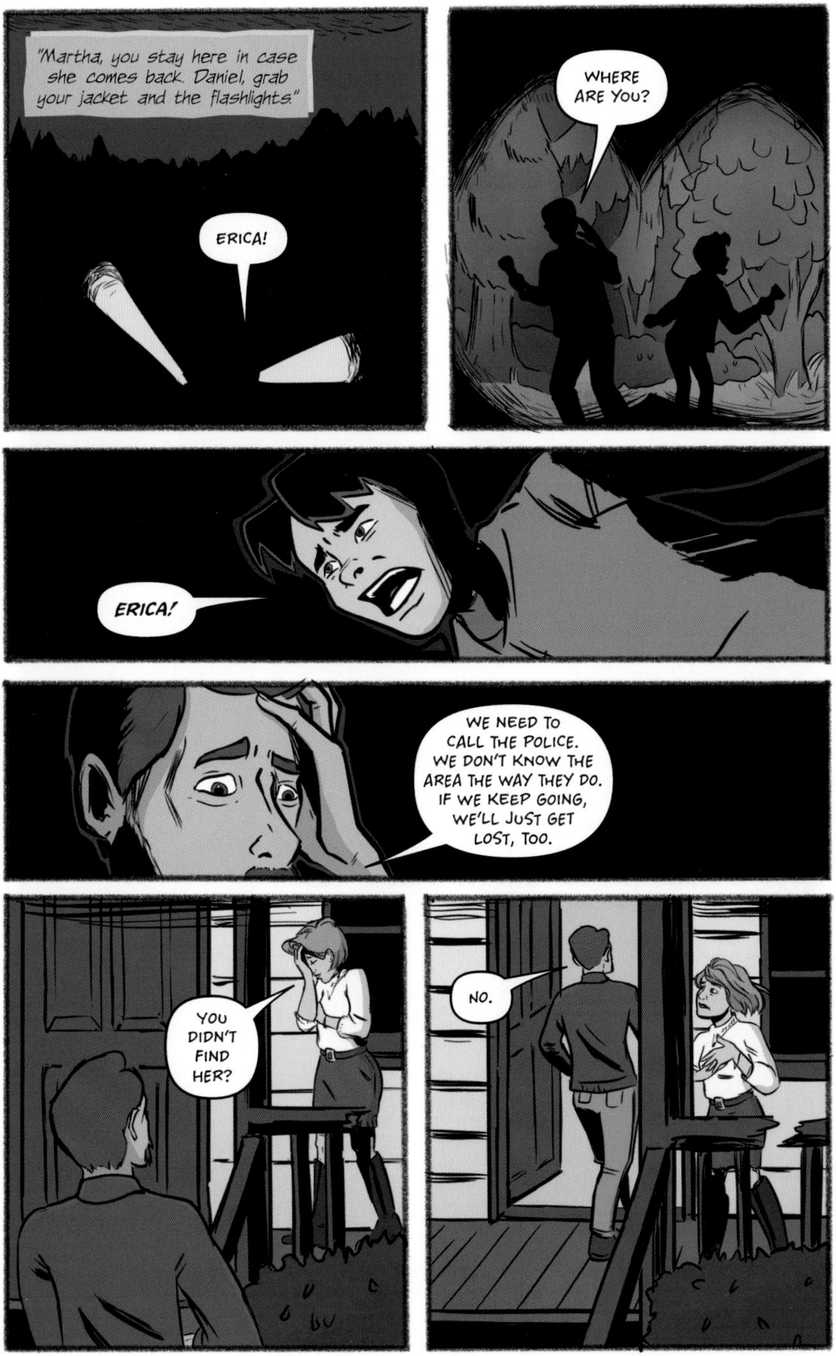
"Martha, you stay here in case she comes back. Daniel, grab your jacket and the flashlights."
ERICA!
WHERE ARE YOU?
ERICA!
WE NEED TO CALL THE POLICE. WE DON'T KNOW THE AREA THE WAY THEY DO. IF WE KEEP GOING, WE'LL JUST GET LOST, TOO.
YOU DIDN'T FIND HER?
NO.

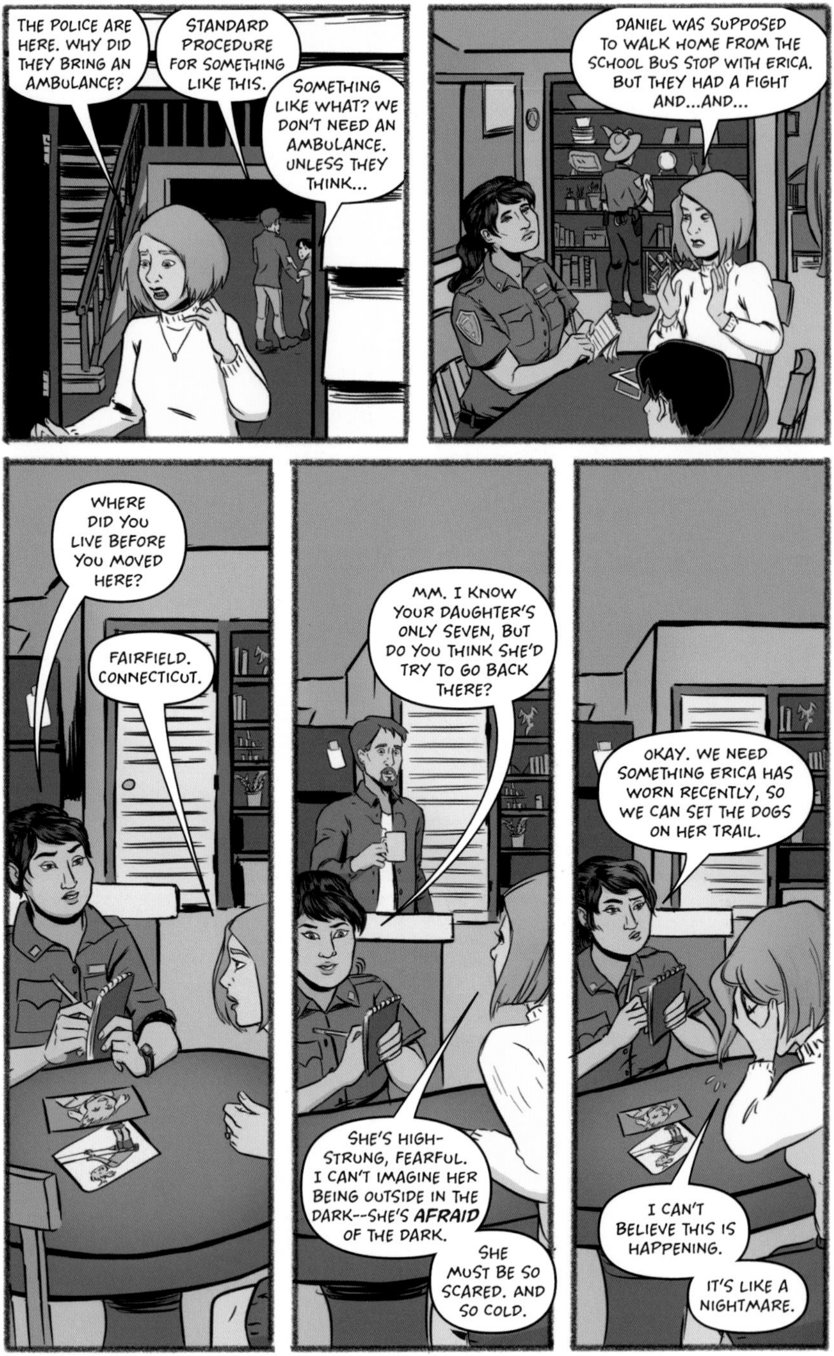
THE POLICE ARE HERE. WHY DID THEY BRING AN AMBULANCE?
STANDARD PROCEDURE FOR SOMETHING LIKE THIS.
SOMETHING LIKE WHAT? WE DON'T NEED AN AMBULANCE. UNLESS THEY THINK...
DANIEL WAS SUPPOSED TO WALK HOME FROM THE SCHOOL BUS STOP WITH ERICA. BUT THEY HAD A FIGHT AND...AND...
WHERE DID YOU LIVE BEFORE YOU MOVED HERE?
FAIRFIELD. CONNECTICUT.
MM. I KNOW YOUR DAUGHTER'S ONLY SEVEN, BUT DO YOU THINK SHE'D TRY TO GO BACK THERE?
SHE'S HIGH-STRUNG, FEARFUL. I CAN'T IMAGINE HER BEING OUTSIDE IN THE DARK--SHE'S ***AFRAID*** OF THE DARK.
SHE MUST BE SO SCARED. AND SO COLD.
OKAY. WE NEED SOMETHING ERICA HAS WORN RECENTLY, SO WE CAN SET THE DOGS ON HER TRAIL.
I CAN'T BELIEVE THIS IS HAPPENING.
IT'S LIKE A NIGHTMARE.

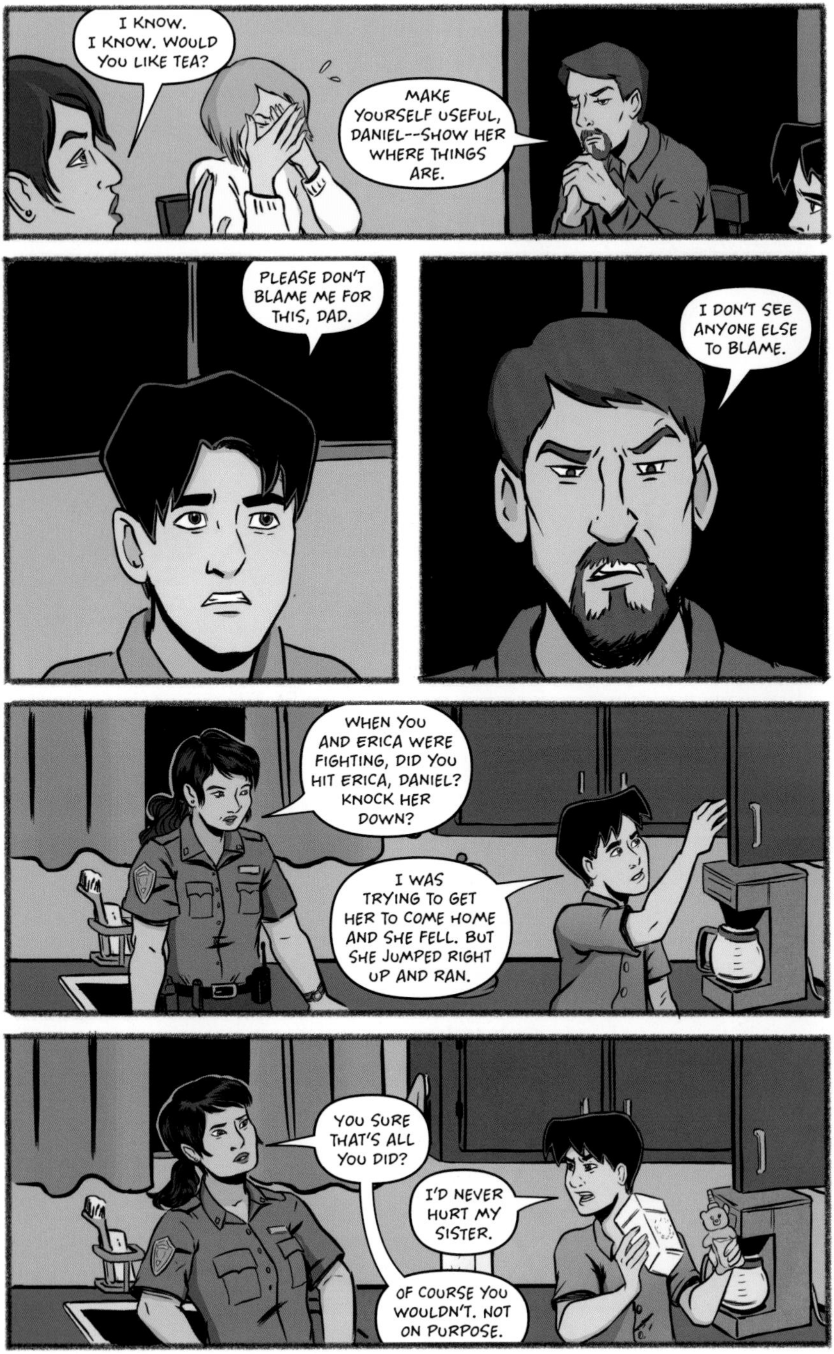
I KNOW. I KNOW. WOULD YOU LIKE TEA?
MAKE YOURSELF USEFUL, DANIEL--SHOW HER WHERE THINGS ARE.
PLEASE DON'T BLAME ME FOR THIS, DAD.
I DON'T SEE ANYONE ELSE TO BLAME.
WHEN YOU AND ERICA WERE FIGHTING, DID YOU HIT ERICA, DANIEL? KNOCK HER DOWN?
I WAS TRYING TO GET HER TO COME HOME AND SHE FELL. BUT SHE JUMPED RIGHT UP AND RAN.
YOU SURE THAT'S ALL YOU DID?
I'D NEVER HURT MY SISTER.
OF COURSE YOU WOULDN'T. NOT ON PURPOSE.

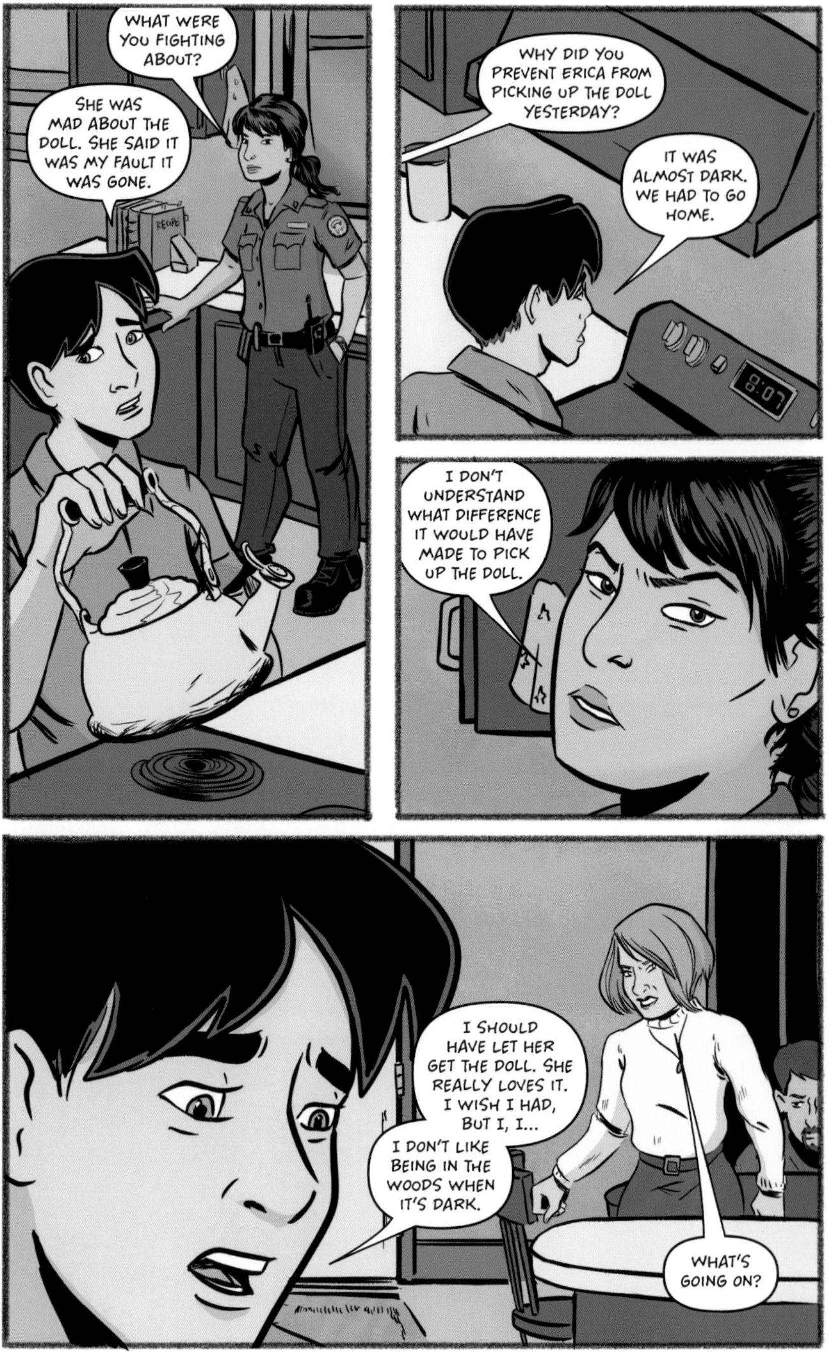
WHAT WERE YOU FIGHTING ABOUT?
SHE WAS MAD ABOUT THE DOLL. SHE SAID IT WAS MY FAULT IT WAS GONE.
RECIPE
WHY DID YOU PREVENT ERICA FROM PICKING UP THE DOLL YESTERDAY?
IT WAS ALMOST DARK. WE HAD TO GO HOME.
I DON'T UNDERSTAND WHAT DIFFERENCE IT WOULD HAVE MADE TO PICK UP THE DOLL.
I SHOULD HAVE LET HER GET THE DOLL. SHE REALLY LOVES IT. I WISH I HAD, BUT I, I...
I DON'T LIKE BEING IN THE WOODS WHEN IT'S DARK.
WHAT'S GOING ON?

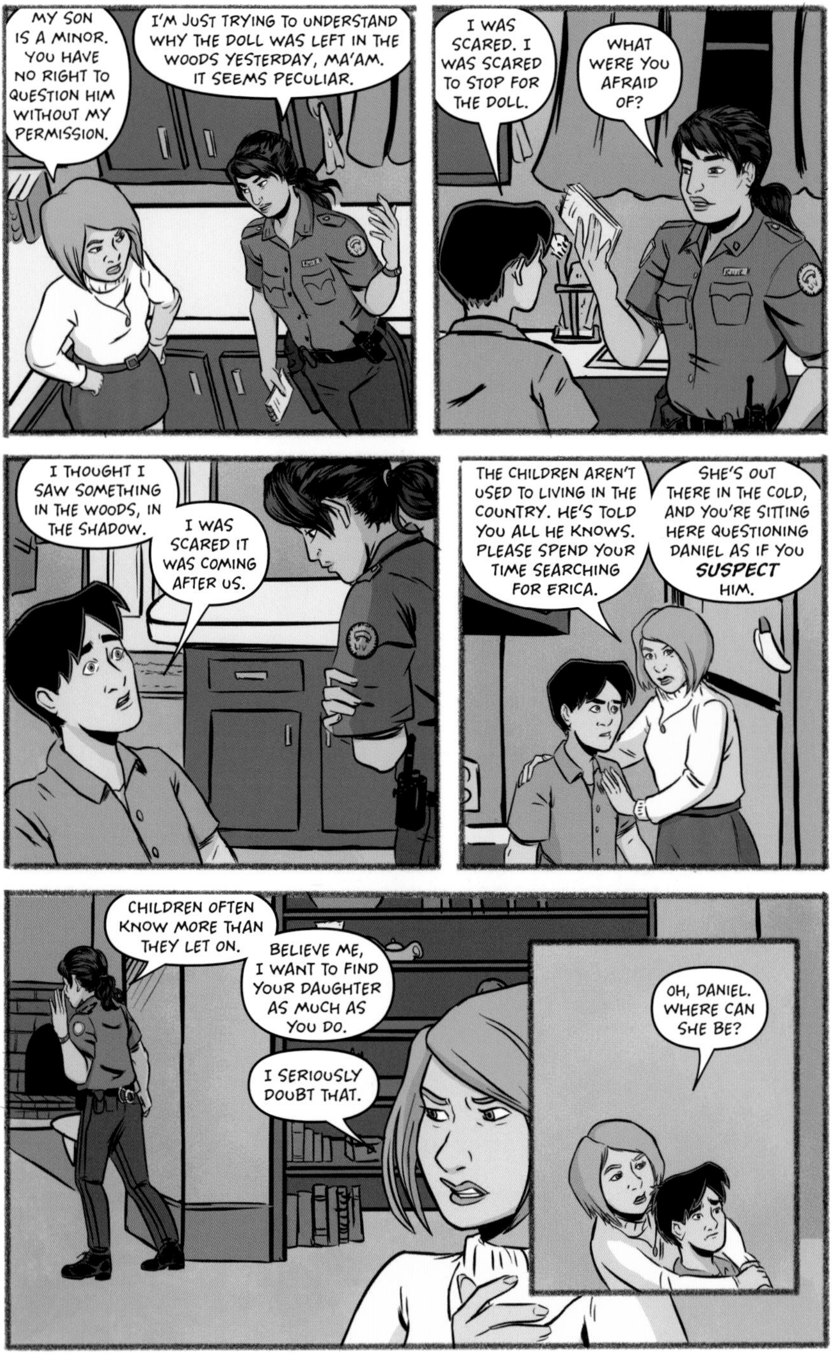
MY SON IS A MINOR. YOU HAVE NO RIGHT TO QUESTION HIM WITHOUT MY PERMISSION.
I'M JUST TRYING TO UNDERSTAND WHY THE DOLL WAS LEFT IN THE WOODS YESTERDAY, MA'AM. IT SEEMS PECULIAR.
I WAS SCARED. I WAS SCARED TO STOP FOR THE DOLL.
WHAT WERE YOU AFRAID OF?
I THOUGHT I SAW SOMETHING IN THE WOODS, IN THE SHADOW.
I WAS SCARED IT WAS COMING AFTER US.
THE CHILDREN AREN'T USED TO LIVING IN THE COUNTRY. HE'S TOLD YOU ALL HE KNOWS. PLEASE SPEND YOUR TIME SEARCHING FOR ERICA.
SHE'S OUT THERE IN THE COLD, AND YOU'RE SITTING HERE QUESTIONING DANIEL AS IF YOU *SUSPECT* HIM.
CHILDREN OFTEN KNOW MORE THAN THEY LET ON.
BELIEVE ME, I WANT TO FIND YOUR DAUGHTER AS MUCH AS YOU DO.
I SERIOUSLY DOUBT THAT.
OH, DANIEL. WHERE CAN SHE BE?

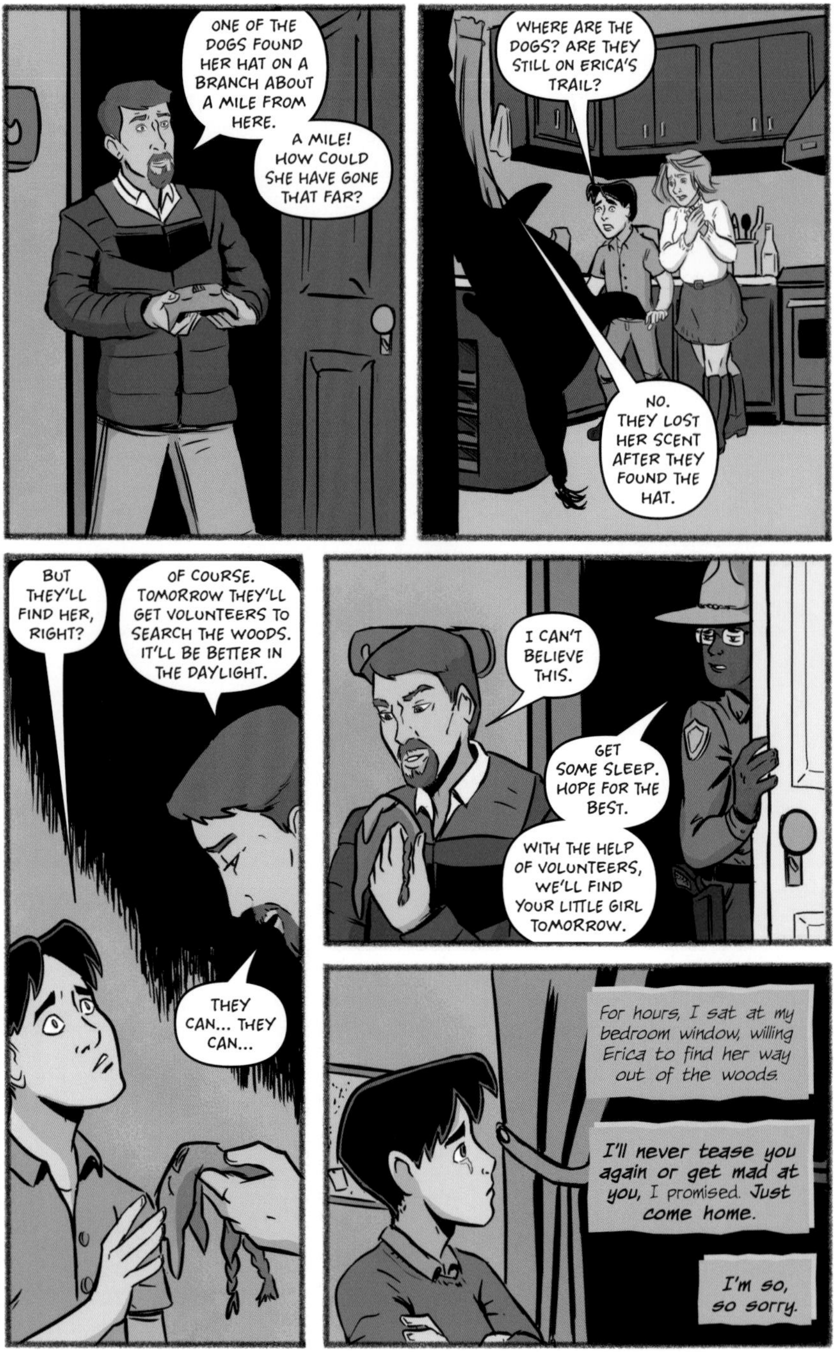
ONE OF THE DOGS FOUND HER HAT ON A BRANCH ABOUT A MILE FROM HERE.
A MILE! HOW COULD SHE HAVE GONE THAT FAR?
WHERE ARE THE DOGS? ARE THEY STILL ON ERICA'S TRAIL?
NO. THEY LOST HER SCENT AFTER THEY FOUND THE HAT.
BUT THEY'LL FIND HER, RIGHT?
OF COURSE. TOMORROW THEY'LL GET VOLUNTEERS TO SEARCH THE WOODS. IT'LL BE BETTER IN THE DAYLIGHT.
THEY CAN... THEY CAN...
I CAN'T BELIEVE THIS.
GET SOME SLEEP. HOPE FOR THE BEST.
WITH THE HELP OF VOLUNTEERS, WE'LL FIND YOUR LITTLE GIRL TOMORROW.
For hours, I sat at my bedroom window, willing Erica to find her way out of the woods.
I'll never tease you again or get mad at you, I promised. Just come home.
I'm so, so sorry.

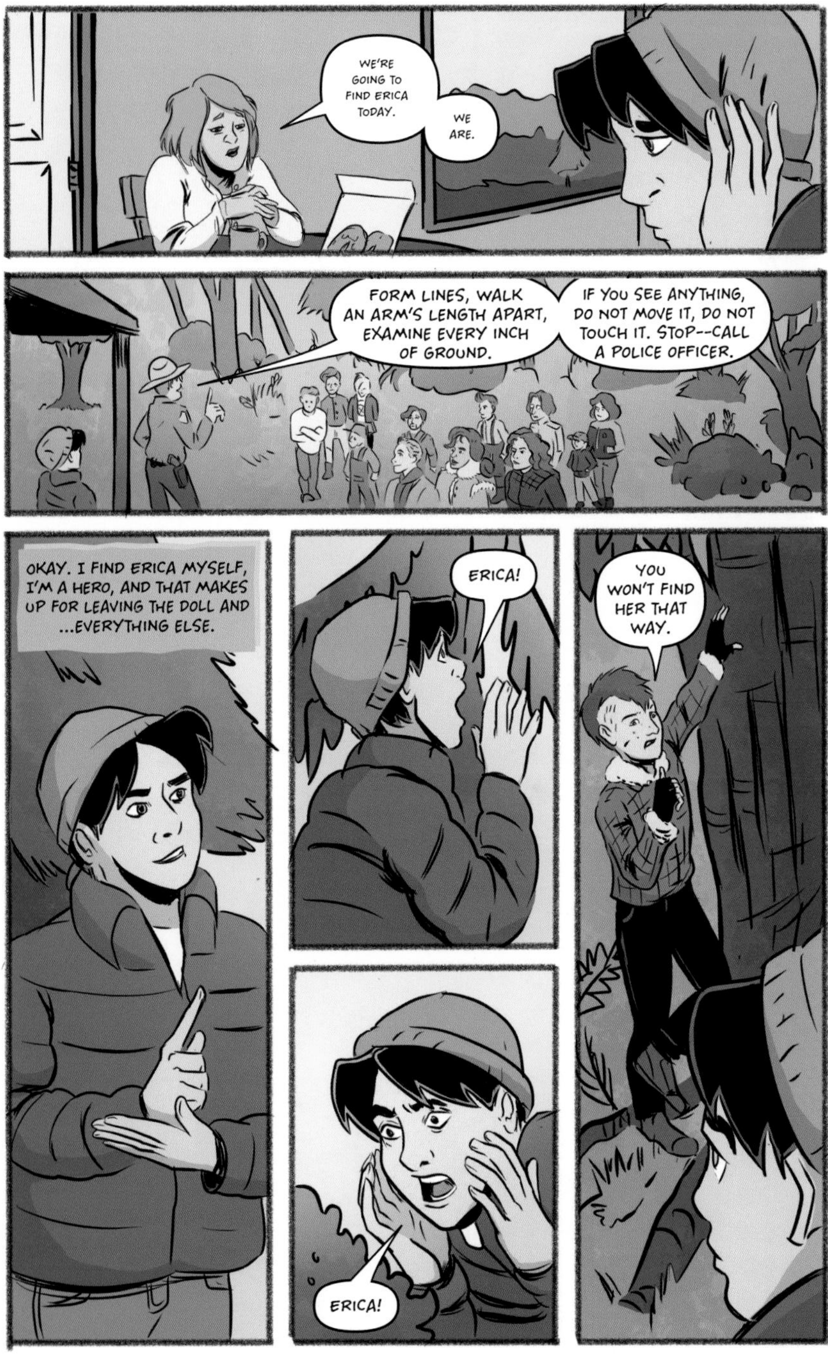
WE'RE GOING TO FIND ERICA TODAY.
WE ARE.
FORM LINES, WALK AN ARM'S LENGTH APART, EXAMINE EVERY INCH OF GROUND.
IF YOU SEE ANYTHING, DO NOT MOVE IT, DO NOT TOUCH IT. STOP--CALL A POLICE OFFICER.
OKAY. I FIND ERICA MYSELF, I'M A HERO, AND THAT MAKES UP FOR LEAVING THE DOLL AND ...EVERYTHING ELSE.
ERICA!
ERICA!
YOU WON'T FIND HER THAT WAY.

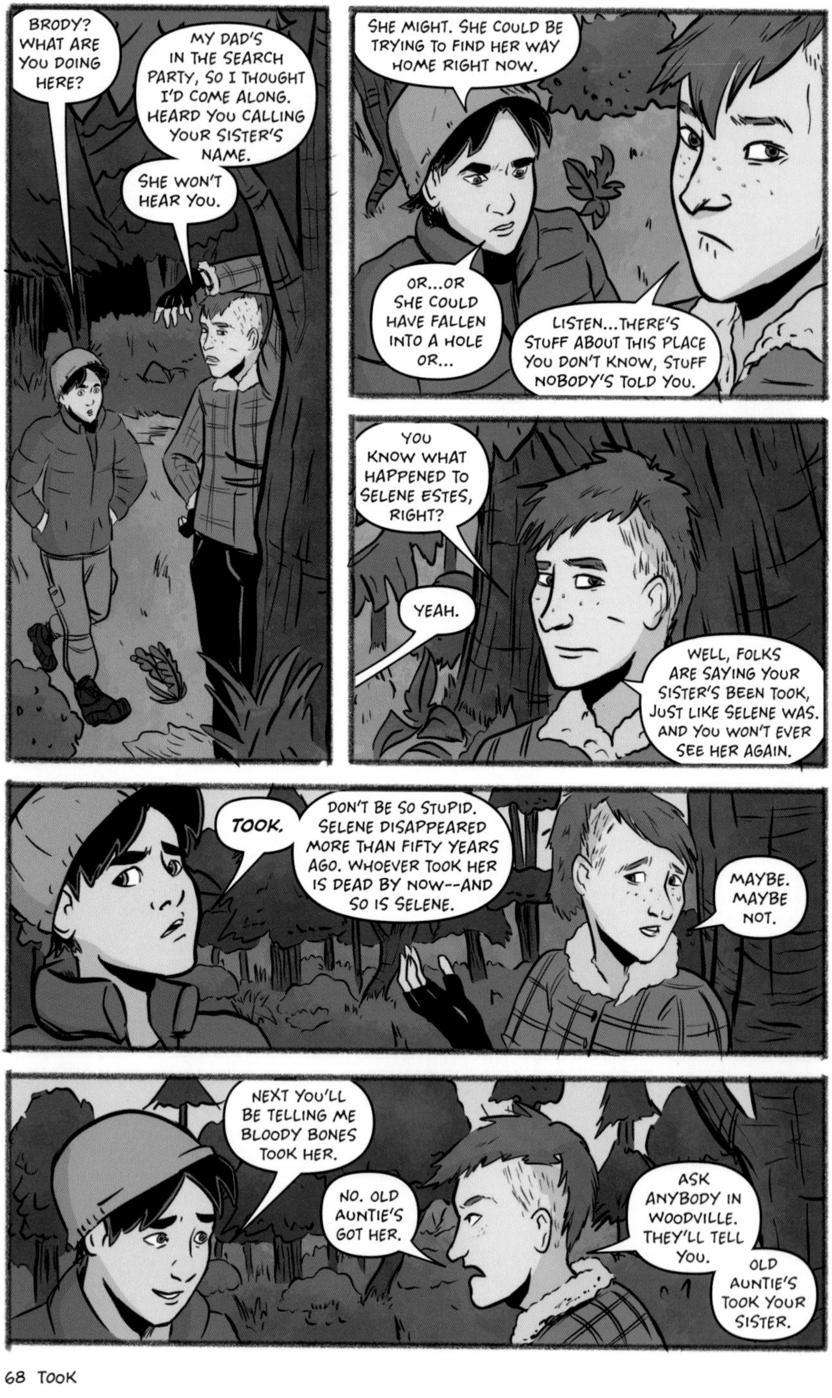
BRODY? WHAT ARE YOU DOING HERE?
MY DAD'S IN THE SEARCH PARTY, SO I THOUGHT I'D COME ALONG. HEARD YOU CALLING YOUR SISTER'S NAME.
SHE WON'T HEAR YOU.
SHE MIGHT. SHE COULD BE TRYING TO FIND HER WAY HOME RIGHT NOW.
OR...OR SHE COULD HAVE FALLEN INTO A HOLE OR...
LISTEN...THERE'S STUFF ABOUT THIS PLACE YOU DON'T KNOW, STUFF NOBODY'S TOLD YOU.
YOU KNOW WHAT HAPPENED TO SELENE ESTES, RIGHT?
YEAH.
WELL, FOLKS ARE SAYING YOUR SISTER'S BEEN TOOK, JUST LIKE SELENE WAS. AND YOU WON'T EVER SEE HER AGAIN.
TOOK.
DON'T BE SO STUPID. SELENE DISAPPEARED MORE THAN FIFTY YEARS AGO. WHOEVER TOOK HER IS DEAD BY NOW--AND SO IS SELENE.
MAYBE. MAYBE NOT.
NEXT YOU'LL BE TELLING ME BLOODY BONES TOOK HER.
NO. OLD AUNTIE'S GOT HER.
ASK ANYBODY IN WOODVILLE. THEY'LL TELL YOU.
OLD AUNTIE'S TOOK YOUR SISTER.

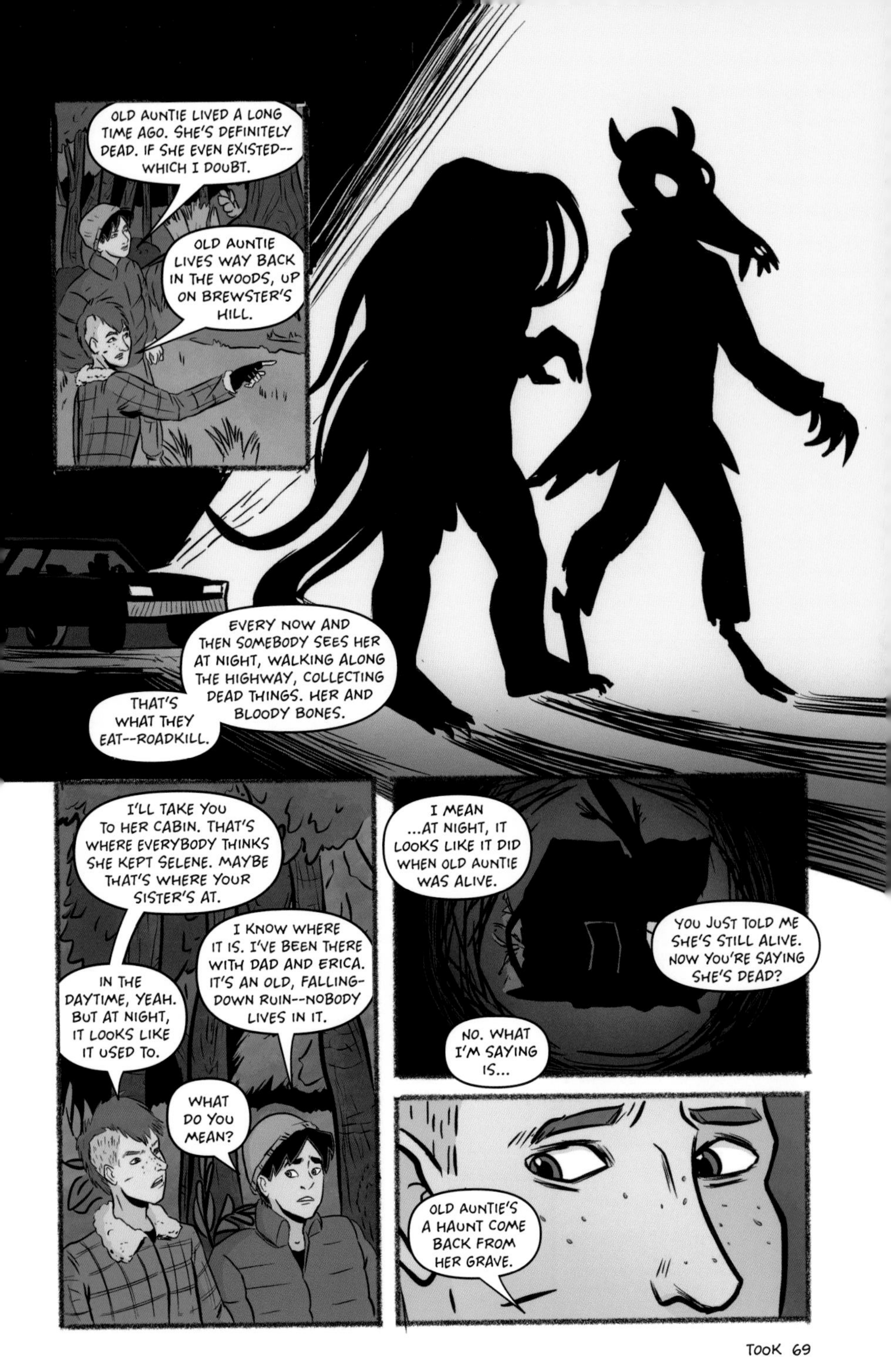
OLD AUNTIE LIVED A LONG TIME AGO. SHE'S DEFINITELY DEAD. IF SHE EVEN EXISTED-- WHICH I DOUBT.
OLD AUNTIE LIVES WAY BACK IN THE WOODS, UP ON BREWSTER'S HILL.
EVERY NOW AND THEN SOMEBODY SEES HER AT NIGHT, WALKING ALONG THE HIGHWAY, COLLECTING DEAD THINGS. HER AND BLOODY BONES.
THAT'S WHAT THEY EAT--ROADKILL.
I'LL TAKE YOU TO HER CABIN. THAT'S WHERE EVERYBODY THINKS SHE KEPT SELENE. MAYBE THAT'S WHERE YOUR SISTER'S AT.
I KNOW WHERE IT IS. I'VE BEEN THERE WITH DAD AND ERICA. IT'S AN OLD, FALLING-DOWN RUIN--NOBODY LIVES IN IT.
IN THE DAYTIME, YEAH. BUT AT NIGHT, IT LOOKS LIKE IT USED TO.
WHAT DO YOU MEAN?
I MEAN ...AT NIGHT, IT LOOKS LIKE IT DID WHEN OLD AUNTIE WAS ALIVE.
YOU JUST TOLD ME SHE'S STILL ALIVE. NOW YOU'RE SAYING SHE'S DEAD?
NO. WHAT I'M SAYING IS...
OLD AUNTIE'S A HAUNT COME BACK FROM HER GRAVE.

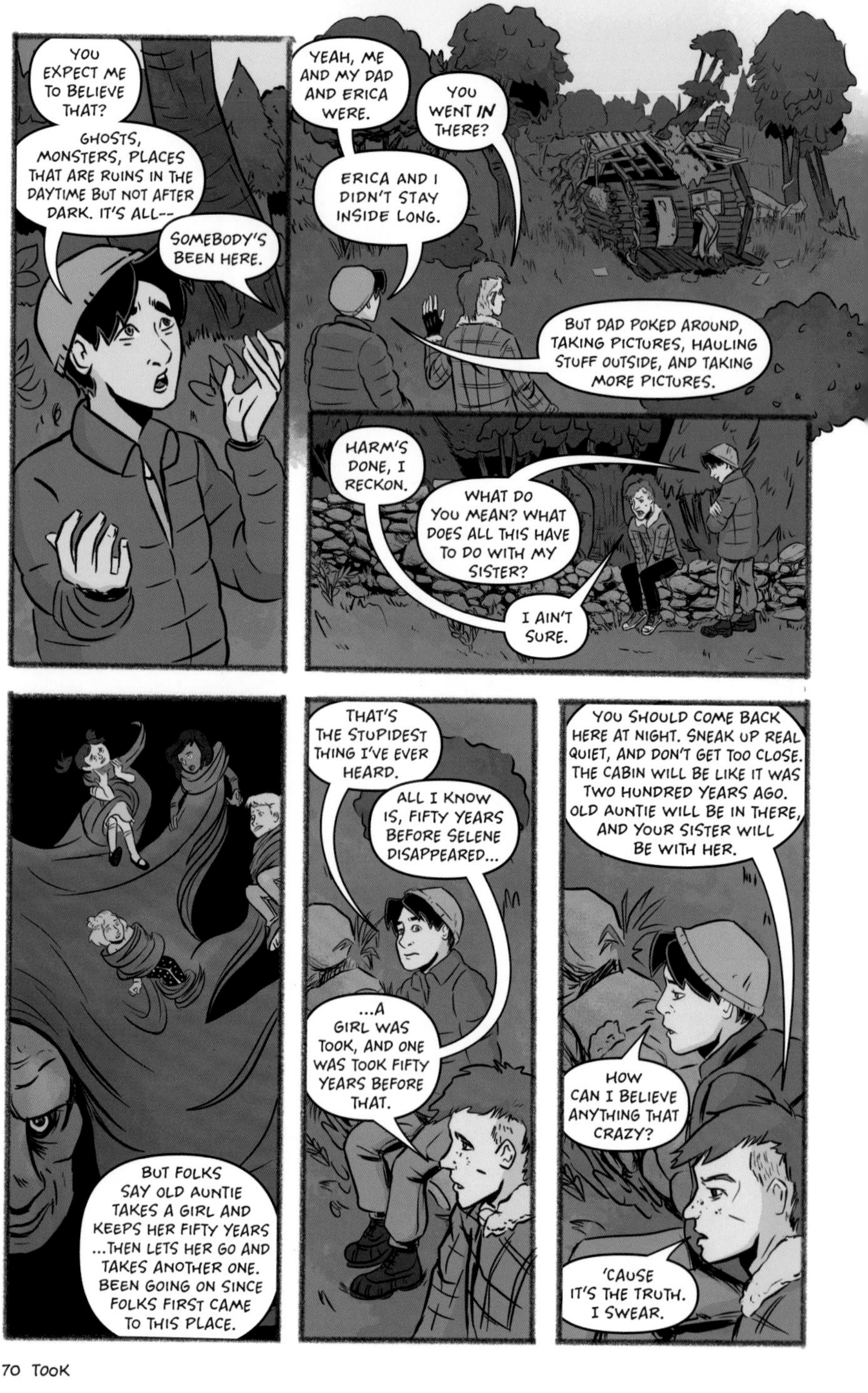
YOU EXPECT ME TO BELIEVE THAT?
GHOSTS, MONSTERS, PLACES THAT ARE RUINS IN THE DAYTIME BUT NOT AFTER DARK. IT'S ALL--
SOMEBODY'S BEEN HERE.
YEAH, ME AND MY DAD AND ERICA WERE.
YOU WENT *IN* THERE?
ERICA AND I DIDN'T STAY INSIDE LONG.
BUT DAD POKED AROUND, TAKING PICTURES, HAULING STUFF OUTSIDE, AND TAKING MORE PICTURES.
HARM'S DONE, I RECKON.
WHAT DO YOU MEAN? WHAT DOES ALL THIS HAVE TO DO WITH MY SISTER?
I AIN'T SURE.
BUT FOLKS SAY OLD AUNTIE TAKES A GIRL AND KEEPS HER FIFTY YEARS ...THEN LETS HER GO AND TAKES ANOTHER ONE. BEEN GOING ON SINCE FOLKS FIRST CAME TO THIS PLACE.
THAT'S THE STUPIDEST THING I'VE EVER HEARD.
ALL I KNOW IS, FIFTY YEARS BEFORE SELENE DISAPPEARED...
...A GIRL WAS TOOK, AND ONE WAS TOOK FIFTY YEARS BEFORE THAT.
YOU SHOULD COME BACK HERE AT NIGHT. SNEAK UP REAL QUIET, AND DON'T GET TOO CLOSE. THE CABIN WILL BE LIKE IT WAS TWO HUNDRED YEARS AGO. OLD AUNTIE WILL BE IN THERE, AND YOUR SISTER WILL BE WITH HER.
HOW CAN I BELIEVE ANYTHING THAT CRAZY?
'CAUSE IT'S THE TRUTH. I SWEAR.

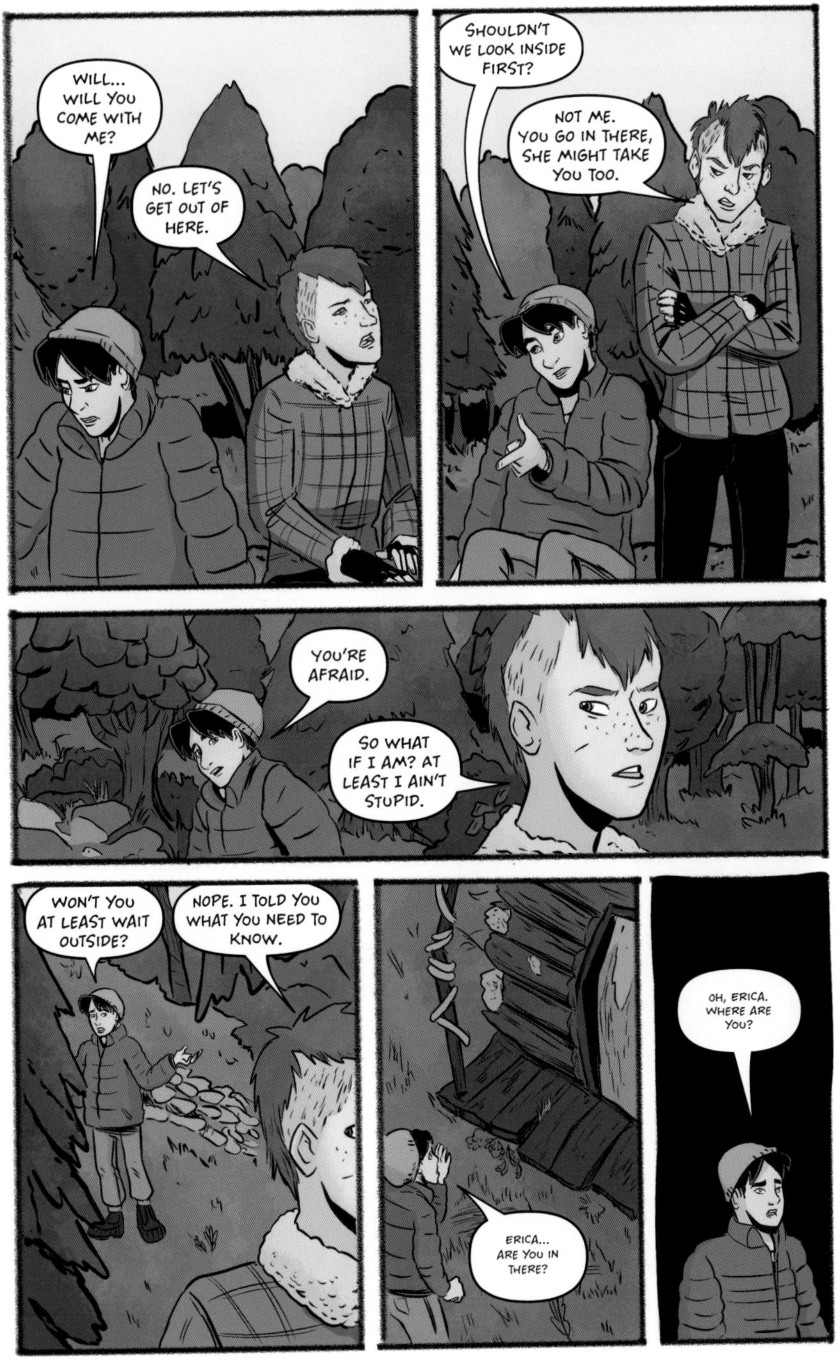

WILL... WILL YOU COME WITH ME?
NO. LET'S GET OUT OF HERE.
SHOULDN'T WE LOOK INSIDE FIRST?
NOT ME. YOU GO IN THERE, SHE MIGHT TAKE YOU TOO.
YOU'RE AFRAID.
SO WHAT IF I AM? AT LEAST I AIN'T STUPID.
WON'T YOU AT LEAST WAIT OUTSIDE?
NOPE. I TOLD YOU WHAT YOU NEED TO KNOW.
ERICA... ARE YOU IN THERE?
OH, ERICA. WHERE ARE YOU?

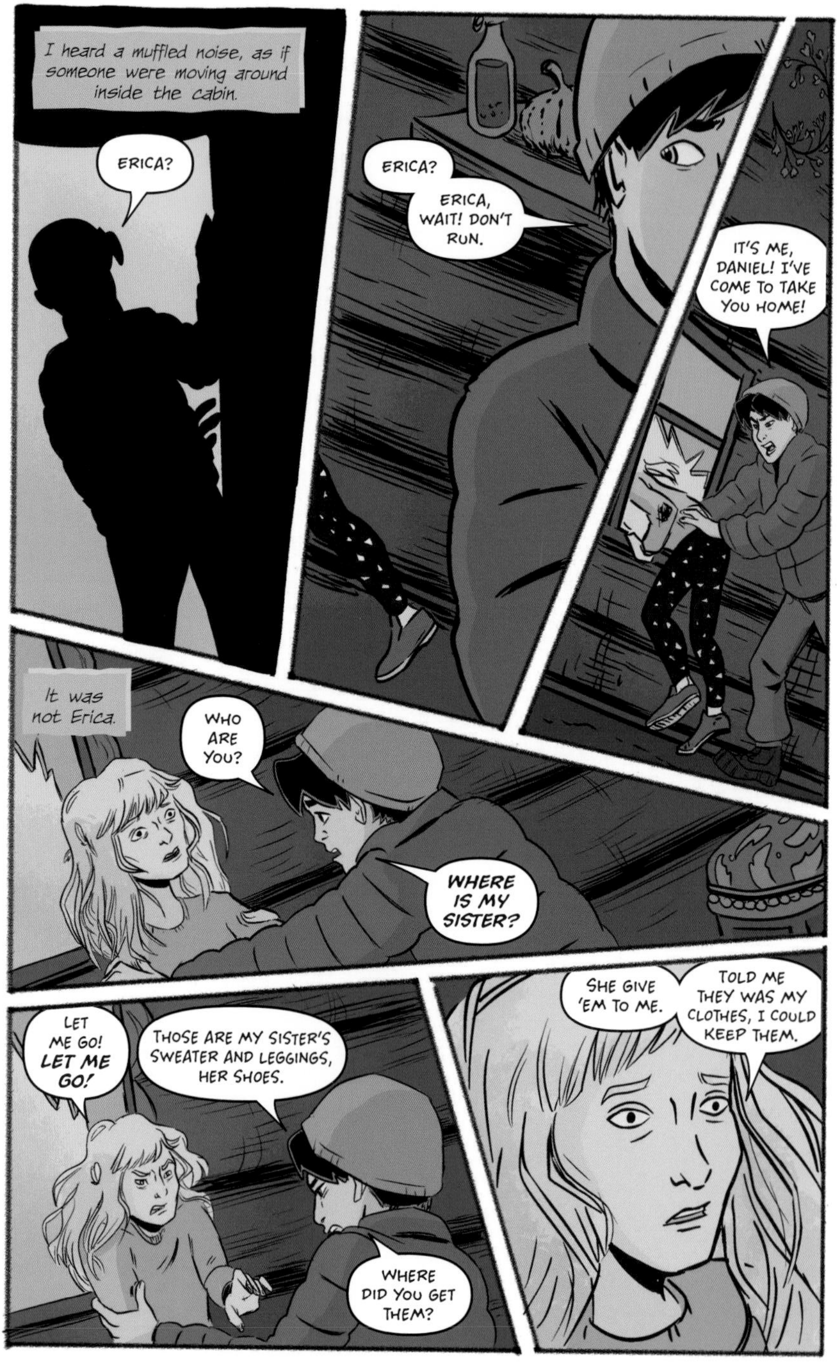
I heard a muffled noise, as if someone were moving around inside the cabin.
ERICA?
ERICA?
ERICA, WAIT! DON'T RUN.
IT'S ME, DANIEL! I'VE COME TO TAKE YOU HOME!
It was not Erica.
WHO ARE YOU?
WHERE IS MY SISTER?
LET ME GO! LET ME GO!
THOSE ARE MY SISTER'S SWEATER AND LEGGINGS, HER SHOES.
WHERE DID YOU GET THEM?
SHE GIVE 'EM TO ME.
TOLD ME THEY WAS MY CLOTHES, I COULD KEEP THEM.

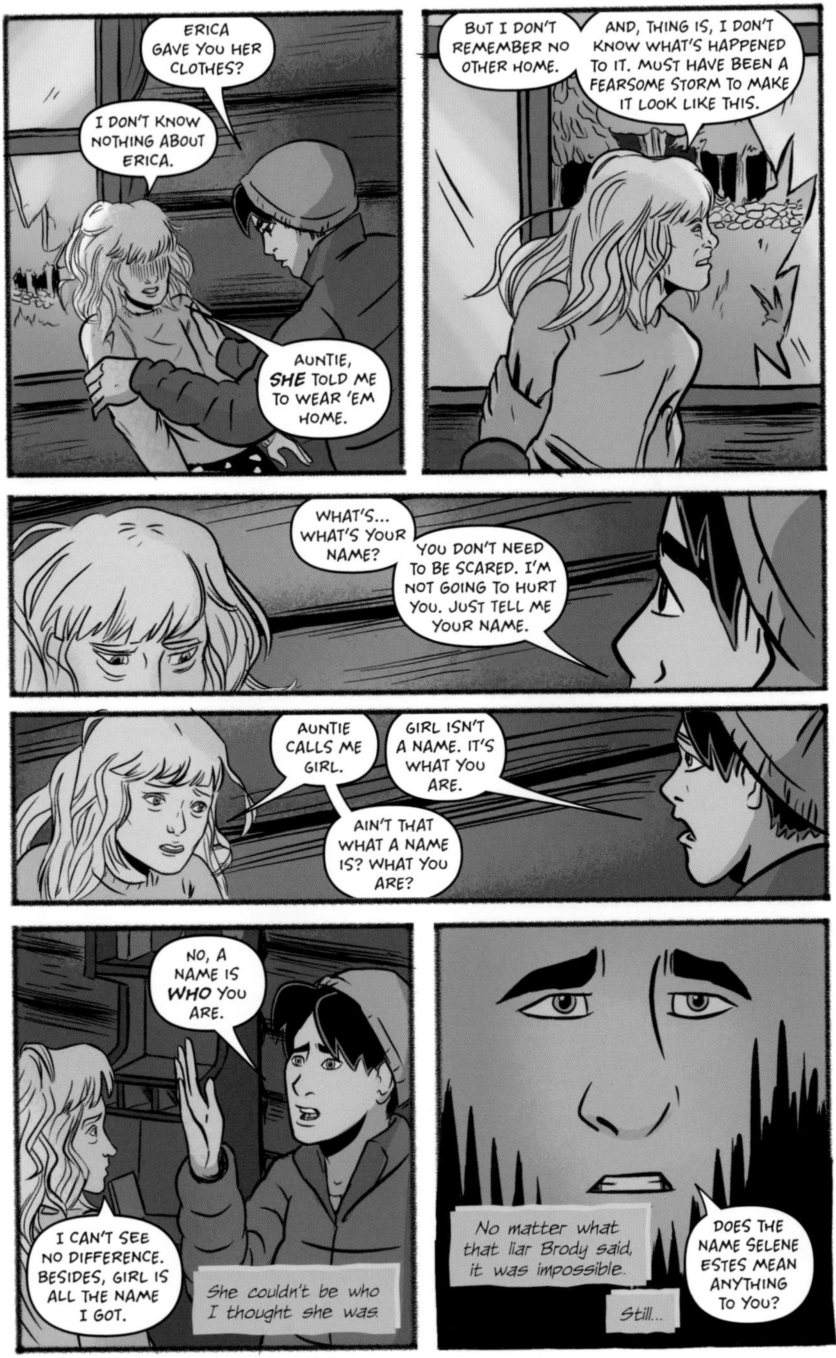
ERICA GAVE YOU HER CLOTHES?
I DON'T KNOW NOTHING ABOUT ERICA.
AUNTIE, SHE TOLD ME TO WEAR 'EM HOME.
BUT I DON'T REMEMBER NO OTHER HOME.
AND, THING IS, I DON'T KNOW WHAT'S HAPPENED TO IT. MUST HAVE BEEN A FEARSOME STORM TO MAKE IT LOOK LIKE THIS.
WHAT'S... WHAT'S YOUR NAME?
YOU DON'T NEED TO BE SCARED. I'M NOT GOING TO HURT YOU. JUST TELL ME YOUR NAME.
AUNTIE CALLS ME GIRL.
GIRL ISN'T A NAME. IT'S WHAT YOU ARE.
AIN'T THAT WHAT A NAME IS? WHAT YOU ARE?
NO, A NAME IS WHO YOU ARE.
I CAN'T SEE NO DIFFERENCE. BESIDES, GIRL IS ALL THE NAME I GOT.
She couldn't be who I thought she was.
No matter what that liar Brody said, it was impossible.
Still...
DOES THE NAME SELENE ESTES MEAN ANYTHING TO YOU?

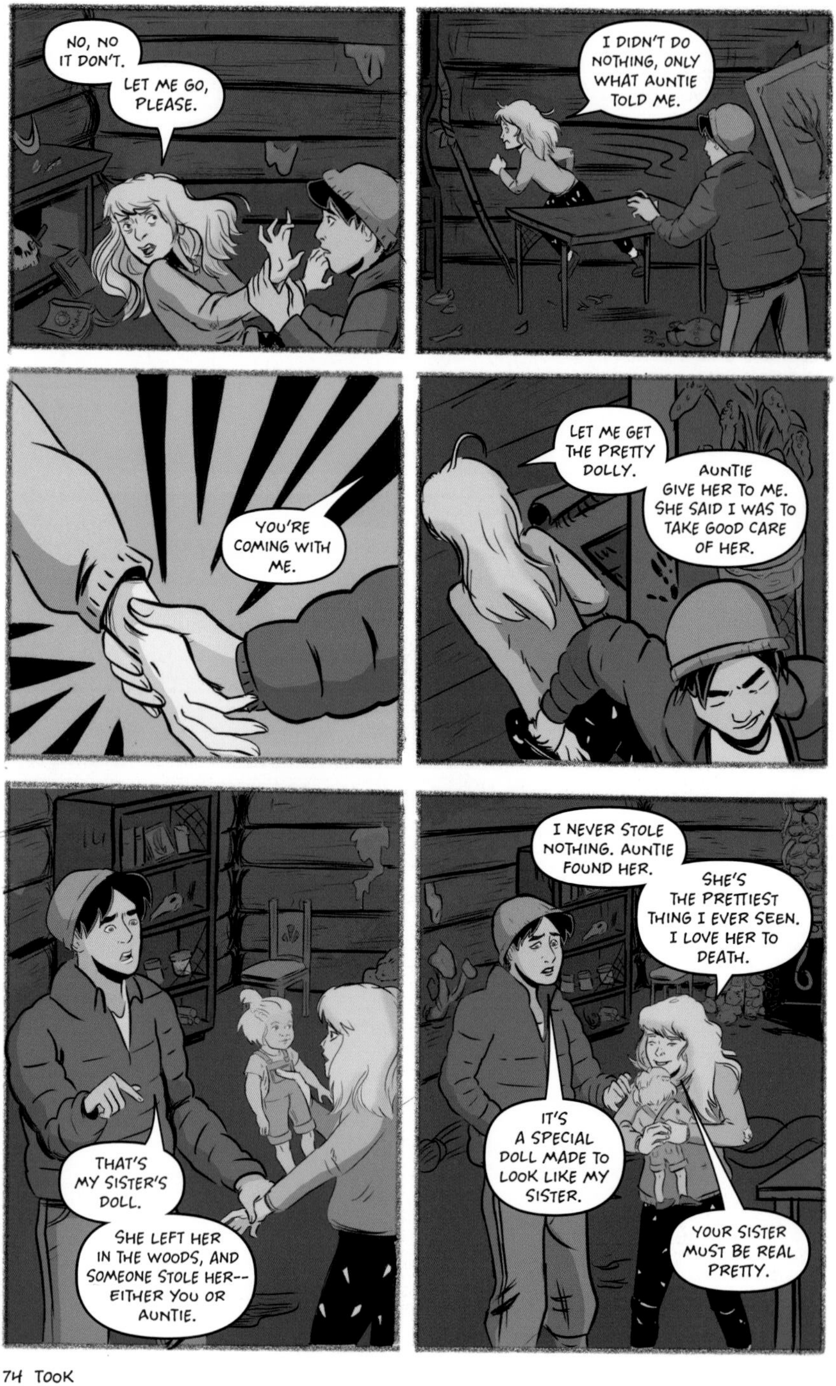
NO, NO IT DON'T.
LET ME GO, PLEASE.
I DIDN'T DO NOTHING, ONLY WHAT AUNTIE TOLD ME.
YOU'RE COMING WITH ME.
LET ME GET THE PRETTY DOLLY.
AUNTIE GIVE HER TO ME. SHE SAID I WAS TO TAKE GOOD CARE OF HER.
THAT'S MY SISTER'S DOLL.
SHE LEFT HER IN THE WOODS, AND SOMEONE STOLE HER-- EITHER YOU OR AUNTIE.
I NEVER STOLE NOTHING. AUNTIE FOUND HER.
SHE'S THE PRETTIEST THING I EVER SEEN. I LOVE HER TO DEATH.
IT'S A SPECIAL DOLL MADE TO LOOK LIKE MY SISTER.
YOUR SISTER MUST BE REAL PRETTY.

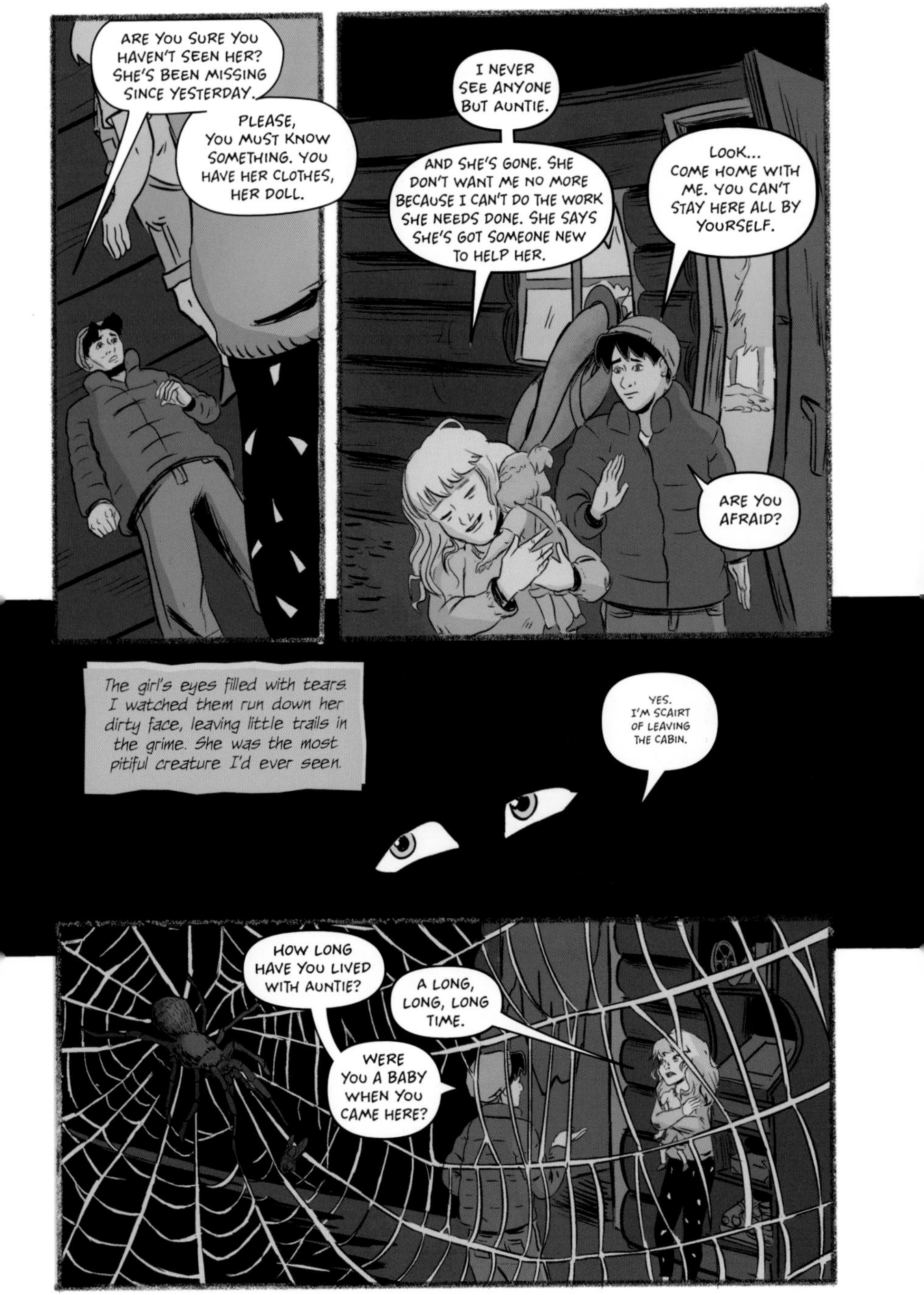
ARE YOU SURE YOU HAVEN'T SEEN HER? SHE'S BEEN MISSING SINCE YESTERDAY.
PLEASE, YOU MUST KNOW SOMETHING. YOU HAVE HER CLOTHES, HER DOLL.
I NEVER SEE ANYONE BUT AUNTIE.
AND SHE'S GONE. SHE DON'T WANT ME NO MORE BECAUSE I CAN'T DO THE WORK SHE NEEDS DONE. SHE SAYS SHE'S GOT SOMEONE NEW TO HELP HER.
LOOK... COME HOME WITH ME. YOU CAN'T STAY HERE ALL BY YOURSELF.
ARE YOU AFRAID?
The girl's eyes filled with tears. I watched them run down her dirty face, leaving little trails in the grime. She was the most pitiful creature I'd ever seen.
YES. I'M SCAIRT OF LEAVING THE CABIN.
HOW LONG HAVE YOU LIVED WITH AUNTIE?
A LONG, LONG, LONG TIME.
WERE YOU A BABY WHEN YOU CAME HERE?

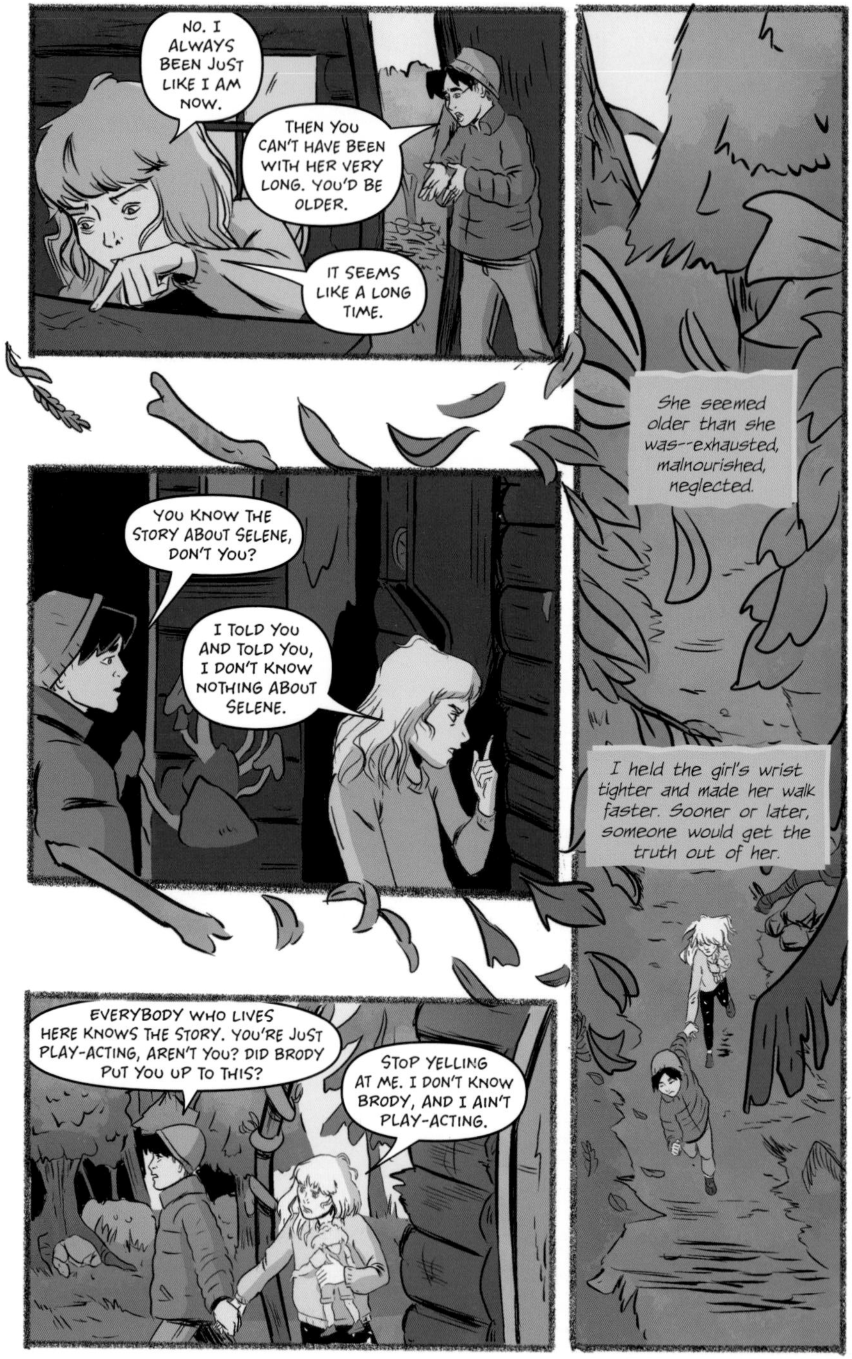
NO. I ALWAYS BEEN JUST LIKE I AM NOW.
THEN YOU CAN'T HAVE BEEN WITH HER VERY LONG. YOU'D BE OLDER.
IT SEEMS LIKE A LONG TIME.
She seemed older than she was--exhausted, malnourished, neglected.
YOU KNOW THE STORY ABOUT SELENE, DON'T YOU?
I TOLD YOU AND TOLD YOU, I DON'T KNOW NOTHING ABOUT SELENE.
I held the girl's wrist tighter and made her walk faster. Sooner or later, someone would get the truth out of her.
EVERYBODY WHO LIVES HERE KNOWS THE STORY. YOU'RE JUST PLAY-ACTING, AREN'T YOU? DID BRODY PUT YOU UP TO THIS?
STOP YELLING AT ME. I DON'T KNOW BRODY, AND I AIN'T PLAY-ACTING.

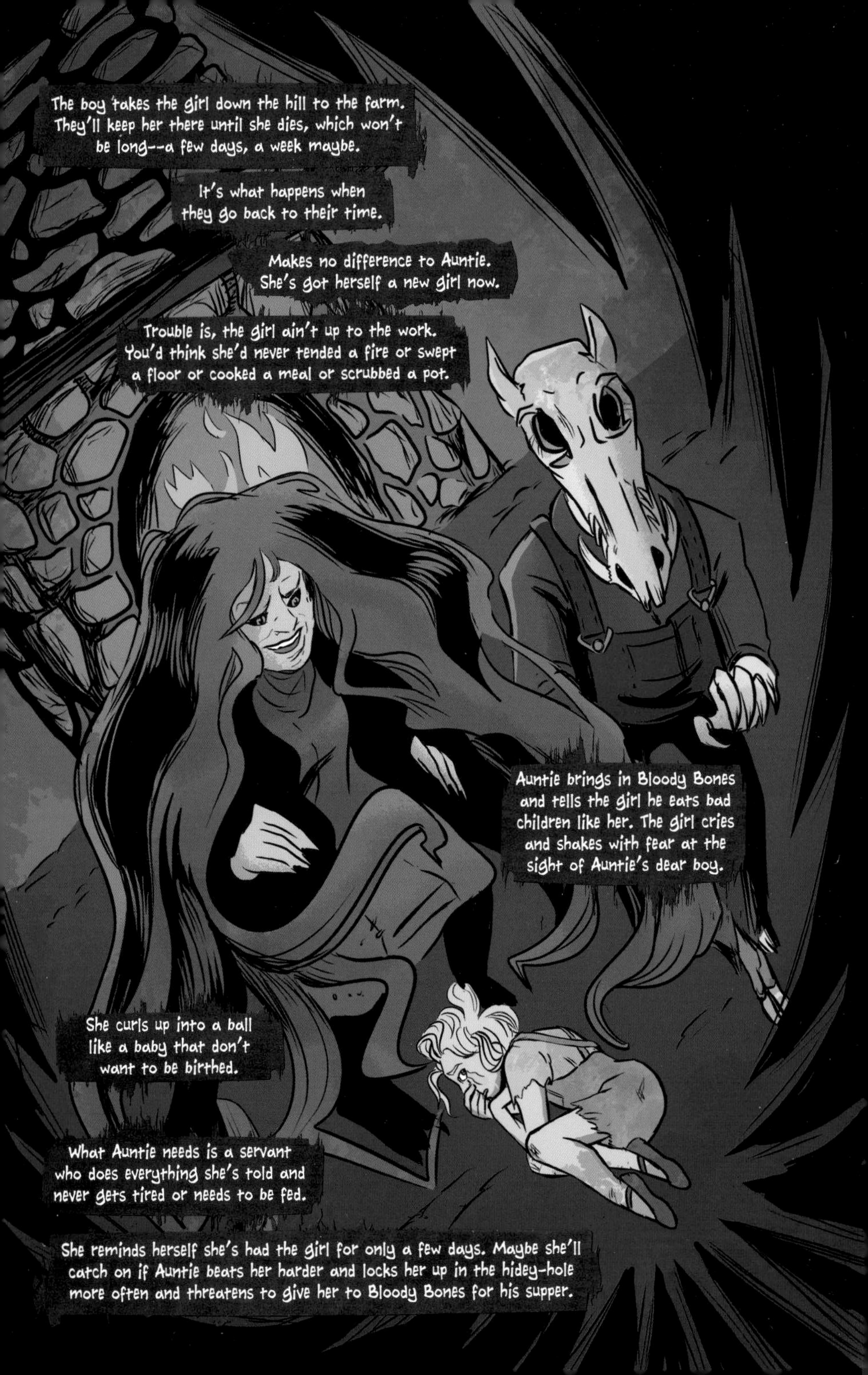

The boy takes the girl down the hill to the farm. They'll keep her there until she dies, which won't be long--a few days, a week maybe.
It's what happens when they go back to their time.
Makes no difference to Auntie. She's got herself a new girl now.
Trouble is, the girl ain't up to the work. You'd think she'd never tended a fire or swept a floor or cooked a meal or scrubbed a pot.
Auntie brings in Bloody Bones and tells the girl he eats bad children like her. The girl cries and shakes with fear at the sight of Auntie's dear boy.
She curls up into a ball like a baby that don't want to be birthed.
What Auntie needs is a servant who does everything she's told and never gets tired or needs to be fed.
She reminds herself she's had the girl for only a few days. Maybe she'll catch on if Auntie beats her harder and locks her up in the hidey-hole more often and threatens to give her to Bloody Bones for his supper.

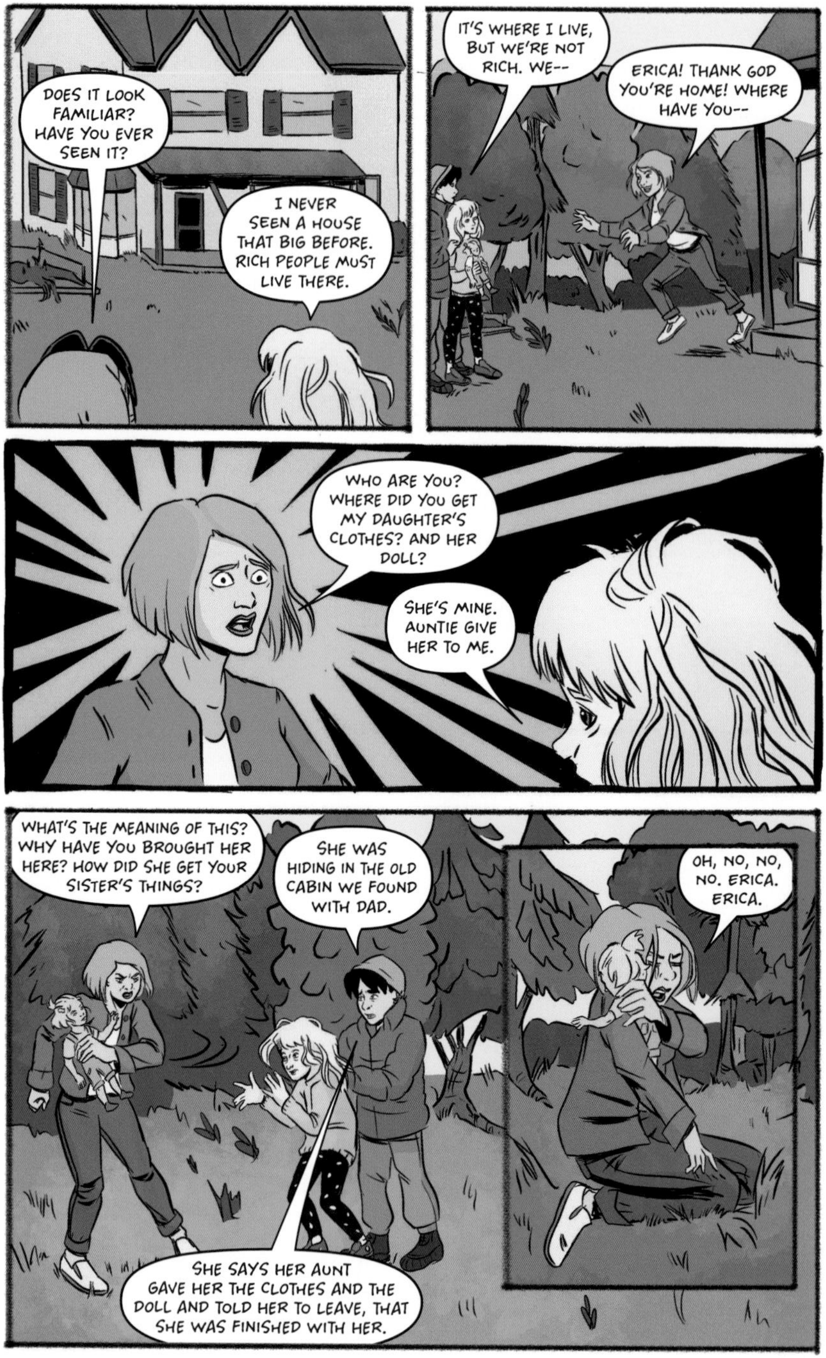
DOES IT LOOK FAMILIAR? HAVE YOU EVER SEEN IT?
I NEVER SEEN A HOUSE THAT BIG BEFORE. RICH PEOPLE MUST LIVE THERE.
IT'S WHERE I LIVE, BUT WE'RE NOT RICH. WE--
ERICA! THANK GOD YOU'RE HOME! WHERE HAVE YOU--
WHO ARE YOU? WHERE DID YOU GET MY DAUGHTER'S CLOTHES? AND HER DOLL?
SHE'S MINE. AUNTIE GIVE HER TO ME.
WHAT'S THE MEANING OF THIS? WHY HAVE YOU BROUGHT HER HERE? HOW DID SHE GET YOUR SISTER'S THINGS?
SHE WAS HIDING IN THE OLD CABIN WE FOUND WITH DAD.
SHE SAYS HER AUNT GAVE HER THE CLOTHES AND THE DOLL AND TOLD HER TO LEAVE, THAT SHE WAS FINISHED WITH HER.
OH, NO, NO, NO. ERICA. ERICA.

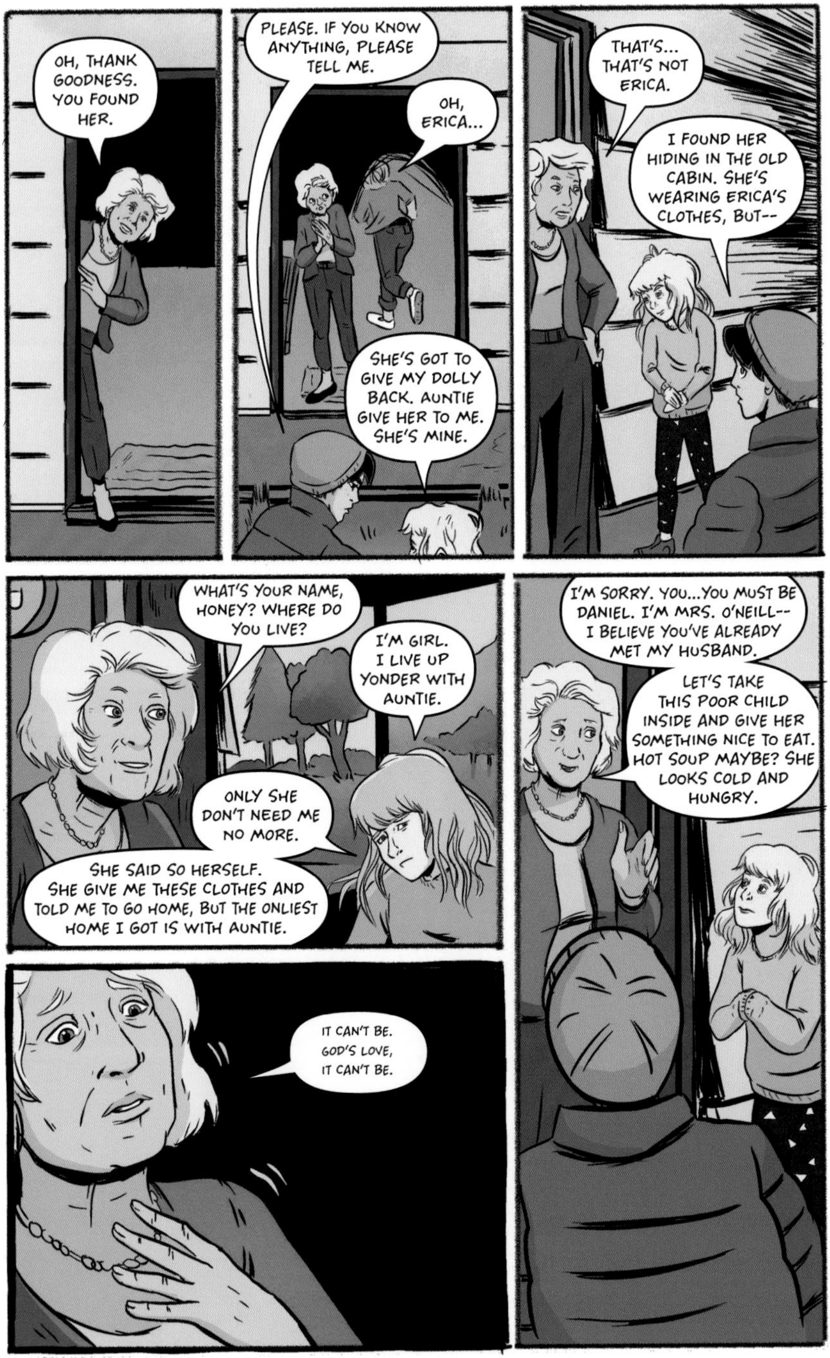
OH, THANK GOODNESS. YOU FOUND HER.
PLEASE. IF YOU KNOW ANYTHING, PLEASE TELL ME.
OH, ERICA...
SHE'S GOT TO GIVE MY DOLLY BACK. AUNTIE GIVE HER TO ME. SHE'S MINE.
THAT'S... THAT'S NOT ERICA.
I FOUND HER HIDING IN THE OLD CABIN. SHE'S WEARING ERICA'S CLOTHES, BUT--
WHAT'S YOUR NAME, HONEY? WHERE DO YOU LIVE?
I'M GIRL. I LIVE UP YONDER WITH AUNTIE.
ONLY SHE DON'T NEED ME NO MORE.
SHE SAID SO HERSELF. SHE GIVE ME THESE CLOTHES AND TOLD ME TO GO HOME, BUT THE ONLIEST HOME I GOT IS WITH AUNTIE.
IT CAN'T BE. GOD'S LOVE, IT CAN'T BE.
I'M SORRY. YOU...YOU MUST BE DANIEL. I'M MRS. O'NEILL-- I BELIEVE YOU'VE ALREADY MET MY HUSBAND.
LET'S TAKE THIS POOR CHILD INSIDE AND GIVE HER SOMETHING NICE TO EAT. HOT SOUP MAYBE? SHE LOOKS COLD AND HUNGRY.

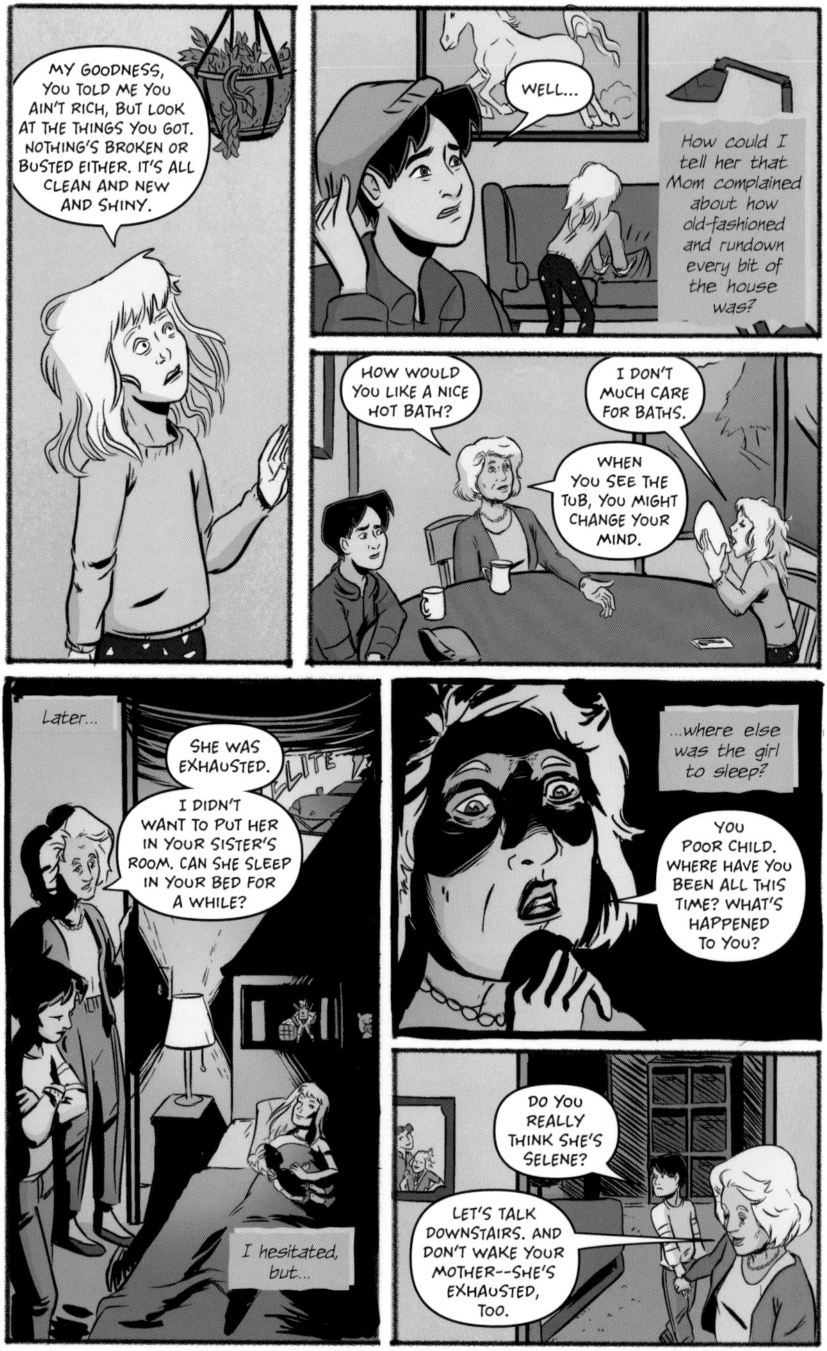
MY GOODNESS, YOU TOLD ME YOU AIN'T RICH, BUT LOOK AT THE THINGS YOU GOT. NOTHING'S BROKEN OR BUSTED EITHER. IT'S ALL CLEAN AND NEW AND SHINY.
WELL...
How could I tell her that Mom complained about how old-fashioned and rundown every bit of the house was?
HOW WOULD YOU LIKE A NICE HOT BATH?
I DON'T MUCH CARE FOR BATHS.
WHEN YOU SEE THE TUB, YOU MIGHT CHANGE YOUR MIND.
Later...
SHE WAS EXHAUSTED.
I DIDN'T WANT TO PUT HER IN YOUR SISTER'S ROOM. CAN SHE SLEEP IN YOUR BED FOR A WHILE?
I hesitated, but...
...where else was the girl to sleep?
YOU POOR CHILD. WHERE HAVE YOU BEEN ALL THIS TIME? WHAT'S HAPPENED TO YOU?
DO YOU REALLY THINK SHE'S SELENE?
LET'S TALK DOWNSTAIRS. AND DON'T WAKE YOUR MOTHER--SHE'S EXHAUSTED, TOO.

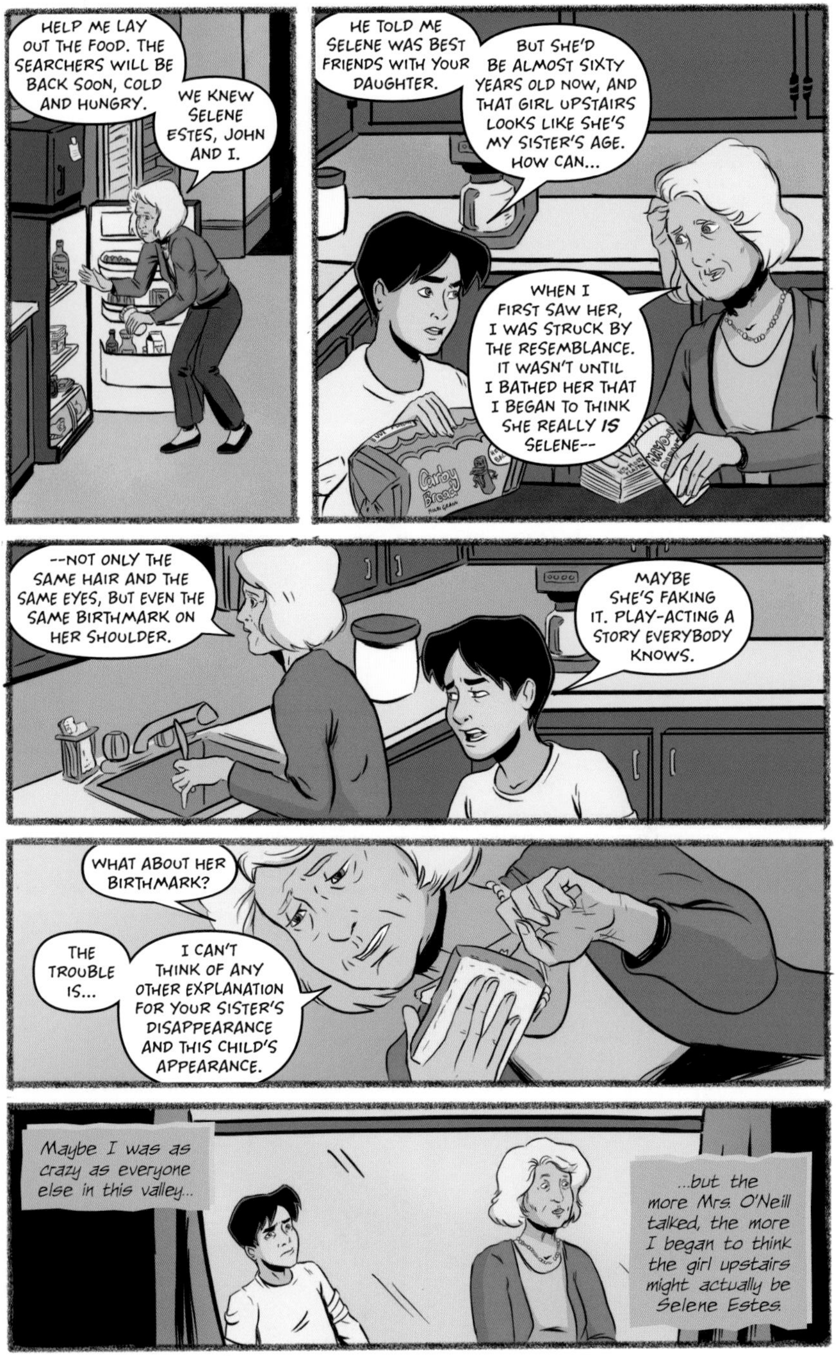
HELP ME LAY OUT THE FOOD. THE SEARCHERS WILL BE BACK SOON, COLD AND HUNGRY.
WE KNEW SELENE ESTES, JOHN AND I.
HE TOLD ME SELENE WAS BEST FRIENDS WITH YOUR DAUGHTER.
BUT SHE'D BE ALMOST SIXTY YEARS OLD NOW, AND THAT GIRL UPSTAIRS LOOKS LIKE SHE'S MY SISTER'S AGE. HOW CAN...
WHEN I FIRST SAW HER, I WAS STRUCK BY THE RESEMBLANCE. IT WASN'T UNTIL I BATHED HER THAT I BEGAN TO THINK SHE REALLY **IS** SELENE--
--NOT ONLY THE SAME HAIR AND THE SAME EYES, BUT EVEN THE SAME BIRTHMARK ON HER SHOULDER.
MAYBE SHE'S FAKING IT. PLAY-ACTING A STORY EVERYBODY KNOWS.
WHAT ABOUT HER BIRTHMARK?
THE TROUBLE IS...
I CAN'T THINK OF ANY OTHER EXPLANATION FOR YOUR SISTER'S DISAPPEARANCE AND THIS CHILD'S APPEARANCE.
Maybe I was as crazy as everyone else in this valley...
...but the more Mrs. O'Neill talked, the more I began to think the girl upstairs might actually be Selene Estes.

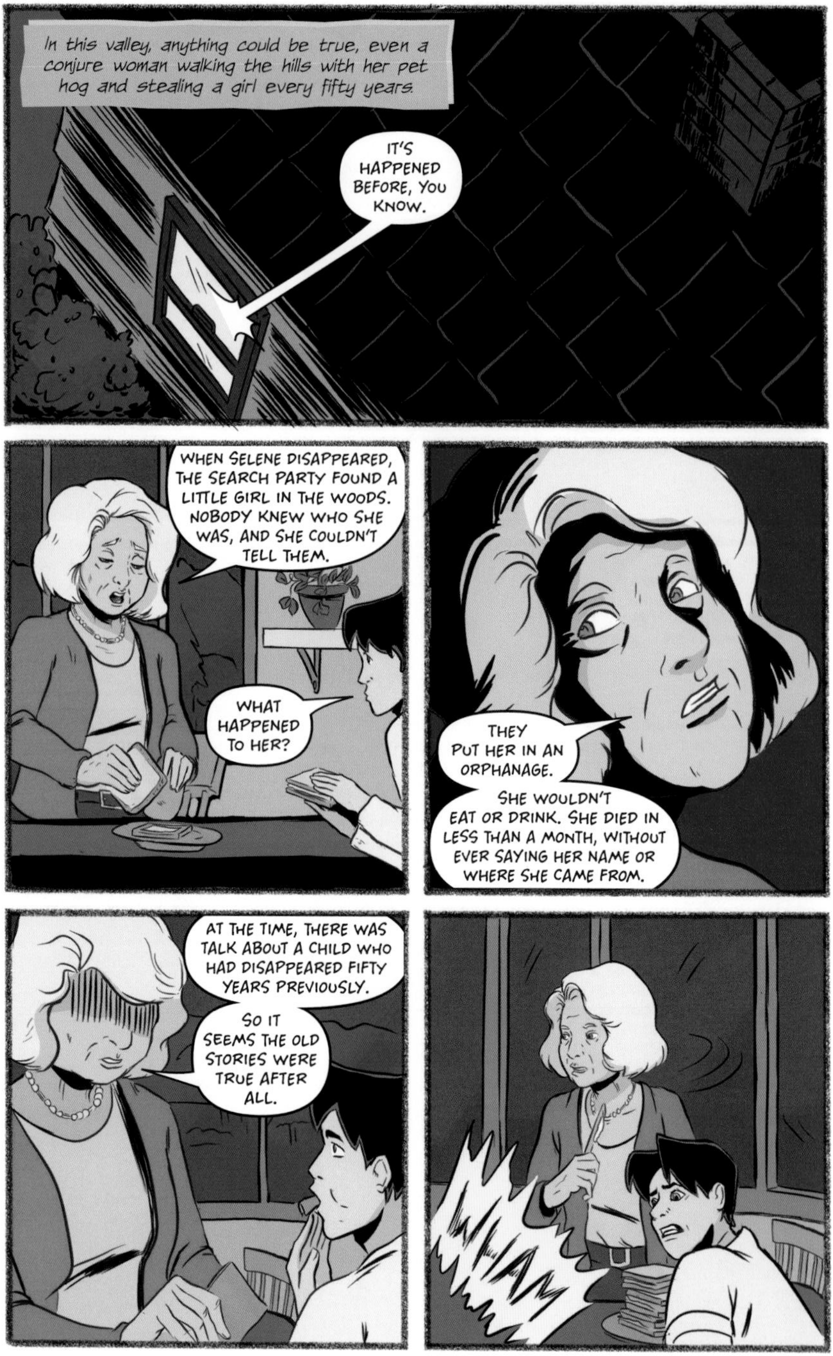
In this valley, anything could be true, even a conjure woman walking the hills with her pet hog and stealing a girl every fifty years.
IT'S HAPPENED BEFORE, YOU KNOW.
WHEN SELENE DISAPPEARED, THE SEARCH PARTY FOUND A LITTLE GIRL IN THE WOODS. NOBODY KNEW WHO SHE WAS, AND SHE COULDN'T TELL THEM.
WHAT HAPPENED TO HER?
THEY PUT HER IN AN ORPHANAGE.
SHE WOULDN'T EAT OR DRINK. SHE DIED IN LESS THAN A MONTH, WITHOUT EVER SAYING HER NAME OR WHERE SHE CAME FROM.
AT THE TIME, THERE WAS TALK ABOUT A CHILD WHO HAD DISAPPEARED FIFTY YEARS PREVIOUSLY.
SO IT SEEMS THE OLD STORIES WERE TRUE AFTER ALL.

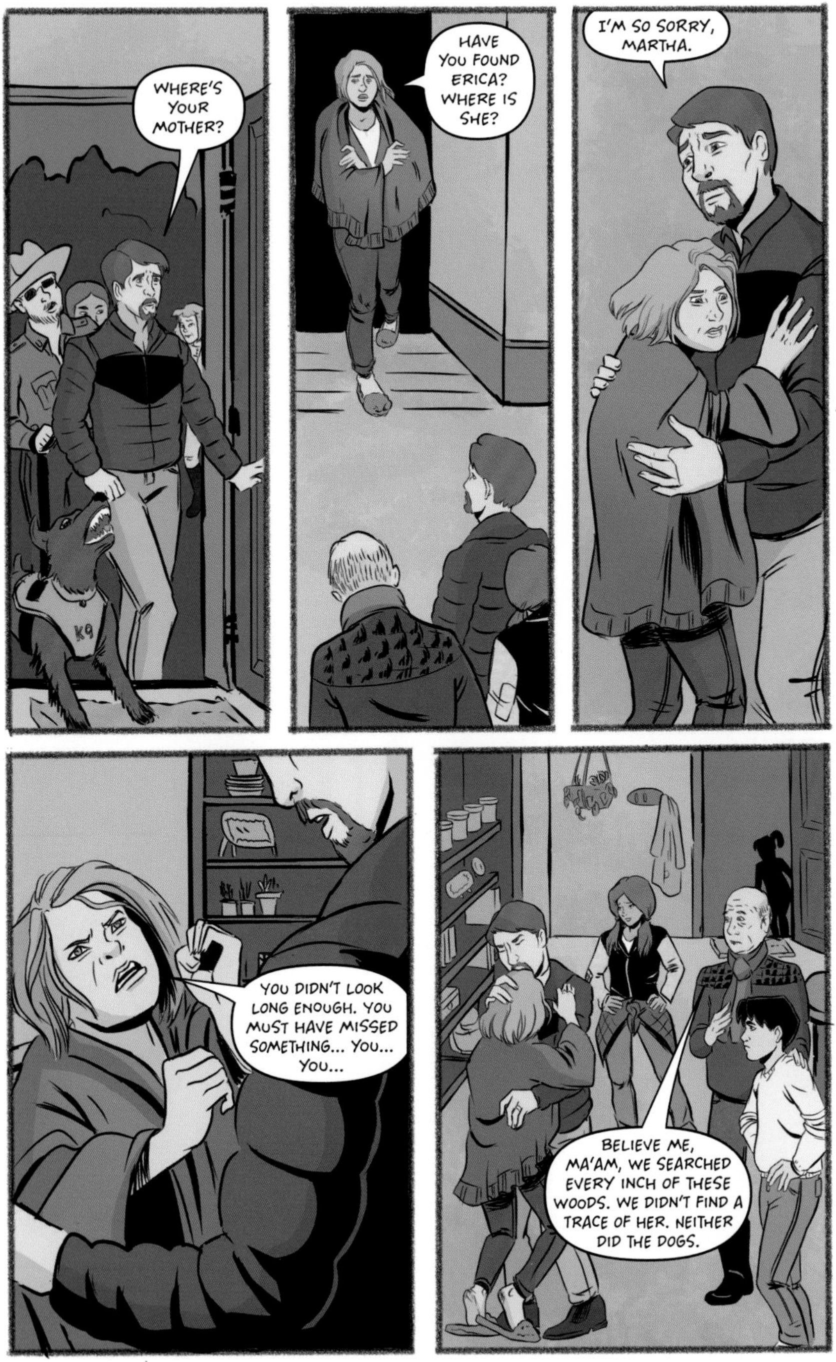
WHERE'S YOUR MOTHER?
HAVE YOU FOUND ERICA? WHERE IS SHE?
I'M SO SORRY, MARTHA.
YOU DIDN'T LOOK LONG ENOUGH. YOU MUST HAVE MISSED SOMETHING... YOU... YOU...
BELIEVE ME, MA'AM, WE SEARCHED EVERY INCH OF THESE WOODS. WE DIDN'T FIND A TRACE OF HER. NEITHER DID THE DOGS.

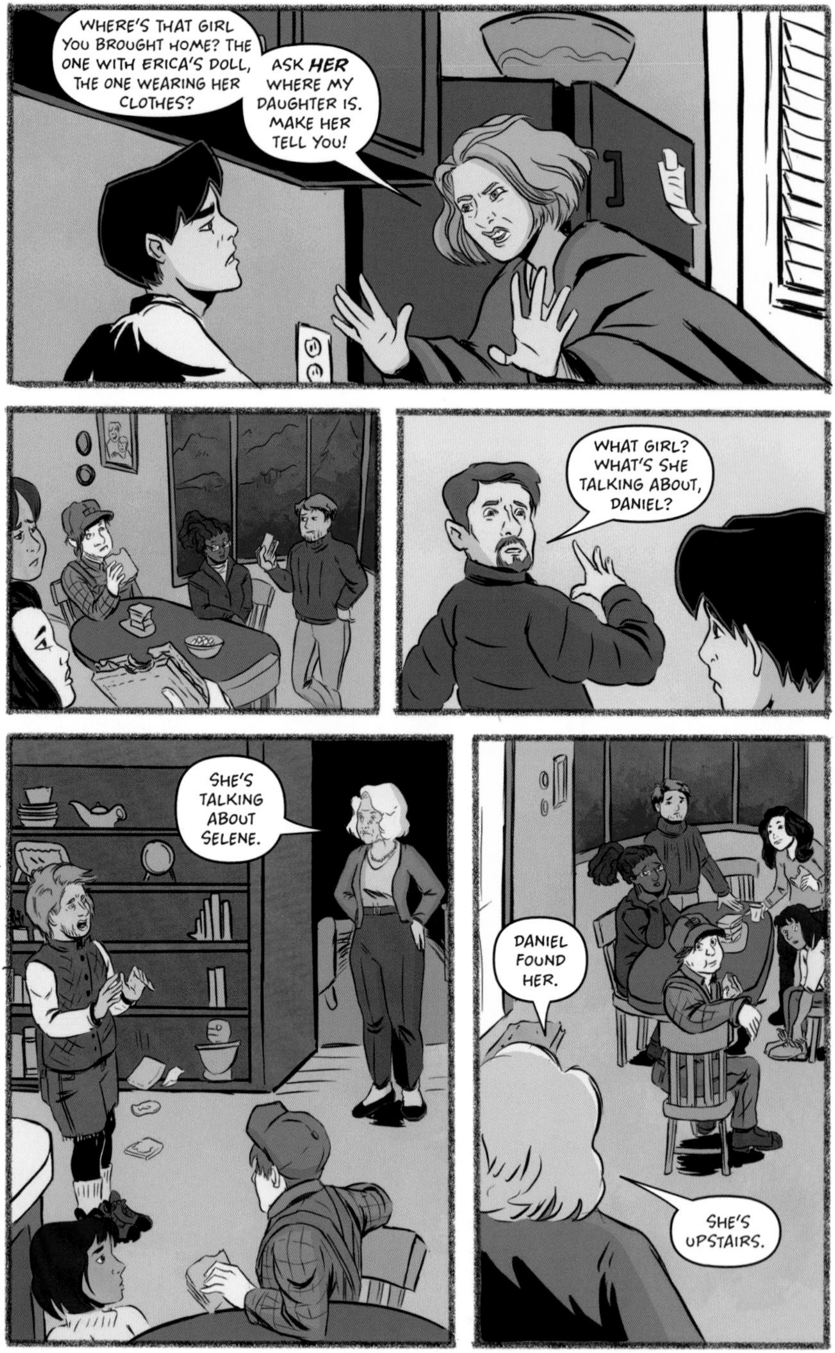
WHERE'S THAT GIRL YOU BROUGHT HOME? THE ONE WITH ERICA'S DOLL, THE ONE WEARING HER CLOTHES?
ASK **HER** WHERE MY DAUGHTER IS. MAKE HER TELL YOU!
WHAT GIRL? WHAT'S SHE TALKING ABOUT, DANIEL?
SHE'S TALKING ABOUT SELENE.
DANIEL FOUND HER.
SHE'S UPSTAIRS.

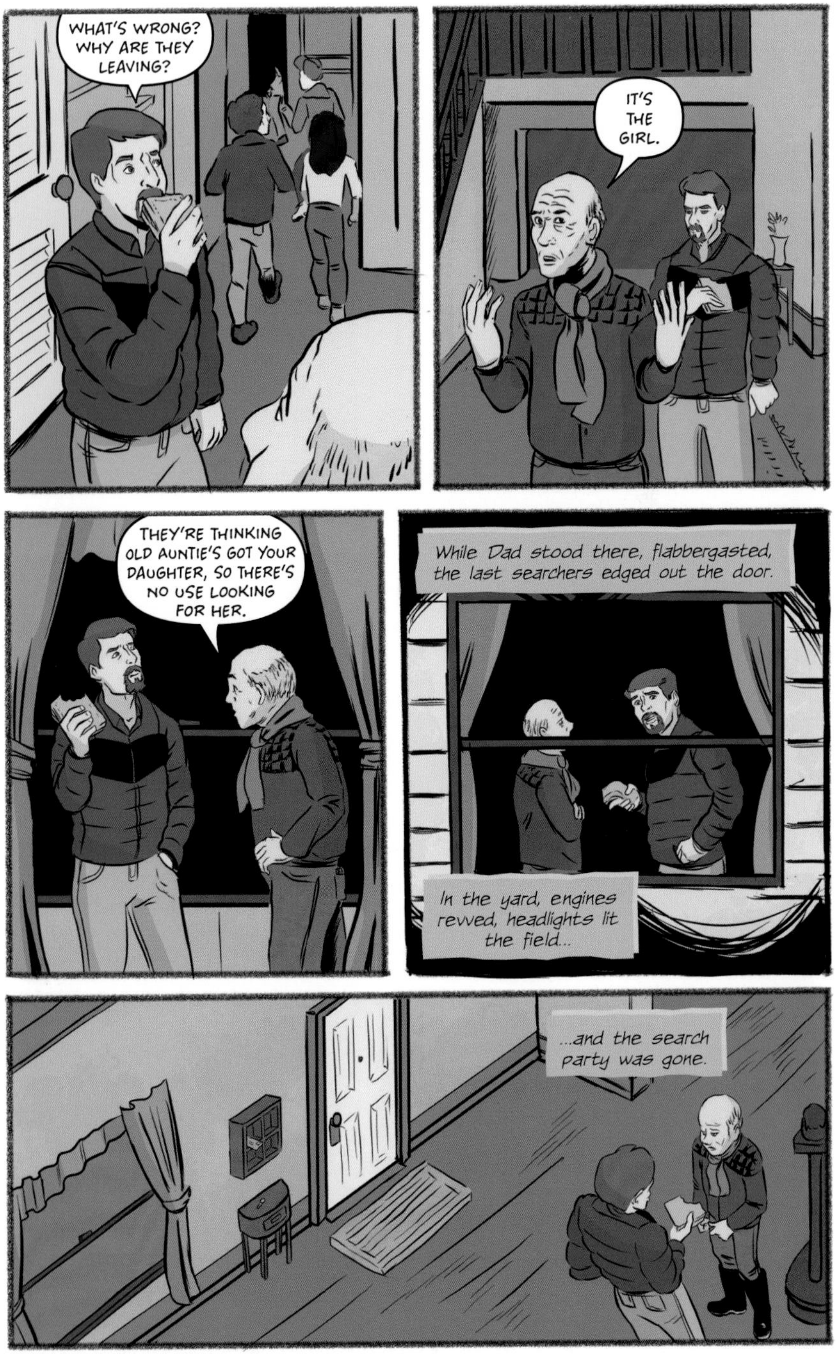
WHAT'S WRONG? WHY ARE THEY LEAVING?
IT'S THE GIRL.
THEY'RE THINKING OLD AUNTIE'S GOT YOUR DAUGHTER, SO THERE'S NO USE LOOKING FOR HER.
While Dad stood there, flabbergasted, the last searchers edged out the door.
In the yard, engines revved, headlights lit the field...
...and the search party was gone.

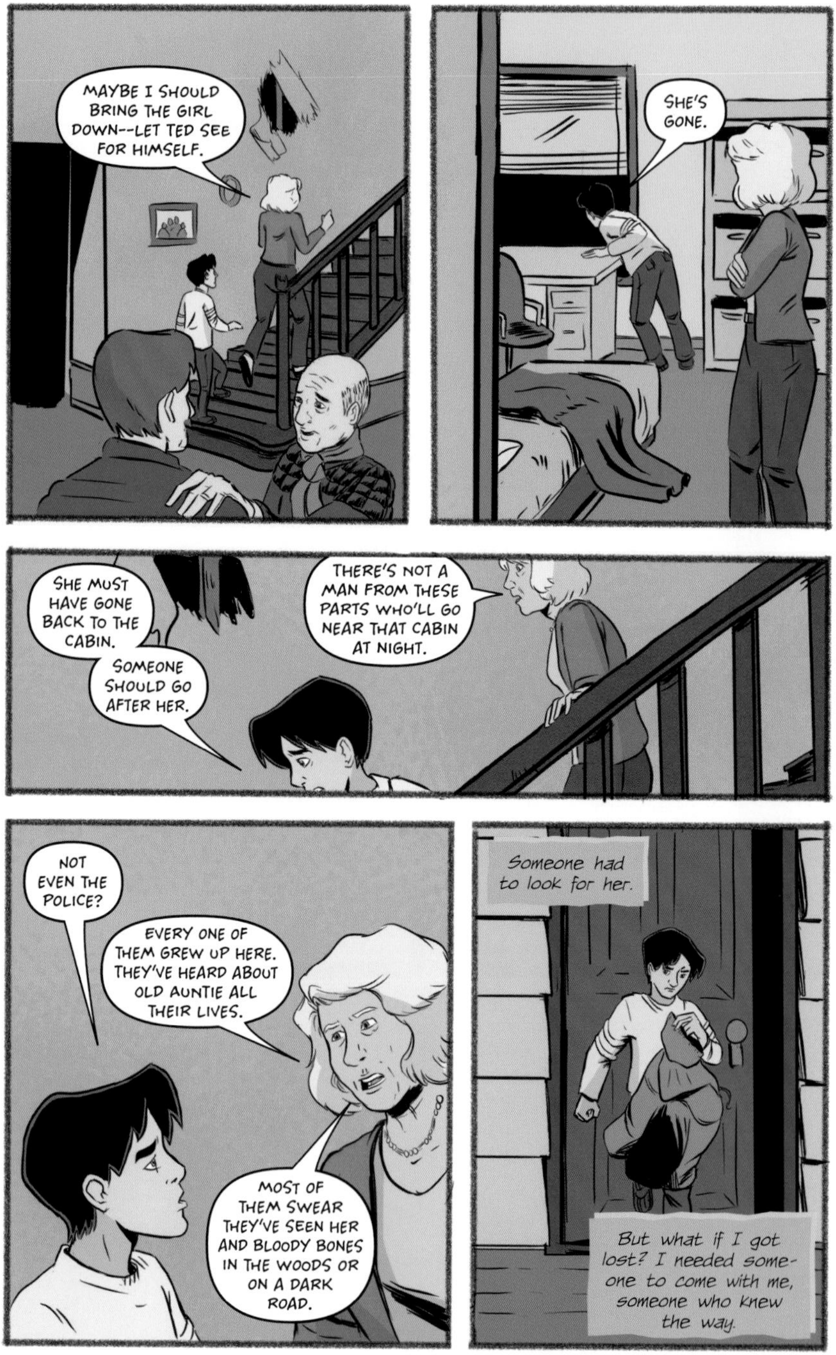
MAYBE I SHOULD BRING THE GIRL DOWN--LET TED SEE FOR HIMSELF.
SHE'S GONE.
SHE MUST HAVE GONE BACK TO THE CABIN.
SOMEONE SHOULD GO AFTER HER.
THERE'S NOT A MAN FROM THESE PARTS WHO'LL GO NEAR THAT CABIN AT NIGHT.
NOT EVEN THE POLICE?
EVERY ONE OF THEM GREW UP HERE. THEY'VE HEARD ABOUT OLD AUNTIE ALL THEIR LIVES.
MOST OF THEM SWEAR THEY'VE SEEN HER AND BLOODY BONES IN THE WOODS OR ON A DARK ROAD.
Someone had to look for her.
But what if I got lost? I needed some-one to come with me, someone who knew the way.

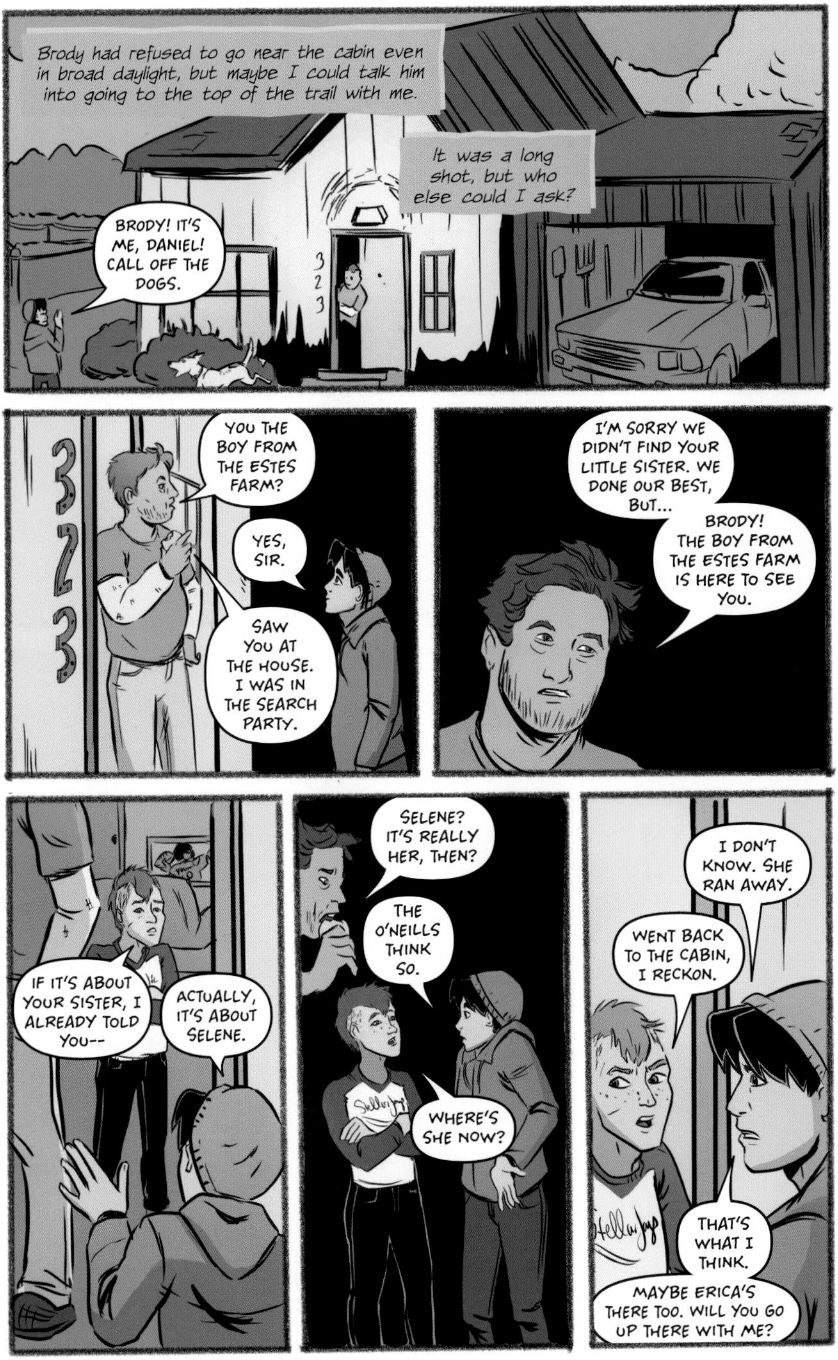

Brody had refused to go near the cabin even in broad daylight, but maybe I could talk him into going to the top of the trail with me.
It was a long shot, but who else could I ask?
BRODY! IT'S ME, DANIEL! CALL OFF THE DOGS.
323
YOU THE BOY FROM THE ESTES FARM?
YES, SIR.
SAW YOU AT THE HOUSE. I WAS IN THE SEARCH PARTY.
I'M SORRY WE DIDN'T FIND YOUR LITTLE SISTER. WE DONE OUR BEST, BUT...
BRODY! THE BOY FROM THE ESTES FARM IS HERE TO SEE YOU.
IF IT'S ABOUT YOUR SISTER, I ALREADY TOLD YOU--
ACTUALLY, IT'S ABOUT SELENE.
SELENE? IT'S REALLY HER, THEN?
THE O'NEILLS THINK SO.
WHERE'S SHE NOW?
I DON'T KNOW. SHE RAN AWAY.
WENT BACK TO THE CABIN, I RECKON.
THAT'S WHAT I THINK.
MAYBE ERICA'S THERE TOO. WILL YOU GO UP THERE WITH ME?

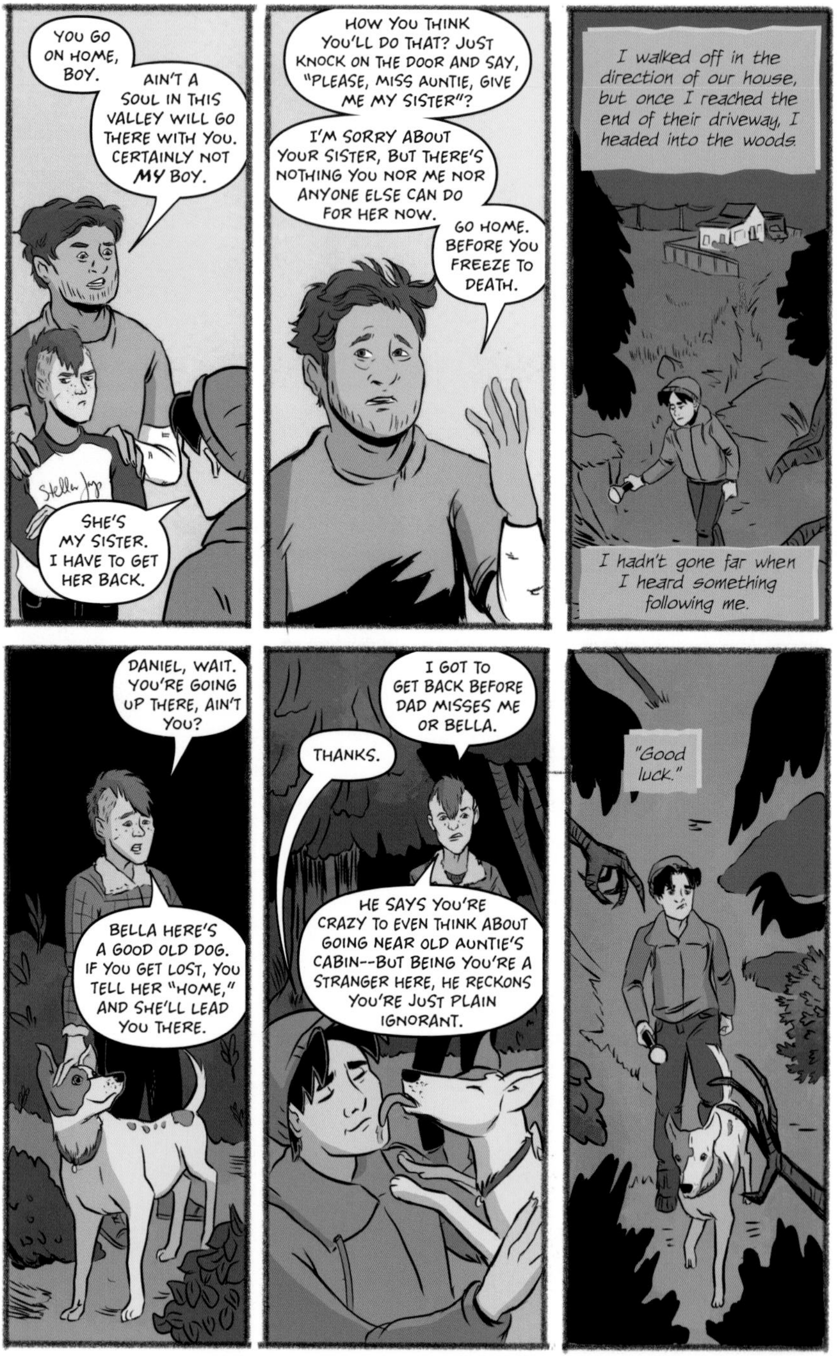
YOU GO ON HOME, BOY.
AIN'T A SOUL IN THIS VALLEY WILL GO THERE WITH YOU. CERTAINLY NOT MY BOY.
SHE'S MY SISTER. I HAVE TO GET HER BACK.
HOW YOU THINK YOU'LL DO THAT? JUST KNOCK ON THE DOOR AND SAY, "PLEASE, MISS AUNTIE, GIVE ME MY SISTER"?
I'M SORRY ABOUT YOUR SISTER, BUT THERE'S NOTHING YOU NOR ME NOR ANYONE ELSE CAN DO FOR HER NOW.
GO HOME. BEFORE YOU FREEZE TO DEATH.
I walked off in the direction of our house, but once I reached the end of their driveway, I headed into the woods.
I hadn't gone far when I heard something following me.
DANIEL, WAIT. YOU'RE GOING UP THERE, AIN'T YOU?
BELLA HERE'S A GOOD OLD DOG. IF YOU GET LOST, YOU TELL HER "HOME," AND SHE'LL LEAD YOU THERE.
I GOT TO GET BACK BEFORE DAD MISSES ME OR BELLA.
THANKS.
HE SAYS YOU'RE CRAZY TO EVEN THINK ABOUT GOING NEAR OLD AUNTIE'S CABIN--BUT BEING YOU'RE A STRANGER HERE, HE RECKONS YOU'RE JUST PLAIN IGNORANT.
"Good luck."

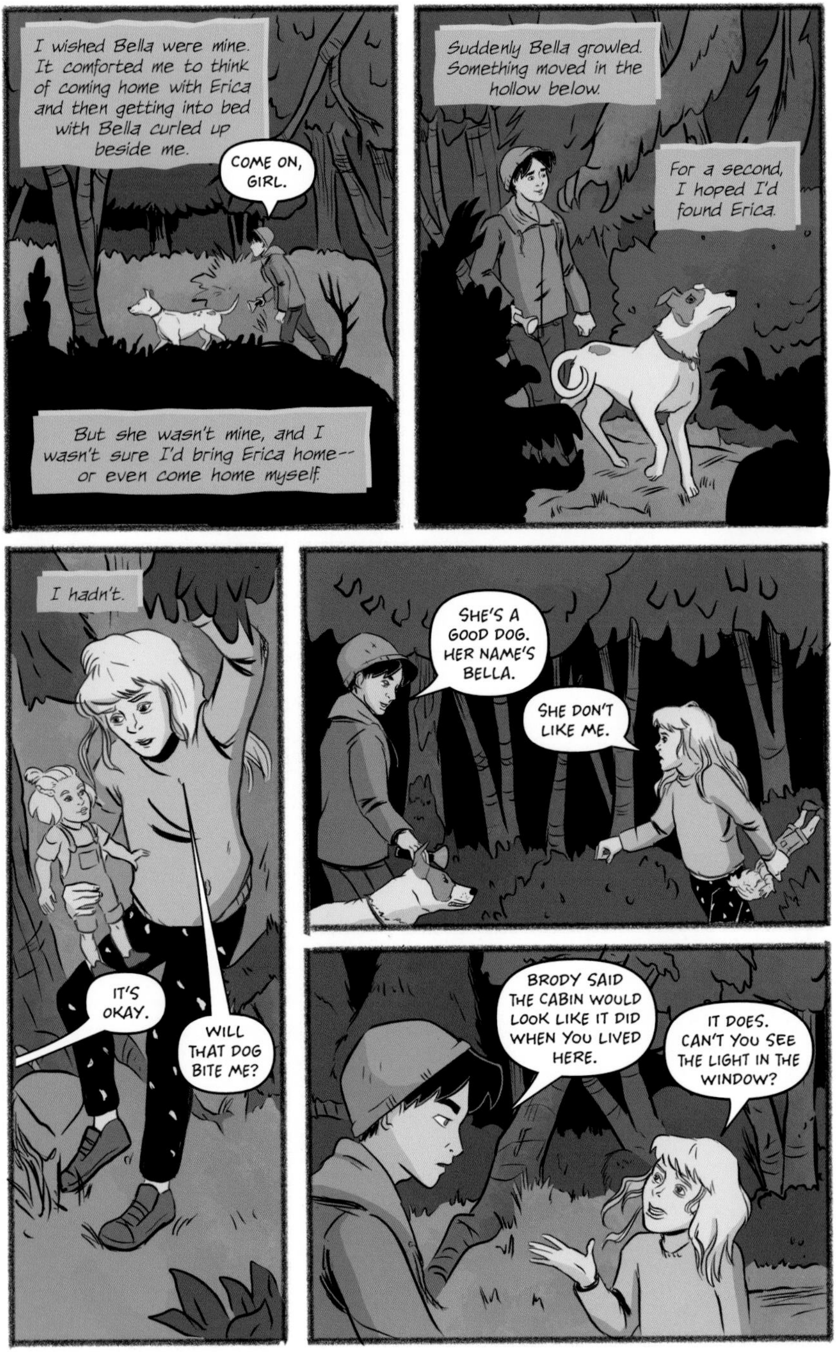
I wished Bella were mine. It comforted me to think of coming home with Erica and then getting into bed with Bella curled up beside me.
COME ON, GIRL.
But she wasn't mine, and I wasn't sure I'd bring Erica home--or even come home myself.
Suddenly Bella growled. Something moved in the hollow below.
For a second, I hoped I'd found Erica.
I hadn't.
WILL THAT DOG BITE ME?
IT'S OKAY.
SHE'S A GOOD DOG. HER NAME'S BELLA.
SHE DON'T LIKE ME.
BRODY SAID THE CABIN WOULD LOOK LIKE IT DID WHEN YOU LIVED HERE.
IT DOES. CAN'T YOU SEE THE LIGHT IN THE WINDOW?

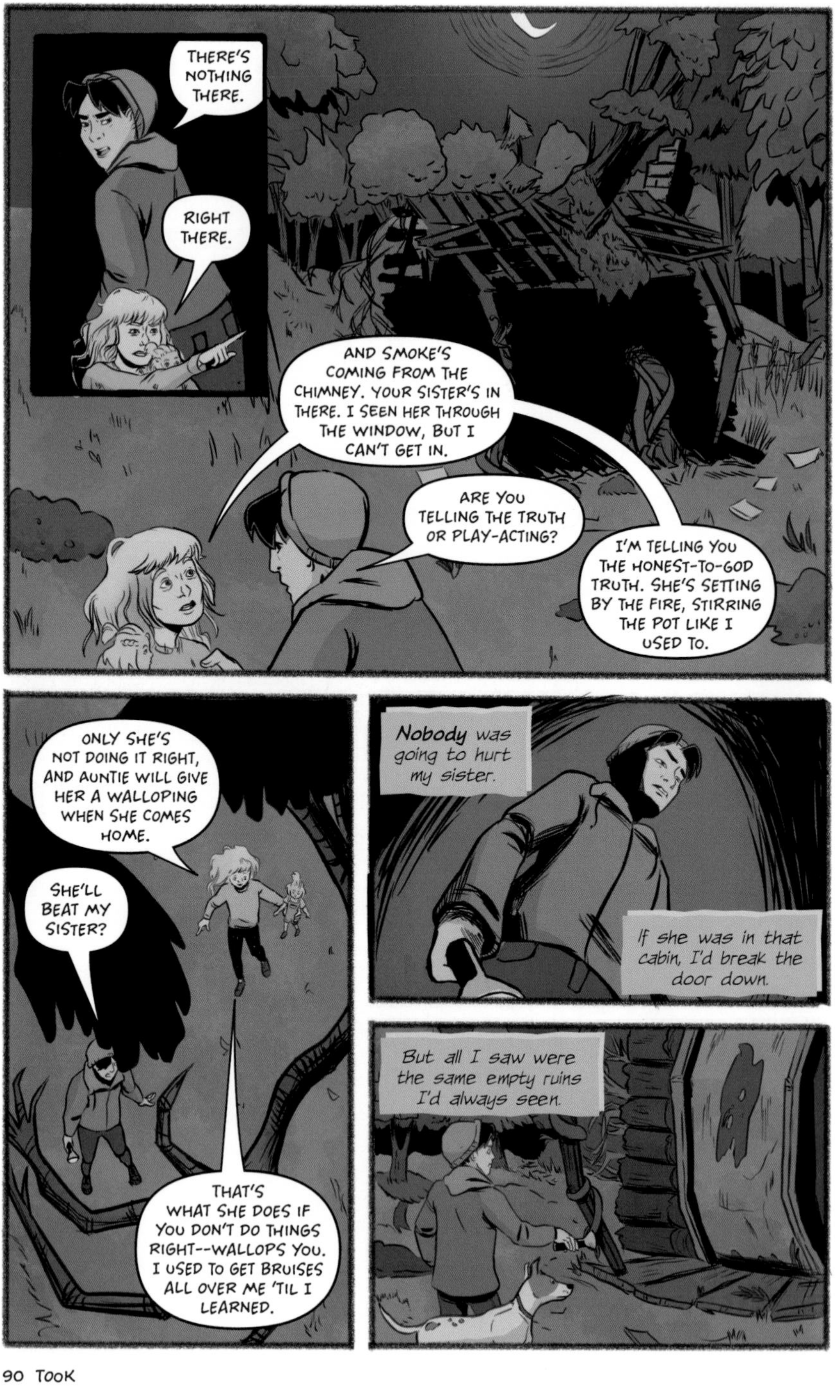

THERE'S NOTHING THERE.
RIGHT THERE.
AND SMOKE'S COMING FROM THE CHIMNEY. YOUR SISTER'S IN THERE. I SEEN HER THROUGH THE WINDOW, BUT I CAN'T GET IN.
ARE YOU TELLING THE TRUTH OR PLAY-ACTING?
I'M TELLING YOU THE HONEST-TO-GOD TRUTH. SHE'S SETTING BY THE FIRE, STIRRING THE POT LIKE I USED TO.
ONLY SHE'S NOT DOING IT RIGHT, AND AUNTIE WILL GIVE HER A WALLOPING WHEN SHE COMES HOME.
SHE'LL BEAT MY SISTER?
THAT'S WHAT SHE DOES IF YOU DON'T DO THINGS RIGHT--WALLOPS YOU. I USED TO GET BRUISES ALL OVER ME 'TIL I LEARNED.
Nobody was going to hurt my sister.
If she was in that cabin, I'd break the door down.
But all I saw were the same empty ruins I'd always seen.

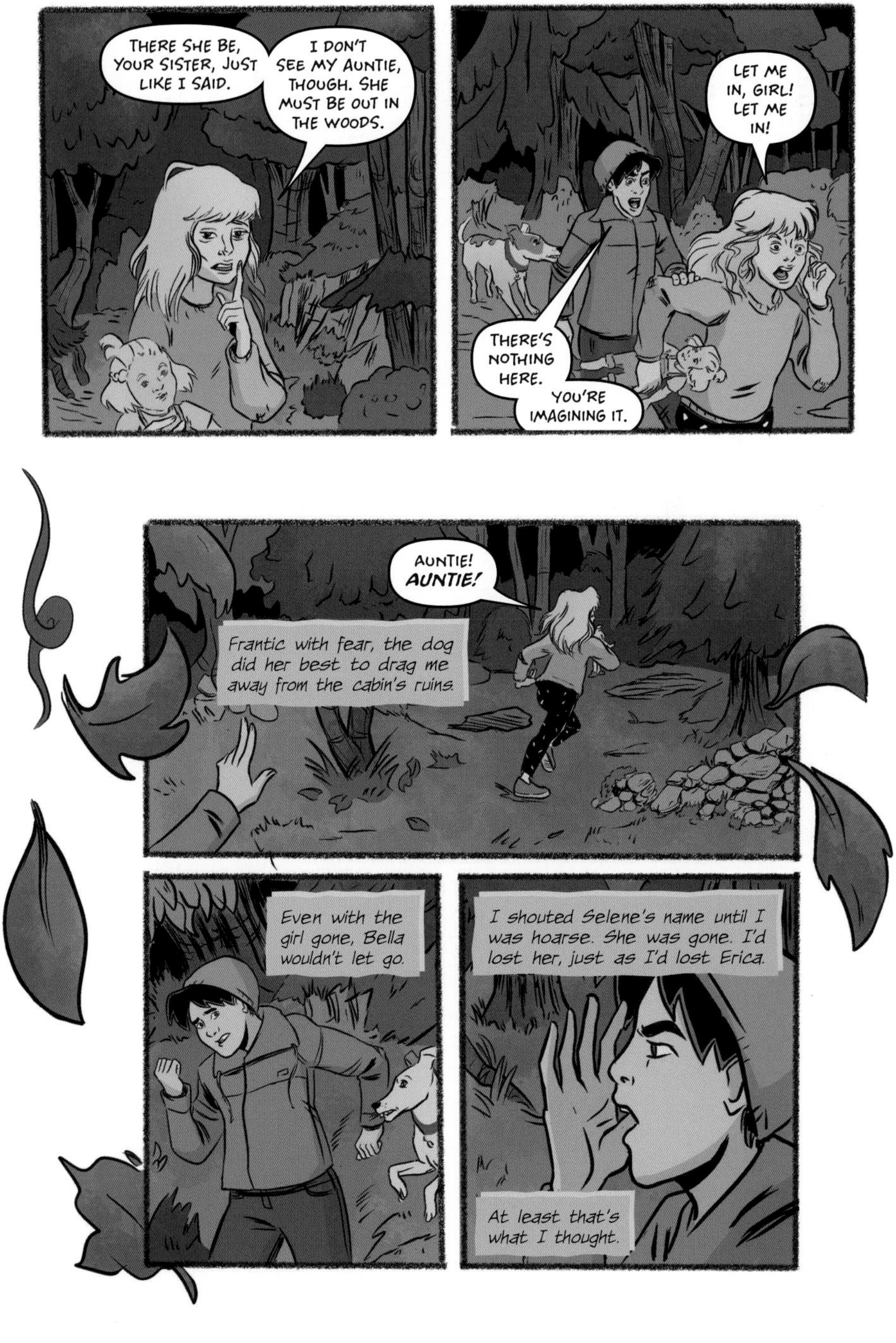
THERE SHE BE, YOUR SISTER, JUST LIKE I SAID.
I DON'T SEE MY AUNTIE, THOUGH. SHE MUST BE OUT IN THE WOODS.
LET ME IN, GIRL! LET ME IN!
THERE'S NOTHING HERE.
YOU'RE IMAGINING IT.
AUNTIE! AUNTIE!
Frantic with fear, the dog did her best to drag me away from the cabin's ruins.
Even with the girl gone, Bella wouldn't let go.
I shouted Selene's name until I was hoarse. She was gone. I'd lost her, just as I'd lost Erica.
At least that's what I thought.

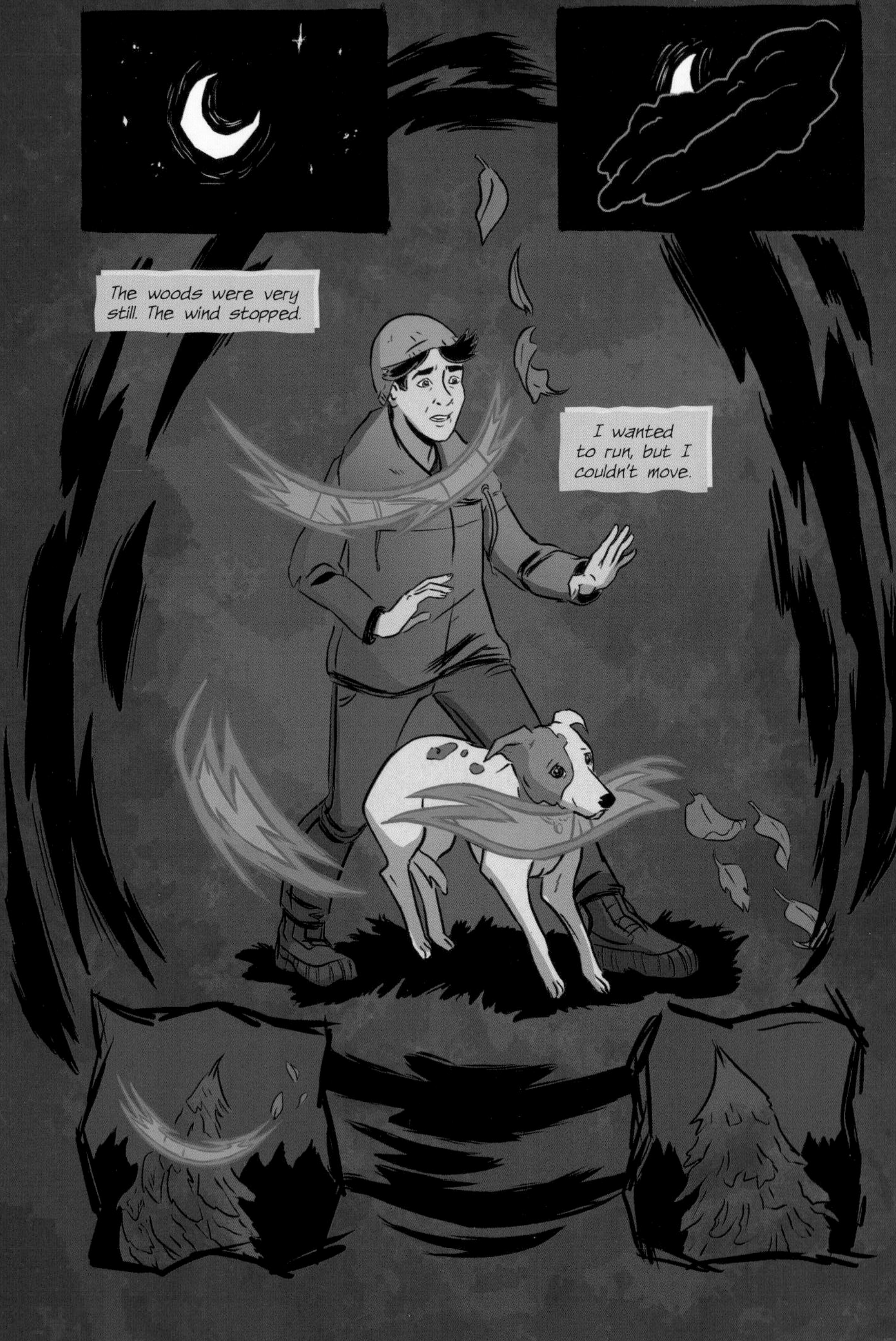
The woods were very still. The wind stopped.
I wanted to run, but I couldn't move.

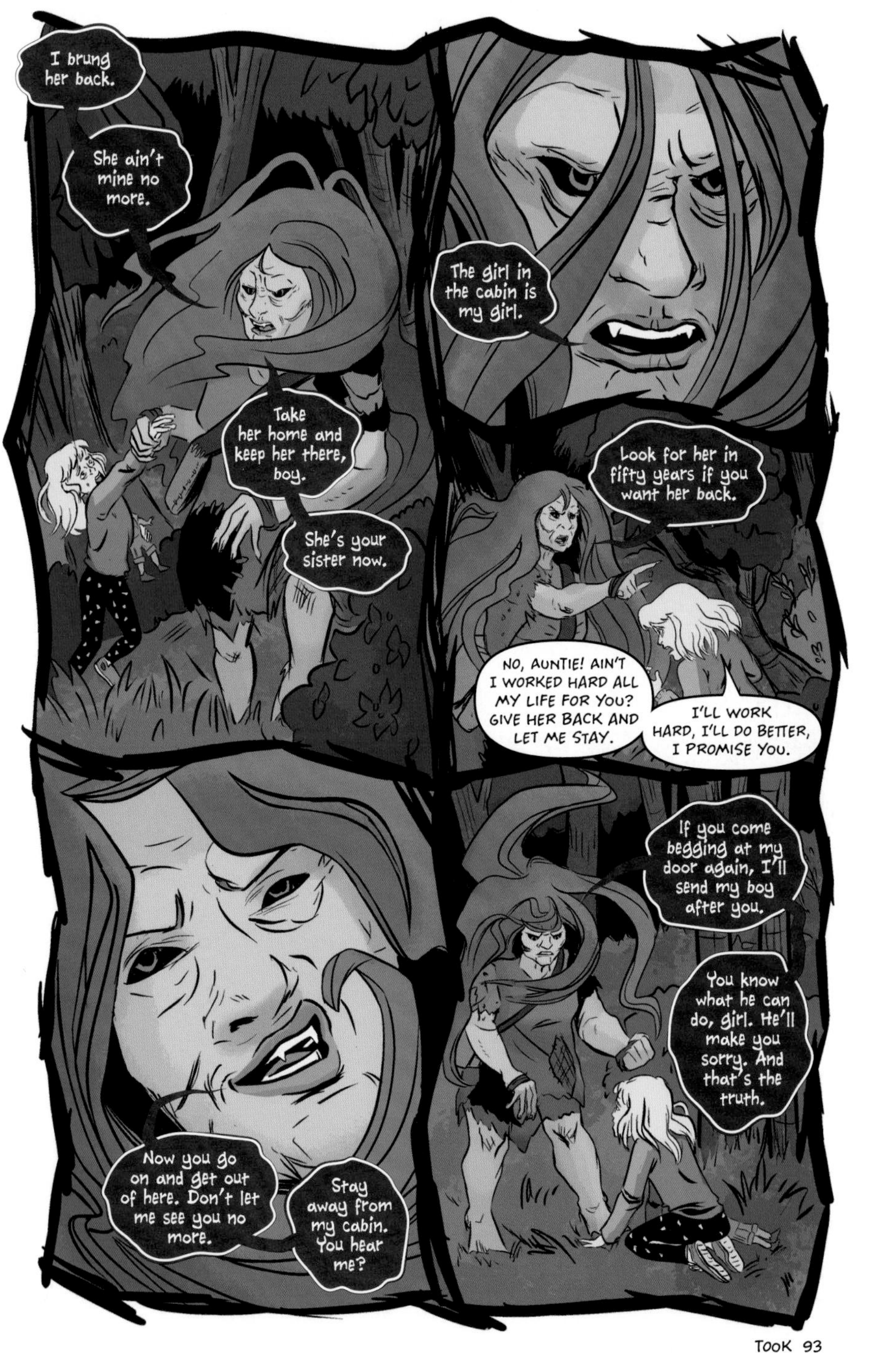
I brung her back.
She ain't mine no more.
Take her home and keep her there, boy.
She's your sister now.
The girl in the cabin is my girl.
Look for her in fifty years if you want her back.
NO, AUNTIE! AIN'T I WORKED HARD ALL MY LIFE FOR YOU? GIVE HER BACK AND LET ME STAY.
I'LL WORK HARD, I'LL DO BETTER, I PROMISE YOU.
Now you go on and get out of here. Don't let me see you no more.
Stay away from my cabin. You hear me?
If you come begging at my door again, I'll send my boy after you.
You know what he can do, girl. He'll make you sorry. And that's the truth.

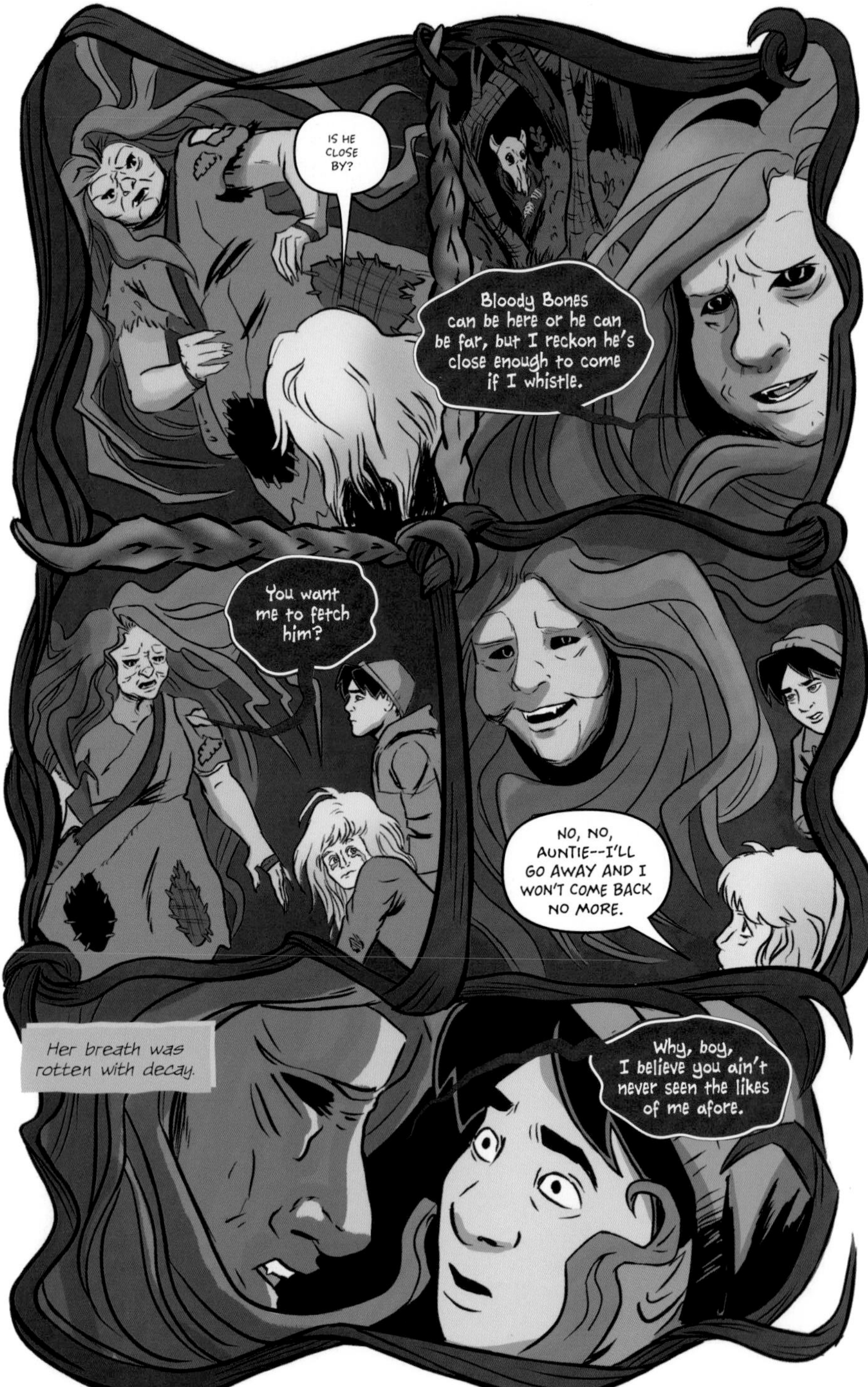
IS HE CLOSE BY?
Bloody Bones can be here or he can be far, but I reckon he's close enough to come if I whistle.
You want me to fetch him?
NO, NO, AUNTIE--I'LL GO AWAY AND I WON'T COME BACK NO MORE.
Her breath was rotten with decay.
Why, boy, I believe you ain't never seen the likes of me afore.

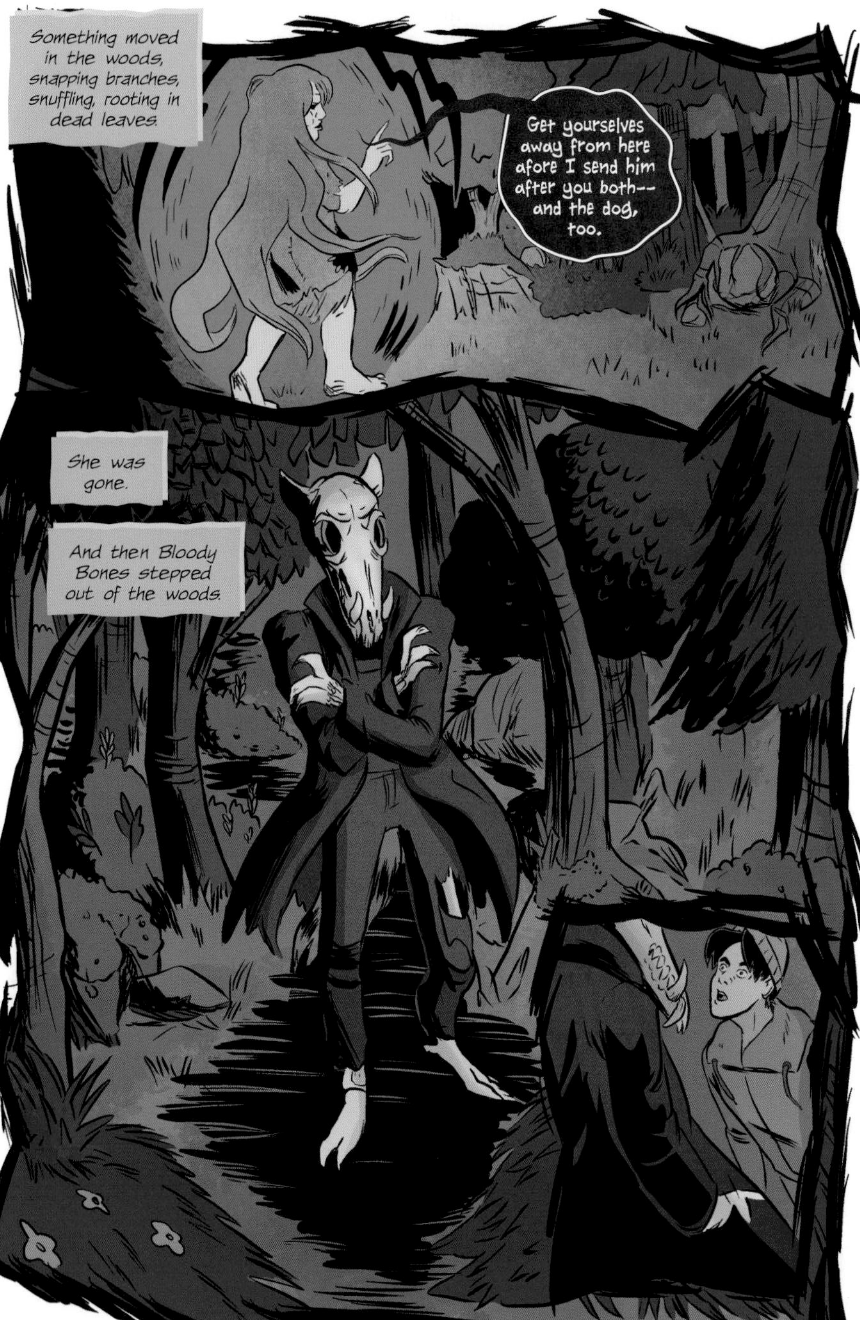
Something moved in the woods, snapping branches, snuffling, rooting in dead leaves.
Get yourselves away from here afore I send him after you both-- and the dog, too.
She was gone.
And then Bloody Bones stepped out of the woods.

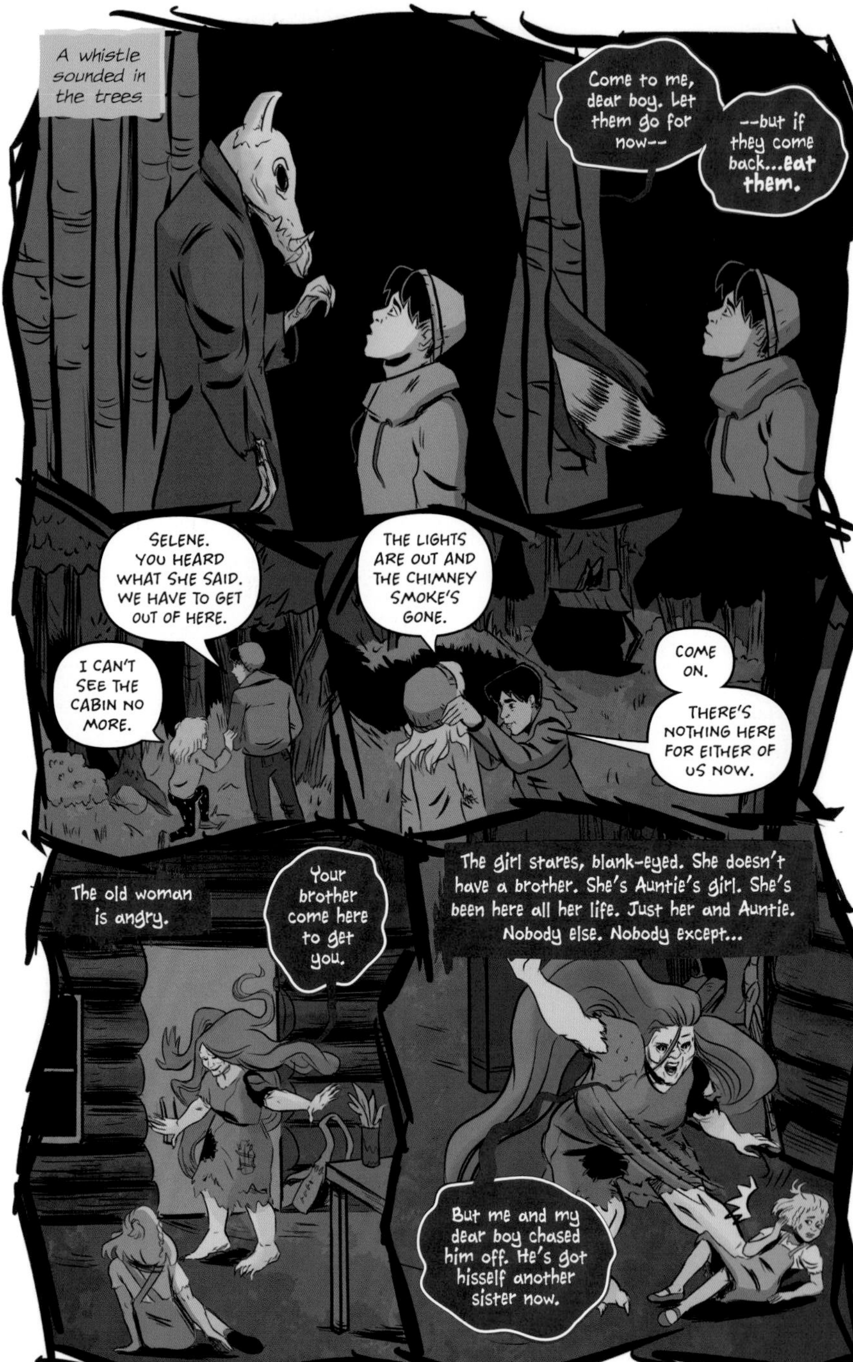
A whistle sounded in the trees.
Come to me, dear boy. Let them go for now--
--but if they come back...**eat them.**
SELENE. YOU HEARD WHAT SHE SAID. WE HAVE TO GET OUT OF HERE.
I CAN'T SEE THE CABIN NO MORE.
THE LIGHTS ARE OUT AND THE CHIMNEY SMOKE'S GONE.
COME ON.
THERE'S NOTHING HERE FOR EITHER OF US NOW.
The old woman is angry.
Your brother come here to get you.
The girl stares, blank-eyed. She doesn't have a brother. She's Auntie's girl. She's been here all her life. Just her and Auntie. Nobody else. Nobody except...
But me and my dear boy chased him off. He's got hisself another sister now.

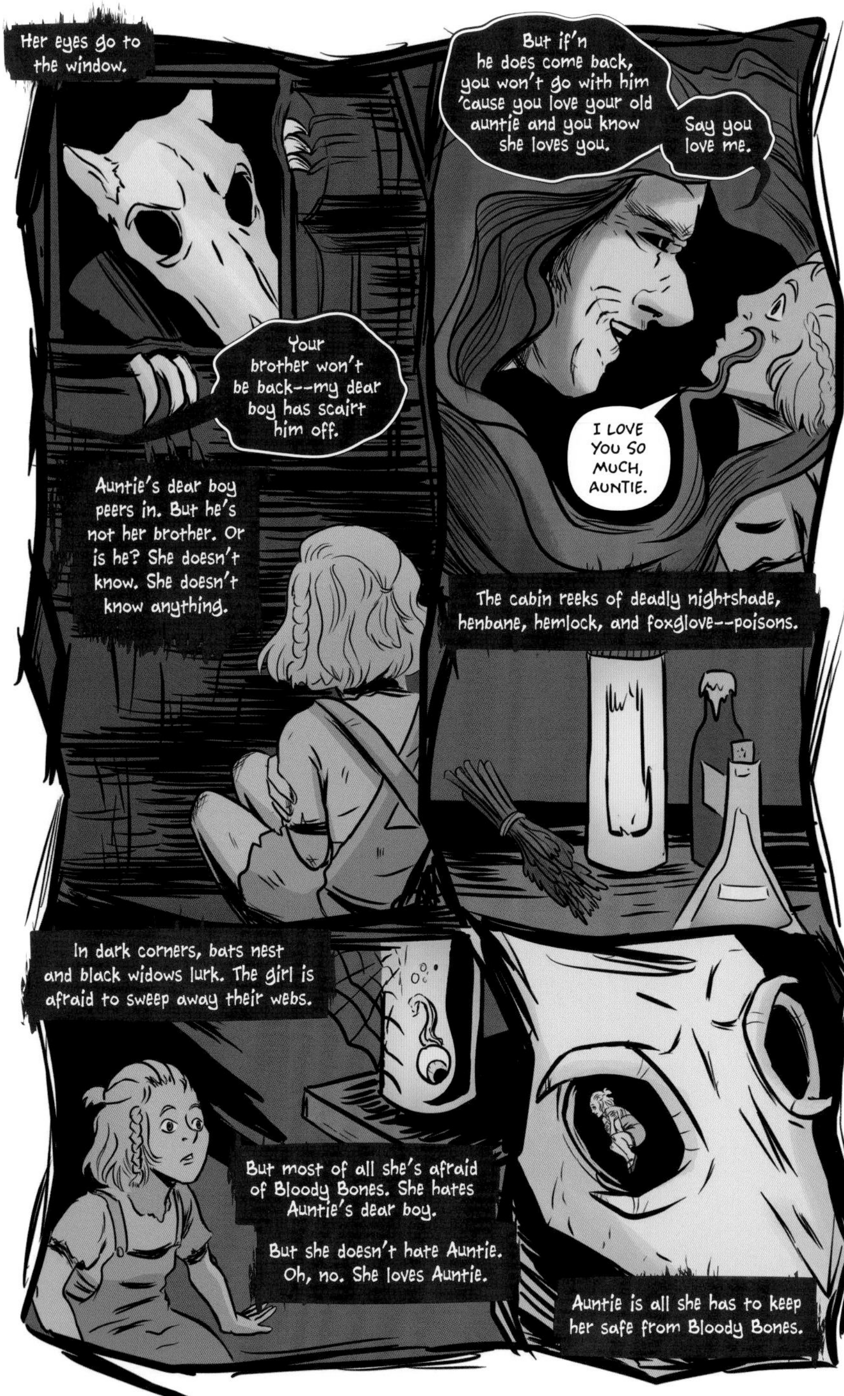

Her eyes go to the window.
Your brother won't be back--my dear boy has scairt him off.
Auntie's dear boy peers in. But he's not her brother. Or is he? She doesn't know. She doesn't know anything.
But if'n he does come back, you won't go with him 'cause you love your old auntie and you know she loves you.
Say you love me.
I LOVE YOU SO MUCH, AUNTIE.
The cabin reeks of deadly nightshade, henbane, hemlock, and foxglove--poisons.
In dark corners, bats nest and black widows lurk. The girl is afraid to sweep away their webs.
But most of all she's afraid of Bloody Bones. She hates Auntie's dear boy.
But she doesn't hate Auntie. Oh, no. She loves Auntie.
Auntie is all she has to keep her safe from Bloody Bones.

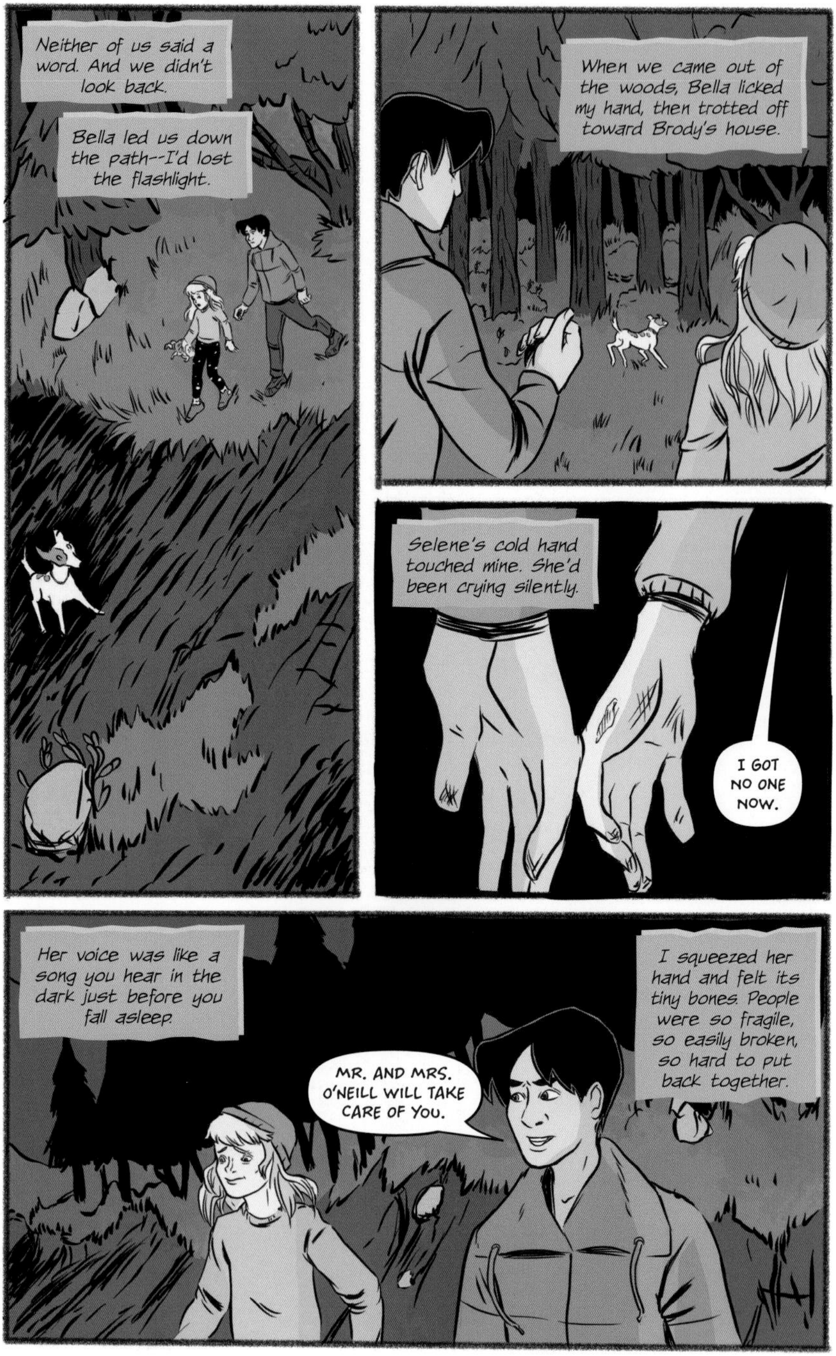
Neither of us said a word. And we didn't look back.
Bella led us down the path--I'd lost the flashlight.
When we came out of the woods, Bella licked my hand, then trotted off toward Brody's house.
Selene's cold hand touched mine. She'd been crying silently.
I GOT NO ONE NOW.
Her voice was like a song you hear in the dark just before you fall asleep.
I squeezed her hand and felt its tiny bones. People were so fragile, so easily broken, so hard to put back together.
MR. AND MRS. O'NEILL WILL TAKE CARE OF YOU.

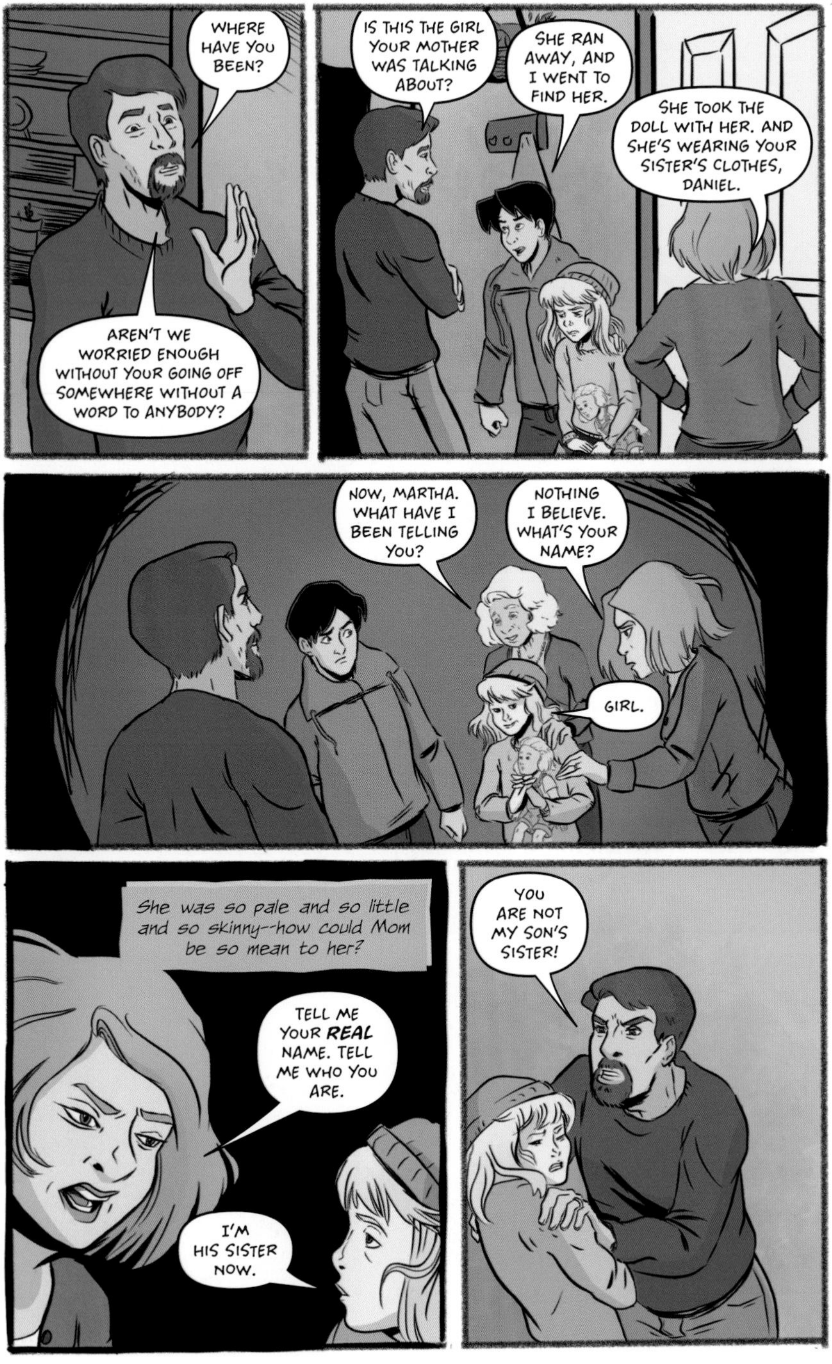
WHERE HAVE YOU BEEN?
AREN'T WE WORRIED ENOUGH WITHOUT YOUR GOING OFF SOMEWHERE WITHOUT A WORD TO ANYBODY?
IS THIS THE GIRL YOUR MOTHER WAS TALKING ABOUT?
SHE RAN AWAY, AND I WENT TO FIND HER.
SHE TOOK THE DOLL WITH HER. AND SHE'S WEARING YOUR SISTER'S CLOTHES, DANIEL.
NOW, MARTHA. WHAT HAVE I BEEN TELLING YOU?
NOTHING I BELIEVE. WHAT'S YOUR NAME?
GIRL.
She was so pale and so little and so skinny--how could Mom be so mean to her?
TELL ME YOUR **REAL** NAME. TELL ME WHO YOU ARE.
I'M HIS SISTER NOW.
YOU ARE NOT MY SON'S SISTER!

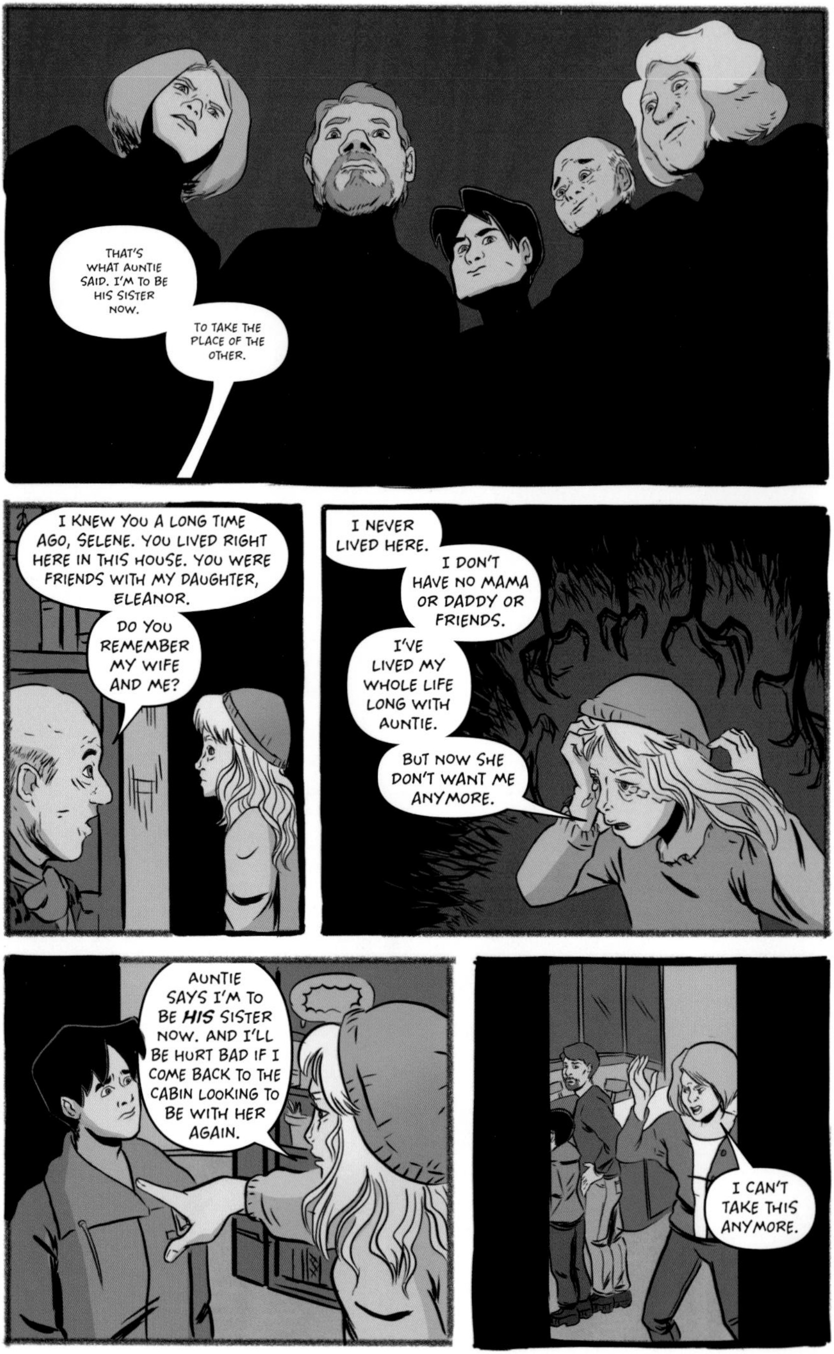
THAT'S WHAT AUNTIE SAID. I'M TO BE HIS SISTER NOW.
TO TAKE THE PLACE OF THE OTHER.
I KNEW YOU A LONG TIME AGO, SELENE. YOU LIVED RIGHT HERE IN THIS HOUSE. YOU WERE FRIENDS WITH MY DAUGHTER, ELEANOR.
DO YOU REMEMBER MY WIFE AND ME?
I NEVER LIVED HERE.
I DON'T HAVE NO MAMA OR DADDY OR FRIENDS.
I'VE LIVED MY WHOLE LIFE LONG WITH AUNTIE.
BUT NOW SHE DON'T WANT ME ANYMORE.
AUNTIE SAYS I'M TO BE ***HIS*** SISTER NOW. AND I'LL BE HURT BAD IF I COME BACK TO THE CABIN LOOKING TO BE WITH HER AGAIN.
I CAN'T TAKE THIS ANYMORE.

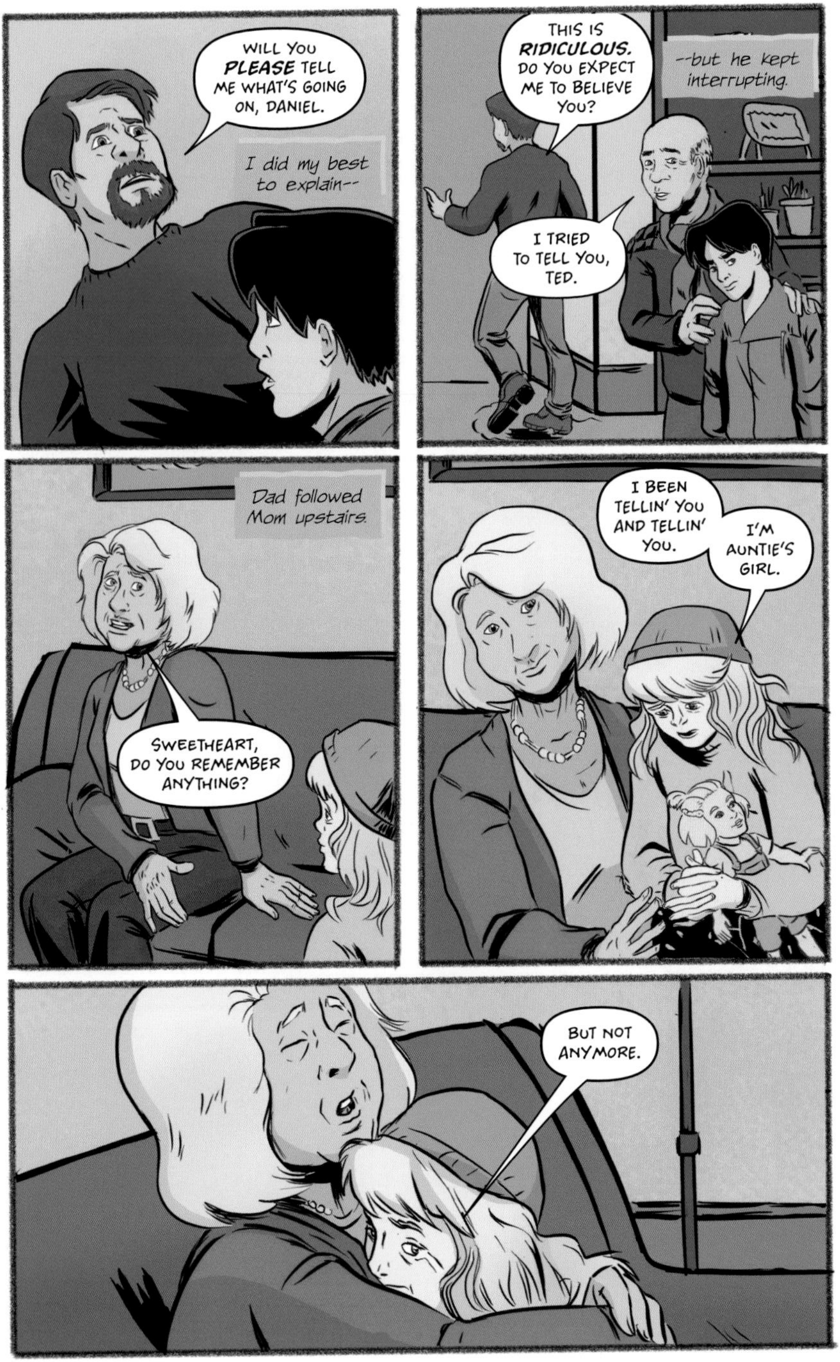
WILL YOU PLEASE TELL ME WHAT'S GOING ON, DANIEL.
I did my best to explain--
THIS IS RIDICULOUS. DO YOU EXPECT ME TO BELIEVE YOU?
--but he kept interrupting.
I TRIED TO TELL YOU, TED.
Dad followed Mom upstairs.
SWEETHEART, DO YOU REMEMBER ANYTHING?
I BEEN TELLIN' YOU AND TELLIN' YOU.
I'M AUNTIE'S GIRL.
BUT NOT ANYMORE.

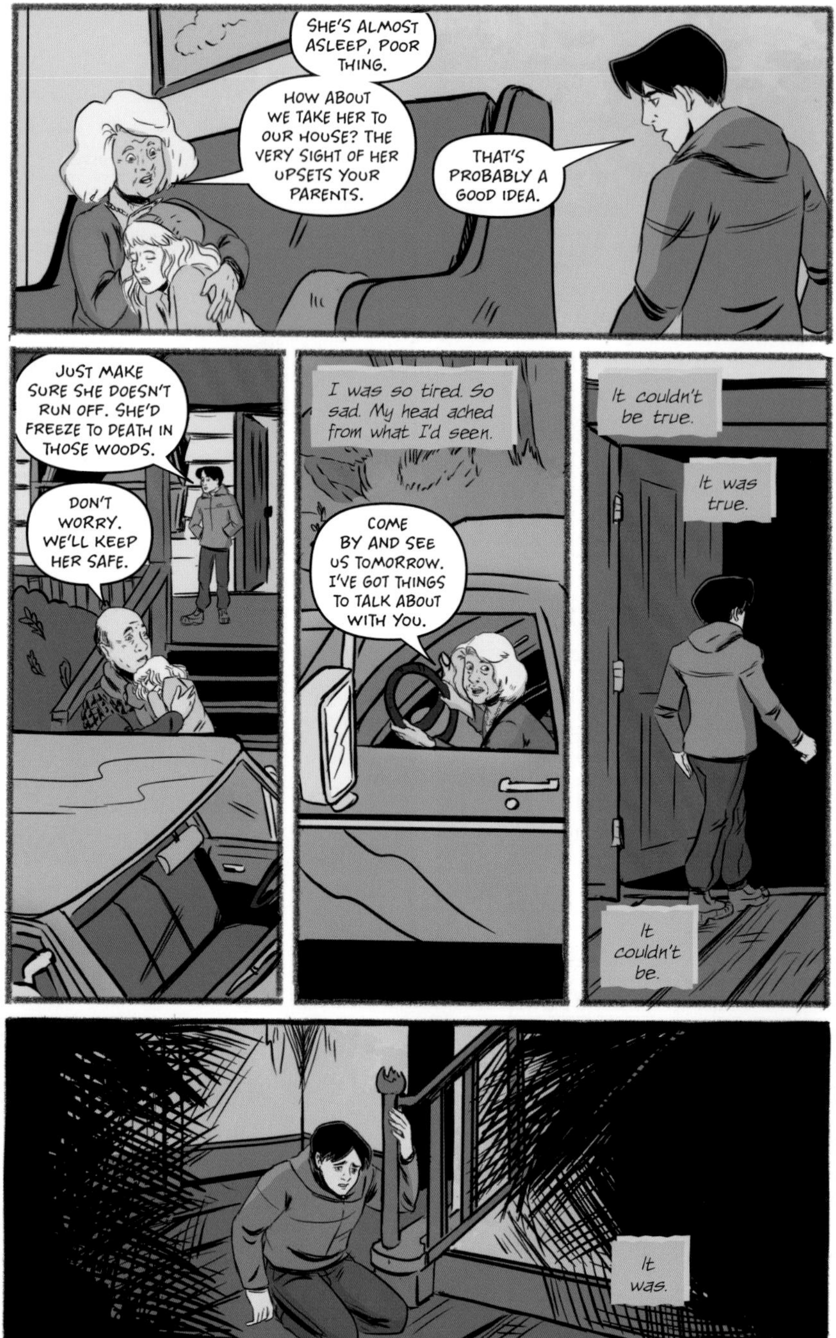
SHE'S ALMOST ASLEEP, POOR THING.
HOW ABOUT WE TAKE HER TO OUR HOUSE? THE VERY SIGHT OF HER UPSETS YOUR PARENTS.
THAT'S PROBABLY A GOOD IDEA.
JUST MAKE SURE SHE DOESN'T RUN OFF. SHE'D FREEZE TO DEATH IN THOSE WOODS.
DON'T WORRY. WE'LL KEEP HER SAFE.
I was so tired. So sad. My head ached from what I'd seen.
COME BY AND SEE US TOMORROW. I'VE GOT THINGS TO TALK ABOUT WITH YOU.
It couldn't be true.
It was true.
It couldn't be.
It was.

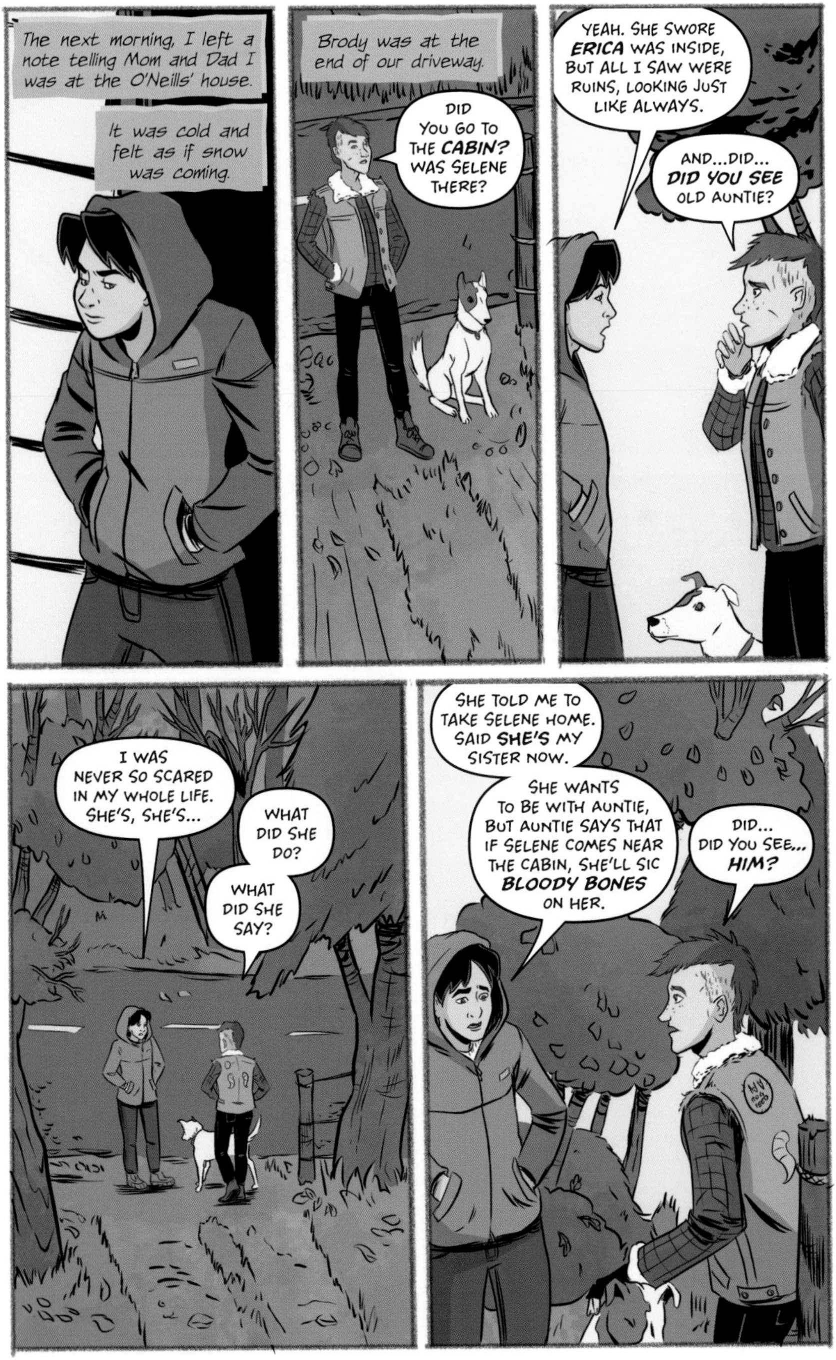
The next morning, I left a note telling Mom and Dad I was at the O'Neills' house.
It was cold and felt as if snow was coming.
Brody was at the end of our driveway.
DID YOU GO TO THE CABIN? WAS SELENE THERE?
YEAH. SHE SWORE ERICA WAS INSIDE, BUT ALL I SAW WERE RUINS, LOOKING JUST LIKE ALWAYS.
AND...DID... DID YOU SEE OLD AUNTIE?
I WAS NEVER SO SCARED IN MY WHOLE LIFE. SHE'S, SHE'S...
WHAT DID SHE DO?
WHAT DID SHE SAY?
SHE TOLD ME TO TAKE SELENE HOME. SAID SHE'S MY SISTER NOW.
SHE WANTS TO BE WITH AUNTIE, BUT AUNTIE SAYS THAT IF SELENE COMES NEAR THE CABIN, SHE'LL SIC BLOODY BONES ON HER.
DID... DID YOU SEE... HIM?

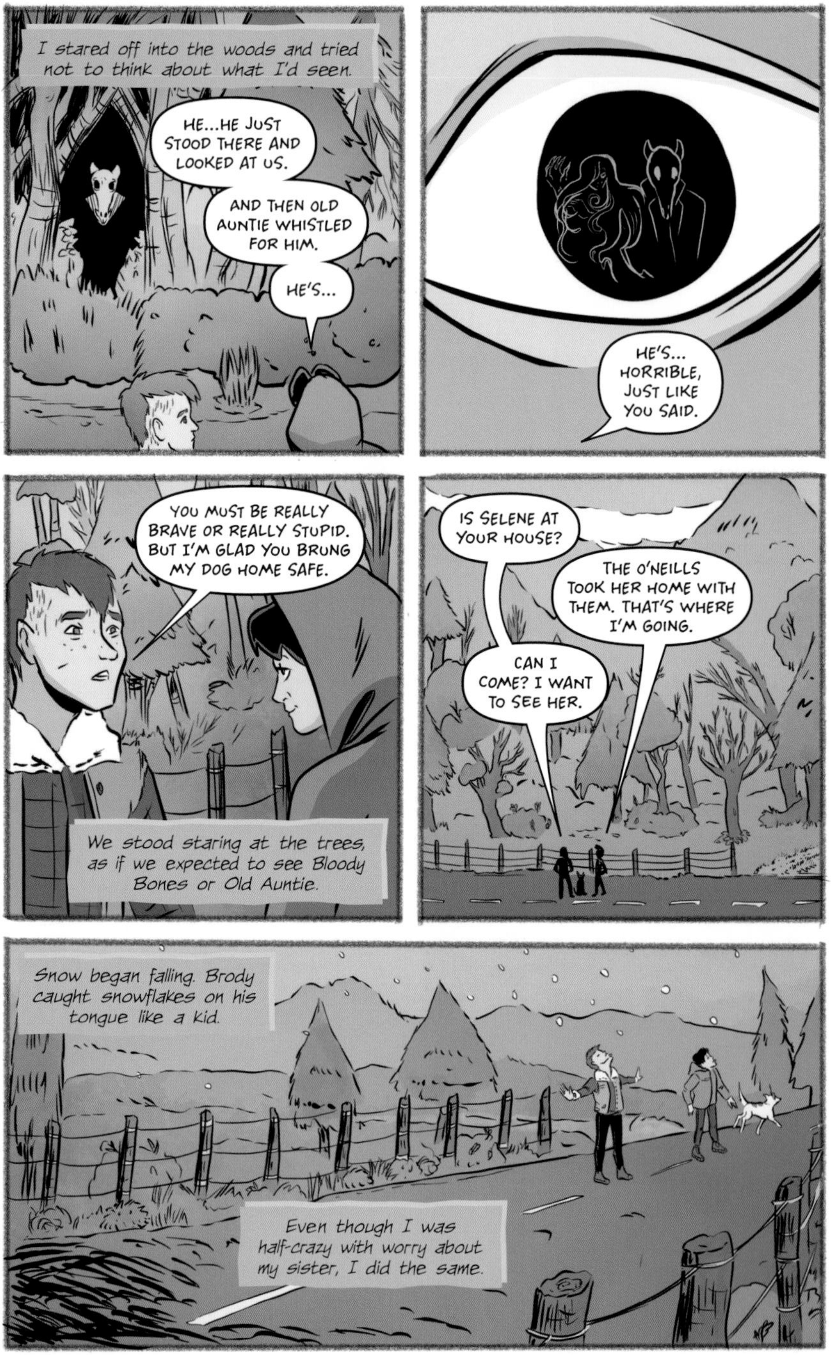
I stared off into the woods and tried not to think about what I'd seen.
HE...HE JUST STOOD THERE AND LOOKED AT US.
AND THEN OLD AUNTIE WHISTLED FOR HIM.
HE'S...
HE'S... HORRIBLE, JUST LIKE YOU SAID.
YOU MUST BE REALLY BRAVE OR REALLY STUPID. BUT I'M GLAD YOU BRUNG MY DOG HOME SAFE.
We stood staring at the trees, as if we expected to see Bloody Bones or Old Auntie.
IS SELENE AT YOUR HOUSE?
THE O'NEILLS TOOK HER HOME WITH THEM. THAT'S WHERE I'M GOING.
CAN I COME? I WANT TO SEE HER.
Snow began falling. Brody caught snowflakes on his tongue like a kid.
Even though I was half-crazy with worry about my sister, I did the same.

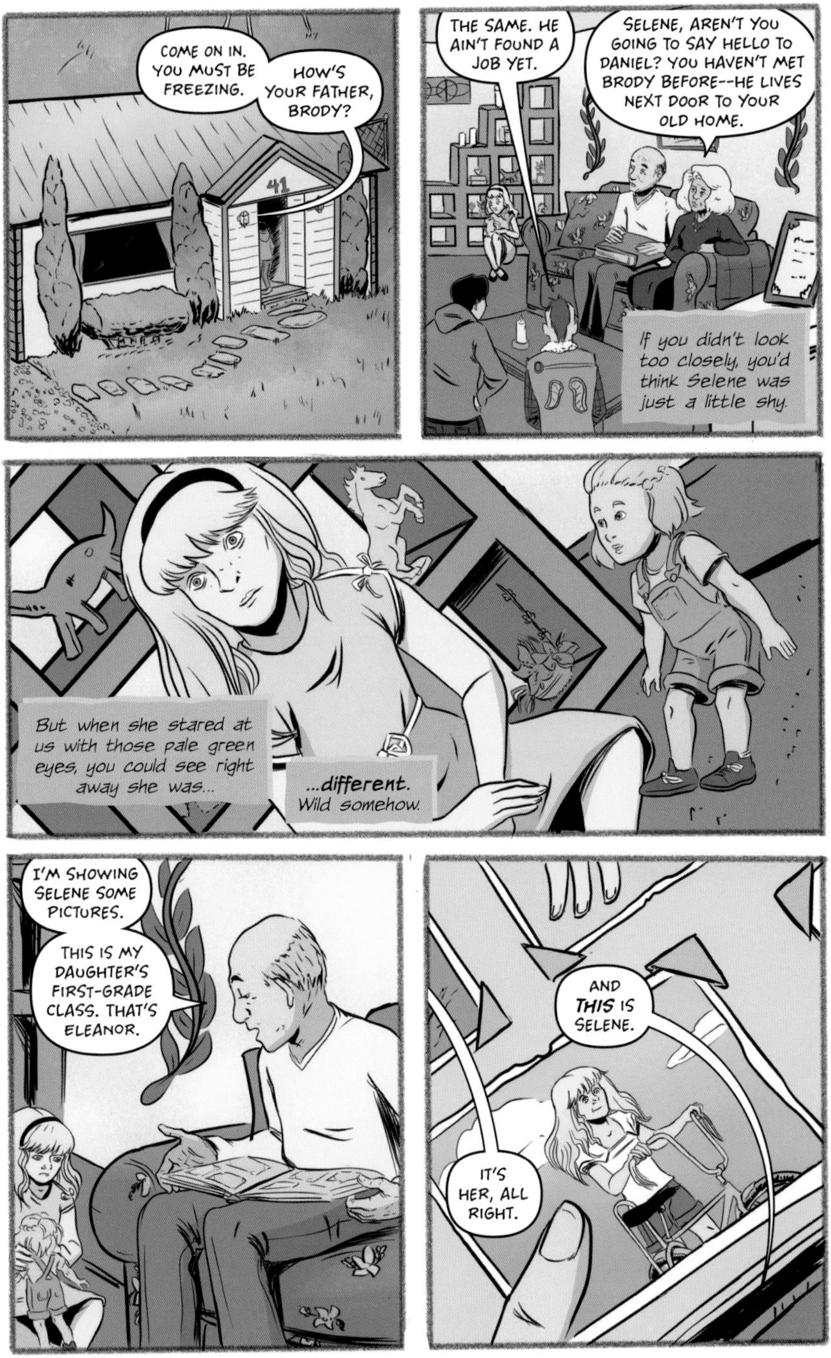
COME ON IN. YOU MUST BE FREEZING.
HOW'S YOUR FATHER, BRODY?
THE SAME. HE AIN'T FOUND A JOB YET.
SELENE, AREN'T YOU GOING TO SAY HELLO TO DANIEL? YOU HAVEN'T MET BRODY BEFORE--HE LIVES NEXT DOOR TO YOUR OLD HOME.
If you didn't look too closely, you'd think Selene was just a little shy.
But when she stared at us with those pale green eyes, you could see right away she was...
...different. Wild somehow.
I'M SHOWING SELENE SOME PICTURES.
THIS IS MY DAUGHTER'S FIRST-GRADE CLASS. THAT'S ELEANOR.
AND THIS IS SELENE.
IT'S HER, ALL RIGHT.

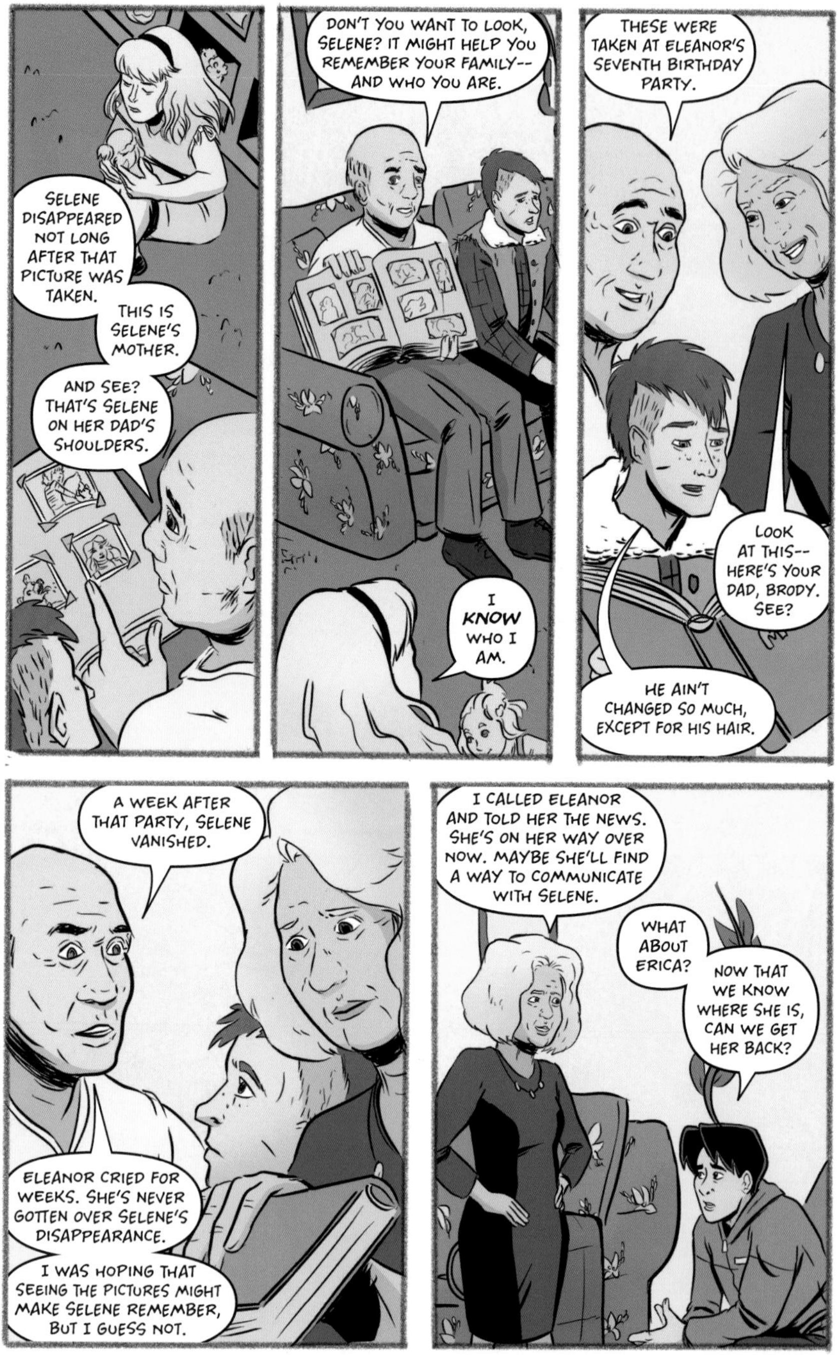
SELENE DISAPPEARED NOT LONG AFTER THAT PICTURE WAS TAKEN.
THIS IS SELENE'S MOTHER.
AND SEE? THAT'S SELENE ON HER DAD'S SHOULDERS.
DON'T YOU WANT TO LOOK, SELENE? IT MIGHT HELP YOU REMEMBER YOUR FAMILY-- AND WHO YOU ARE.
I KNOW WHO I AM.
THESE WERE TAKEN AT ELEANOR'S SEVENTH BIRTHDAY PARTY.
LOOK AT THIS-- HERE'S YOUR DAD, BRODY. SEE?
HE AIN'T CHANGED SO MUCH, EXCEPT FOR HIS HAIR.
A WEEK AFTER THAT PARTY, SELENE VANISHED.
ELEANOR CRIED FOR WEEKS. SHE'S NEVER GOTTEN OVER SELENE'S DISAPPEARANCE.
I WAS HOPING THAT SEEING THE PICTURES MIGHT MAKE SELENE REMEMBER, BUT I GUESS NOT.
I CALLED ELEANOR AND TOLD HER THE NEWS. SHE'S ON HER WAY OVER NOW. MAYBE SHE'LL FIND A WAY TO COMMUNICATE WITH SELENE.
WHAT ABOUT ERICA?
NOW THAT WE KNOW WHERE SHE IS, CAN WE GET HER BACK?

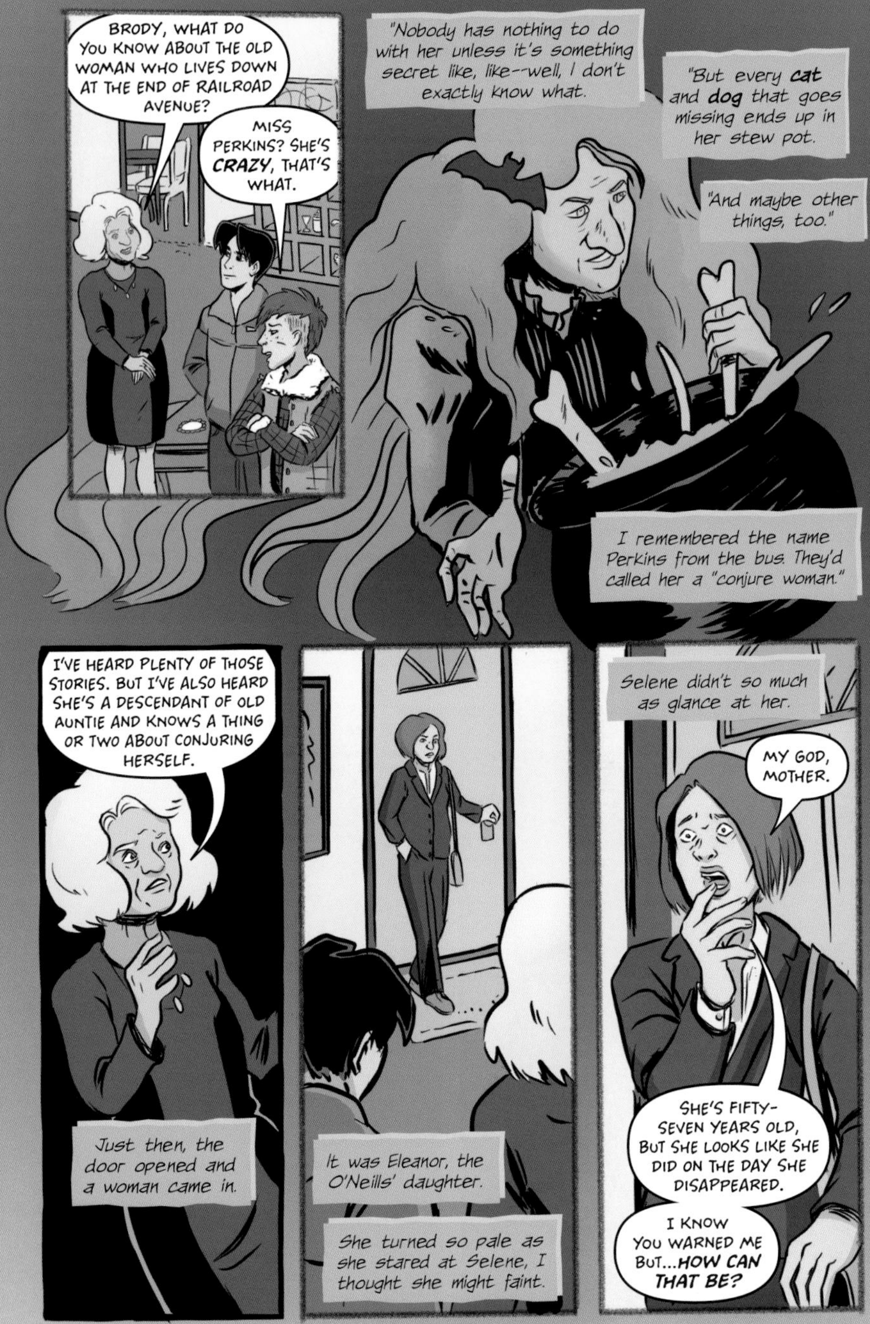
BRODY, WHAT DO YOU KNOW ABOUT THE OLD WOMAN WHO LIVES DOWN AT THE END OF RAILROAD AVENUE?
MISS PERKINS? SHE'S CRAZY, THAT'S WHAT.
"Nobody has nothing to do with her unless it's something secret like, like--well, I don't exactly know what.
"But every cat and dog that goes missing ends up in her stew pot.
"And maybe other things, too."
I remembered the name Perkins from the bus. They'd called her a "conjure woman."
I'VE HEARD PLENTY OF THOSE STORIES. BUT I'VE ALSO HEARD SHE'S A DESCENDANT OF OLD AUNTIE AND KNOWS A THING OR TWO ABOUT CONJURING HERSELF.
Just then, the door opened and a woman came in.
It was Eleanor, the O'Neills' daughter.
She turned so pale as she stared at Selene, I thought she might faint.
Selene didn't so much as glance at her.
MY GOD, MOTHER.
SHE'S FIFTY-SEVEN YEARS OLD, BUT SHE LOOKS LIKE SHE DID ON THE DAY SHE DISAPPEARED.
I KNOW YOU WARNED ME BUT...HOW CAN THAT BE?

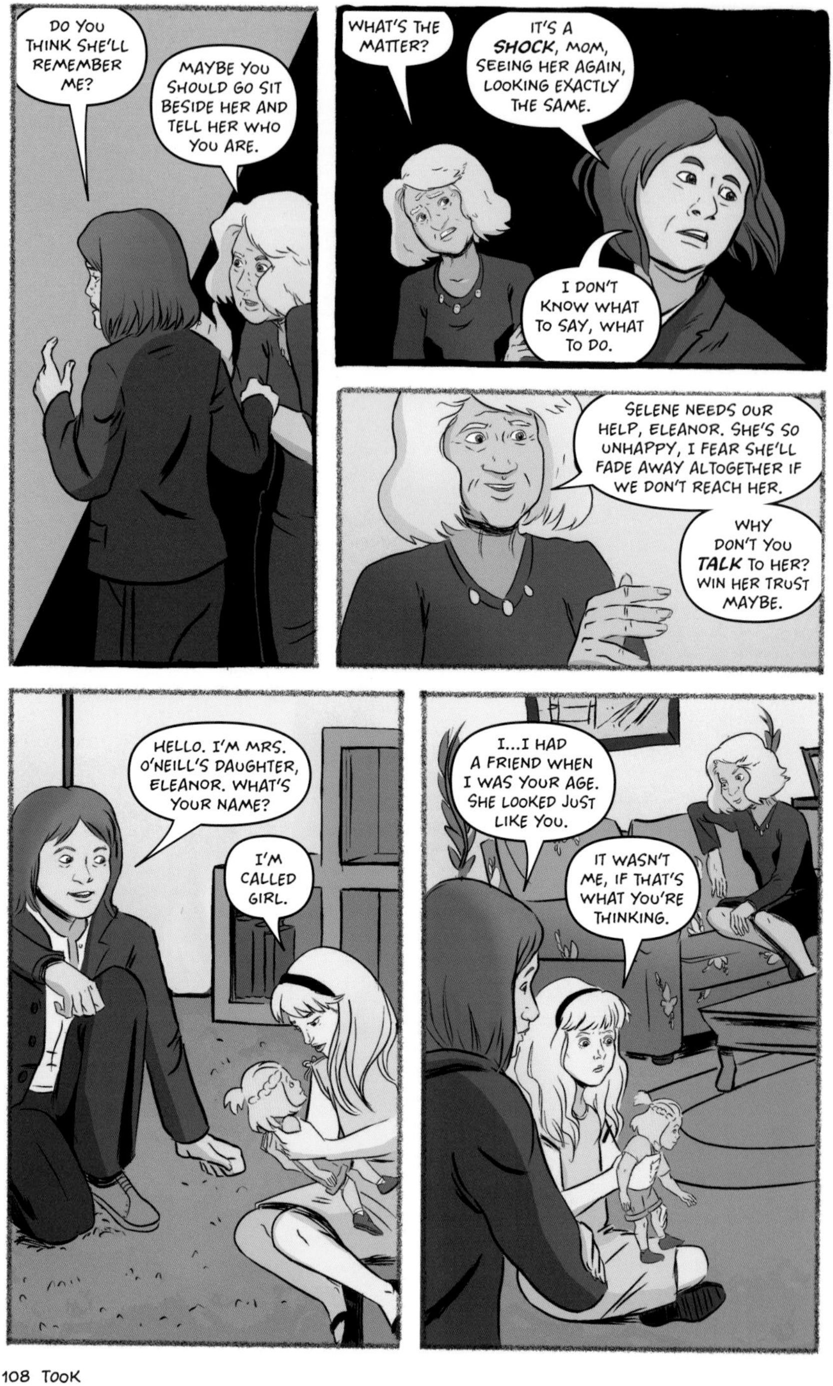
DO YOU THINK SHE'LL REMEMBER ME?
MAYBE YOU SHOULD GO SIT BESIDE HER AND TELL HER WHO YOU ARE.
WHAT'S THE MATTER?
IT'S A SHOCK, MOM, SEEING HER AGAIN, LOOKING EXACTLY THE SAME.
I DON'T KNOW WHAT TO SAY, WHAT TO DO.
SELENE NEEDS OUR HELP, ELEANOR. SHE'S SO UNHAPPY, I FEAR SHE'LL FADE AWAY ALTOGETHER IF WE DON'T REACH HER.
WHY DON'T YOU TALK TO HER? WIN HER TRUST MAYBE.
HELLO. I'M MRS. O'NEILL'S DAUGHTER, ELEANOR. WHAT'S YOUR NAME?
I'M CALLED GIRL.
I...I HAD A FRIEND WHEN I WAS YOUR AGE. SHE LOOKED JUST LIKE YOU.
IT WASN'T ME, IF THAT'S WHAT YOU'RE THINKING.

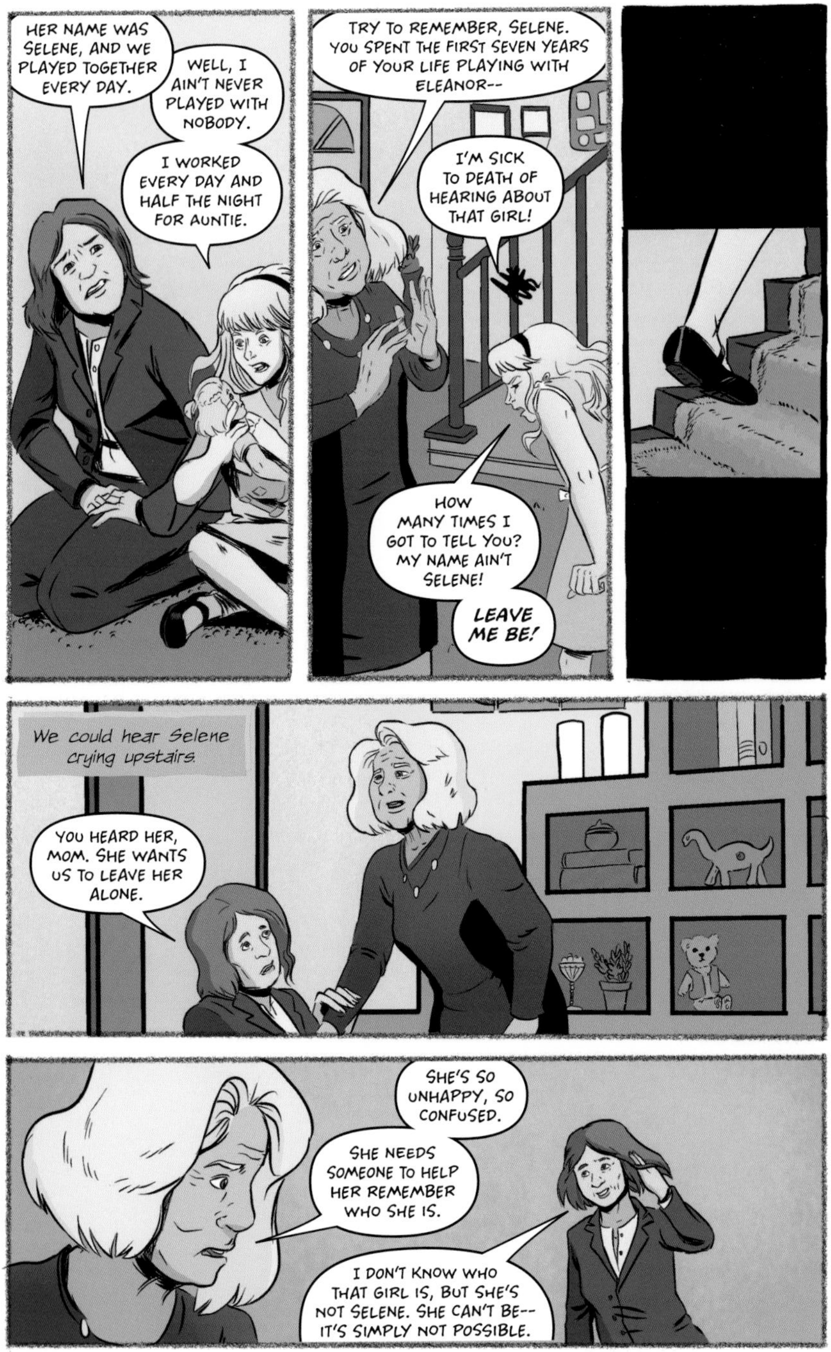

HER NAME WAS SELENE, AND WE PLAYED TOGETHER EVERY DAY.
WELL, I AIN'T NEVER PLAYED WITH NOBODY.
I WORKED EVERY DAY AND HALF THE NIGHT FOR AUNTIE.
TRY TO REMEMBER, SELENE. YOU SPENT THE FIRST SEVEN YEARS OF YOUR LIFE PLAYING WITH ELEANOR--
I'M SICK TO DEATH OF HEARING ABOUT THAT GIRL!
HOW MANY TIMES I GOT TO TELL YOU? MY NAME AIN'T SELENE!
LEAVE ME BE!
We could hear Selene crying upstairs.
YOU HEARD HER, MOM. SHE WANTS US TO LEAVE HER ALONE.
SHE'S SO UNHAPPY, SO CONFUSED.
SHE NEEDS SOMEONE TO HELP HER REMEMBER WHO SHE IS.
I DON'T KNOW WHO THAT GIRL IS, BUT SHE'S NOT SELENE. SHE CAN'T BE-- IT'S SIMPLY NOT POSSIBLE.

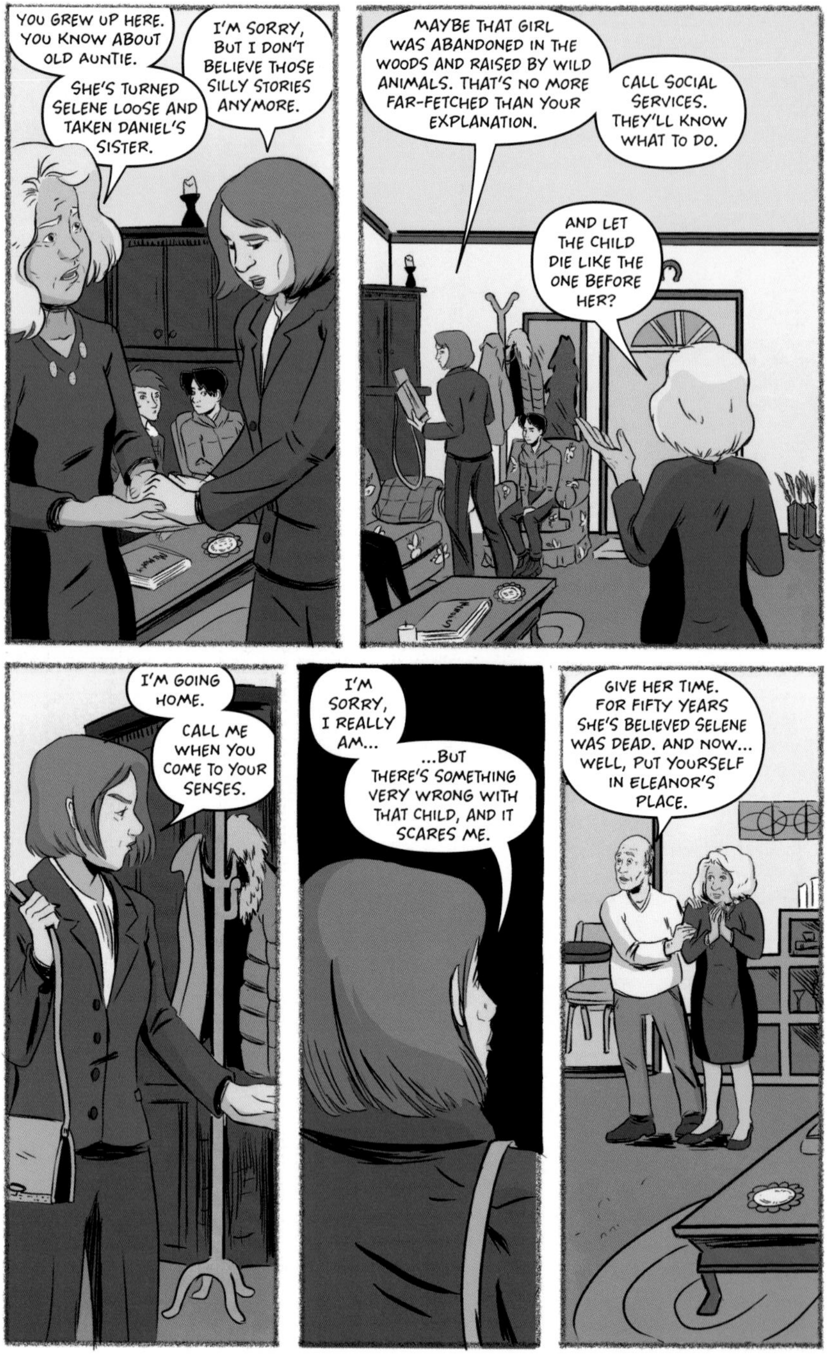
YOU GREW UP HERE. YOU KNOW ABOUT OLD AUNTIE.
SHE'S TURNED SELENE LOOSE AND TAKEN DANIEL'S SISTER.
I'M SORRY, BUT I DON'T BELIEVE THOSE SILLY STORIES ANYMORE.
MAYBE THAT GIRL WAS ABANDONED IN THE WOODS AND RAISED BY WILD ANIMALS. THAT'S NO MORE FAR-FETCHED THAN YOUR EXPLANATION.
CALL SOCIAL SERVICES. THEY'LL KNOW WHAT TO DO.
AND LET THE CHILD DIE LIKE THE ONE BEFORE HER?
I'M GOING HOME.
CALL ME WHEN YOU COME TO YOUR SENSES.
I'M SORRY, I REALLY AM...
...BUT THERE'S SOMETHING VERY WRONG WITH THAT CHILD, AND IT SCARES ME.
GIVE HER TIME. FOR FIFTY YEARS SHE'S BELIEVED SELENE WAS DEAD. AND NOW... WELL, PUT YOURSELF IN ELEANOR'S PLACE.

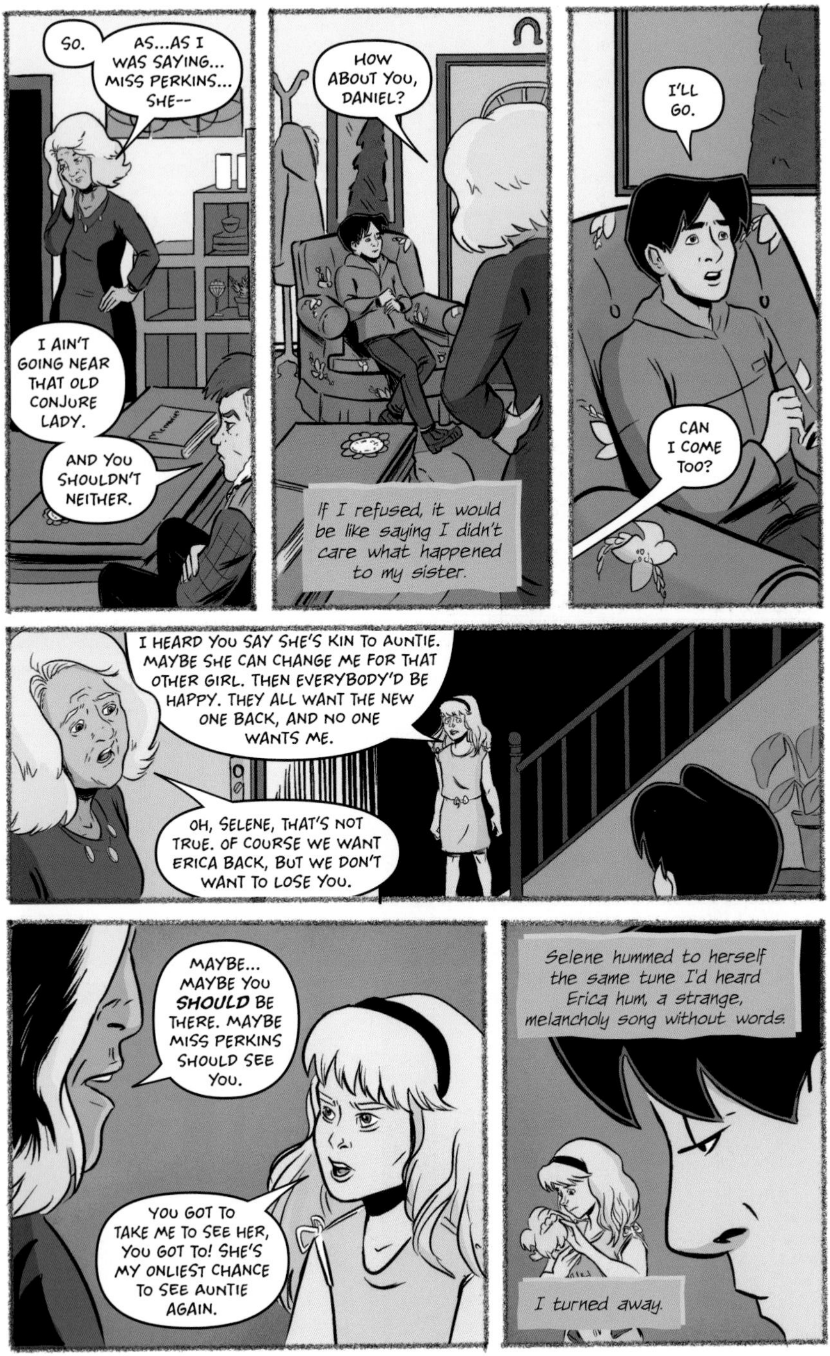
SO.
AS...AS I WAS SAYING... MISS PERKINS... SHE--
I AIN'T GOING NEAR THAT OLD CONJURE LADY.
AND YOU SHOULDN'T NEITHER.
HOW ABOUT YOU, DANIEL?
If I refused, it would be like saying I didn't care what happened to my sister.
I'LL GO.
CAN I COME TOO?
I HEARD YOU SAY SHE'S KIN TO AUNTIE. MAYBE SHE CAN CHANGE ME FOR THAT OTHER GIRL. THEN EVERYBODY'D BE HAPPY. THEY ALL WANT THE NEW ONE BACK, AND NO ONE WANTS ME.
OH, SELENE, THAT'S NOT TRUE. OF COURSE WE WANT ERICA BACK, BUT WE DON'T WANT TO LOSE YOU.
MAYBE... MAYBE YOU SHOULD BE THERE. MAYBE MISS PERKINS SHOULD SEE YOU.
YOU GOT TO TAKE ME TO SEE HER, YOU GOT TO! SHE'S MY ONLIEST CHANCE TO SEE AUNTIE AGAIN.
Selene hummed to herself the same tune I'd heard Erica hum, a strange, melancholy song without words.
I turned away.

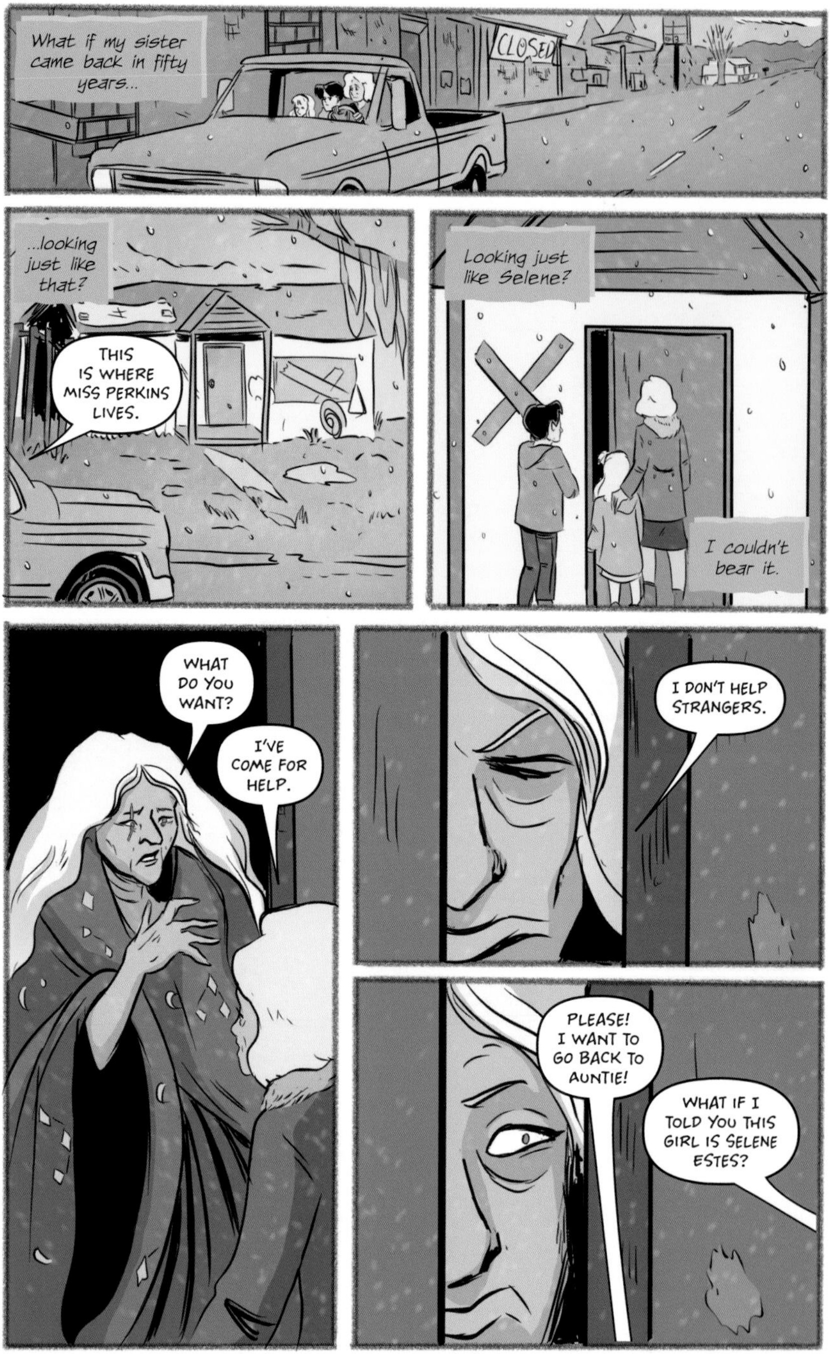
What if my sister came back in fifty years...
CLOSED
...looking just like that?
THIS IS WHERE MISS PERKINS LIVES.
Looking just like Selene?
I couldn't bear it.
WHAT DO YOU WANT?
I'VE COME FOR HELP.
I DON'T HELP STRANGERS.
PLEASE! I WANT TO GO BACK TO AUNTIE!
WHAT IF I TOLD YOU THIS GIRL IS SELENE ESTES?

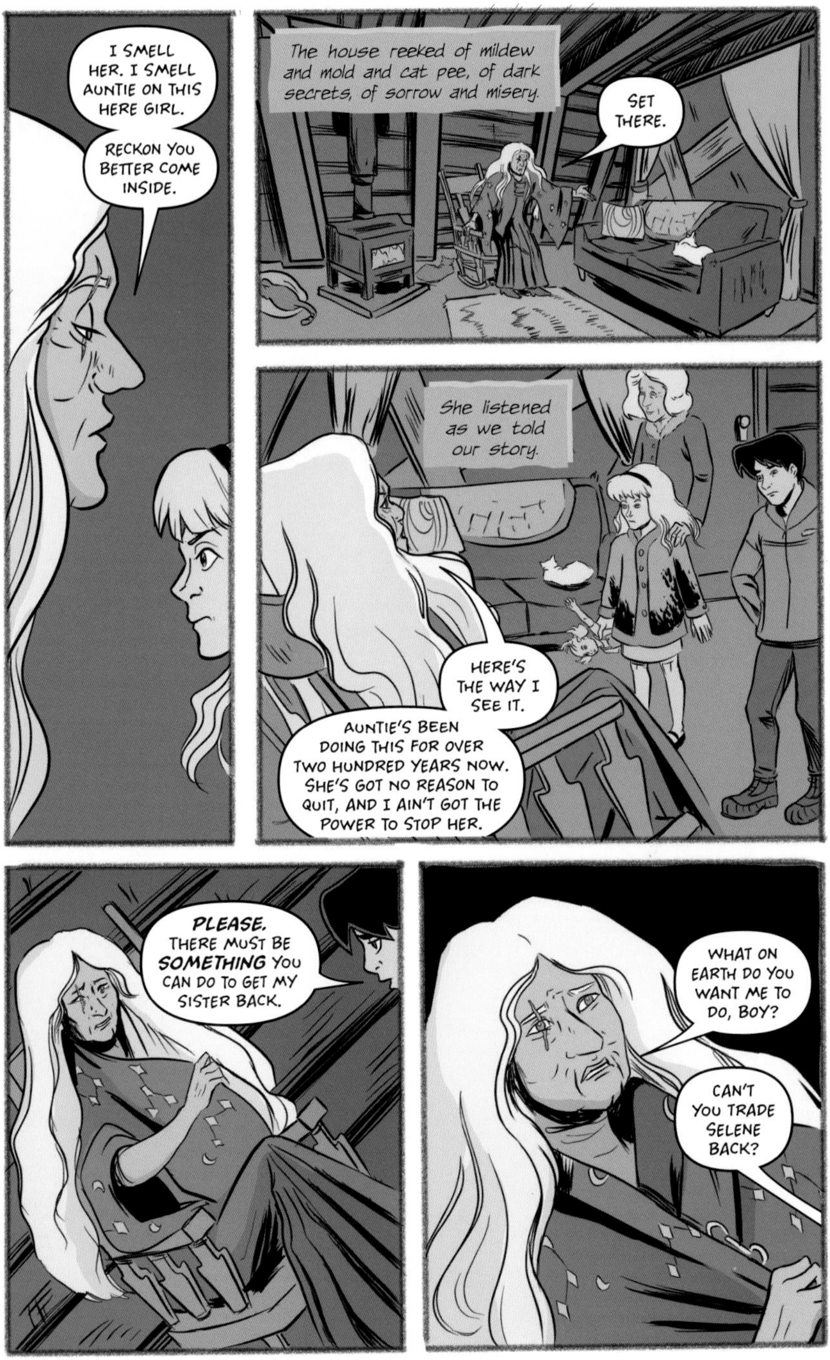
I SMELL HER. I SMELL AUNTIE ON THIS HERE GIRL.
RECKON YOU BETTER COME INSIDE.
The house reeked of mildew and mold and cat pee, of dark secrets, of sorrow and misery.
SET THERE.
She listened as we told our story.
HERE'S THE WAY I SEE IT.
AUNTIE'S BEEN DOING THIS FOR OVER TWO HUNDRED YEARS NOW. SHE'S GOT NO REASON TO QUIT, AND I AIN'T GOT THE POWER TO STOP HER.
PLEASE. THERE MUST BE SOMETHING YOU CAN DO TO GET MY SISTER BACK.
WHAT ON EARTH DO YOU WANT ME TO DO, BOY?
CAN'T YOU TRADE SELENE BACK?

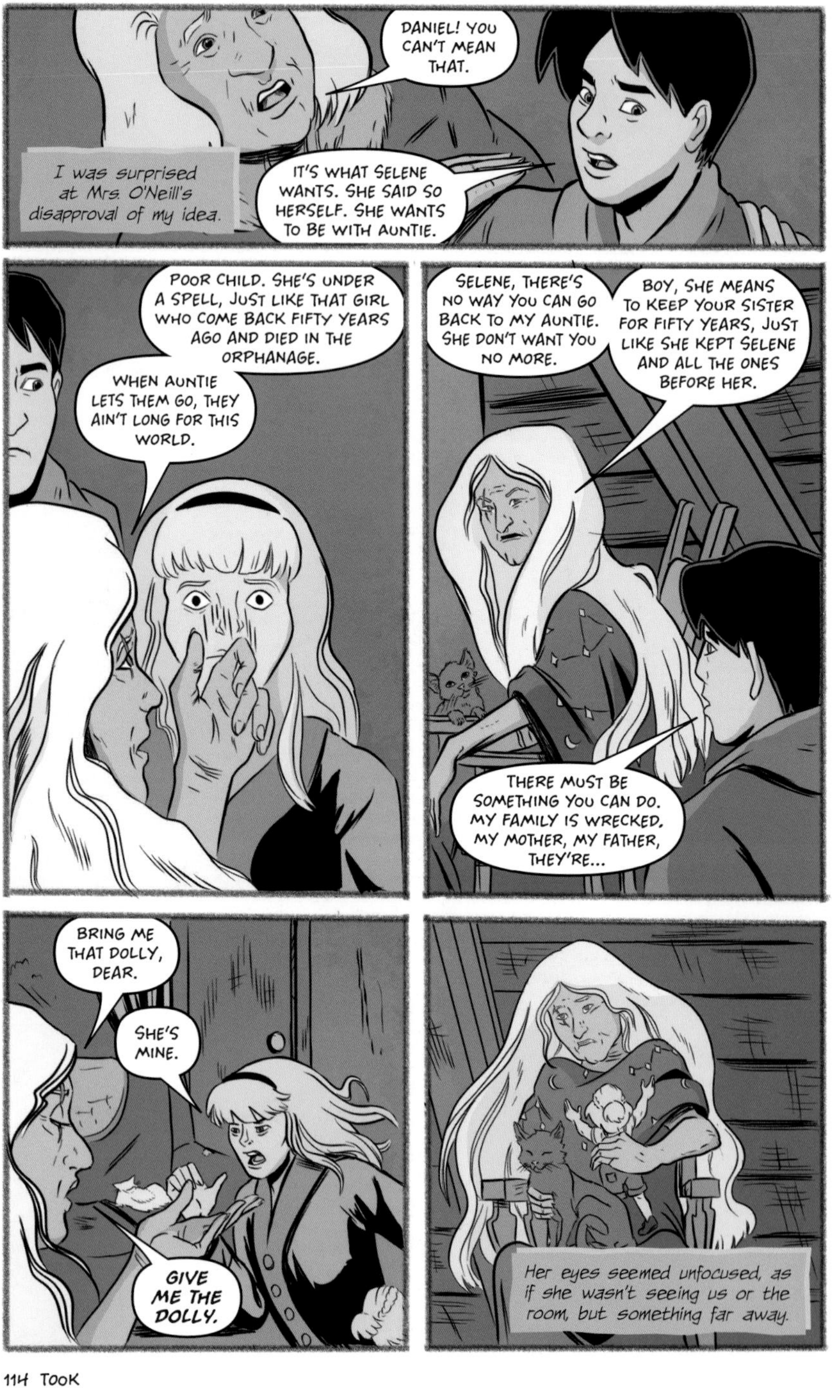
DANIEL! YOU CAN'T MEAN THAT.
I was surprised at Mrs. O'Neill's disapproval of my idea.
IT'S WHAT SELENE WANTS. SHE SAID SO HERSELF. SHE WANTS TO BE WITH AUNTIE.
POOR CHILD. SHE'S UNDER A SPELL, JUST LIKE THAT GIRL WHO COME BACK FIFTY YEARS AGO AND DIED IN THE ORPHANAGE.
WHEN AUNTIE LETS THEM GO, THEY AIN'T LONG FOR THIS WORLD.
SELENE, THERE'S NO WAY YOU CAN GO BACK TO MY AUNTIE. SHE DON'T WANT YOU NO MORE.
BOY, SHE MEANS TO KEEP YOUR SISTER FOR FIFTY YEARS, JUST LIKE SHE KEPT SELENE AND ALL THE ONES BEFORE HER.
THERE MUST BE SOMETHING YOU CAN DO. MY FAMILY IS WRECKED. MY MOTHER, MY FATHER, THEY'RE...
BRING ME THAT DOLLY, DEAR.
SHE'S MINE.
GIVE ME THE DOLLY.
Her eyes seemed unfocused, as if she wasn't seeing us or the room, but something far away.

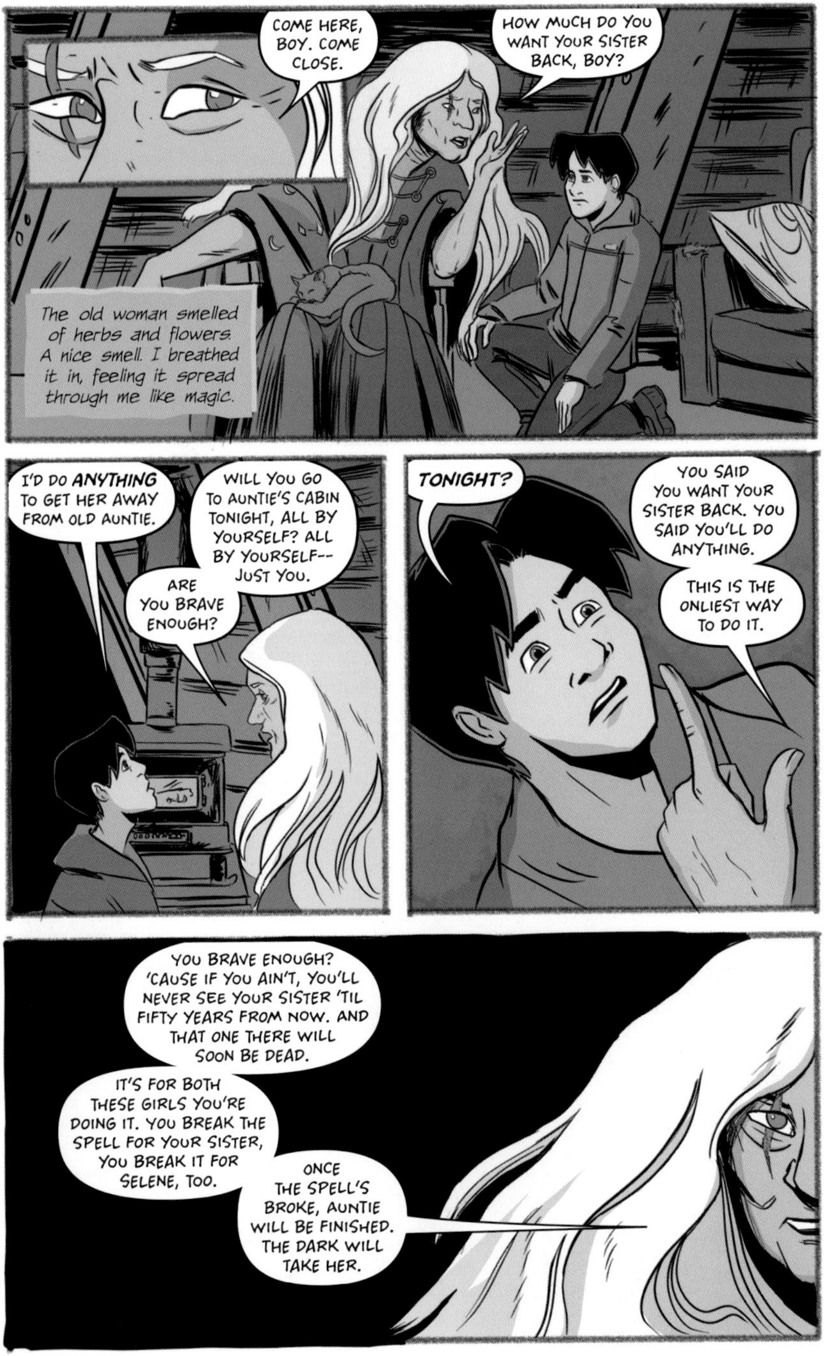
COME HERE, BOY. COME CLOSE.
HOW MUCH DO YOU WANT YOUR SISTER BACK, BOY?
The old woman smelled of herbs and flowers. A nice smell. I breathed it in, feeling it spread through me like magic.
I'D DO **ANYTHING** TO GET HER AWAY FROM OLD AUNTIE.
WILL YOU GO TO AUNTIE'S CABIN TONIGHT, ALL BY YOURSELF? ALL BY YOURSELF-- JUST YOU.
ARE YOU BRAVE ENOUGH?
TONIGHT?
YOU SAID YOU WANT YOUR SISTER BACK. YOU SAID YOU'LL DO ANYTHING.
THIS IS THE ONLIEST WAY TO DO IT.
YOU BRAVE ENOUGH? 'CAUSE IF YOU AIN'T, YOU'LL NEVER SEE YOUR SISTER 'TIL FIFTY YEARS FROM NOW. AND THAT ONE THERE WILL SOON BE DEAD.
IT'S FOR BOTH THESE GIRLS YOU'RE DOING IT. YOU BREAK THE SPELL FOR YOUR SISTER, YOU BREAK IT FOR SELENE, TOO.
ONCE THE SPELL'S BROKE, AUNTIE WILL BE FINISHED. THE DARK WILL TAKE HER.

Maybe if I *acted* brave, I'd be brave.

WHAT DO I HAVE TO DO?

She told me.

BUT WHEN SHE SEES ME, SHE'LL KNOW WHO I AM.

AUNTIE AIN'T THE *ONLIEST* ONE THAT KNOWS HER WAY AROUND THE DARK SIDE OF THE MOON.

I GOT TRICKS OF MY OWN, BOY. SHE WON'T KNOW YOU-- I'LL SEE TO THAT.

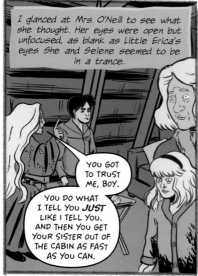

I glanced at Mrs. O'Neill to see what she thought. Her eyes were open but unfocused, as blank as Little Erica's eyes. She and Selene seemed to be in a trance.

YOU GOT TO TRUST ME, BOY.

YOU DO WHAT I TELL YOU *JUST* LIKE I TELL YOU. AND THEN YOU GET YOUR SISTER OUT OF THE CABIN AS FAST AS YOU CAN.

SHE WON'T WANT TO COME. YOU'LL HAVE TO DRAG HER AWAY.

RUN FOR HOME LIKE YOU GOT WINGS ON YOUR HEELS OR SEVEN-LEAGUE BOOTS ON YOUR FEET.

BUT WHAT IF--

DON'T VEX ME NO MORE, BOY. DO WHAT I TELL YOU, BRING YOUR SISTER HOME, AND THE SPELL WILL BUST AT SUNRISE-- FOR BOTH GIRLS.

THEY'LL REMEMBER WHO THEY ARE IN THIS WORLD, BUT THEY WON'T REMEMBER NOTHING ABOUT AUNTIE'S WORLD.

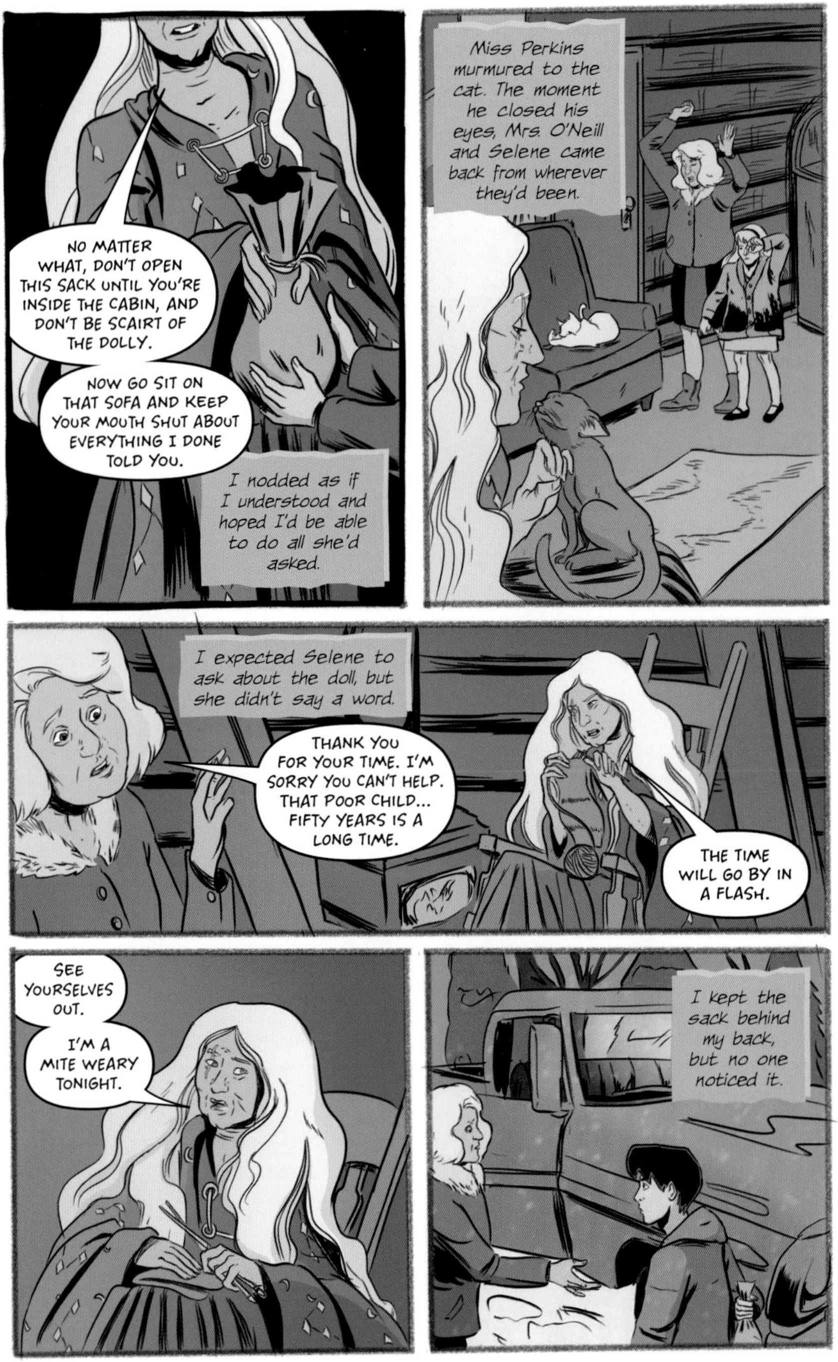
NO MATTER WHAT, DON'T OPEN THIS SACK UNTIL YOU'RE INSIDE THE CABIN, AND DON'T BE SCAIRT OF THE DOLLY.
NOW GO SIT ON THAT SOFA AND KEEP YOUR MOUTH SHUT ABOUT EVERYTHING I DONE TOLD YOU.
I nodded as if I understood and hoped I'd be able to do all she'd asked.
Miss Perkins murmured to the cat. The moment he closed his eyes, Mrs. O'Neill and Selene came back from wherever they'd been.
I expected Selene to ask about the doll, but she didn't say a word.
THANK YOU FOR YOUR TIME. I'M SORRY YOU CAN'T HELP. THAT POOR CHILD... FIFTY YEARS IS A LONG TIME.
THE TIME WILL GO BY IN A FLASH.
SEE YOURSELVES OUT.
I'M A MITE WEARY TONIGHT.
I kept the sack behind my back, but no one noticed it.

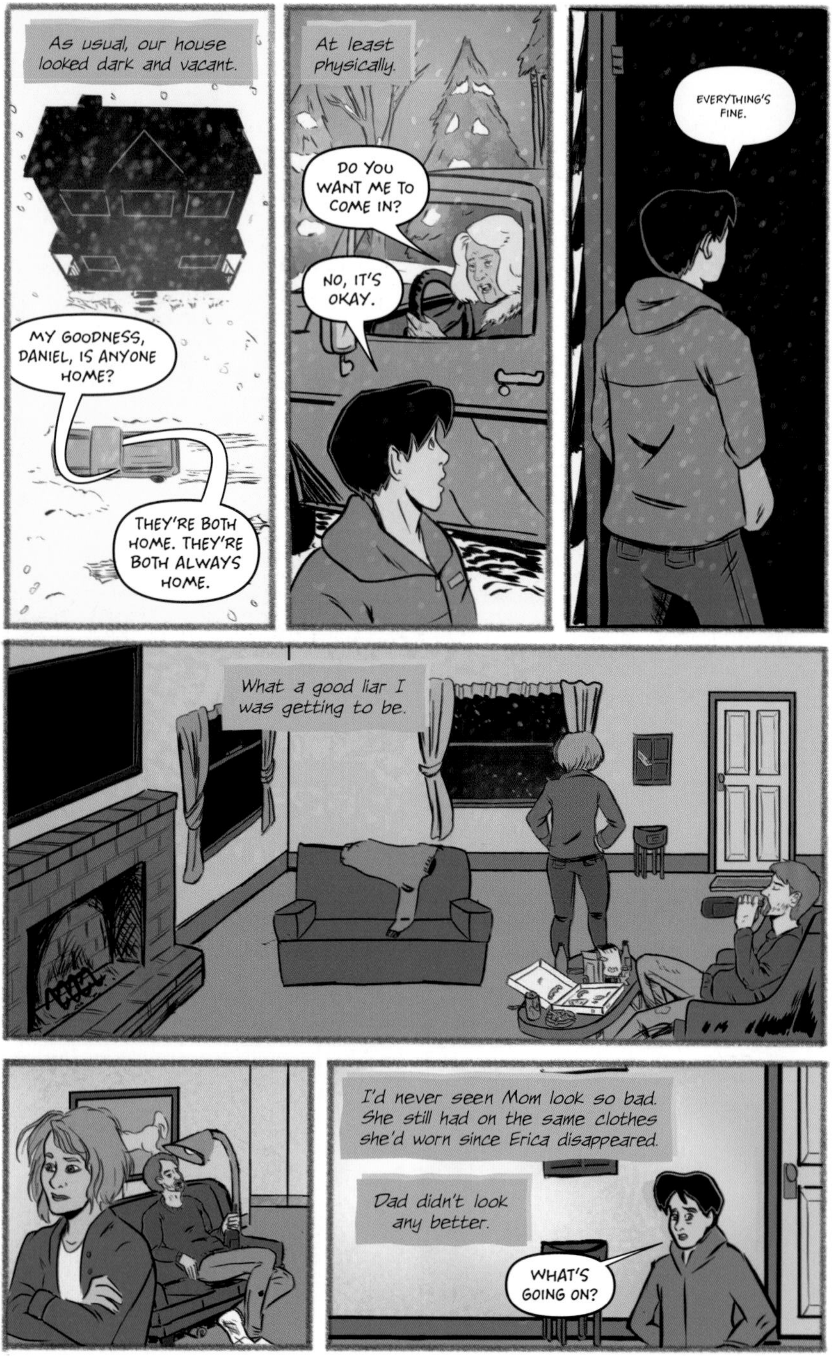
As usual, our house looked dark and vacant.
MY GOODNESS, DANIEL, IS ANYONE HOME?
THEY'RE BOTH HOME. THEY'RE BOTH ALWAYS HOME.
At least physically.
DO YOU WANT ME TO COME IN?
NO, IT'S OKAY.
EVERYTHING'S FINE.
What a good liar I was getting to be.
I'd never seen Mom look so bad. She still had on the same clothes she'd worn since Erica disappeared.
Dad didn't look any better.
WHAT'S GOING ON?

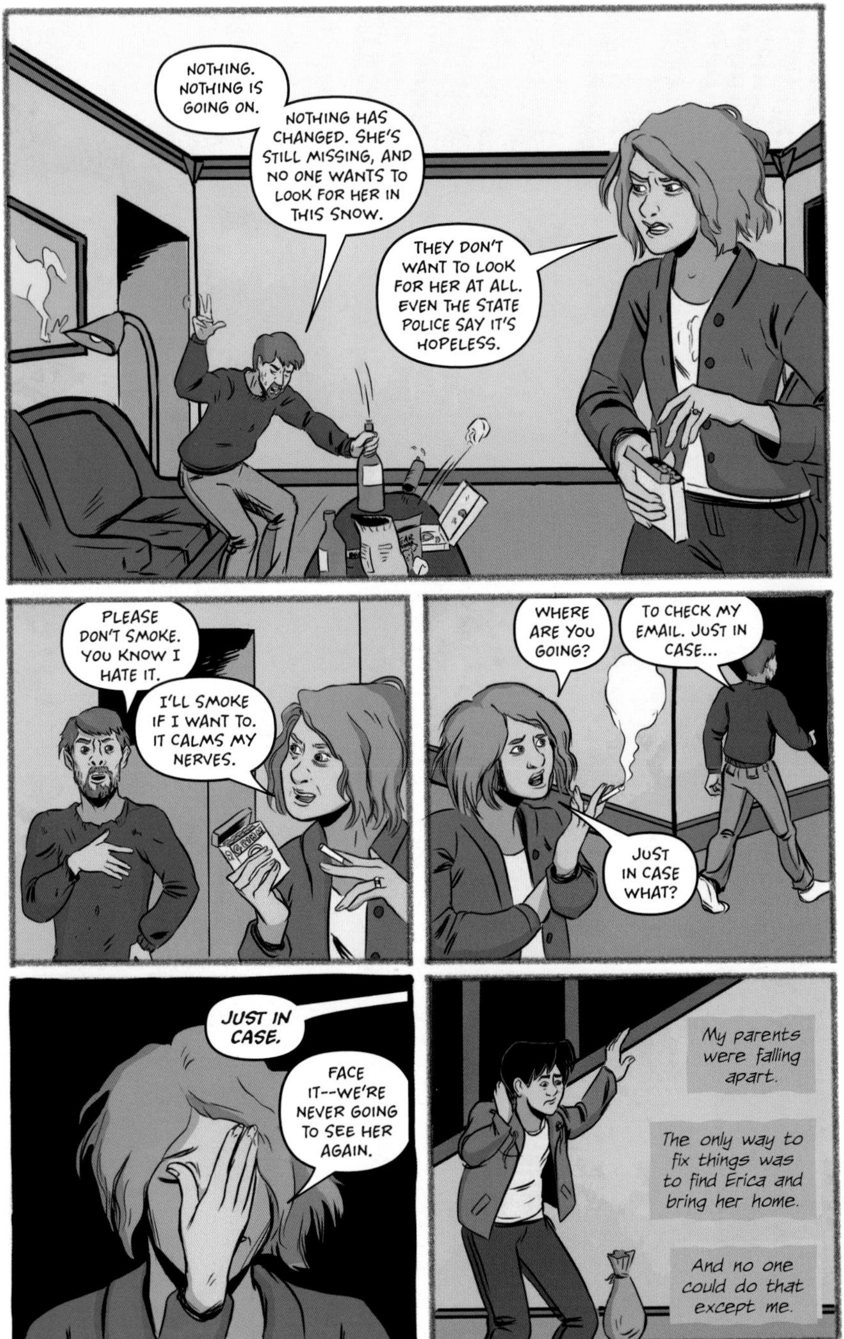
NOTHING. NOTHING IS GOING ON.
NOTHING HAS CHANGED. SHE'S STILL MISSING, AND NO ONE WANTS TO LOOK FOR HER IN THIS SNOW.
THEY DON'T WANT TO LOOK FOR HER AT ALL. EVEN THE STATE POLICE SAY IT'S HOPELESS.
PLEASE DON'T SMOKE. YOU KNOW I HATE IT.
I'LL SMOKE IF I WANT TO. IT CALMS MY NERVES.
WHERE ARE YOU GOING?
TO CHECK MY EMAIL. JUST IN CASE...
JUST IN CASE WHAT?
JUST IN CASE.
FACE IT--WE'RE NEVER GOING TO SEE HER AGAIN.
My parents were falling apart.
The only way to fix things was to find Erica and bring her home.
And no one could do that except me.

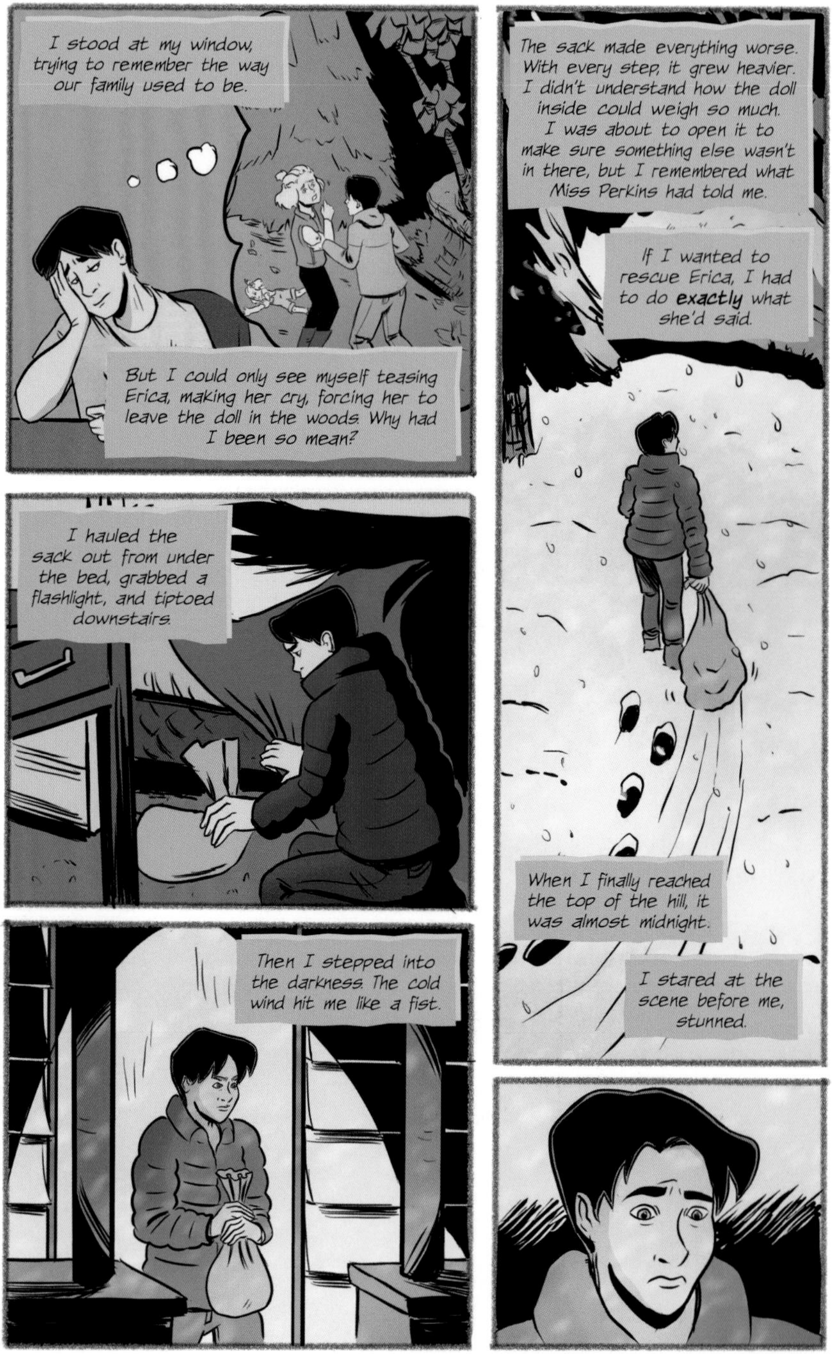
I stood at my window, trying to remember the way our family used to be.
But I could only see myself teasing Erica, making her cry, forcing her to leave the doll in the woods. Why had I been so mean?
I hauled the sack out from under the bed, grabbed a flashlight, and tiptoed downstairs.
Then I stepped into the darkness. The cold wind hit me like a fist.
The sack made everything worse. With every step, it grew heavier. I didn't understand how the doll inside could weigh so much. I was about to open it to make sure something else wasn't in there, but I remembered what Miss Perkins had told me.
If I wanted to rescue Erica, I had to do **exactly** what she'd said.
When I finally reached the top of the hill, it was almost midnight.
I stared at the scene before me, stunned.

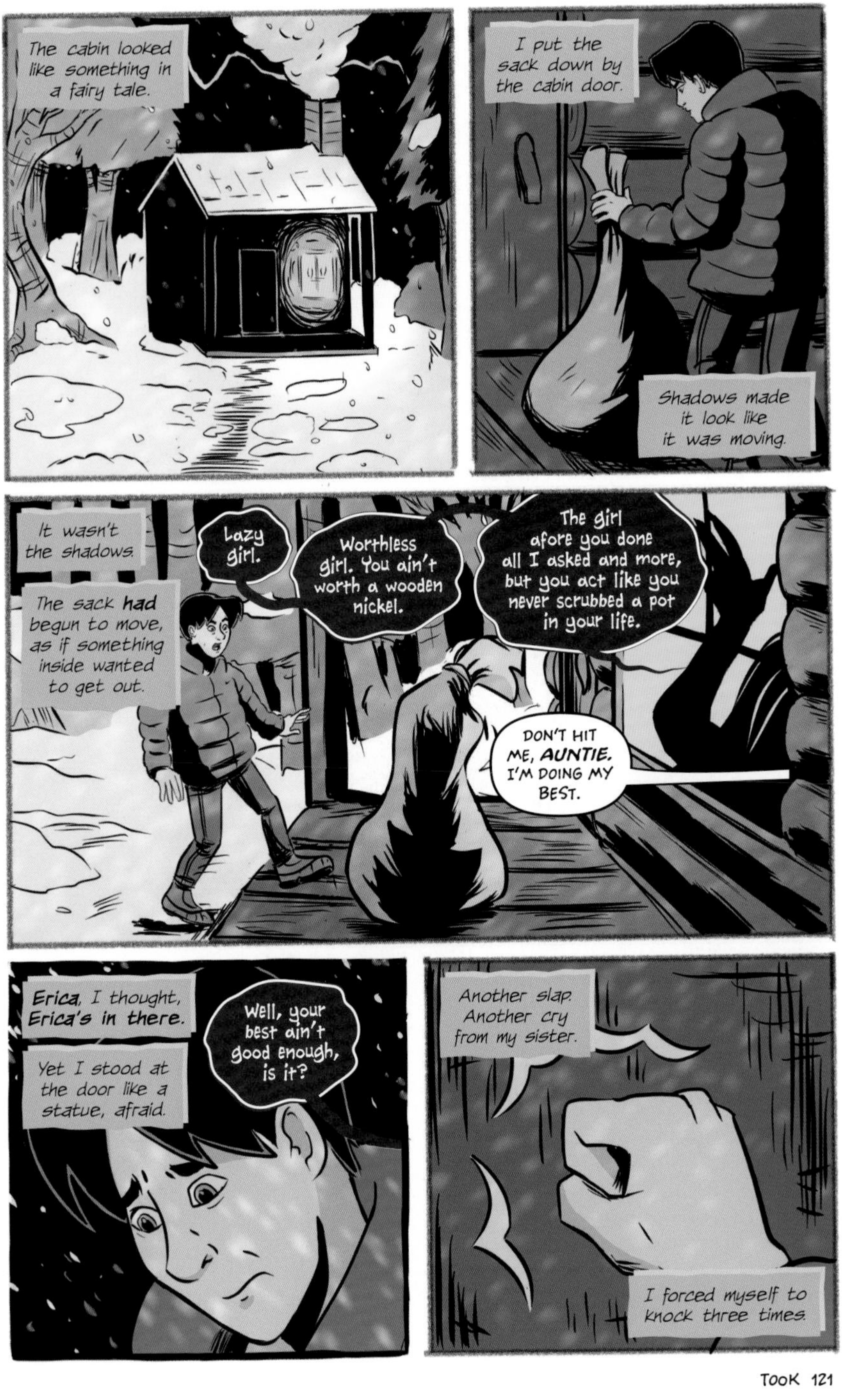

The cabin looked like something in a fairy tale.
I put the sack down by the cabin door.
Shadows made it look like it was moving.
It wasn't the shadows.
The sack **had** begun to move, as if something inside wanted to get out.
Lazy girl.
Worthless girl. You ain't worth a wooden nickel.
The girl afore you done all I asked and more, but you act like you never scrubbed a pot in your life.
DON'T HIT ME, **AUNTIE.** I'M DOING MY BEST.
Erica, I thought, **Erica's in there.**
Yet I stood at the door like a statue, afraid.
Well, your best ain't good enough, is it?
Another slap. Another cry from my sister.
I forced myself to knock three times.

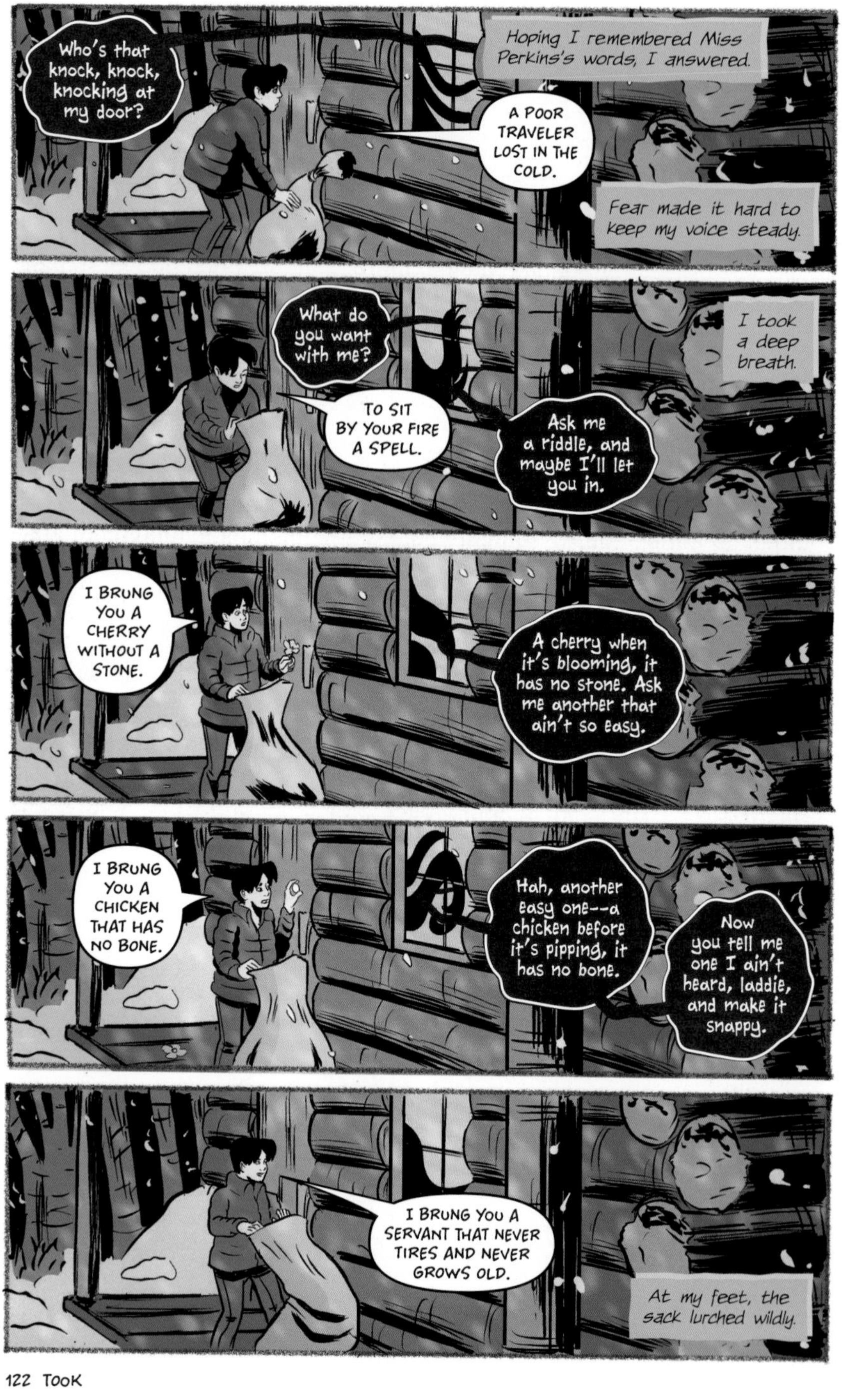
Hoping I remembered Miss Perkins's words, I answered.
Who's that knock, knock, knocking at my door?
A POOR TRAVELER LOST IN THE COLD.
Fear made it hard to keep my voice steady.
What do you want with me?
TO SIT BY YOUR FIRE A SPELL.
I took a deep breath.
Ask me a riddle, and maybe I'll let you in.
I BRUNG YOU A CHERRY WITHOUT A STONE.
A cherry when it's blooming, it has no stone. Ask me another that ain't so easy.
I BRUNG YOU A CHICKEN THAT HAS NO BONE.
Hah, another easy one--a chicken before it's pipping, it has no bone.
Now you tell me one I ain't heard, laddie, and make it snappy.
I BRUNG YOU A SERVANT THAT NEVER TIRES AND NEVER GROWS OLD.
At my feet, the sack lurched wildly.

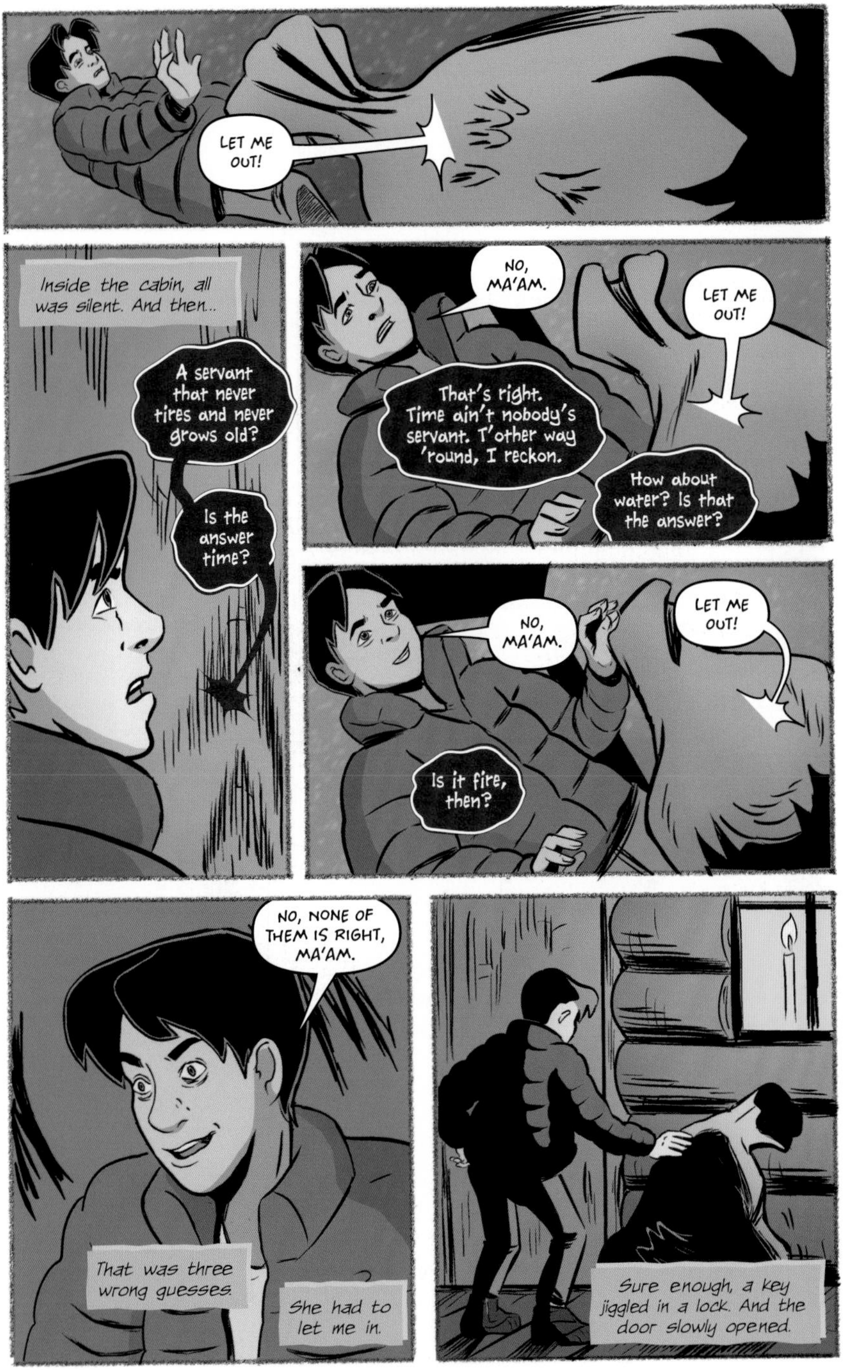
LET ME OUT!
Inside the cabin, all was silent. And then...
A servant that never tires and never grows old?
Is the answer time?
NO, MA'AM.
LET ME OUT!
That's right. Time ain't nobody's servant. T'other way 'round, I reckon.
How about water? Is that the answer?
NO, MA'AM.
LET ME OUT!
Is it fire, then?
NO, NONE OF THEM IS RIGHT, MA'AM.
That was three wrong guesses.
She had to let me in.
Sure enough, a key jiggled in a lock. And the door slowly opened.

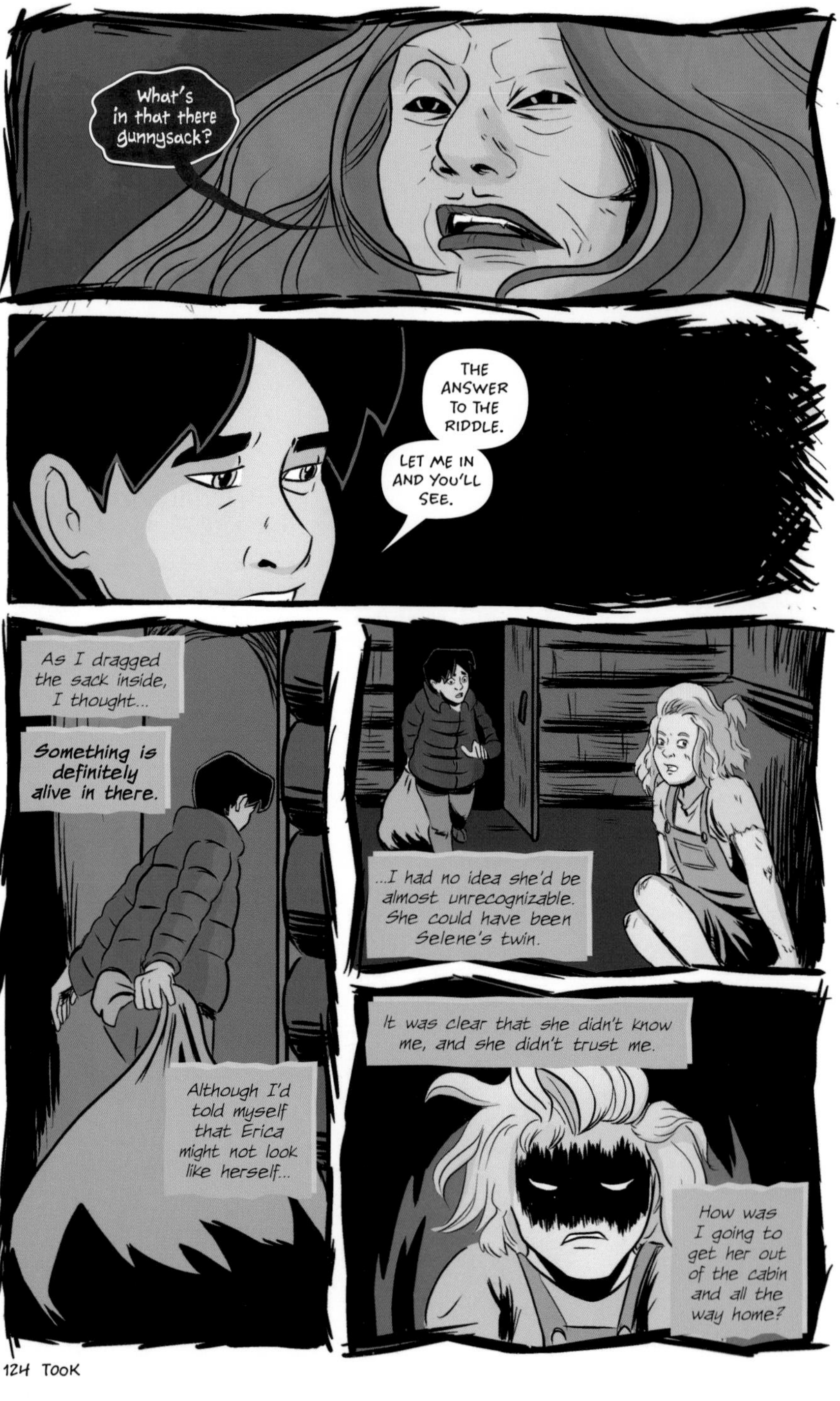
What's in that there gunnysack?
THE ANSWER TO THE RIDDLE.
LET ME IN AND YOU'LL SEE.
As I dragged the sack inside, I thought...
Something is definitely alive in there.
Although I'd told myself that Erica might not look like herself...
...I had no idea she'd be almost unrecognizable. She could have been Selene's twin.
It was clear that she didn't know me, and she didn't trust me.
How was I going to get her out of the cabin and all the way home?

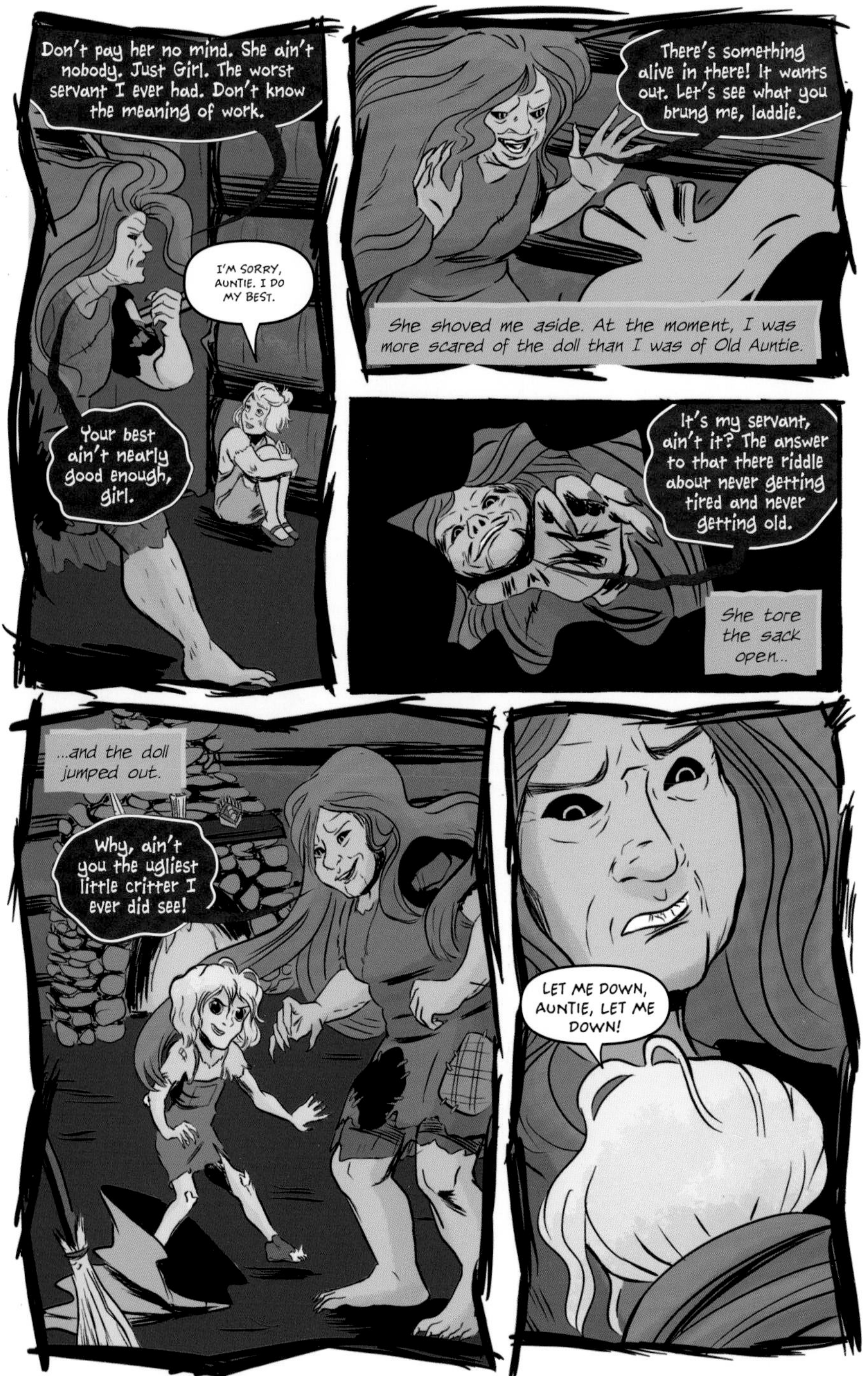
Don't pay her no mind. She ain't nobody. Just Girl. The worst servant I ever had. Don't know the meaning of work.
I'M SORRY, AUNTIE. I DO MY BEST.
Your best ain't nearly good enough, girl.
There's something alive in there! It wants out. Let's see what you brung me, laddie.
She shoved me aside. At the moment, I was more scared of the doll than I was of Old Auntie.
It's my servant, ain't it? The answer to that there riddle about never getting tired and never getting old.
She tore the sack open...
...and the doll jumped out.
Why, ain't you the ugliest little critter I ever did see!
LET ME DOWN, AUNTIE, LET ME DOWN!

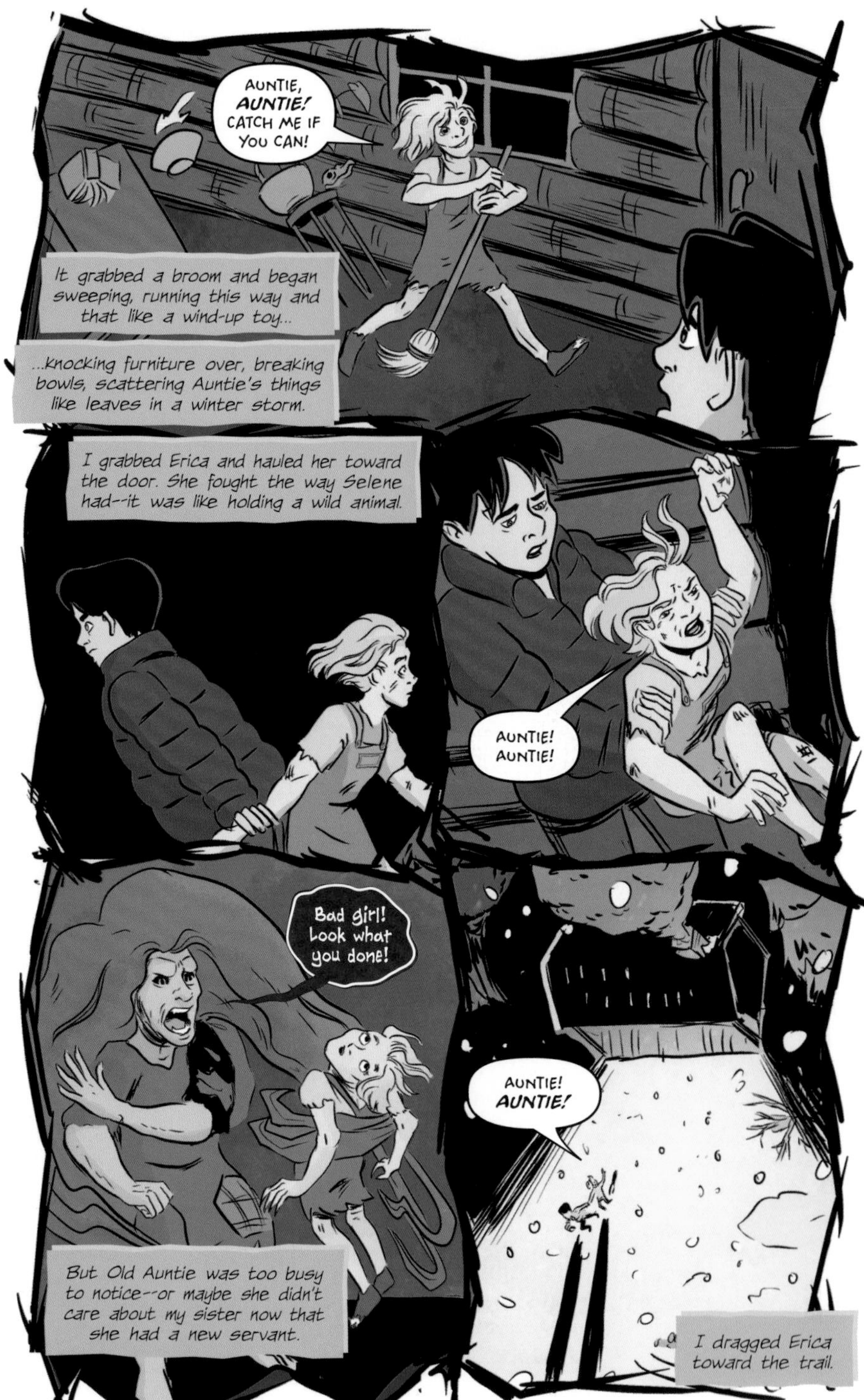
AUNTIE, AUNTIE! CATCH ME IF YOU CAN!
It grabbed a broom and began sweeping, running this way and that like a wind-up toy...
...knocking furniture over, breaking bowls, scattering Auntie's things like leaves in a winter storm.
I grabbed Erica and hauled her toward the door. She fought the way Selene had--it was like holding a wild animal.
AUNTIE! AUNTIE!
Bad girl! Look what you done!
But Old Auntie was too busy to notice--or maybe she didn't care about my sister now that she had a new servant.
AUNTIE! AUNTIE!
I dragged Erica toward the trail.

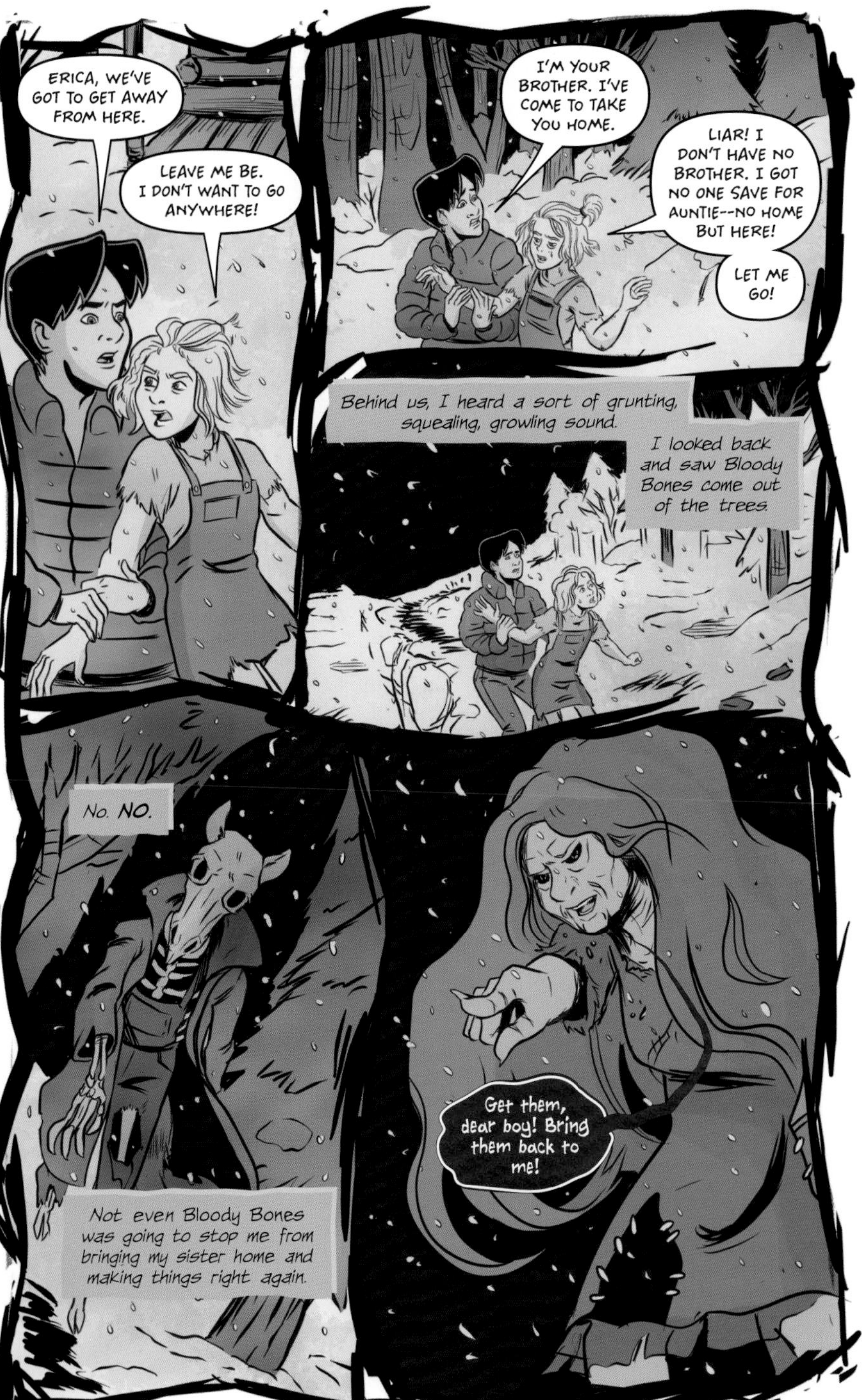
ERICA, WE'VE GOT TO GET AWAY FROM HERE.
LEAVE ME BE. I DON'T WANT TO GO ANYWHERE!
I'M YOUR BROTHER. I'VE COME TO TAKE YOU HOME.
LIAR! I DON'T HAVE NO BROTHER. I GOT NO ONE SAVE FOR AUNTIE--NO HOME BUT HERE!
LET ME GO!
Behind us, I heard a sort of grunting, squealing, growling sound.
I looked back and saw Bloody Bones come out of the trees.
No. NO.
Not even Bloody Bones was going to stop me from bringing my sister home and making things right again.
Get them, dear boy! Bring them back to me!

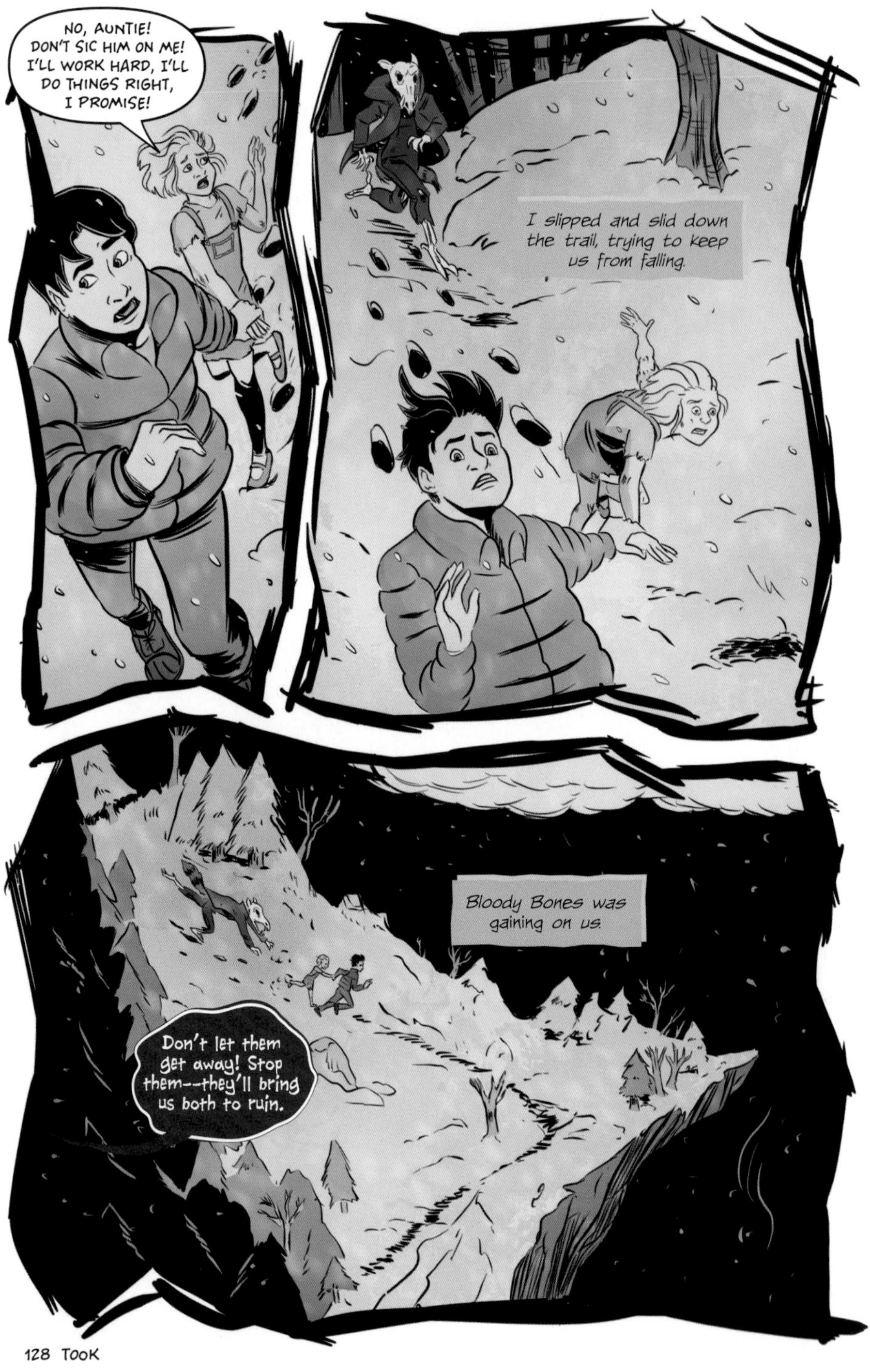
NO, AUNTIE! DON'T SIC HIM ON ME! I'LL WORK HARD, I'LL DO THINGS RIGHT, I PROMISE!
I slipped and slid down the trail, trying to keep us from falling.
Bloody Bones was gaining on us.
Don't let them get away! Stop them--they'll bring us both to ruin.

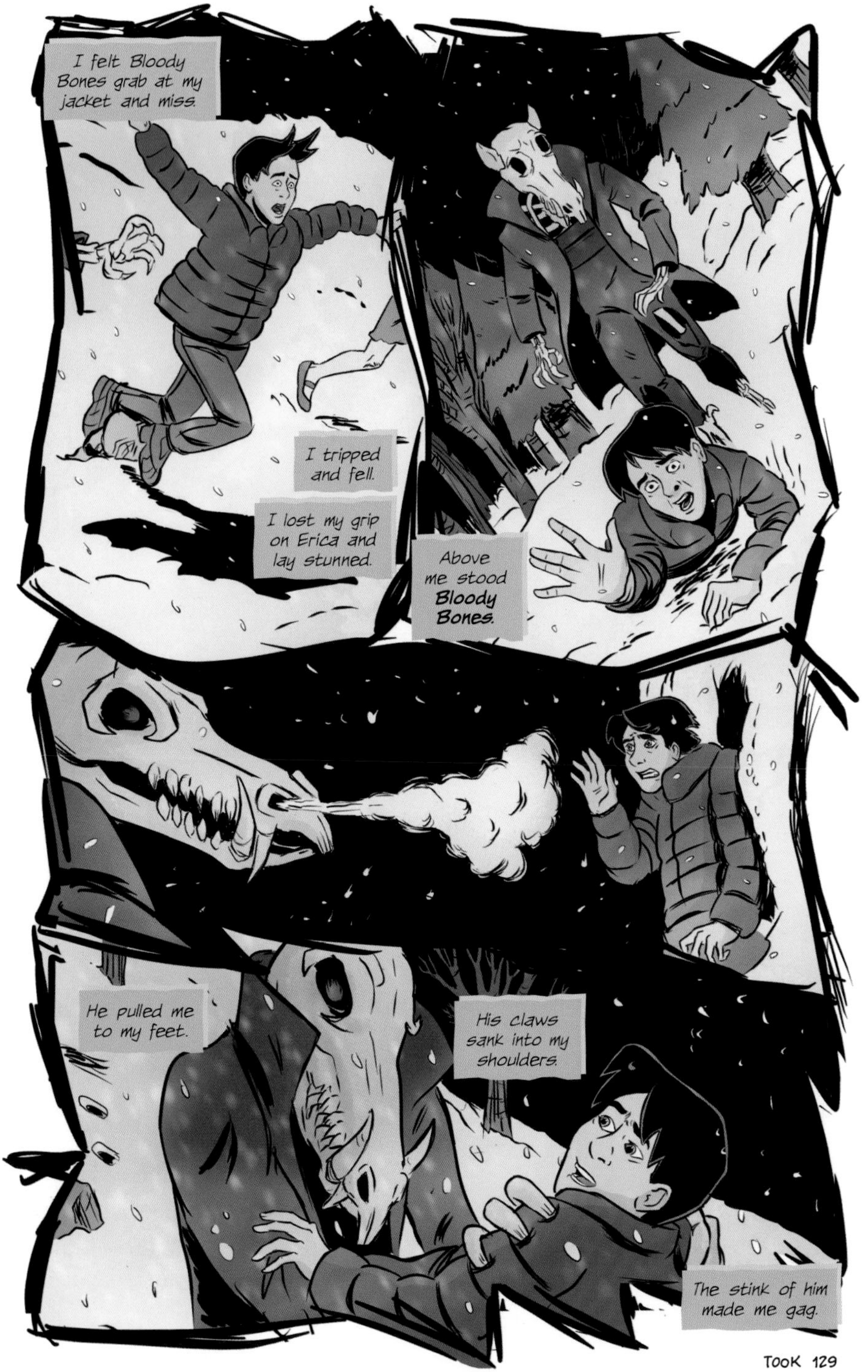
I felt Bloody Bones grab at my jacket and miss.
I tripped and fell.
I lost my grip on Erica and lay stunned.
Above me stood **Bloody Bones.**
He pulled me to my feet.
His claws sank into my shoulders.
The stink of him made me gag.

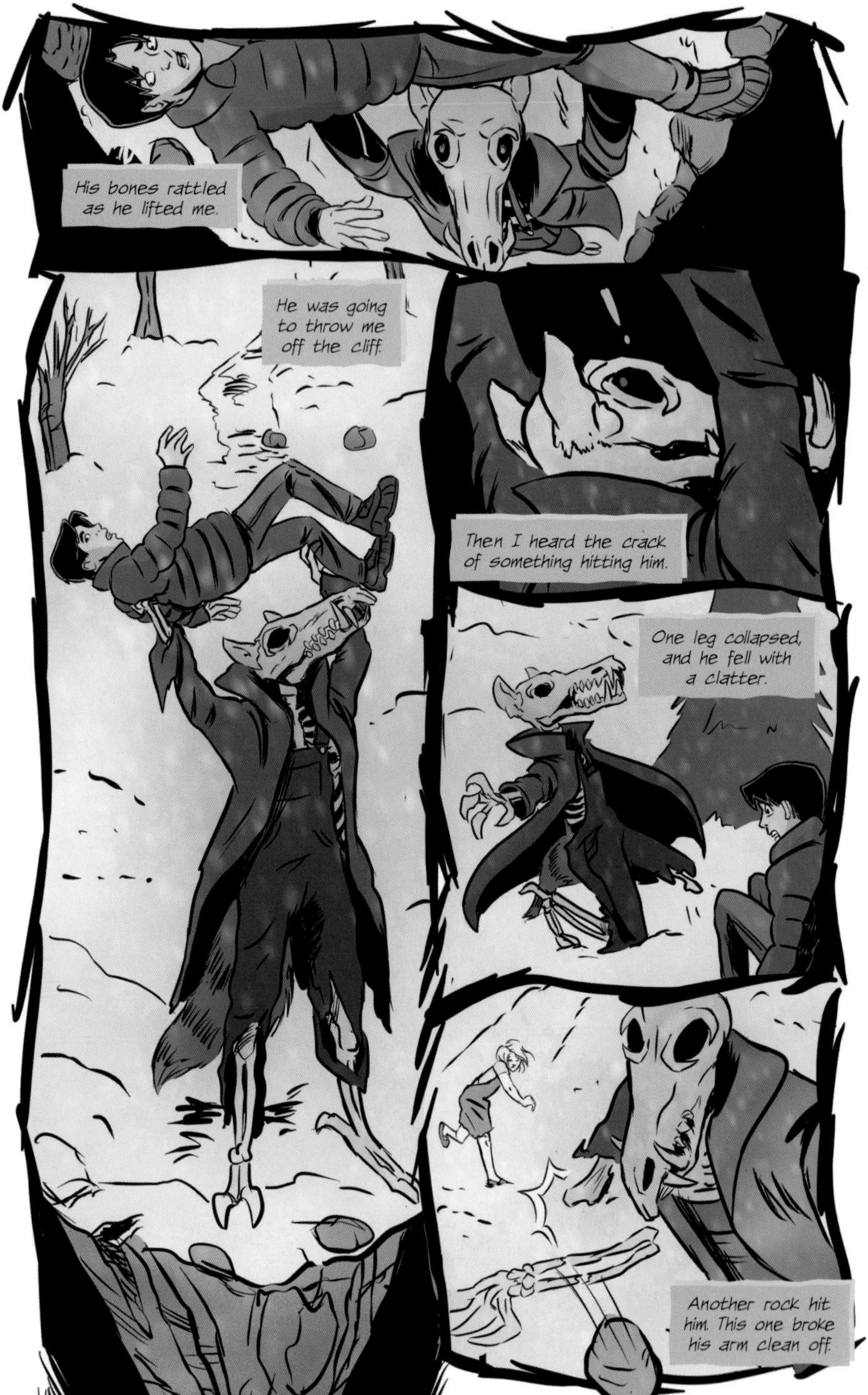
His bones rattled as he lifted me.
He was going to throw me off the cliff.
Then I heard the crack of something hitting him.
One leg collapsed, and he fell with a clatter.
Another rock hit him. This one broke his arm clean off.

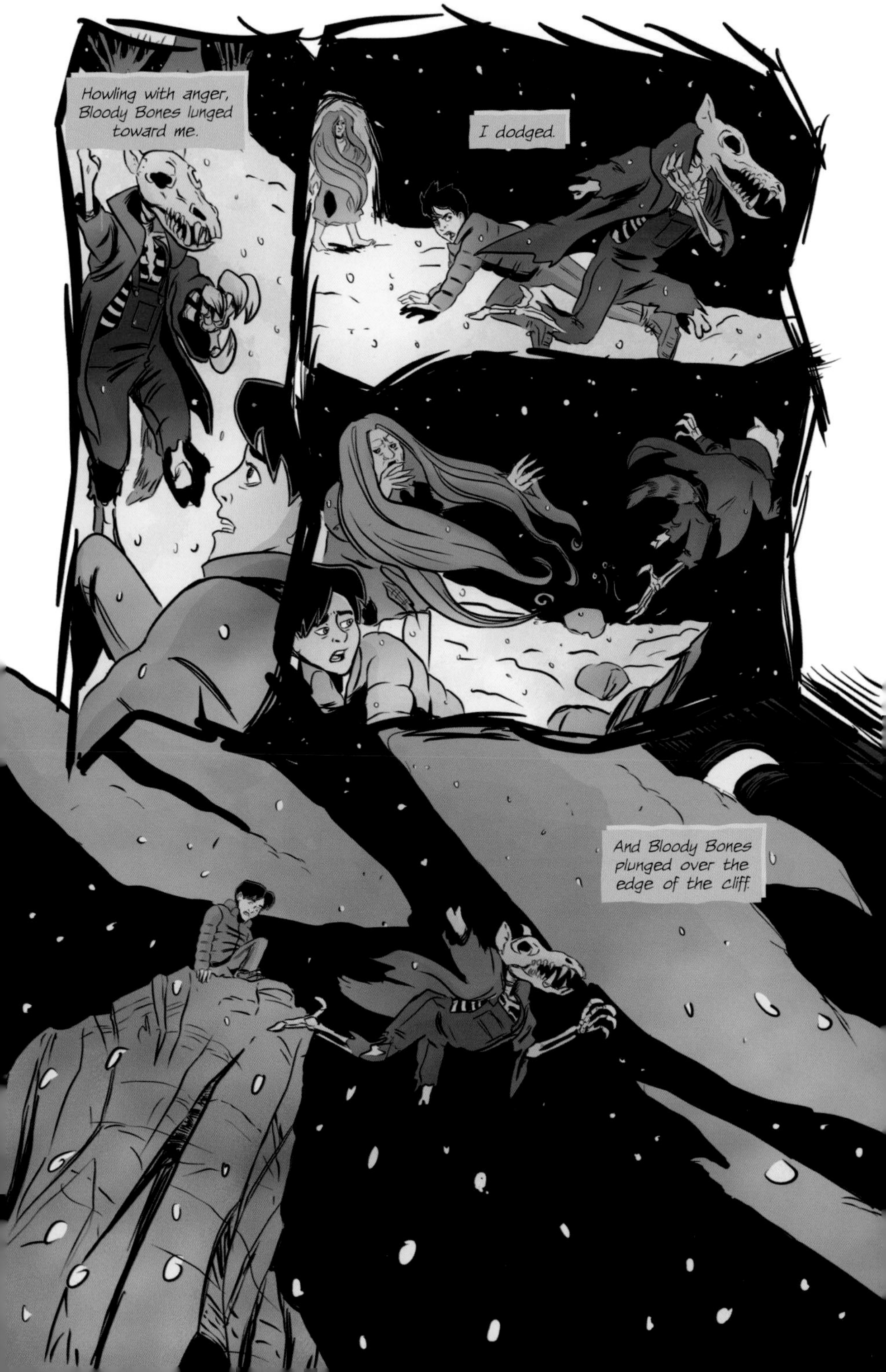

Howling with anger, Bloody Bones lunged toward me.
I dodged.
And Bloody Bones plunged over the edge of the cliff.

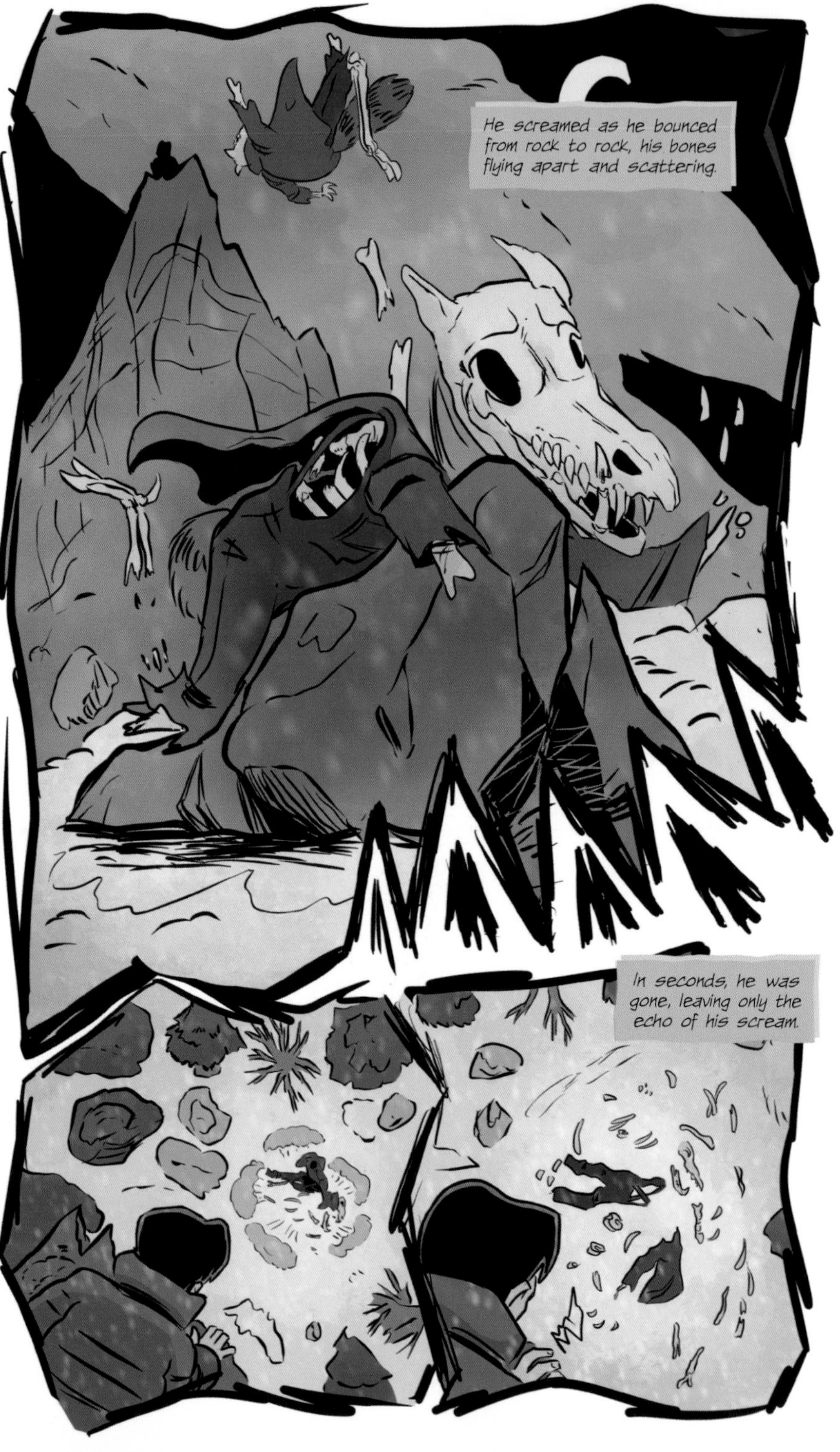
He screamed as he bounced from rock to rock, his bones flying apart and scattering.
In seconds, he was gone, leaving only the echo of his scream.

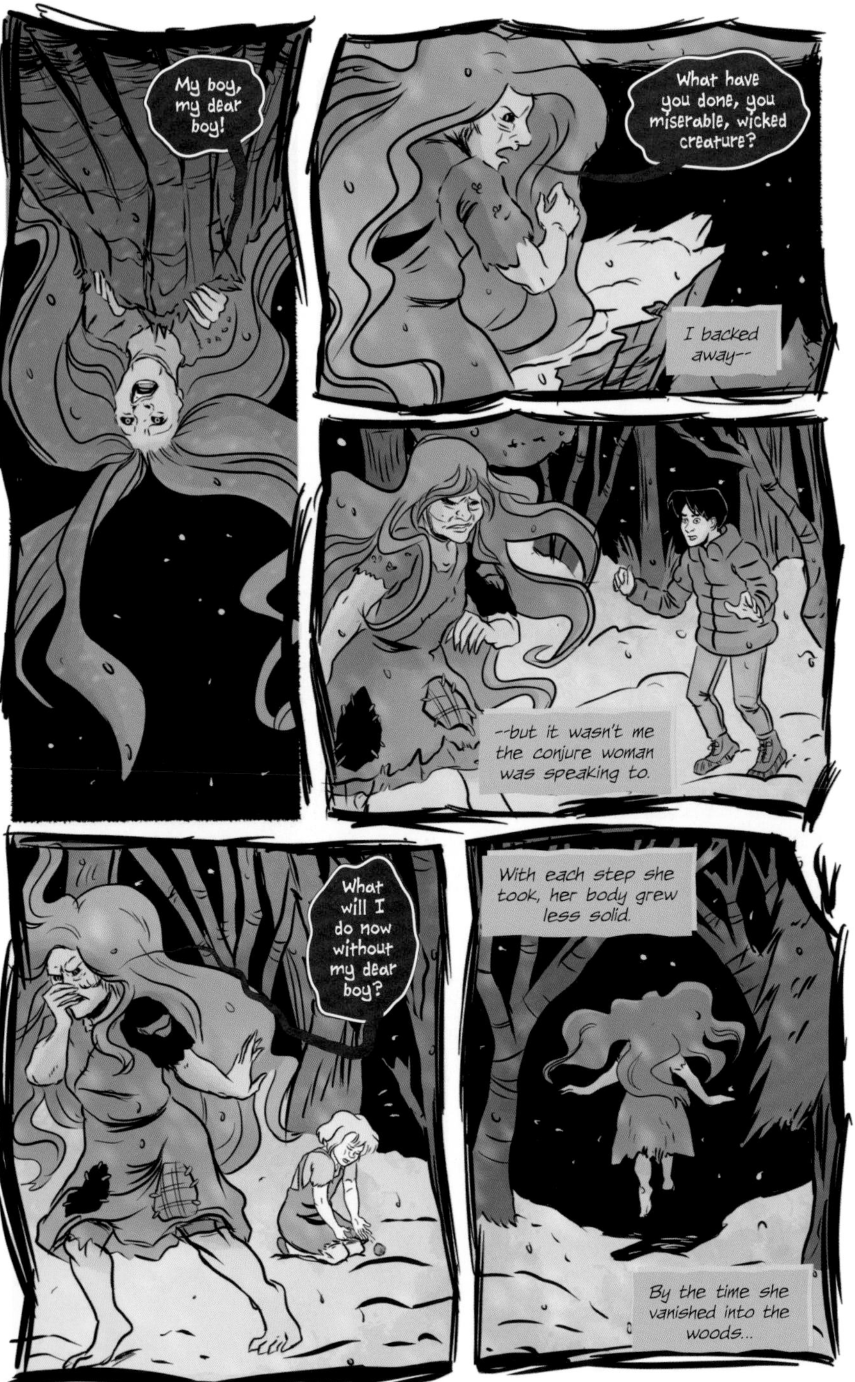
My boy, my dear boy!
What have you done, you miserable, wicked creature?
I backed away--
--but it wasn't me the conjure woman was speaking to.
What will I do now without my dear boy?
With each step she took, her body grew less solid.
By the time she vanished into the woods...

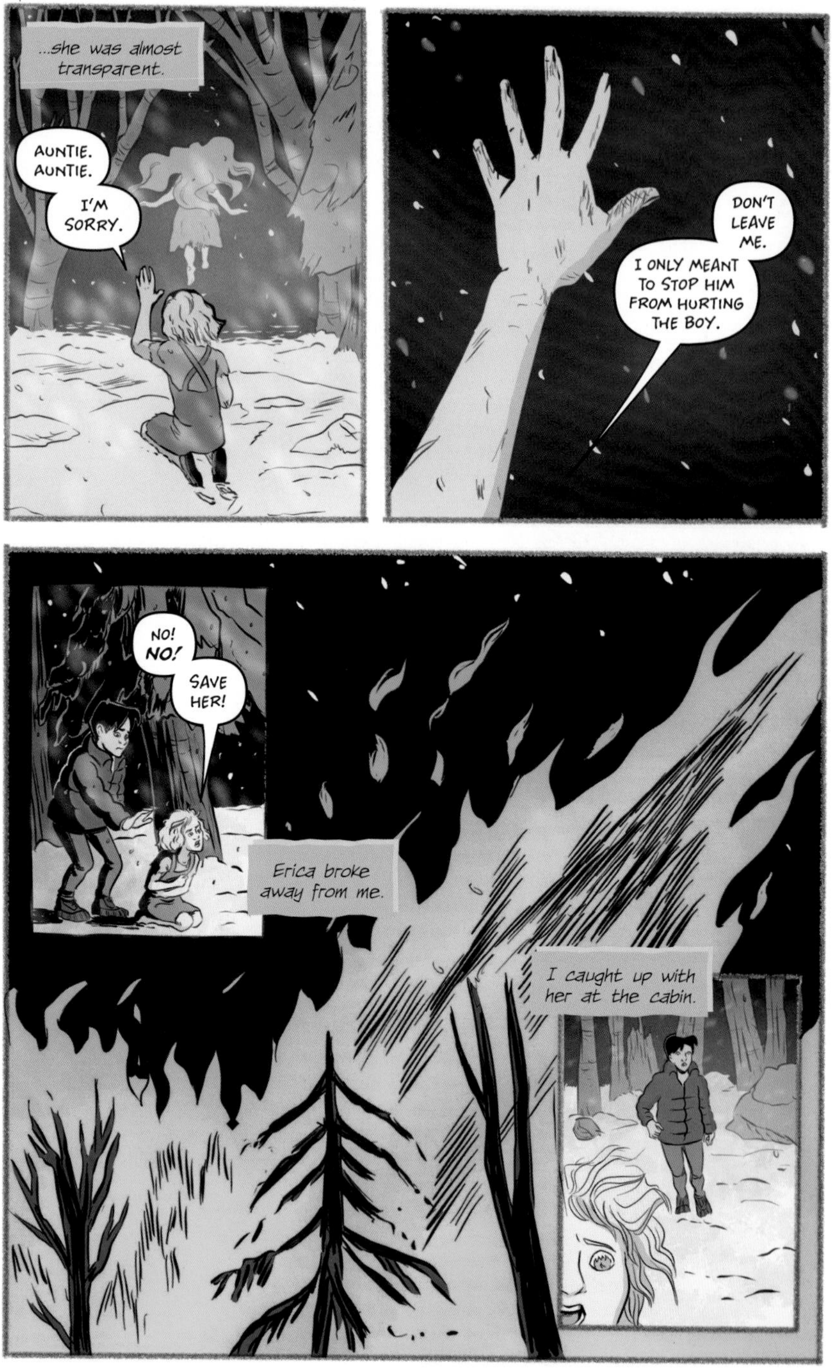

...she was almost transparent.
AUNTIE. AUNTIE.
I'M SORRY.
DON'T LEAVE ME.
I ONLY MEANT TO STOP HIM FROM HURTING THE BOY.
NO! **NO!**
SAVE HER!
Erica broke away from me.
I caught up with her at the cabin.

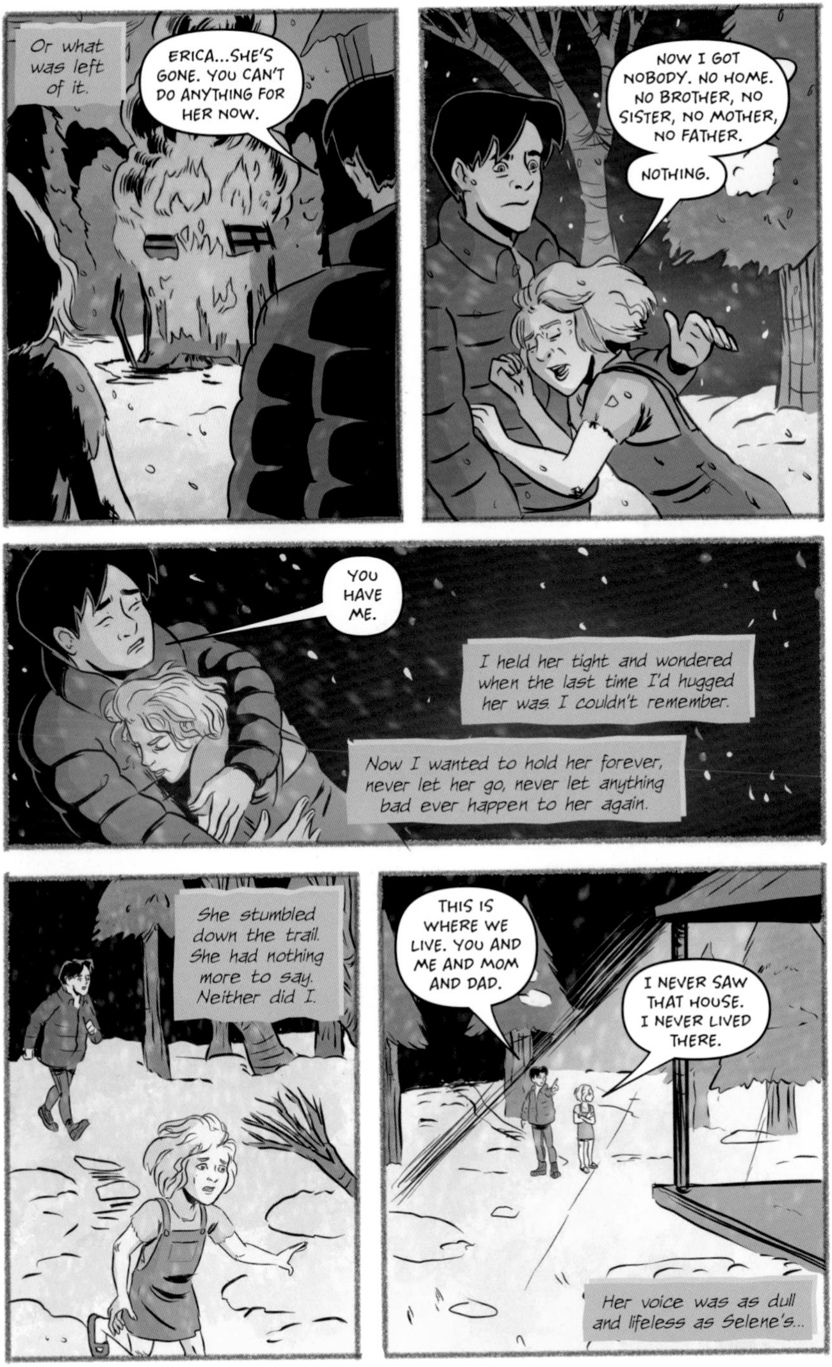

Or what was left of it.
ERICA...SHE'S GONE. YOU CAN'T DO ANYTHING FOR HER NOW.
NOW I GOT NOBODY. NO HOME. NO BROTHER, NO SISTER, NO MOTHER, NO FATHER.
NOTHING.
YOU HAVE ME.
I held her tight and wondered when the last time I'd hugged her was. I couldn't remember.
Now I wanted to hold her forever, never let her go, never let anything bad ever happen to her again.
She stumbled down the trail. She had nothing more to say. Neither did I.
THIS IS WHERE WE LIVE. YOU AND ME AND MOM AND DAD.
I NEVER SAW THAT HOUSE. I NEVER LIVED THERE.
Her voice was as dull and lifeless as Selene's...

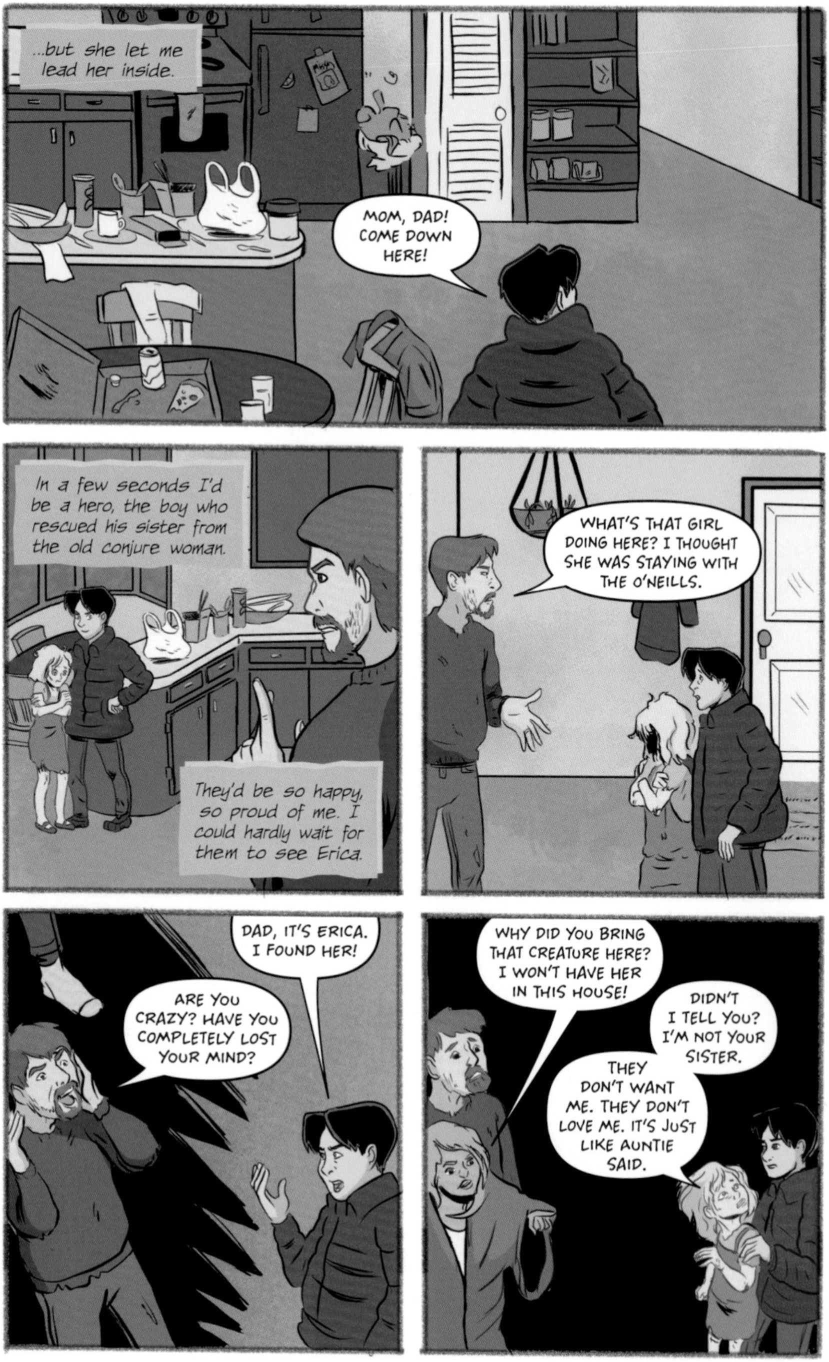
...but she let me lead her inside.
MOM, DAD! COME DOWN HERE!
In a few seconds I'd be a hero, the boy who rescued his sister from the old conjure woman.
They'd be so happy, so proud of me. I could hardly wait for them to see Erica.
WHAT'S THAT GIRL DOING HERE? I THOUGHT SHE WAS STAYING WITH THE O'NEILLS.
DAD, IT'S ERICA. I FOUND HER!
ARE YOU CRAZY? HAVE YOU COMPLETELY LOST YOUR MIND?
WHY DID YOU BRING THAT CREATURE HERE? I WON'T HAVE HER IN THIS HOUSE!
DIDN'T I TELL YOU? I'M NOT YOUR SISTER.
THEY DON'T WANT ME. THEY DON'T LOVE ME. IT'S JUST LIKE AUNTIE SAID.

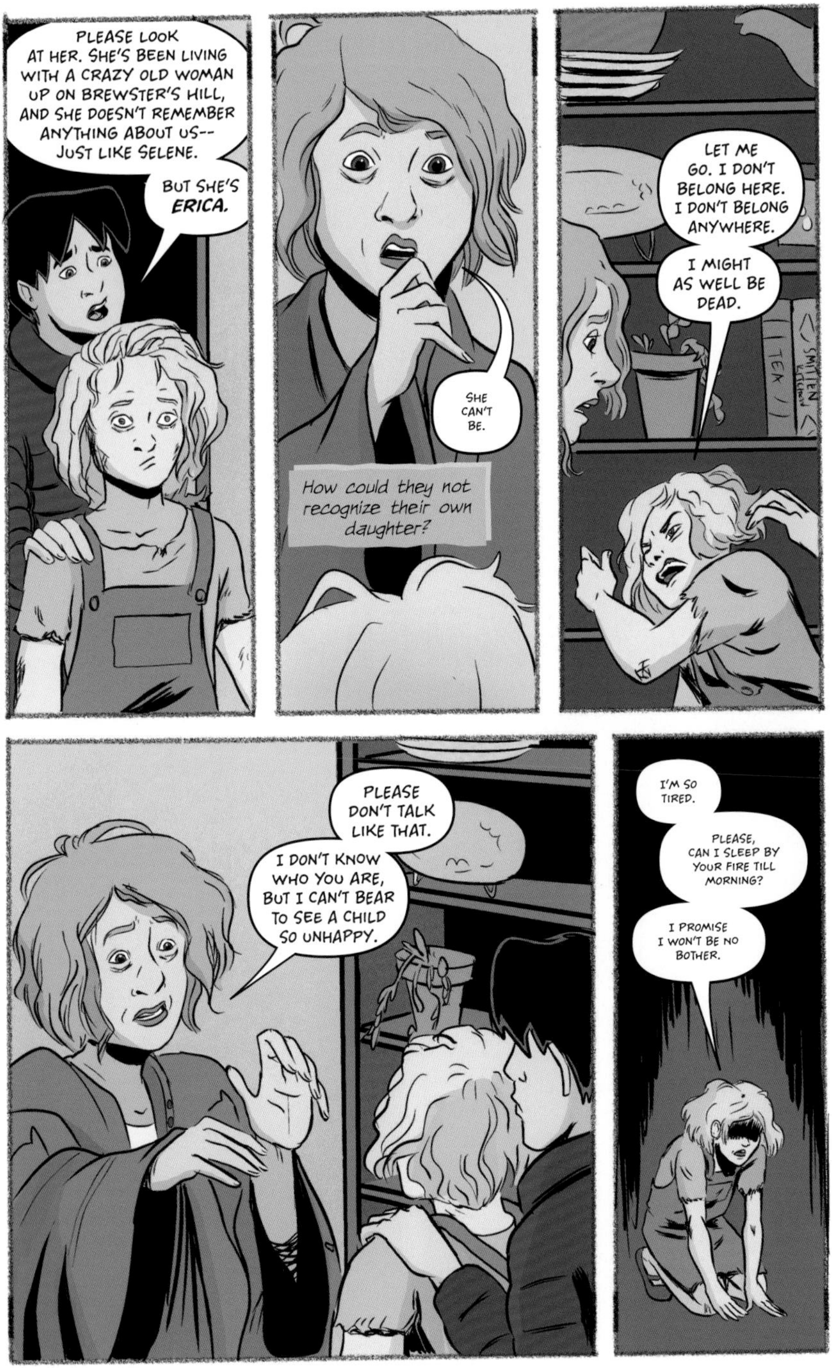
PLEASE LOOK AT HER. SHE'S BEEN LIVING WITH A CRAZY OLD WOMAN UP ON BREWSTER'S HILL, AND SHE DOESN'T REMEMBER ANYTHING ABOUT US-- JUST LIKE SELENE.
BUT SHE'S *ERICA.*
SHE CAN'T BE.
How could they not recognize their own daughter?
LET ME GO. I DON'T BELONG HERE. I DON'T BELONG ANYWHERE.
I MIGHT AS WELL BE DEAD.
PLEASE DON'T TALK LIKE THAT.
I DON'T KNOW WHO YOU ARE, BUT I CAN'T BEAR TO SEE A CHILD SO UNHAPPY.
I'M SO TIRED.
PLEASE, CAN I SLEEP BY YOUR FIRE TILL MORNING?
I PROMISE I WON'T BE NO BOTHER.

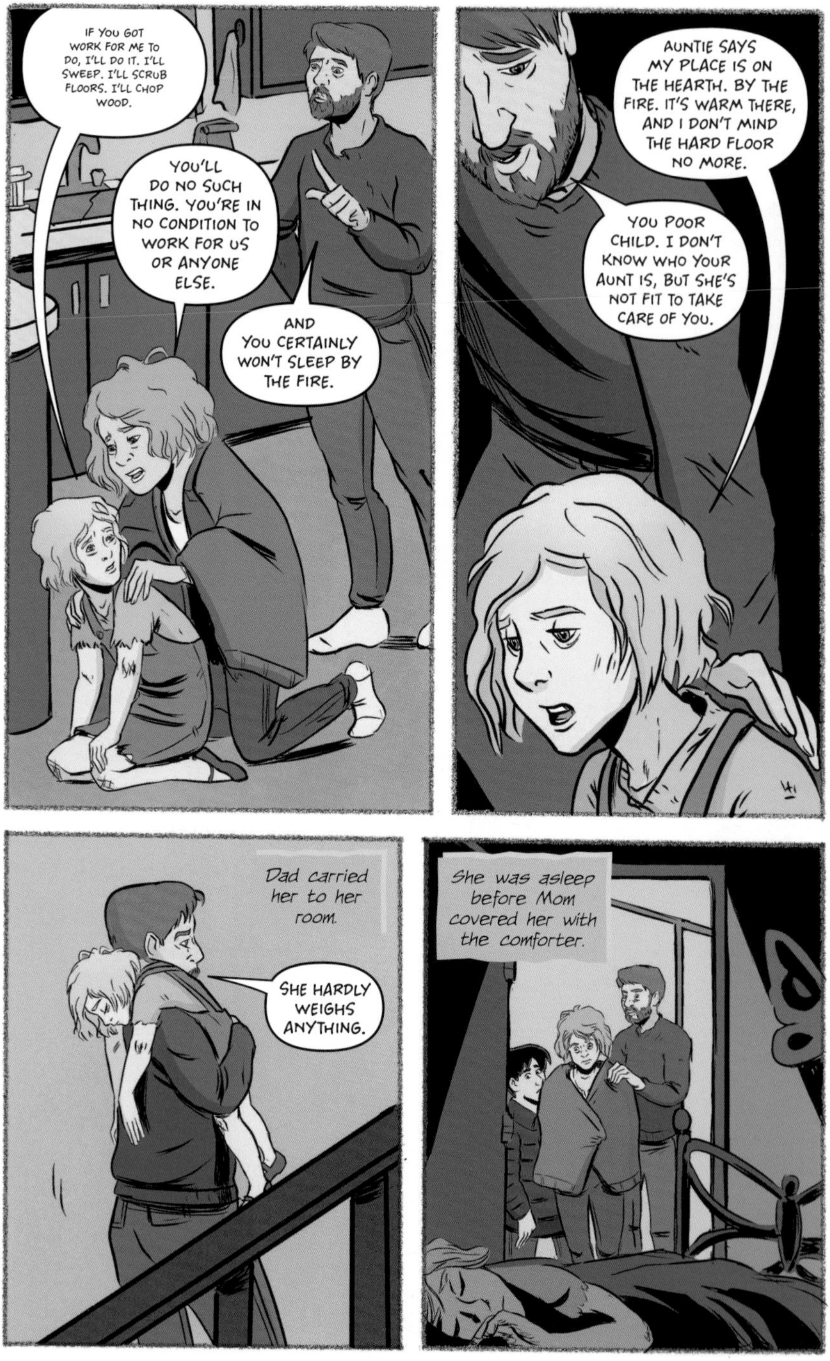
IF YOU GOT WORK FOR ME TO DO, I'LL DO IT. I'LL SWEEP. I'LL SCRUB FLOORS. I'LL CHOP WOOD.
YOU'LL DO NO SUCH THING. YOU'RE IN NO CONDITION TO WORK FOR US OR ANYONE ELSE.
AND YOU CERTAINLY WON'T SLEEP BY THE FIRE.
AUNTIE SAYS MY PLACE IS ON THE HEARTH. BY THE FIRE. IT'S WARM THERE, AND I DON'T MIND THE HARD FLOOR NO MORE.
YOU POOR CHILD. I DON'T KNOW WHO YOUR AUNT IS, BUT SHE'S NOT FIT TO TAKE CARE OF YOU.
Dad carried her to her room.
SHE HARDLY WEIGHS ANYTHING.
She was asleep before Mom covered her with the comforter.

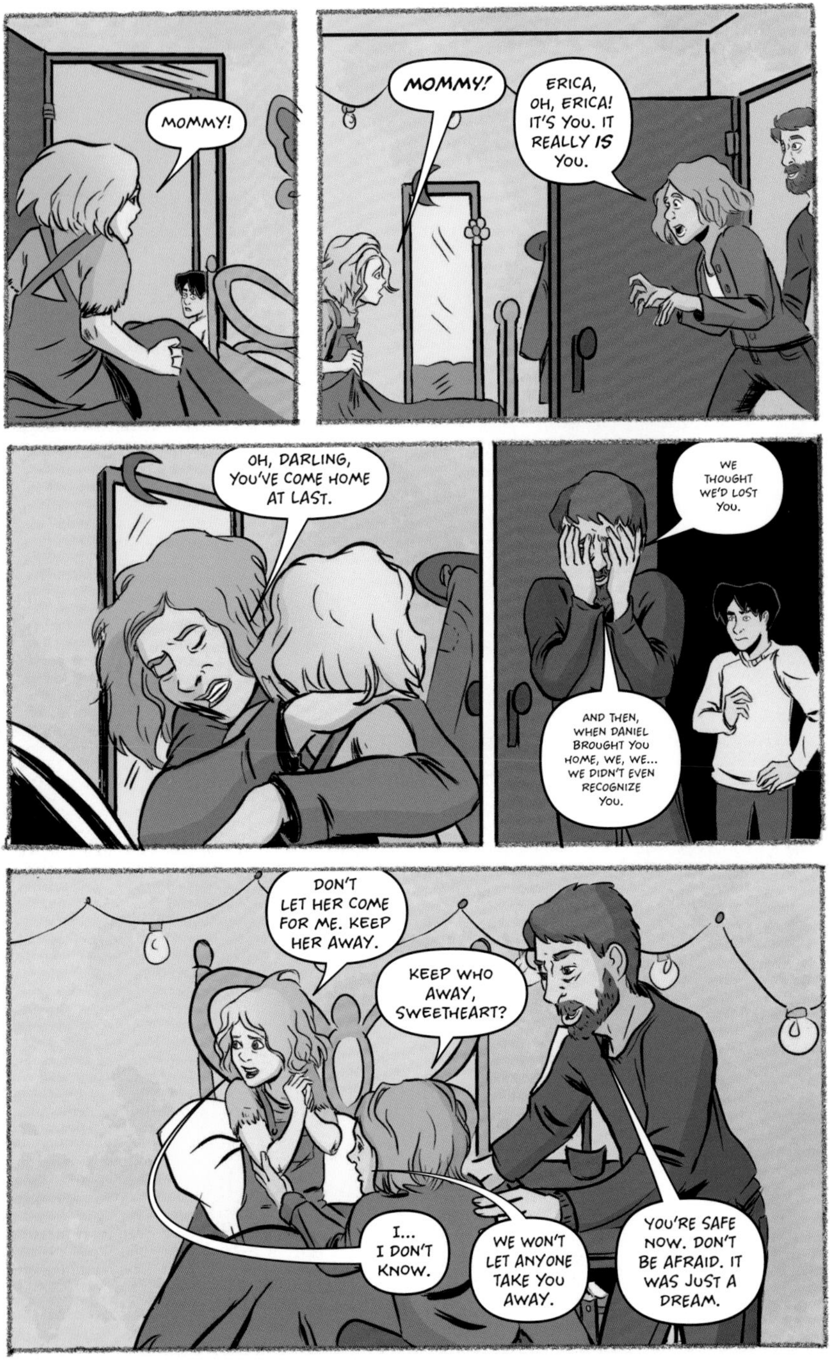
MOMMY!
MOMMY!
ERICA, OH, ERICA! IT'S YOU. IT REALLY IS YOU.
OH, DARLING, YOU'VE COME HOME AT LAST.
WE THOUGHT WE'D LOST YOU.
AND THEN, WHEN DANIEL BROUGHT YOU HOME, WE, WE... WE DIDN'T EVEN RECOGNIZE YOU.
DON'T LET HER COME FOR ME. KEEP HER AWAY.
KEEP WHO AWAY, SWEETHEART?
I... I DON'T KNOW.
WE WON'T LET ANYONE TAKE YOU AWAY.
YOU'RE SAFE NOW. DON'T BE AFRAID. IT WAS JUST A DREAM.

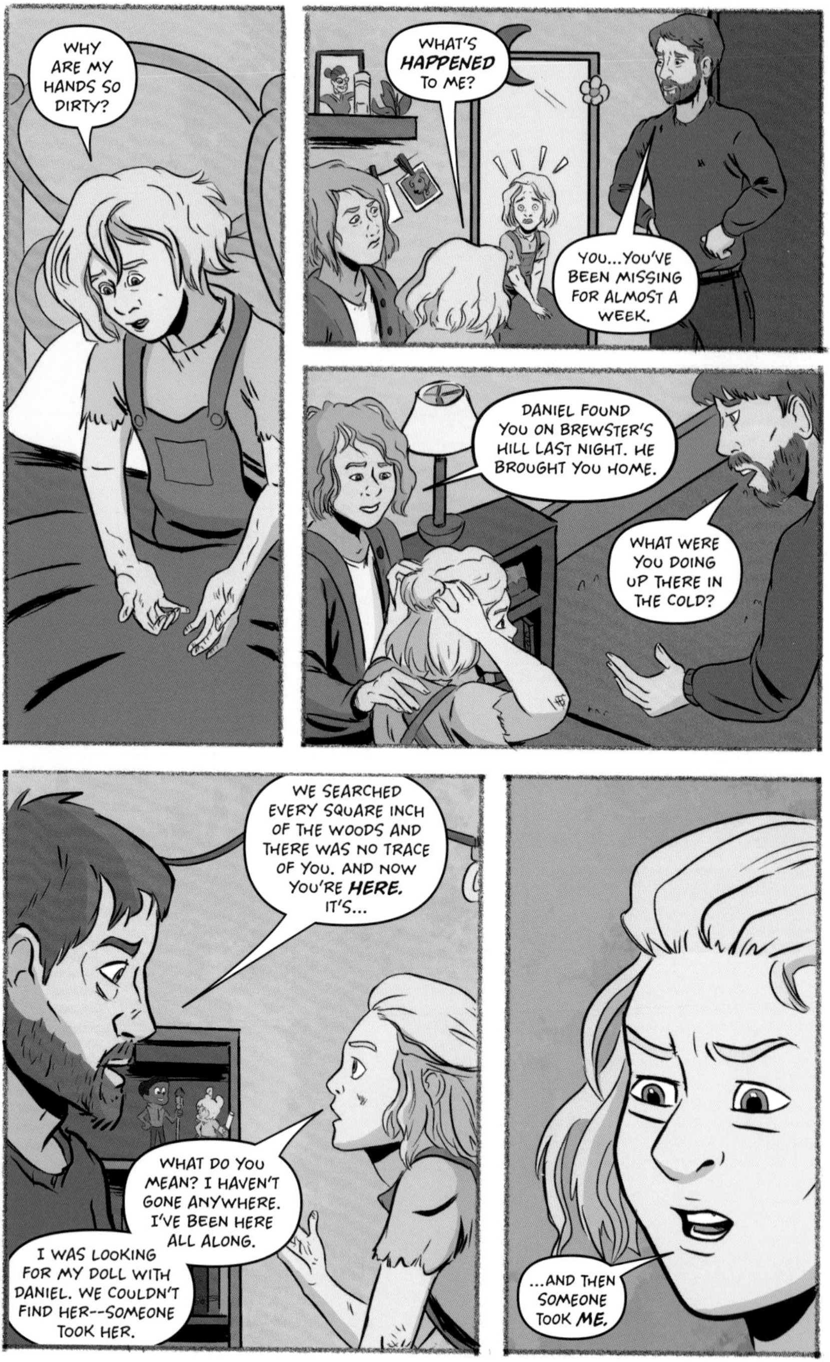
WHY ARE MY HANDS SO DIRTY?
WHAT'S *HAPPENED* TO ME?
YOU...YOU'VE BEEN MISSING FOR ALMOST A WEEK.
DANIEL FOUND YOU ON BREWSTER'S HILL LAST NIGHT. HE BROUGHT YOU HOME.
WHAT WERE YOU DOING UP THERE IN THE COLD?
WE SEARCHED EVERY SQUARE INCH OF THE WOODS AND THERE WAS NO TRACE OF YOU. AND NOW YOU'RE *HERE.* IT'S...
WHAT DO YOU MEAN? I HAVEN'T GONE ANYWHERE. I'VE BEEN HERE ALL ALONG.
I WAS LOOKING FOR MY DOLL WITH DANIEL. WE COULDN'T FIND HER--SOMEONE TOOK HER.
...AND THEN SOMEONE TOOK *ME.*

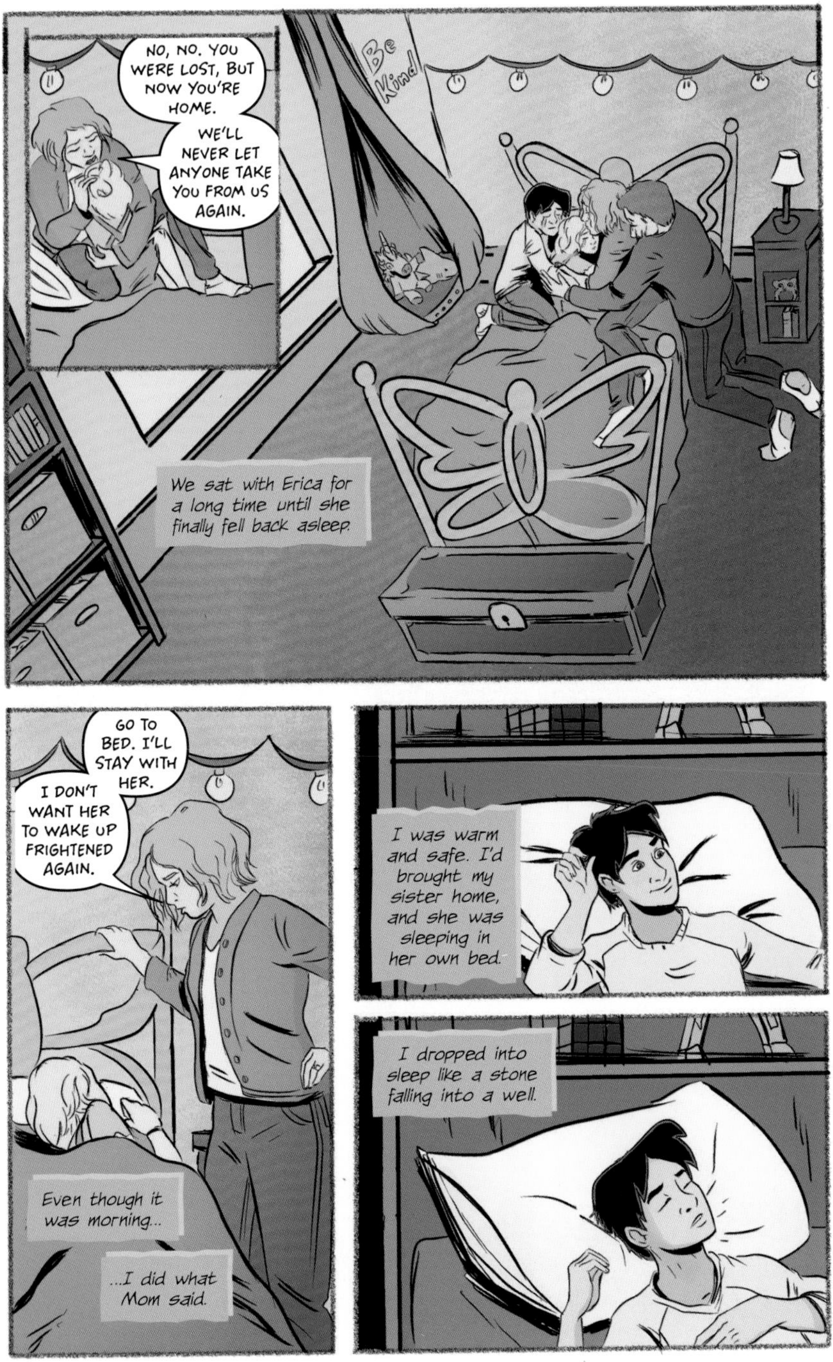

NO, NO. YOU WERE LOST, BUT NOW YOU'RE HOME.
WE'LL NEVER LET ANYONE TAKE YOU FROM US AGAIN.
Be Kind!
We sat with Erica for a long time until she finally fell back asleep.
GO TO BED. I'LL STAY WITH HER.
I DON'T WANT HER TO WAKE UP FRIGHTENED AGAIN.
Even though it was morning...
...I did what Mom said.
I was warm and safe. I'd brought my sister home, and she was sleeping in her own bed.
I dropped into sleep like a stone falling into a well.

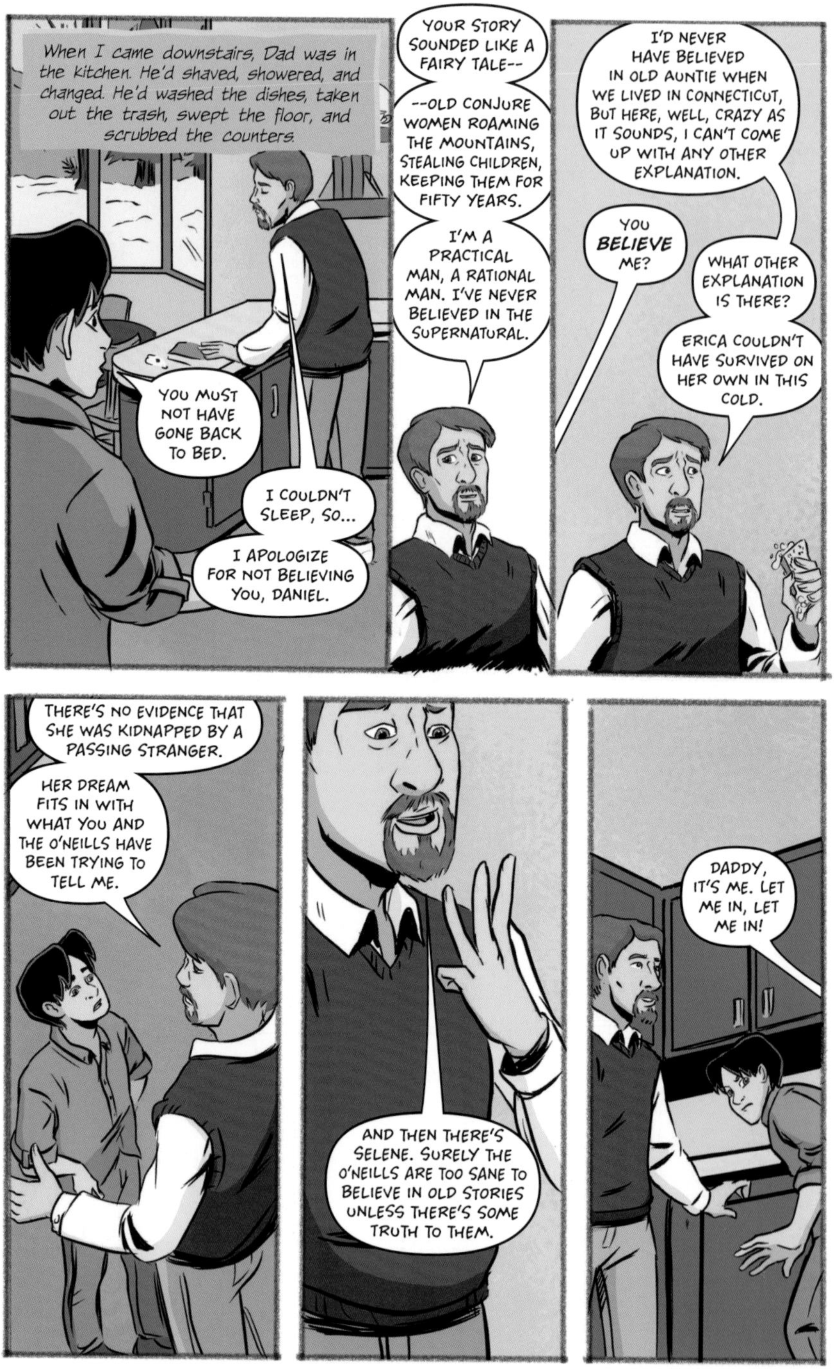
When I came downstairs, Dad was in the kitchen. He'd shaved, showered, and changed. He'd washed the dishes, taken out the trash, swept the floor, and scrubbed the counters.
YOU MUST NOT HAVE GONE BACK TO BED.
I COULDN'T SLEEP, SO...
I APOLOGIZE FOR NOT BELIEVING YOU, DANIEL.
YOUR STORY SOUNDED LIKE A FAIRY TALE--
--OLD CONJURE WOMEN ROAMING THE MOUNTAINS, STEALING CHILDREN, KEEPING THEM FOR FIFTY YEARS.
I'M A PRACTICAL MAN, A RATIONAL MAN. I'VE NEVER BELIEVED IN THE SUPERNATURAL.
I'D NEVER HAVE BELIEVED IN OLD AUNTIE WHEN WE LIVED IN CONNECTICUT, BUT HERE, WELL, CRAZY AS IT SOUNDS, I CAN'T COME UP WITH ANY OTHER EXPLANATION.
YOU **BELIEVE** ME?
WHAT OTHER EXPLANATION IS THERE?
ERICA COULDN'T HAVE SURVIVED ON HER OWN IN THIS COLD.
THERE'S NO EVIDENCE THAT SHE WAS KIDNAPPED BY A PASSING STRANGER.
HER DREAM FITS IN WITH WHAT YOU AND THE O'NEILLS HAVE BEEN TRYING TO TELL ME.
AND THEN THERE'S SELENE. SURELY THE O'NEILLS ARE TOO SANE TO BELIEVE IN OLD STORIES UNLESS THERE'S SOME TRUTH TO THEM.
DADDY, IT'S ME. LET ME IN, LET ME IN!

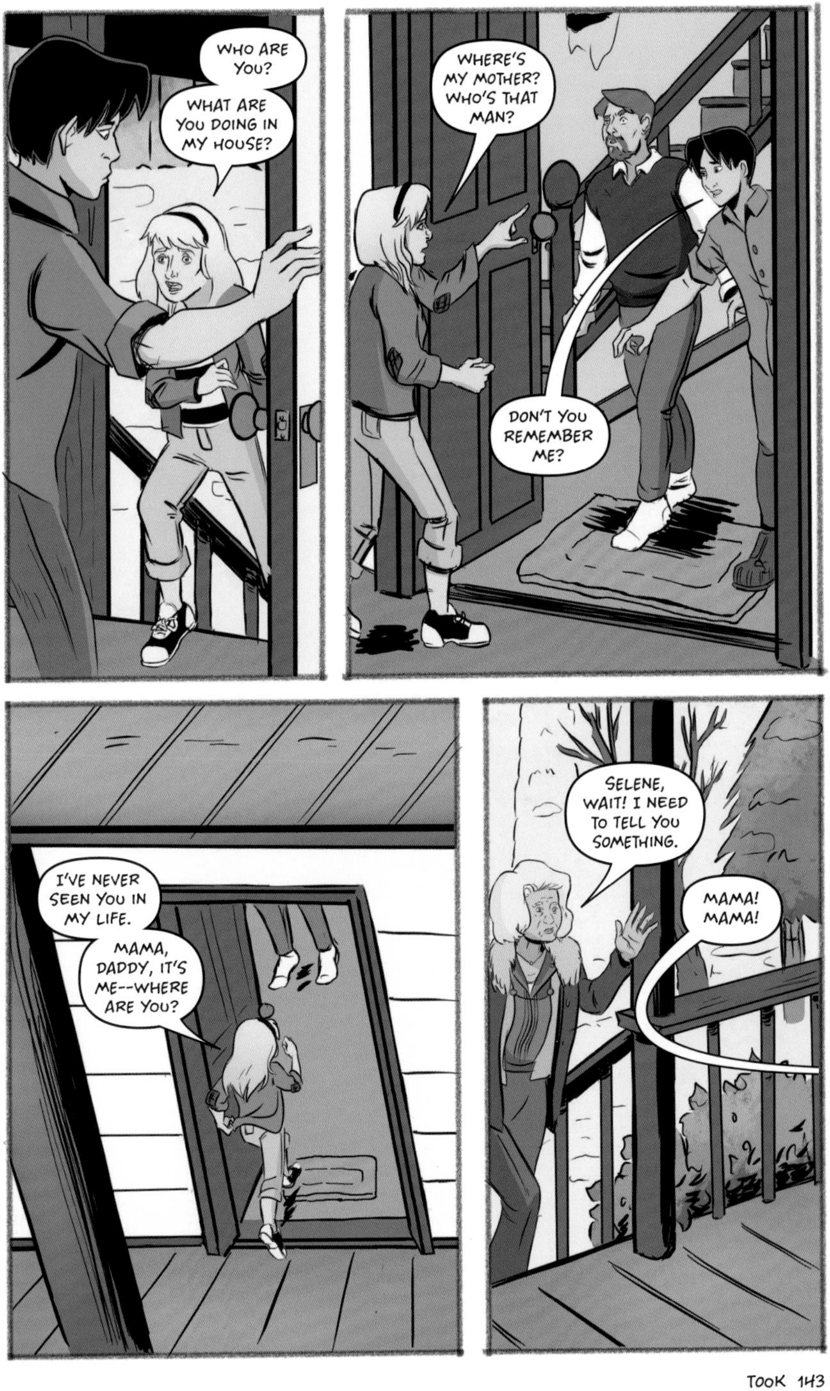
WHO ARE YOU?
WHAT ARE YOU DOING IN MY HOUSE?
WHERE'S MY MOTHER? WHO'S THAT MAN?
DON'T YOU REMEMBER ME?
I'VE NEVER SEEN YOU IN MY LIFE.
MAMA, DADDY, IT'S ME--WHERE ARE YOU?
SELENE, WAIT! I NEED TO TELL YOU SOMETHING.
MAMA! MAMA!

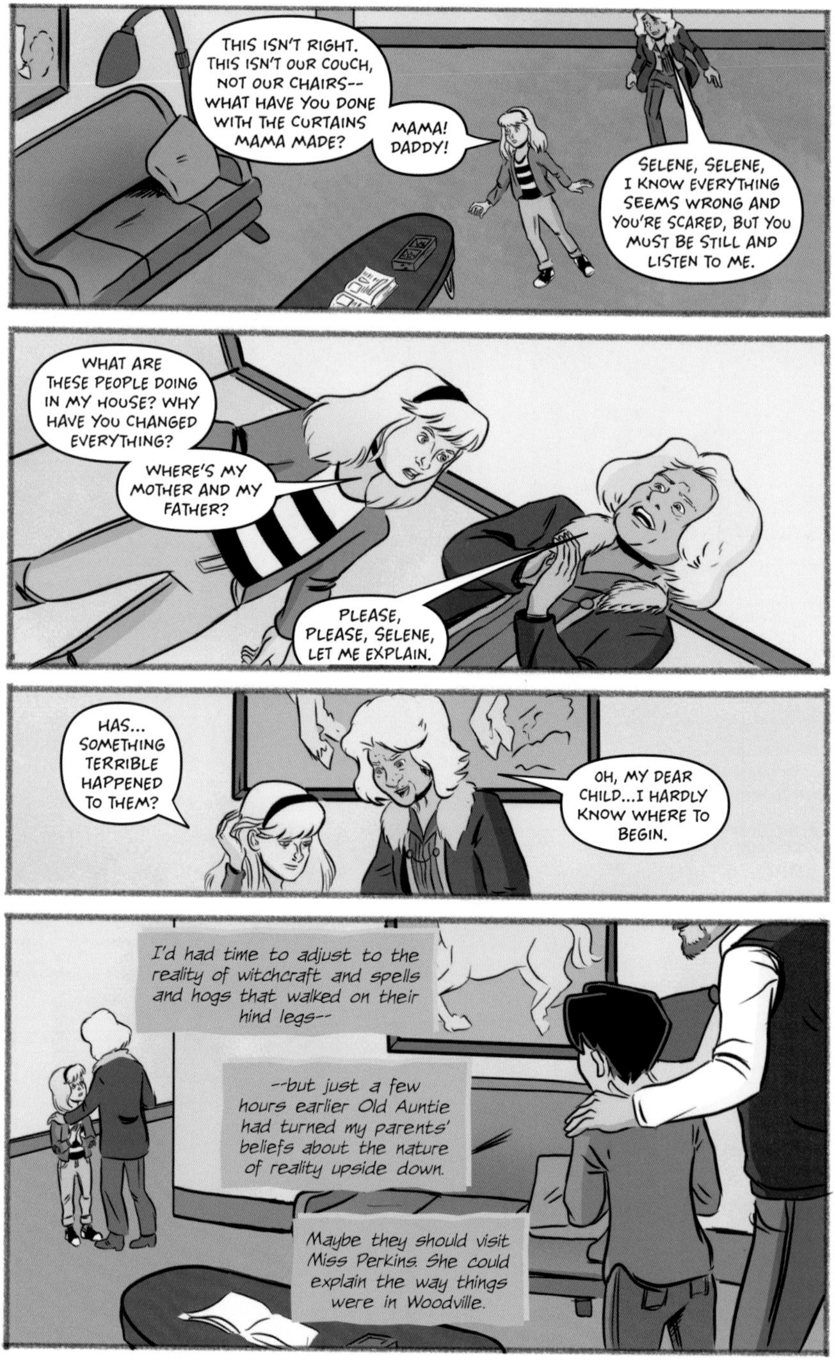
THIS ISN'T RIGHT. THIS ISN'T OUR COUCH, NOT OUR CHAIRS-- WHAT HAVE YOU DONE WITH THE CURTAINS MAMA MADE?
MAMA! DADDY!
SELENE, SELENE, I KNOW EVERYTHING SEEMS WRONG AND YOU'RE SCARED, BUT YOU MUST BE STILL AND LISTEN TO ME.
WHAT ARE THESE PEOPLE DOING IN MY HOUSE? WHY HAVE YOU CHANGED EVERYTHING?
WHERE'S MY MOTHER AND MY FATHER?
PLEASE, PLEASE, SELENE, LET ME EXPLAIN.
HAS... SOMETHING TERRIBLE HAPPENED TO THEM?
OH, MY DEAR CHILD...I HARDLY KNOW WHERE TO BEGIN.
I'd had time to adjust to the reality of witchcraft and spells and hogs that walked on their hind legs--
--but just a few hours earlier Old Auntie had turned my parents' beliefs about the nature of reality upside down.
Maybe they should visit Miss Perkins. She could explain the way things were in Woodville.

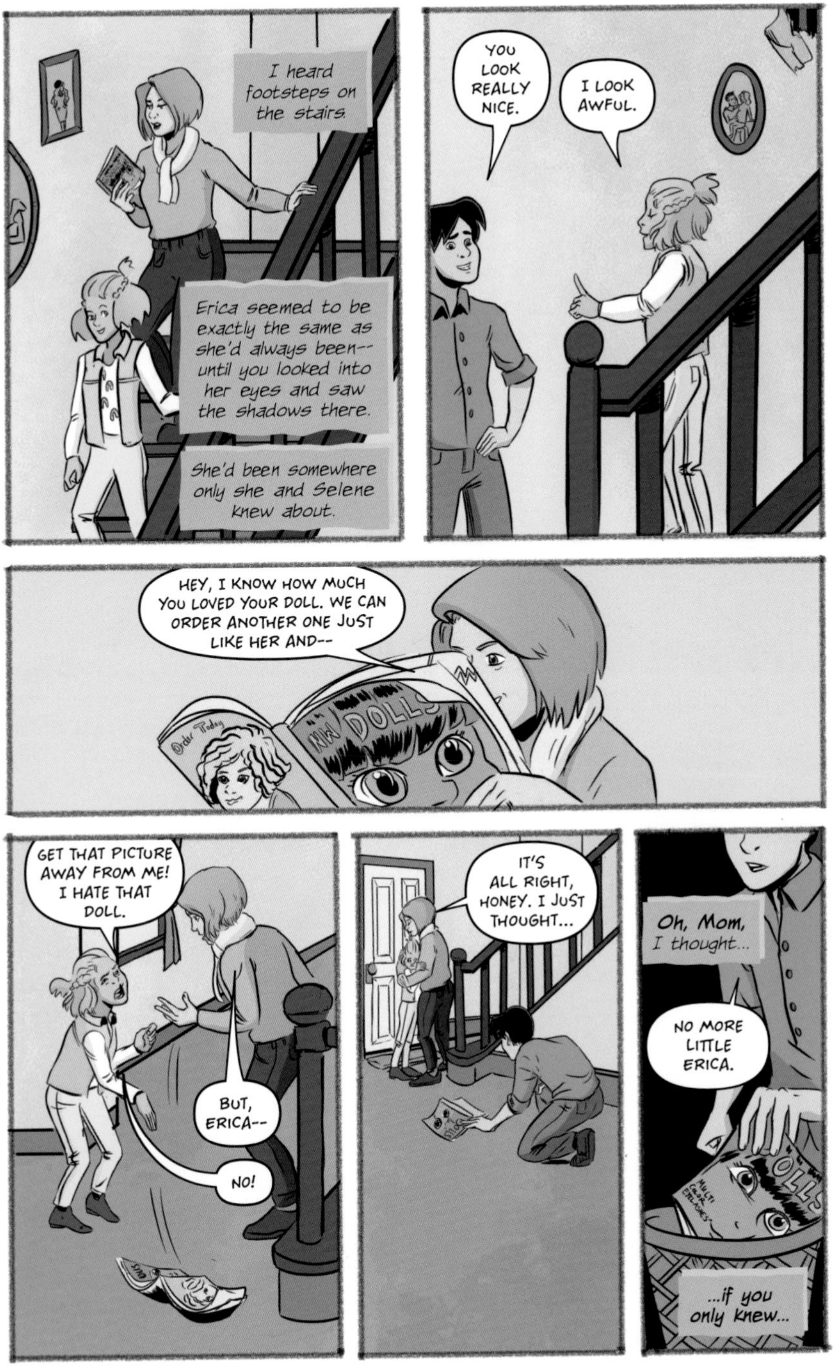

I heard footsteps on the stairs.
Erica seemed to be exactly the same as she'd always been--until you looked into her eyes and saw the shadows there.
She'd been somewhere only she and Selene knew about.
YOU LOOK REALLY NICE.
I LOOK AWFUL.
HEY, I KNOW HOW MUCH YOU LOVED YOUR DOLL. WE CAN ORDER ANOTHER ONE JUST LIKE HER AND--
Order Today
DOLLS
GET THAT PICTURE AWAY FROM ME! I HATE THAT DOLL.
BUT, ERICA--
NO!
IT'S ALL RIGHT, HONEY. I JUST THOUGHT...
Oh, Mom, I thought...
NO MORE LITTLE ERICA.
DOLLS
...if you only knew...

WHO WANTS PANCAKES FOR BREAKFAST?

PANCAKES WOULD BE WONDERFUL!

WHO'S THAT?

THIS IS SELENE. SHE LIVES DOWN THE ROAD WITH MR. AND MRS. O'NEILL.

SHE'S YOUR AGE.

COME SIT BESIDE ME.

WE'RE GOING TO BE FRIENDS, YOU AND ME. I JUST KNOW IT.

DO YOU LIKE PANCAKES?

WITH MAPLE SYRUP.

COMING RIGHT UP!

ROUND TABLE PANCAKE MIX

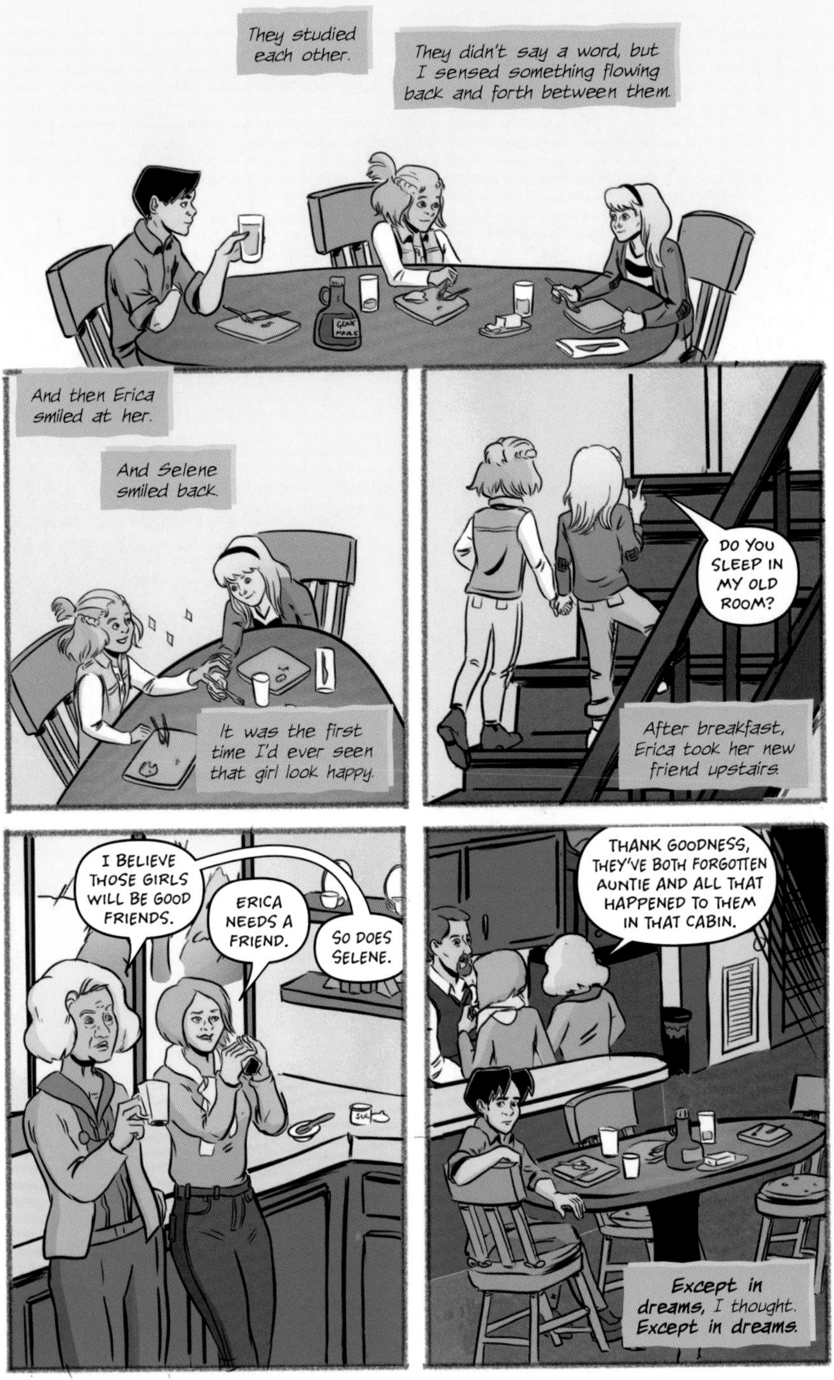
They studied each other.
They didn't say a word, but I sensed something flowing back and forth between them.
And then Erica smiled at her.
And Selene smiled back.
It was the first time I'd ever seen that girl look happy.
DO YOU SLEEP IN MY OLD ROOM?
After breakfast, Erica took her new friend upstairs.
I BELIEVE THOSE GIRLS WILL BE GOOD FRIENDS.
ERICA NEEDS A FRIEND.
SO DOES SELENE.
THANK GOODNESS, THEY'VE BOTH FORGOTTEN AUNTIE AND ALL THAT HAPPENED TO THEM IN THAT CABIN.
Except in dreams, I thought. Except in dreams.

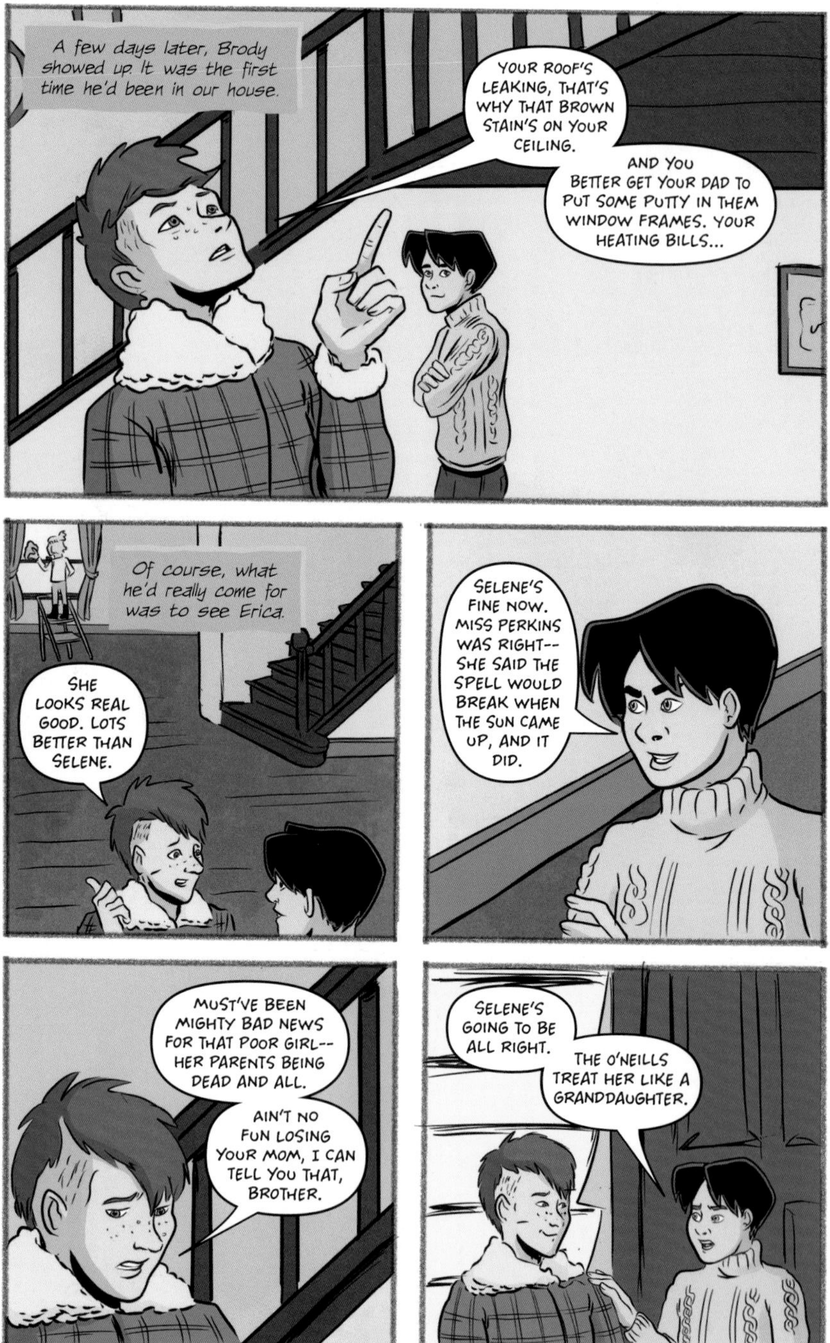
A few days later, Brody showed up. It was the first time he'd been in our house.
YOUR ROOF'S LEAKING, THAT'S WHY THAT BROWN STAIN'S ON YOUR CEILING.
AND YOU BETTER GET YOUR DAD TO PUT SOME PUTTY IN THEM WINDOW FRAMES. YOUR HEATING BILLS...
Of course, what he'd really come for was to see Erica.
SHE LOOKS REAL GOOD. LOTS BETTER THAN SELENE.
SELENE'S FINE NOW. MISS PERKINS WAS RIGHT-- SHE SAID THE SPELL WOULD BREAK WHEN THE SUN CAME UP, AND IT DID.
MUST'VE BEEN MIGHTY BAD NEWS FOR THAT POOR GIRL-- HER PARENTS BEING DEAD AND ALL.
AIN'T NO FUN LOSING YOUR MOM, I CAN TELL YOU THAT, BROTHER.
SELENE'S GOING TO BE ALL RIGHT.
THE O'NEILLS TREAT HER LIKE A GRANDDAUGHTER.

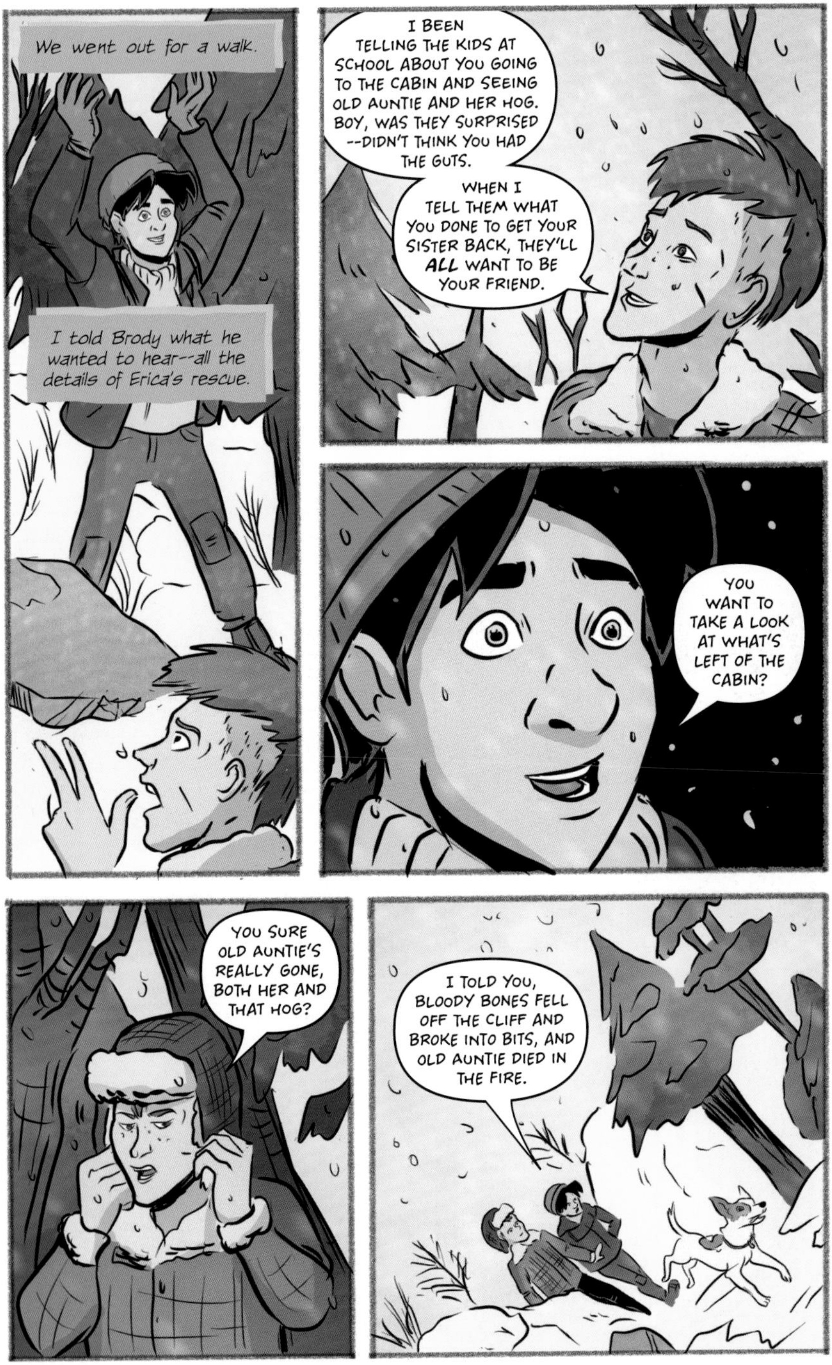
We went out for a walk.
I told Brody what he wanted to hear--all the details of Erica's rescue.
I BEEN TELLING THE KIDS AT SCHOOL ABOUT YOU GOING TO THE CABIN AND SEEING OLD AUNTIE AND HER HOG. BOY, WAS THEY SURPRISED --DIDN'T THINK YOU HAD THE GUTS.
WHEN I TELL THEM WHAT YOU DONE TO GET YOUR SISTER BACK, THEY'LL ALL WANT TO BE YOUR FRIEND.
YOU WANT TO TAKE A LOOK AT WHAT'S LEFT OF THE CABIN?
YOU SURE OLD AUNTIE'S REALLY GONE, BOTH HER AND THAT HOG?
I TOLD YOU, BLOODY BONES FELL OFF THE CLIFF AND BROKE INTO BITS, AND OLD AUNTIE DIED IN THE FIRE.

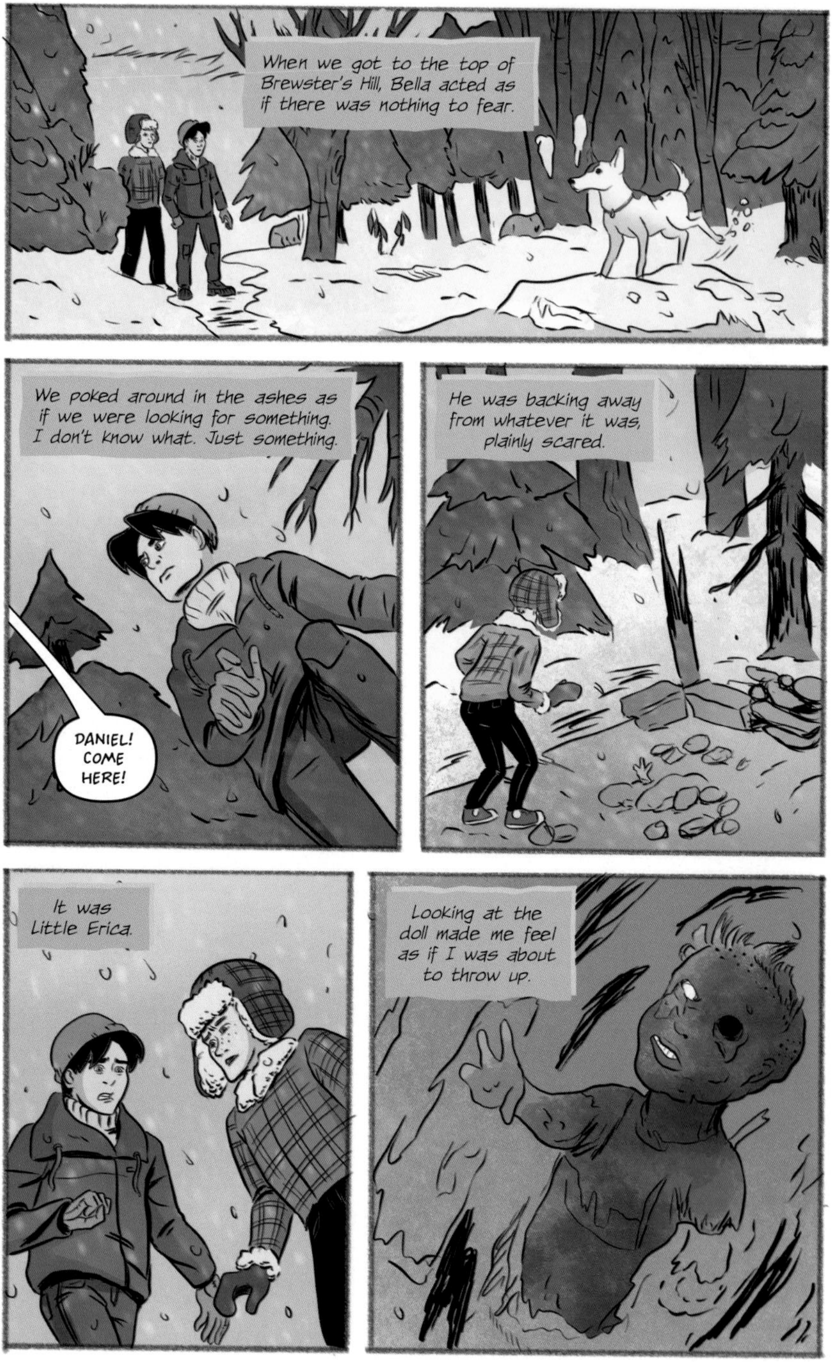
When we got to the top of Brewster's Hill, Bella acted as if there was nothing to fear.
We poked around in the ashes as if we were looking for something. I don't know what. Just something.
DANIEL! COME HERE!
He was backing away from whatever it was, plainly scared.
It was Little Erica.
Looking at the doll made me feel as if I was about to throw up.

IT'S MY SISTER'S DOLL.

THE ONE THAT STARTED ALL THE TROUBLE?

BUT SHE'S LITTLE, LIKE A PLAIN OLD, ORDINARY KID'S DOLL.

YOU TOLD ME SHE GROWED BIG AND COME TO LIFE.

WHEN THE SPELL BROKE, I GUESS SHE CHANGED BACK TO WHAT SHE REALLY WAS--A LUMP OF PLASTIC, MOSTLY MELTED NOW.

YOU AIN'T GOING TO GIVE HER BACK TO YOUR SISTER, ARE YOU?

ERICA DOESN'T WANT ANYTHING TO DO WITH DOLLS ANYMORE.

As soon as Bella saw the doll, she started growling.

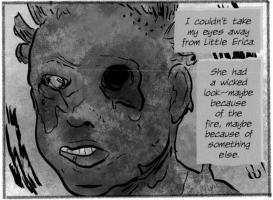

I couldn't take my eyes away from Little Erica.

She had a wicked look--maybe because of the fire, maybe because of something else.

YOU THINK IT'S OKAY TO LEAVE IT HERE?

TOOK 151

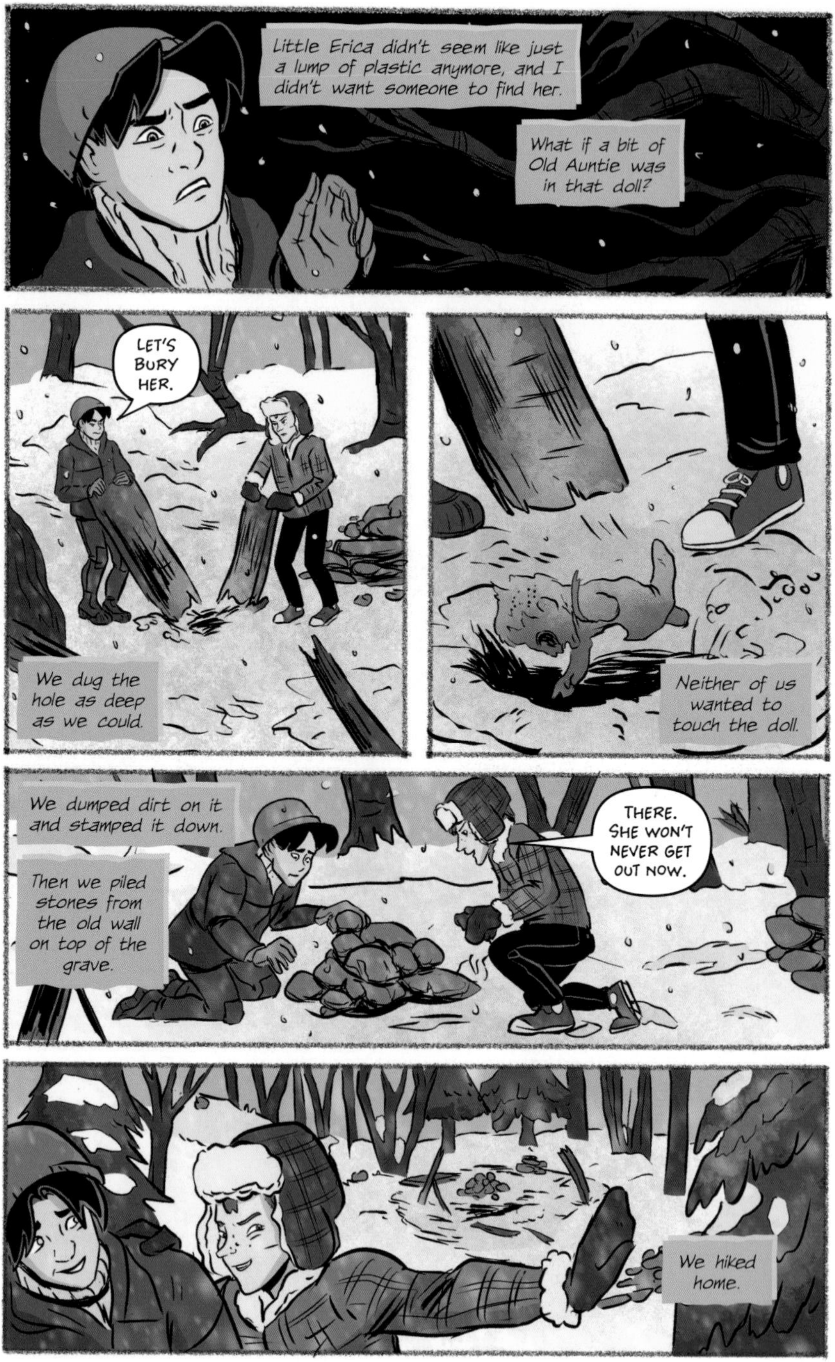
Little Erica didn't seem like just a lump of plastic anymore, and I didn't want someone to find her.
What if a bit of Old Auntie was in that doll?
LET'S BURY HER.
We dug the hole as deep as we could.
Neither of us wanted to touch the doll.
We dumped dirt on it and stamped it down.
Then we piled stones from the old wall on top of the grave.
THERE. SHE WON'T NEVER GET OUT NOW.
We hiked home.

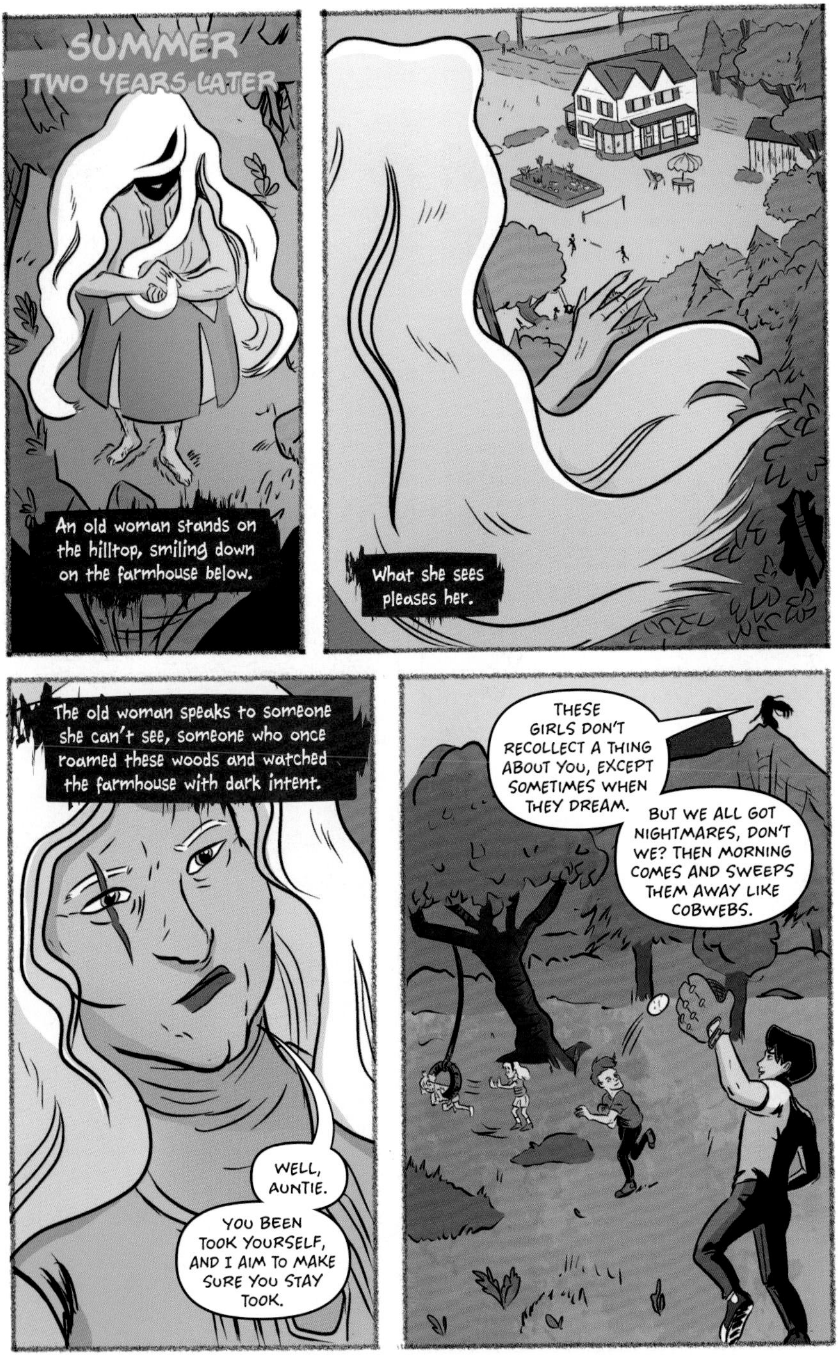

SUMMER
TWO YEARS LATER
An old woman stands on the hilltop, smiling down on the farmhouse below.
What she sees pleases her.
The old woman speaks to someone she can't see, someone who once roamed these woods and watched the farmhouse with dark intent.
WELL, AUNTIE.
YOU BEEN TOOK YOURSELF, AND I AIM TO MAKE SURE YOU STAY TOOK.
THESE GIRLS DON'T RECOLLECT A THING ABOUT YOU, EXCEPT SOMETIMES WHEN THEY DREAM.
BUT WE ALL GOT NIGHTMARES, DON'T WE? THEN MORNING COMES AND SWEEPS THEM AWAY LIKE COBWEBS.

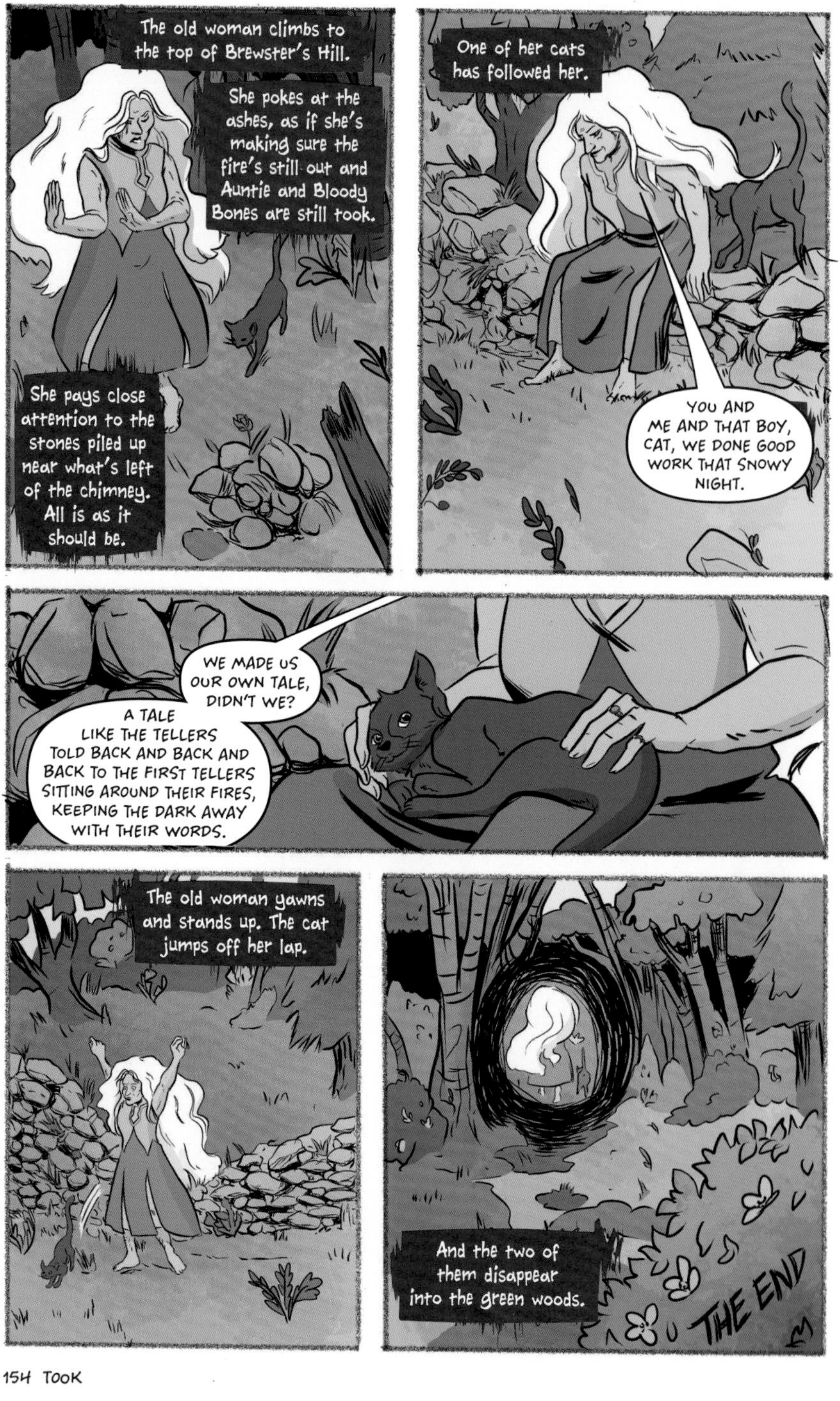

The old woman climbs to the top of Brewster's Hill.
She pokes at the ashes, as if she's making sure the fire's still out and Auntie and Bloody Bones are still took.
She pays close attention to the stones piled up near what's left of the chimney. All is as it should be.
One of her cats has followed her.
YOU AND ME AND THAT BOY, CAT, WE DONE GOOD WORK THAT SNOWY NIGHT.
WE MADE US OUR OWN TALE, DIDN'T WE?
A TALE LIKE THE TELLERS TOLD BACK AND BACK AND BACK TO THE FIRST TELLERS SITTING AROUND THEIR FIRES, KEEPING THE DARK AWAY WITH THEIR WORDS.
The old woman yawns and stands up. The cat jumps off her lap.
And the two of them disappear into the green woods.
THE END